Justice On My Mind

Justice On My Mind

Clara Hunter King

MILLIGAN BOOKS, INC.   BOOKS   CALIFORNIA

Printed and Bound in the United States of America
Published and Distributed by:
Milligan Books

Cover Design: Rufus Nelson, Sr.
Formatting: Milligan Books

First Printing, January 2009
10 9 8 7 6 5 4 3 2 1

ISBN# 978-0-9815783-7-8

Library of Congress Cataloging-in-Publication Data

Justice On My Mind, King Clara Hunter

Milligan Books
1425 W. Manchester Blvd., Suite C
Los Angeles, CA 90047
www.milliganbooks.com
drrosie@aol.com
(323) 750-3592

FOR

My dad, the late Simon Owen Hunter,
the greatest dad that ever walked on the planet.

And my grandson, Anthony Omari King,
The sweetest baby to "light" the planet.

About The Author

C lara Hunter King was born and raised in Como, Mississippi. After high school, she migrated to Los Angeles, California where she earned a Bachelor of Arts in Sociology at California State University at Los Angeles. She worked for a number of government agencies, including the Los Angeles Board of Education, Social Security Administration, and Internal Revenue Service. She moved to Atlanta, Georgia in May of 1979, where she earned her Juris Doctorate degree at John Marshall Law School.

When she began her practice as a criminal defense attorney, she was appalled by the number of young people entering the criminal justice system. She, along with four other attorneys and a private investigator, has written a series of short stories titled *This Is Not Cool, Volumes I and II*, that are based on cases they have handle in court and show clearly and directly, how one wrong decision can have lifetime consequences.

Her passion is to decrease the number of young people entering the criminal justice system. She is founder and president of Watchdogs For Justice, a non-profit organization founded specifically for that purpose.

Acknowledgment

Special thanks to my sister, Dr. Rosie Milligan, and my friend, Attorney Lawanda O'Bannon, for taking the time to read my manuscript and offer rewriting tips.

To my son, Anthony King, who always encourages me to write and thinks I'm the greatest writer who ever put fingers to the keyboard.

To my good friend and editor, Renae Spencer.

To all my family, friends, and fellow church members who encouraged me to keep writing. The list is too long to tackle. I really appreciate you guys.

He who dwells in the secret place of the Most High,

Shall abide under the shadow of the Almighty

Psalms 91:1

1

Mark LaNear had worked hard to become senior assistant district attorney in Butler County, while he also struggled to keep his marriage together. It had been a harrowing time in his life, and he had, at one point, even considered divorcing his wife of five years. But, things had changed in the past year. Now he felt like a king sitting on his throne, like Courtroom D belonged to him, and he ruled it with an iron fist. The courthouse was located in Winston, Georgia, a small town on the outskirts of Atlanta. Mark was tall and muscular. He enjoyed towering over people. He had blond hair and brown eyes that turned black when he was angry. And he seemed to be angry more often than not. He wanted everyone in his courtroom to know that he was in charge and put forth every effort to be sure that everything revolved around him. Finally, everything was going his way. Everything.

Monday, June 13, 2006, was just another day for Mark. But, his attention was drawn to the new assistant public defender that he had met on Friday when her predecessor showed her around the courtroom and introduced her to the courtroom personnel. Monday was her first day as one of the public defenders in Courtroom D. She seemed to be watching and analyzing everything and everybody in the courtroom. There was something about her that made Mark a little uneasy.

Justiana Fullilove, called Justice by her friends, stood five feet, seven inches tall. Her perfectly shaped oval face was a sable brown, and her jet-black hair was pilled on top of her head with a few strands dangling around her ears. She was slender, shapely, and appeared to have already bonded with Brad Hollis, the other public defender in Courtroom D. After Mark completed his negotiations with the last defense attorney in line, he turned to Justice, who had not bothered to get in the line.

"Miss Fullilove, are you ready to pretry your case?"

"No, my client doesn't want to plea bargain. We are going to waive arraignment and ask to have the case placed on the trial calendar," she answered without really looking at him.

She was stunned by Mark's reaction. He stood and literally screamed at her. "Your client does not decide how I run my courtroom. Every case in my courtroom will be pretried. Now ... are you ready to pretry your case or not?"

Brad Hollis and Lionel Weeks, the two attorneys she had been talking with at the time Mark addressed her, began to protest. Brad was short with shoulder-length blond hair and gray eyes. Lionel, who was in private practice, was tall and ball headed. His friends called him the ginger bread man. He and Brad were good friends and often referred to as "salt and pepper."

"Hey man, that was uncalled for," Lionel said.

"That's right ..." Brad began, but stopped short when Justice stood and walked quickly toward Mark. She walked so close that he had to take a step backward.

"Now you listen to me, Buddy Boy!" she hissed. "Once upon a time this was your courtroom, but I'm here now and it's my courtroom as well. Things are never going to be the same around here again. From this day forward, it's a new day and a new courtroom. We will operate by new rules." She took a few steps back and drew a line between the defense table and the prosecutor's table with her foot. "When I'm in this courtroom, this is my side and that's yours, if you so much as step on this line, I'll wipe you out, do we understand each other, Buddy Boy?"

Mark's face turned red, the veins stood out in his neck, his nostrils began to flare, and his eyes became little slits, as he clenched and unclenched his fists.

"Is that a threat, Miss Fullilove," he whispered. He had intended to yell, but only a whisper came out.

"No, it's not a threat, it's a promise." She stepped back and moved around Mark toward the calendar clerk.

"What's the trial date for this case," she asked the clerk. The clerk nervously thumbed through her paperwork.

"Let's see here . . . it's August, 15 Miss Fullilove."

"Thank you, we'll be ready to go forward at that time," Justice said as she turned and walked back to the defense table.

Mark continued to stare at Justice as she gathered her belongings and headed for the door. All eyes went from Mark to Justice. When she reached the door she had an irresistible urge to turn and look back to see what he was doing. She stopped, turned slowly and looked at him, she glanced around the courtroom and all eyes were on her. She wanted to shake her fist at Mark, or stick out her tongue and make a face at him. A thought came to her mind that was so strong; it was almost like an audible voice. "No, just turn around and go your way." She obeyed immediately, turned slowly, and walked out of the courtroom.

As soon as Justice left the courtroom she began to scold herself. *When will you learn to control your temper? Why were you the only attorney who had to scream at the prosecutor? Why couldn't you have said that you would talk with your client, or just pretried the case and then said your client would not accept the offer?* Justice stomped the sidewalk in anger. "I hope this doesn't get back to my boss," she said out loud. But she knew Antonio, the public defender for Butler County, would get the news sooner or later. She was glad she had walked to the courthouse. She needed the time to calm down and regain her composure as she walked back to the office. Justice was quite disgusted with herself. *I was fortunate enough to get the job after that horrible interview, and I blew it the first day. How can I make this right? What can I do? What can I say? I really thought I had my temper under control.*

⌒

ANTONIO'S PHONE BEGAN to ring as soon as Justice left the courtroom. Two attorneys rushed out into the hallway and another snuck a call from the courtroom. Antonio was well aware of what had happened before Justice reached the office. *That girl doesn't waste any time* he thought, as he grabbed the phone and dialed Vanessa's extension. Antonio had been the public defender for Butler County as long as most people in Winston could remember. He was a tall, handsome man whose mother was Filipino and his father Black. When people met him for the first time, they were always surprised to find that he was not Hispanic. With a name like Antonio Vegas, who could blame them? Vanessa, his chief assistant, was a plump redhead who got along with everyone and kept the office running smoothly.

"Vanessa, I have some news I think you will be glad to hear."

"What is it?" Vanessa asked.

"I think you will want to hear this in person, and straight from the horse's mouth, well, let's say Justice's mouth." Vanessa hung up and hurried to Antonio's office. As Justice entered the building she saw Vanessa going into Antonio's office, and groaned. She knew it had to be about her conduct. She wanted to kick herself. She went to her office and waited for the phone call she knew would soon come. She sat at her desk and put her head in her hands. *What will I say? How will I explain this? Oh God, Why? Why? Why? Why can't I control this lousy temper?* She thought about that for a moment, and then said softly, "It was Mark's fault. He provoked me." She knew that was not good enough. She didn't have a defense. She stood and walked to the window, turned and stared at the phone, stood there, waiting for it to ring.

Vanessa rushed into Antonio's office and closed the door. She was anxious to hear what Justice had done. She knew this had to be good.

"Well, did she threaten the judge or what?"

"You're close, she threatened Mark, and that's better than the judge, and my phone has not stopped ringing since she left the courtroom."

"This I gotta hear," Vanessa said as she pulled up a chair.

"She is just what the doctor ordered for that courtroom," Antonio said as he picked up the phone and dialed Justice's extension.

"This is Justice," she answered on the first ring.

"Justice, would you come to my office for a moment," Antonio said and hung up without waiting for a reply. He was as excited as a little kid with a new toy. Vanessa didn't know which she would enjoy more, watching Antonio's excitement or hearing what Justice had done to shake up Courtroom D.

Antonio walked over to the door and waited for Justice. Vanessa turned to look at a man in whom she had not seen such excitement in a long time.

⸎

VANESSA LEANED BACK in her chair and thought about the day they interviewed Justice for the job. She was laid back, pleasant, and had a ready answer for every question about her career goals and desires. When she was asked the "what would you do if" question, Justice frowned, and from that point on it was all downhill.

"If you were an officer and you saw two cars run a red light, one with a woman and one child and one with a man and five children, and you could only stop one, which one would you stop?" Antonio asked.

"Am I being considered for a job as assistant public defender or police officer?" Justice asked. "Because if I become a police officer, I think I could figure out the correct answer from what they taught me at the academy."

Antonio and Vanessa glanced at each other, and Vanessa asked the next question.

"If you had the job of detaining shoplifters, and you observed an older lady on a walker who was shoplifting and a young man who seemed to be mentally challenged who was shoplifting, and you could only detain one, which one would you detain?"

Justice picked up her purse, stood, and pushed her chair back.

"I'm not going to try and answer that, and I'm not going to take up anymore of your time. But I do appreciate your taking the time to talk with me."

She walked to the door and turned around. Both Vanessa and Antonio were standing and staring at her.

"Good afternoon, Ms. Allen ... Mr. Vegas." Justice turned, walked out, and closed the door.

"Did you ever?" Antonio asked Vanessa.

"What happened?" Vanessa asked. They both took their seat and remained silent for what seemed like a long time to Vanessa.

Antonio picked up the folder. "Who made up these questions?"

"I have no idea," Vanessa answered. "But, it does seem that they were developed for someone at the police academy."

"What kind of answers did the other candidates give when asked those questions?"

"Well," Vanessa said. "We don't really pay any attention to the answer. We are only interested in how they express themselves and whether or not they provide a logical reason for their choice."

Antonio took the stack of questions out of the folder and slowly began to tear them into small pieces. Vanessa sat and watched in silence. Their minds were working overtime.

"She is just the person for Courtroom D," they both said at the same time.

"Call her and ask her if she still wants the job," Antonio said. "No, wait until later tonight, maybe after supper. Give her time to cool off. She has the kind of nerve I wish I'd had when I was her age. Make sure she takes the job Vanessa!"

"She's doesn't seem to be the type that you can make sure she does anything, but I will give it my best shot."

"I'm sure you'll succeed," Antonio said, as he dismissed her with a wave of his hand.

⤢

JUSTICE WALKED INTO Antonio's office and he pointed to the seat next to Vanessa, "Have a seat, Justice." He walked back around his desk and waited until she was seated. He took his seat and smiled at Justice. "You wanna tell us what happened in Courtroom D today?"

"Mark and I had a little disagreement." She wasn't sure if they had heard all the details of that little indiscretion.

"Little disagreement!" Antonio exclaimed. "I heard that you came close to striking the man. And I'm sure he deserved it. Now give us the details."

Justice relaxed a bit and told them the entire story. She was surprised by their interest in Mark's reaction. They wanted to know what he said, how he reacted, and whether he seemed surprised. She told them how he stood clenching and unclenching his fist, how the veins stood out in his neck, how his eyes became little slits, and how she could hear him breathing all the way to the back of the courtroom. They loved it. Justice relaxed and decided that she was not in as much trouble as she had imagined. They didn't seem to be upset with her at all. But it would never happen again, she vowed. She would get her temper under control and never allow anyone else to make her that angry.

"Mark has been asking for this a long time. I'm happy someone had the guts to stand up to him," Antonio said. " He won't forget this day for a long time. Congratulations Justice, I'm sure you are going to be a real asset to this office and that courtroom." He walked around the desk and shook her hand.

"And let me add my congratulations to that," Vanessa said as she stood and prepared to leave. "I'll see you guys later; I have work to do."

"Thank you," Justice said as she looked from Antonio to Vanessa. "I guess I'll get back to my work, too." Antonio walked them to the door. He closed the door and shook his head. *They are certainly women of different temperaments. Vanessa would never scream at anyone, and Justice, well... one day she just might burn the courthouse down. I wouldn't be a bit surprised.*

2

Justice was a little apprehensive and embarrassed as she entered the courtroom the following day. She was relieved when everyone acted as if nothing unusual had happened the day before. She sat in the chair across from Mark and thumbed through her case file. Mark looked up and said, "Good morning, Ms. Fullilove."

"Good morning, Mr. LaNear." She hadn't known what to expect, but Mark acted as though nothing had happened. The negotiation went smoothly. She had two cases on this plea and arraignment calendar. There was the case of Jerame Willis, a young man charged with aggravated assault. His girl friend, Shemika Hoskins, claimed that he broke her arm by knocking her down and stomping her arm during one of their many fights. He claimed she fell as she ran away from him in a fit of anger, after he told her that his other girl friend was pregnant. The state's offer to Willis was a five-year prison term.

The second case was Abdullah Hasid, a 23-year-old man accused of possession of cocaine, for which the state was offering two years in prison and two on probation. Justice told the prosecutor that she would discuss the offers with her clients and get back with him. *That's what you should have done yesterday, idiot.*

The judge in Courtroom D, the Honorable Charles Denver, was a 47 year old, slightly overweight, gambler with light-brown hair and blue eyes—who had lived on junk food since his wife and two children moved to California to live with her parents eleven months earlier. During calendar call, he took the time to explain the courtroom procedures to Justice and two court-appointed attorneys, all relatively new to his courtroom. He encouraged them to always pretry every case before asking to have it placed on the trial calendar. Justice knew this was really meant for her and vowed to make every effort to conform to his expectations.

When Justice visited Jerame, one of the first clients scheduled for trial, he was hostile and uncooperative.

"I know you are overworked and underpaid and don't care what happens to me. So why take up my time asking silly questions?" He stared past Justice and tapped his finger on the window that separated them.

"Okay," Justice said, as she placed her file back into her briefcase. "I apologize for attempting to take up your time. Please, go back to whatever you were doing, I won't bother you again until you come to court for your trial in two months"

"Wait a minute, you're not going to try and find out what happened?" he stammered.

"I'll see you at trial," Justice said as she stood and walked out of the holding cage.

"Hey, I'm . . . " he heard the door cling shut behind her. He sat there for another five minutes; he was in shock. He didn't know what he had expected. He quickly decided he would not try that with her again. He returned to his cell and wrote her a letter apologizing for his behavior and asking her to come back to see him. Justice had already decided to let him stew for a few days and planned to go back the next week.

⌐

PETER CHAMPION, ONE of the most popular attorneys in Georgia, was in courtroom D on July 11, 2006. He sat next to Justice and began a conversation with her. Justice knew his name and reputation, but had no idea what the man looked like. So she had no idea she was talking with Peter Champion.

"What kind of case do you have today," she asked.

"Felony murder," he answered. "I'm here to request a continuance. I have two other murder cases before the Supreme Court." He was impressed with her because she was not impressed with him.

"Wow," she said.

He could tell that she was a new attorney and wondered if she knew anything about him.

"What kind of case do you have today?" Peter asked.

"I have two cases on the plea and arraignment calendar, one is aggravated assault and the other is possession of cocaine, and I'm arguing a motion to suppress for a fellow public defender," she said proudly. "He had to rush his mom to the hospital last night."

"Mind if I stay and watch, I'm free the rest of the day, which is a rarity."

"I'd love that she said, and maybe you could give me some feedback afterwards, this is my first motion."

"Okay," he said with a big smile. New attorneys always reminded him of his beginning years. He never missed a chance to encourage them. He liked Justice. *She seems so innocent and refreshing. How did she get into criminal defense? I like the lighthearted and hopeful spirit of new attorneys.*

"What made you decide to go into criminal defense?" Peter asked.

"My dad. He was a criminal defense attorney. He connected everything he did to the legal system in some way, including naming his only child Justiana Jurisprudence Fullilove. And he never gave me much choice. I think he decided that I would follow in his footsteps before I was born." Peter noticed that her eyes seemed to cloud a bit, and then she smiled and continued. "He died while I was in law school. If he were still here, there's no way he would have missed sitting in on my first motion."

"Then I guess I'll just have to sit in for him, that is if you don't mind," he added quickly.

"I don't mind at all. I think he would like that. I think people in Heaven can see us sometimes, especially when we are involved in something really important."

Peter chuckled. *So you think arguing a motion to suppress is something really important.*

~

BRAD, WHO WAS also a public defender in Courtroom D, had asked Justice to fill in for him because the judge warned him when he granted a continuance two months ago that he would not grant another continuance in the case. When the motions calendar was called, Justice stood and answered for Brad.

"Your Honor, I'm Justiana Fullilove, and I'm standing in for Mr. Hollis because he had a family emergency and can't be here today. I have the case file and just need an opportunity to speak with the defendant and we will be ready to proceed."

"Is Mr. Bart Orr in the courtroom?" the judge asked.

"Yes, your Honor, but I didn't know my attorney wouldn't be here until this morning," the defendant said. "And he didn't give me all the details about the person who would be representing me."

"And just which details didn't he give you, Mr. Orr?"

"Well . . . he didn't tell me she would be Black and a female." Some of the defendants snickered.

"Well, you need to know that your case will go forward today with or without an attorney. If I were you, I wouldn't risk "biting the hand" that's trying to help me. Miss Fullilove is not required to represent you, if she chooses not to, you will have to go forward on your own."

"Oh, that's okay, your Honor," Justice said. "Brad didn't tell me a couple of things about him either. So we are even."

"And what didn't he tell you about the defendant, Miss Fullilove?"

"That he is stupid and a red neck."

All of the spectators laughed and the defendant was embarrassed and a little frightened. He wondered if he had cooked his own goose. *I'm in trouble. What kind of attorney would say such a thing about the client?*

When Justice's cases were called she announced not guilty on her two cases and the judge excused her so that she could meet with the defendant. When they went into the witness room, the defendant began to apologize.

"Look, I'm sorry about shooting off my big mouth. I hope you won't hold it against me. I'm really innocent of this crime. I didn't know the lady had drugs in her bag. I hope you will do everything you can to help me."

"You can count on that," Justice said. "When I'm on your case, I'm on it one hundred percent. So relax, you'll get the best defense possible. Okay?"

Justice began to prepare the Defendant to testify, should it become necessary. "I don't think you will need to testify because your attorney has done all the research and thoroughly prepared your case. However, it never hurts to be prepared for the unexpected."

She seemed so serious and efficient; the defendant was beginning to think he had misjudged her. He finally relaxed. She had put him in his place and he wasn't mad at her. As a matter of fact, he felt he was in pretty good hands.

They returned to the courtroom just as a motion to suppress, involving the Defendant's confession to armed robbery, was concluded. The judge said he would take the motion under advisement. The defendant was returned to jail to await the judge's decision.

Justice sat next to Peter Champion and began discussing the case with him. He took the file and began to thumb through it. He knew the judge would be a little more inclined to make a fair ruling if he knew an old timer like him was looking on. He whispered to Justice and gave her some pointers about the case and made sure the judge could see what he was doing. Judge Denver was known as the hanging judge and Peter had taken a liking to Justice and hoped that his interest in the case would win some brownie points with the judge.

When the case was called, Justice moved to the defense table and beckoned for the defendant to join her. Peter smiled because she seemed to think that this was really a court of law, fairness, and justice. He hoped his presence would be to her advantage.

After Justice and Mark gave brief opening statements, the judge moved right into the testimonies.

"You may call your first witness, Mr. LaNear."

Mark called one of the arresting officers, Frank Hood. After the preliminary questions establishing his role as federal narcotic agent, he turned and pointed to Bart.

"Mr. Hood, were you one of the officers involved in the arrest of the defendant in this case, Bart Orr?"

"Yes, I was."

"And would you tell us the basis for his arrest?"

"We received a call from the Los Angeles police office that two people suspected of illegal drug activity were traveling to Columbia, South Carolina, with a stop in Atlanta. We were given the description and went to the airport to investigate."

"And what happened when you stopped them?" Mark asked.

"We searched their bags and found a plastic bag containing a substance that appeared to be heroine."

"What happened after that?"

"Both parties denied ownership of the drugs. Mr. Orr said the bag belonged to his female companion, and she said it belonged to him. So we arrested both of them."

"Did the lab report show that the substance was heroine?"

"Yes, the lab report showed that the bag contained 85 grams of heroine."

"Thank you Mr. Hood. Your witness counsel," Mark said.

Justice moved to the podium and opened her notebook. "Officer Hood, you were able to identify the defendant by the description given to you by . . . was it a phone call?"

"Yes, it was a phone call."

"And you went up to the defendants, identified yourself and asked to search their bags?"

"Well, we asked if they would mind if we searched their bags. I told them that it was my job to stop drugs and drug proceeds coming through the airport."

"And they agreed to the search?"

"Well, not exactly, they refused and asked if we had a search warrant. And we asked them if they would mind stepping into the office so we could talk in private."

"And did you have a search warrant?"

"No."

"Did you ask this defendant for identification?" Justice pointed to Bart.

"Yes."

"Did he provide it, and did it match the name on his luggage?"

"Yes, he provided it, and it matched the name on the luggage."

"Did you ask him where he was going and why?"

"Yes."

"Did he provide that information?"

"Yes."

"Did you ask for the identification first, or ask him to step into the office first?"

"Objection, your Honor," Mark said. "Irrelevant. What difference does it make what the order was?"

"Your Honor," Justice said. "The motion to suppress was filed on the basis that the search was illegal and in violation of the defendant's 4th Amendment rights to be free from unreasonable searches and seizures. And if the defendant was . . ."

"Objection overruled, the officer will answer the question."

"We asked for the identification and where he was going first."

"So, let me see if I understand what happened. He provided you with his identification, which matched the name on his luggage, he told you where he was going and why, and you did not have a search warrant for this defendant's luggage. Is that correct?"

"Yes."

"Tell me officer, if this statement is correct. The defendant answered all your questions, provided you with all the information you requested, and you still asked him to step into the office so that you could interrogate him further?"

The officer shifted in his seat. "Basically."

"Does basically mean yes, or no?" Justice asked.

"It means yes," the officer said and glanced at the judge.

Justice turned to the judge. "Your Honor, I have a case that is exactly on point for the case before this court: Pullano v. Georgia."

The judge moved to his computer, opened up a screen, put in his password, and turned to Justice.

"Do you have a cite, Counselor?"

"Yes," Justice said. "As a matter of fact, I have copies of the case. She opened a folder and removed three sheets of paper. She placed one on top of her notebook, handed one to the prosecutor, and handed one to the deputy to give to the judge. She waited for the judge to read the facts of the case. When he finished reading, he turned to look at Justice.

"I have no further questions for this witness at this time, your Honor."

The examination and cross-examination of the second officer was pretty much the same as that for the first officer. When Justice finished her cross-examination, the judge turned to Mark.

"You may present your closing argument counselor."

"She can go first," Mark said and pointed to Justice. She moved to the podium, arranged her papers, glanced at Peter, and turned to looked at the judge.

"Your Honor, in this case, Pullano v. Georgia, the defendant was stopped in an airport by drug agents. He was asked for his identification--where he was going--and the purpose of his trip. He complied with each request. But the officers still searched his bags even though he never gave them permission to do so, and they did not have a search warrant. He was convicted. But the Appellate Court overturned the conviction.

"The Court of Appeals ruled that once the defendant gave the officers his identification, told them where he was going and why, and the identification matched that on his luggage, he should have been allowed to leave. To continue to detain him was a clear violation of his 4th amendment right to be free from unreasonable searches and seizures.

"The facts in the case before this court today is exactly the same as in that case. The officers testified that the defendant provided them with his identification, told them where he was going, and why. When they asked the defendant to step into the office for further questioning and searched his luggage, without his permission, they violated his 4th amendment right. Therefore, any contraband confiscated as a result of this illegal search, is the fruit of the poison tree, and *must* be suppressed as a matter of law." She returned to her seat and Mark moved to the podium.

"Your Honor, it's sometimes impossible, due to time constraints, to get a search warrant before searching a defendant. These officers are charged with stopping drugs and drug proceeds that come through the airport. They will not be able to do that if they must take the time to get a search warrant each time a defendant demands one. For that reason, the state is asking that the motion to suppress be denied." Mark took his seat and Justice moved back to the podium.

"Your Honor, convenience is not the issue here. Time constraint is not the issue. A clear violation of the defendant's constitutional rights under both the constitution of the United States and the state of Georgia is at issue. It's not always convenient to follow the law. But the law must be followed nonetheless. In the case before this court, the officers did not follow the law, they violated the defendants constitutional rights and *all evidence* must be suppressed as a matter of law."

Judge Denver sat there and pretended to be reading his notes and the case file. He had already made up his mind to grant the motion. He did so primarily because Peter Champion was sitting there taking notes during the hearing. The judge was a little weary of Justice Fullilove.

Judge Denver granted the motion and scolded the officers. He reminded them that they, as enforcers of the law, must also uphold the law. Mark was stunned and Justice was overjoyed. She ran to Peter and shook his hand. He patted her on the back and wished her luck in her practice. Judge Denver wondered why Justice had so much favor with Peter Champion. He had no idea that Justice did not even know with whom she had just interacted.

When Brad thanked Justice for taking over his case and told her that he heard that Peter Champion helped her, she was floored.

"No," she said. "Please don't tell me that was Peter Champion. I could have gotten his autograph or asked him more questions. No, it couldn't have been. Why didn't he say so?"

"Everyone in Winston knows him except you. I guess he thought you knew who he was. He's on the news all the time. Don't you watch TV?" Brad asked.

"No, not very often. The news always make me sad."

"Once in a while, they tell something good on the news. You ought to watch it sometimes."

"Maybe I will."

3

Jerame's case took Justice to Oaktree Downs, a housing project not far from the courthouse. The defendant's grandmother, who was a witness in the case, lived in Oaktree Downs. A petite, sad looking lady who appeared to be in her early 50's greeted Justice, and introduced herself as Josie Willis. A little girl, who appeared to be about seven years old, followed Josie and clung to her arm. She told the little girl to go watch TV as she motioned for Justice to follow her to the kitchen. The child looked as sad as the lady and refused to let go of her arm. Josie threatened to spank the child, and she dropped her head and went to watch TV.

"Why isn't she in school?" Justice asked.

"She wasn't feeling well today. She has missed a lot of days from school since her twin sister was killed in an accident near the school."

"What happened?" Justice asked as she turned to look at the little girl.

"She ran out in the street when the ice cream man parked near her school and was hit by a cement truck."

"How long ago was that?" Justice asked.

"Almost a year."

"The cement company, did they provide any help or counseling for ...what is your daughter's name?"

"She's my granddaughter and her name is LaQuita, her mother is a crack addict. So I was left to raise them, even though I have taken care of their brother, Jerame, since birth. The twins were a handful when I had the two of them. I was always complaining about raising two little kids, now

I would give anything if I had both of them to raise. And no, the cement company didn't provide any help, said the accident was not their fault, that she ran into the truck. A lawyer took the case and told us there was nothing he could do after three months. He said they were not willing to settle and he was not willing to go to trial. My sister said they paid him off."

"Did you try to find another attorney? *At least the statute of limitation has not expired.*

"No, I didn't … what do you want to know about Jerame?"

Justice opened her folder and thumbed through the papers. Her mind was still on the little girl. "One final question about the accident … do you plan to try and find another attorney?"

"No." Josie clearly wanted to leave that conversation.

"Okay," Justice said. "Let's get to the reason for my visit. Did you see what took place between Shemika and Jerame?"

"No, I was in the kitchen when she came in. She spoke to me and went to watch TV in the living room. They were back and forward, you know, he popped popcorn, and came in to get cold drinks a few times. I didn't pay any attention to them. She usually came over two or three times a week. I didn't hear any arguing; just heard her scream and went to see what was wrong. She was lying on the floor and he was trying to help her up. She told him to get away from her. I "shooed" him away and helped her up. Then she stormed out of the house, got in her car, and drove away."

"Did he tell you what had happened?"

"Not at first, I think he was a little embarrassed. Said he didn't want to talk about it, but that she wouldn't be coming back. The relationship was over. He didn't tell me what had happened until after he was arrested. We were surprised; we had no idea her arm had been broken. He said he told her that his other girlfriend was pregnant. I never knew he had two girlfriends. He said she knew about it. What women will put up with from men these days. Anyhow, I never want to see her again."

"So you don't really know what happened?" Justice asked.

"No, not really. Have you talked to him yet?"

"Yes, I spoke with him yesterday," Justice said. "I think Jerame believes that you know more than you do. Thanks for your time Ms. Willis, I'll keep you posted." Justice shook Josie's hand and left. She just couldn't get the little girl off her mind. She looked so sad.

When Justice returned to her car, a gray Mercedes Benz, there were approximately 20 young people standing around admiring the car. "Here she comes," several of the boys said, as if she couldn't hear them. They knew she was the attorney that represented Jerame. She stopped and smiled.

"You're Miss Justice aren't you? She nodded her head.

"How much does a car like this cost?" asked Leroy, an-overweight, eleven-year old.

"A lot more than it's worth," Justice answered. "If you were going to buy a car, what kind would you buy?" They all began talking at once. She heard a Mercedes Benz, a BMW, a Cadillac, Infinity, and finally a little girl pushed her way to the front of the crowd and said, "I would buy a Toyota Camry."

"What's your name?" Justice pointed to the little girl who had pushed her way up front.

"Katrina, like the hurricane."

"She's as dangerous as a hurricane," one of the boys said, and they all snickered.

"That's a pretty name, do you know what Katrina means?"

"No," they answered in unison.

"It means pure, pretty, and smart," Justice said. "Hurricanes are given names so we can keep track of them and the damage they cause. The name doesn't have anything to do with how dangerous the hurricane is. But Katrina meant pure, pretty, and smart long before Hurricane Katrina came along."

Katrina held her head high, crossed her arms, and smiled. The children pushed in close. "What does Tony mean, I mean Anthony," a little boy asked.

"Anthony means a brilliant warrior. But he's not the kind of warrior that fights in a war; he's the kind of warrior who fights invisible enemies, like ignorance and poverty, hatred and lack of self-respect. Anthony is the type of warrior who fights ignorance by studying and acquiring a lot of knowledge and information. He fights poverty by using his knowledge to get a good job or starting his own business and hiring people to work for him. He fights hatred by treating everyone the way he wants to be treated. He develops self respect by respecting himself first, then respecting others."

"What does David mean?" asked a little boy by that name.

"David means one loved by God, while God loves everyone, he has a special love for people named David because they always try to obey Him. They are natural leaders in the Kingdom of God."

"What about Eugenia?" a little girl asked.

"Eugenia means a beautiful plant. It's usually green and has beautiful flowers that turn into a reddish fruit. People named Eugenia usually make their parents happy and proud of them because they always bare good fruit by obeying their parents and staying out of trouble."   They were all raising their hands and calling out their names.

Justice held up her hands. "That's it for today, but I will be back and we will go over each and every name. If I don't know what your name means, I promise I'll find out. Fair enough?"

"When will you be back?" they asked in unison.

"Soon."

"We are forming a club, we would like for you to become a member? Please, pretty please," Katrina pleaded.

"Well, you guys vote on it. You may not want an outsider to be a member. But I will consider it, and we'll talk about it the next time I'm here."

"I have an Aunt that works as a private investigator. She can find anything or anybody you need to find," said Leroy as he reached in his pocket and handed Justice one of his aunt's business cards.

"Thanks," Justice said as she got into her car to leave. "I'll be sure and give her a call if I need to locate someone. Good bye, and remember, I'll be back." They all followed the car about ten feet after she drove away. She watched them in the rearview mirror. She smiled and said out loud, "following a car a few feet is a dumb human habit."

Hmmm, I think I need to get rid of the Mercedes. Maybe I'll get me a Toyota Avalon. Justice called Uncle Henry, her accountant, who was also the trustee over the trust her father set up for her. When she told him she wanted to trade the Mercedes in for a Toyota Avalon, he tried to convince her that that was improper. She reminded him that she was over the age of twenty-four and could take over her own trust if she chose to do so. He sold the Mercedes and bought her a Toyota Avalon. She was pretty sure she would become a member of the club at Oaktree Downs; she did not want the kids gawking at her car every time she went out there.

☙

JUSTICE WAS IN a hurry because she was running late for her best friend's housewarming.

She and Lela had been best friends since fifth grade. Their families live in Washington, DC until Lela's dad, a pharmacist, was transferred to Atlanta just after they finished the 11th grade. It was all so unexpected. Justice was in a state of shock. She and Lela had both planned to attend Howard University. When Lela moved to Atlanta, Justice lost all interest in attending Howard.

Lela was tall and hippy, her skin tone was milk chocolate and she had grayish green eyes and dark brown hair. For years she was infuriated with people who told her that her skin tone did not match her eye color. One day she realized it didn't bother her anymore. She loved her eye color. The guys seemed to love it, too.

Lela had always known she wanted to be a pharmacist. Justice had known from the time she was a little girl that she was going to be a lawyer, like it or not. Harold Fullilove, Justice's father, had made the decision that his daughter would be a lawyer before she was born. After Lela's family moved to Atlanta, Harold came up with the idea of Justice attending Spelman College in Atlanta. However, she ended up at Lincoln University with Lela instead.

Justice's mother had been killed by a drunk driver when she was 18 months old. Harold had never recovered from her death, and he was torn because he had never found a way to make up to Justice for that loss. He enrolled her in karate classes when she was six years old, and she had earned a Black Belt by the time she was 12.

Justice had objected; she didn't want to leave her dad. "I'll never go to Atlanta and leave you alone," she protested.

"I will not be alone, there are more than half a million people in DC, and I know almost half of them. Besides, if you don't go to Atlanta, you will make me a sad, old man."

"You are not an old man, and I would never do anything to make you sad."

"Then you'll go?"

"Dad, you are not being fair."

"How did that word get into our conversation? There is no fairness in this world, and we both know it."

"I'm not leaving you." She folded her arms and glared at him.

"Then I'll close my law practice and move to Atlanta myself. Because it really isn't fair. You miss Lela and she misses you. I can be just as happy in Atlanta as I am in DC. He knew Justice would never allow him to close his practice. He loved his work and he loved DC.

"Okay," she said. "And you are right; there is no fairness in this world. I'll go to Atlanta. You are just trying to get rid of me because I can't cook. I'll show you, I'm going to become a first class chef, and you'll be sorry you sent your only daughter away."

Harold came over and put his arms around her. "I don't know why God has been so good to me. I don't deserve a daughter like you. I'm the most blessed man on this planet. What would I do without you?'

"I have to admit, you would be pretty pitiful without me," Justice said as she sighed and hugged her dad. She was already beginning to dread how much she would miss him.

JUSTICE PARKED BEHIND a blue Mercedes, glanced at her watch, got out of her car and stopped to looked around at the houses. She took the time to admire the beauty and diversity of the neighborhood, once again. She had driven out with Lela on several occasions to look at the houses while Lela's house was under construction. Each one was different; each one was beautiful. As she turned toward Lela's house she stopped in her tracks when the garage door of the house in front of her zoomed up. She turned and saw Alou standing in the garage. He was a builder and had gone into the garage of a house three doors from Lela's house to check the garage door switch. He had developed a garage door opener that would open the door in two seconds. He never missed an opportunity to play with his new toy. No one was on the street when he went into the house. He did a quick inspection and headed for the garage. When the door zoomed up, he heard a muffled scream and turned to see the most beautiful sight he had ever seen in his entire life. She was beautiful, shapely, and covered from her neck to just below the knees. She left everything to the imagination. Not your typical Winston woman Alou thought. They were always generous enough in their dress to show a man a little cleavage and the knees if not a bit of the thigh. She stood with wide eyes and her hand over her mouth. She had the softest brown eyes he had ever seen. She placed one hand on her chest when she saw him. Fear was written all over her face.

"Hi," he said from inside the garage. He didn't want to advance toward her too quickly. "My name is Alou Hambrick, and I'm just checking the garage door switch. It's new, and the fastest garage door opener in the whole wide world."

"I can see," Justice said as she tried to regain her composure. There was something about her obvious fear and vulnerability that caused him to want to take her in his arms and protect her. He never wanted her to experience such fear again. The feeling startled him because he had never felt that way about a woman before. As he stood there looking at her, he realized that in that instant he had fallen completely in love with her.

He touched his face with both hands. "Do I look like a man-eating monster or something, correction, a woman-eating monster or something?"

She sighed and tried to smile. "I didn't think there was anyone else around and the door went up so fast. I certainly didn't expect to see anyone standing there ... I guess I shocked you," she stammered.

"No, you didn't," he said as he ventured out of the garage slowly. He walked to within a few feet of her and said, "I'm going to let it down now."

"Okay," she said. "I won't scream."

"Are you going to Lela's house warming?"

"Yes." *He must think I'm awfully silly.*

"So am I," he said. "Let me introduce myself, my name is Alou Hambrick, I'm not married, never been married. I don't have any children. I graduated from college, I work full time, and I don't live with my mother. And if I lived with my mother, I would think it was okay. Since I obviously shocked you, it's only fair that I watch over you all evening to be sure you are okay. That is, if you are not meeting someone else." He took care not to use the word frighten.

26

"My name is Justiana Fullilove, my friends call me Justice. And no, I'm not meeting anyone, but that sounded more like some kind of a resume than an introduction." She was not about to object, she hated going to social events alone, but she couldn't miss Lela's big day. Now that she was over the shock, she was kind of glad she had run into him. He wore an expensive blue suit, was a little over six-feet tall, and had broad shoulders and a neat waistline. His hair and beard were cut low and seemed to run together. It was a work of art. His skin was milk chocolate, almost the same color as eyes that were so sleepy looking he seemed ready to fall over. *If Lela invited him to her house he must be okay. And he's very handsome.*

Alou gave Justice a brief overview of his life as they walked slowly down the street. She didn't tell him anything about herself. When they entered the house, Lela hurried to them because she was surprised to see them together.

"Justice, Alou . . . I didn't know you two knew each other."

"We don't, I met him outside," Justice said.

"But it seems as if we have known each other all our lives," Alou said.

"I'm glad you could come," Lela said and took both of them by the hand. "Justice, my husband wants to see you, he has a bone to pick with you."

"Why? What could I have done that offended Ted?" Justice asked. "Come with me Lela, he's not going to beat me up is he?"

"No, silly. Now run along, he just wants to ask you a few questions." She let Justice's hand go but not Alou's.

"What's wrong?" he asked when the look on her face changed.

"How did you arrange this?" she asked. He saw fire in her eyes.

"Arrange what?" Alou was stunned by her reaction.

"You stay away from Justice, you are up to no good, I've heard how you treat women and I've seen you with at least a dozen different women in the short time I've known you. She's not your type. So leave her alone. I warn you, I will not stand by and watch you hurt her."

"All I did was meet the lady on the street in front of your house and walk with her to your door. I didn't ask for her phone number. I didn't ask her to marry me. I didn't ask her to help me rob a bank. I just spoke to her and asked if she was coming to your house and walked with her to the door. Where is the crime in that?"

" Maybe I overacted, but I still know you and I will not allow anyone to hurt my friend. Besides, I know you don't have any respect for women."

"Now you hold up, you don't know anything about how I feel about women."

It was Alou's turn to be angry. "Who told you that I don't have any respect for women? In the first place, whoever told you that gave you incorrect information about me. In the second place, you don't know anything about my type of woman. In the third place, how do you know the women you saw me with weren't the ones looking for a one-night stand, all women may not be like you and your friend. In the fourth place," he paused and collected himself. "I promise you--I will never do anything to hurt your friend. Never. And you can count on that."

He seemed so sincere that Lela relaxed and said "okay, I'll hold you to that, and if I am wrong, I apologize."

"You are, and I accept your apology ... I know your heart is in the right place, but I did promise the lady that I would watch over her all evening, and I mean to keep my promise." He smiled at Lela, kissed both her hands, and hurried off to find Justice.

True to his word, Alou stayed close to Justice all evening. When she was ready to leave, he walked her to her car. He let her drive away without asking for her phone number. He cursed Lela for butting into his life. He had fallen in love with a woman he saw standing on the sidewalk looking frightened, and a loud mouth female, for whom he had designed a home, had threatened him and caused him to let her walk out of his life. He cursed Lela again. *Why couldn't she have mined her own business?*

4

Lela had called Justice ten days in a row to see if she had heard from Alou since the housewarming. She had not. Lela was a little surprised. She decided she had better have a talk with her husband, Ted, about her suspicion; maybe she had misjudged Alou.

She smiled when she thought about how she met Ted. During her first week on campus as a new pharmacy student, she had gone to the wrong classroom and did not realize her mistake until the professor walked into the room. She looked around and didn't recognize any of the students. She was almost too embarrassed to leave. When she picked up her books to leave, they all spilled out onto the floor. She thought she was going to die of embarrassment. Ted had walked over and said, "Hey, I'll get those for you." He picked up the books, took her by the hand and led her out of the classroom. "What classroom are you supposed to be in?"

"How did you know I was in the wrong class?" she asked as she pulled out her schedule to check for the correct classroom.

"If you had been in that class before, I would have noticed you."

"Room 104 is correct, but it's South Hall, instead of North," she said, and reached for her books.

"C'mon, I'll walk you over there, and I'll carry your books. I'm from the old school. The gentleman carries the books and the lady just walks along and looks pretty. By the way, my name is Ted. Ted Bolton."

Lela looked straight ahead. She was afraid she was blushing. "Thank you. Is it really Ted, or is it Edward?"

Ted laughed. "It's Edward. But sometimes I forget. And what, may I ask, is your name?"

"Lela Weston, and this is my first semester here."

"I know, if you had been here last semester, I would have noticed you."

Lela felt as if she were all ankles and thumbs. She couldn't think of anything to say. He told her that he was a senior and already had a job at a hospital pharmacy in Winston. When she got to her class, Ted walked into the classroom with her, pointed to Lela and mouthed to the professor, "my fault." The professor nodded okay, and Lela wanted to go through the floor. She took her seat and didn't hear one word the professor said. Ted Bolton had taken over her thoughts.

As Lela left her first class on Thursday and headed for room 104, she stopped short. She saw Ted watching her as he leaned against a tree with his arms folded and a big smile on his face. He had waited for her every day after that for two weeks. He said he wanted to be sure she made it to the right class. By the time they went on their second date, Lela realized that she was already in love with Ted. He was twenty-eight years old, tall, slender, and handsome with honey colored skin, long side burns, and a cleft in his chin. Lela felt that he was the wisest and most sensitive man she had ever met.

After dinner, she began her conversation with her husband. "Ted, what do you think of Alou?"

"What do you mean, what do I think of him?"

"What kind of guy is he?" Is he conceited? A womanizer?"

"I don't think so. He seems like a nice guy. What brought this on?

"Justice."

"Justice?" Ted asked. He was surprised. "What's the connection between Justice and Alou?"

"Well, none yet, but I could tell by the way he looked at her at the house warming party that he was interested in her."

"And has he called her, I'm sure you asked. And what makes women think that all good-looking men are conceited or a womanizer? You, of all people, should know better. Look how good looking I am, and I treat you like a queen."

"Yeah, right, but no, he hasn't called. But I think that's because I let him know in no uncertain terms that I would not stand by and watch him hurt Justice."

"Lela, Justice is a big girl, what makes you think you have to protect her from men? What do you have against Alou, he seem like a nice enough fellow."

"Every time we see him at a social event, he's with a different woman. He's like, love'em and throw'em away."

"I personally think Alou's too nice for his own good. Have you ever noticed that most of those women seem to be gold diggers looking for an opportunity to move into what they see as the in crowd? They are actually using Alou. I think he's just trying to give them an opportunity to experience The Club. He has never liked the idea of excluding people from The Club. When you think about it, a lot of those woman have good looks or a good figure, but no money, no profession and no other means of breaking into what they see as the in crowd. And what about that Ericka, who came to The Club with Alou and immediately latched onto that doctor, Samuel, and how she went after Alou again when Samuel ditched her, remember that?"

"Yes," Lela said. She had forgotten that little escapade. She hadn't noticed all the things Ted mentioned. She just knew she was disgusted with Alou because he always seemed to have a different woman on his arm.

"Any more questions," Ted asked as he moved to the den and picked up the TV remote to indicate the end of the discussion. Lela shook her head. *How could I have missed all that?*

JUSTICE WENT BACK to Oaktree Downs and met with the kids. They formed a Club, "My Brother's Keeper." They all made a pledge to look out for each other. They would meet Every 4th Friday. Katrina was elected to serve as president. She had a photographic memory and made a list of what each person's name meant and tried to hold them to its meaning.

At the second meeting, Justice learned that the only non-African-American kids, Amy, a 9-year old white girl, and Raul an 11-year-old Hispanic boy, would not be permitted to join My Brother's Keeper. Their mothers were apparently concerned about their safety. Justice talked with them and they made excuses. Mrs. Lawrence said Amy was small for her age, couldn't handle the rough play, and needed to catch up because she was behind in her homework. Mrs. Romero said she would probably allow Raul to join later, but not now. Justice was frustrated because she could see Amy and Raul watching the activities from their windows. She knew they wanted to join. *God, touch each mother's heart and open an avenue for Amy and Raul to join the club. Amen.*

They lined up and sang their theme song.

"I am somebody, I really am somebody, I am somebody,

I've been washed in His blood; I've been filled with His love, and I'm a child of the Most High King."

Each child looked forward to his or her turn to dance with Miss Justice. Even Leroy, who was secretly called "fat and stinking," had hopes of dancing with Miss Justice. Justice kept a record of each kid with whom she danced. She wanted to be sure she danced with every kid in the club. Leroy was high on the list because the kids were always picking on him. When Justice picked a kid to dance with, it seemed to raise his status. She made special note of those who were not highly esteemed by the other kids. *Kids can be so cruel.*

Chapter

5

Justice walked out of the courtroom three weeks after she met Alou at Lela's house-warming party, and saw him standing outside Courtroom C. She stood there for a second trying to decide whether she should go over and say hello. She had decided against it and turned to walk away when Alou turned and called to her.

"Hey, is that who I think it is?"

"Depends on who you think it is," Justice said, as she stopped and turned to face him.

"I think it's the lady that stole my heart and ran away in the middle of the night. What are you doing here?"

"I work here, well, I work in the Public Defender's Office and I'm assigned to Courtroom D."

"What do you do?"

"I defend people accused of crimes."

"Then you deserve a break. May I take you to lunch?"

"You haven't told me why you are here. Are we going to get a new courthouse?"

"I don't think so," he said. "I drove Jan, my secretary, down here to be with her aunt, whose son is in trouble. Her car wouldn't start after she came to work early to get a head start on her projects for today. Can't see that I had much choice."

"So how is she getting back to the office?"

"Her aunt is meeting a friend for lunch and Jan is going with them." Alou made up the answers as he went along. He had a full dossier on Justice and he liked everything about her.

'This is my fast food day. I have one every month. Today it's Dexter's," Justice said as she turned and started toward the parking lot.

Alou followed. "I haven't had Dexter's in a long time, it should be fun. Why don't I drive? That way we can talk going and coming, and you get a free ride."

"Okay," Justice said. She wondered if Lela would approve of her going to lunch with Alou. She chided herself for always wondering if Lela would approve of her actions. *Grow up and take charge of your own life.*

Justice ordered a grilled chicken sandwich, French fries, and a chocolate shake. Alou ordered the same. They ate on the picnic tables and watched the people and cars go by. It was the most fun Alou and had had in a long time. He had never been to Dexter's on a date before. And he wasn't sure if this was a real date, but he certainly hoped so. He dragged it out as long as he could. Justice was so refreshing. It was one of those rare occasions that he had been out with a woman who didn't want anything from him. They all seemed to want something--money, marriage, to break into the in crowd, to be on the arm of a good-looking man. It was never about the real Alou. He often asked himself why he even bothered. When they finished and began to clean their table to leave, Justice placed her hand on the table and looked into his eyes.

"So, what do you want from me, Alou?"

"I want to marry you and take you home." Justice began laughing and couldn't stop. When she looked at Alou and he just sat there without a trace of a smile, it was even funnier. As they cleared the table, Justice tried her best to stop laughing.

"I don't know why that was so funny," she finally said.

"You ought to be ashamed. A man pours his heart out to you in honesty, and you make fun of him."

"I wasn't making fun, that was funny. You don't know anything about me, so you couldn't want to marry me. You can't be serious."

"But I am serious."

"Come on Alou ... let's just change the subject. I shouldn't have put you on the spot like that."

"We can change the subject, but it won't change my mind."

"So what do you think of Lela," Justice asked, changing the subject.

"I think she's a great lady, and we always got along until I showed up at her door with you. That was the beginning of World War III. You would think I was trying to get you to rob a bank. She is certainly her sister's keeper."

"She sees me as an orphan and she and Ted are my best friends."

"So why does she think she needs to protect you? Is it just me, or men in general?"

"Probably men in general. We have been friends a long time, and she saw me go through a real tough time because of a break up with a guy. I think it hurt her almost as much as it did me. I don't blame her for not wanting to go through that again."

"So, did she kill the guy or what?"

Justice laughed. "No, but when she finished with him, I'm sure he wished she had killed him. He changed his mind later and said we should give it another try, but I would not have been able to take him back if I wanted to. Lela would not have stood for it. Besides, I knew I could never trust him again."

"So what did the guy do, kill his grandmother or something?"

Justice was quiet for what seemed like a long time to Alou. He waited. She finally sighed, looked at him, and began to recount the painful experience. "We dated for almost two years. He was the first guy I dated after moving to Georgia, we were in undergrad school together. We were what we called committed Christians. No sex before marriage. We had everything planned: We would get married when I finished law school; he would have one more year in school. We would have our first child a year after he finished school. I would stay home until the baby was two years old. That kind of stuff. But something changed when he went to grad school and ... long story short; he not only changed his mind about abstaining from sex before marriage, he began to make fun of everything we had cherished. Those things didn't make sense to him anymore. He was a completely different person, and said I was thinking like a little girl. I was quite broken hearted and mourned for weeks with Lela trying to comfort me. By God's grace, I survived and eventually got over him completely. You know, I didn't think I would ever be happy again. I vowed I would never fall in love again, and Lela plans to hold me to it. So you see, she's protecting both of us."

"He must have been a real idiot," Alou said as he took both of Justice's hands in his. "I promised Lela, the night of her house warming, that I would never do anything to hurt you, and I make that same promise to you now."

"And I told you all of my personal business so that you would understand why I am not interested in a relationship. I know that I may change my mind about a relationship in the distant future, and I do mean distant. But I want you to know that any promise you make, can and will be used against you by Lela."

"Fair enough," Alou said. They finished clearing the table and walked to the car. When they reached the courthouse parking lot, he parked and walked Justice to her car.

"I would like to take you to a special place this weekend, no strings attached. I know you'll enjoy it. How about Saturday night?"

"Where is this special place?" she asked.

"Can I surprise you?"

"Okay, but I'll call you to confirm on Friday," Justice said as she unlocked the door and slid into her car. She waved and drove away. Alou stood there and watched her until she was out of sight.

Alou had asked Justice out on a date every weekend after the first date. She felt guilty for refusing so often, because he was always such a gentleman, and she always enjoyed herself. Still, she didn't want to lead him on. She had vowed that she would keep it cool and convince him that she was not interested in a romantic relationship.

⁓

ON THEIR FOURTH DATE, Justice and Alou went to Six Flags. He convinced her that she was the only person in Georgia who had not been to Six Flags, and she agreed to go with him. She had a wonderful time. She felt like an idiot because she wanted to get home before midnight so that she could call Lela. She knew Lela would wait up for her call. She also felt that Lela wouldn't like it if she stayed out too late with Alou. *I'm a grown woman, and Lela is not in charge of my life. I am free to do what I want to do without wondering how she will feel about it.*

Alou was sure that Justice would provide Lela with every detail of their date. He decided to take it real slow. He didn't want anything to go wrong. He could not afford to lose Justice. He knew it would be difficult to have a real relationship with her without Lela's approval. *She's the one I've been waiting for all this time.*

Justice called Lela as soon as she walked into her condo. "I'm home," she said when Lela answered the phone.

"Did he try to get in your pants?' Lela got right to the point.

"No, he did not."

"Justice, you know he doesn't even go to Church. Tell me why you are dating him, you weren't raised like that."

"Ocie went to church and read the Bible all the time, and look what he put us through. Besides, I'm not going to fall in love with him or marry him; I just want to go out on a date once in a while. What's wrong with that?"

"Nothing I guess," Lela said and sighed. "What did he do or say when he brought you home, did he try to come in?"

"No, he walked me to my door, kissed both my hands, said good night, waited until I was inside, and went home. He said he would call when he got home and let me know he made it home safe, and that he expected me to call him if I ever drove home after dark by myself to let him know that I made it home safe."

"Maybe I was wrong about him," Lela said grudgingly. "Just be careful Justice, you know men are not like women. We always treat them right, but they don't always do the same for us."

"I will." Justice was glad Lela was not so dead set against Alou. He really seemed like a nice fellow. But she concluded that she was not about to fall in love with him, and he was not about to get in her pants. She had begun to think about him on a regular basis, and took note of the fact that he always put forth a special effort to be sure she had a good time. *Yep, I like him a lot, but that's all it will ever be.*

Justice knew that it wasn't wise for a Christian to date an unbeliever. So she invited Alou to come over to her condo for their next date. She prepared dinner for him. After dinner, she got right to the point.

"Alou, I need to know something about your eternal estate."

"What kind of estate?"

"To put it in plain English, are you a Christian?"

"I think so, I haven't done anything really bad. Except maybe rolling in the hay with women. And I'm all done with that now."

"If you died tonight, where would you spend eternity? Would you go to Heaven?"

"Well," Alou said and looked down at his hands. "I hope . . ."

"If you are not sure, you probably won't. Would you like to be sure?"

"Justice, I know this sounds awful, but I am so put out with church, that I dread the thought of ever going to church again. Some of the most awful people I know are there every Sunday. If Christianity doesn't make you any better than that, why bother? Besides, how can I know for sure if I'm a Christian or not?"

"Are you a citizen of the United States?"

"Yes."

"How do you know?" she asked.

"Because the constitution says so."

"Good, so you are relying on the document that spells out the criteria for citizenship. Are you aware of the fact that there's a document that spells out the criteria for becoming a Christian?"

"Well, no," Alou said. "But, I guess I never really thought about it."

Justice picked up her Bible and turned to the 10th chapter of Romans. "In the 10th chapter of Romans, verse nine, it reads, 'that if you confess with your mouth the Lord Jesus and believe in your heart that God has raised Him from the dead, you will be saved." She placed the Bible back on the table.

"All you have to do is *believe* in your heart and confess with your mouth. Now, let me explain what you are required to *believe* and what you are required to *confess*. You must believe that you are a sinner and that you need a savior. You must believe that Jesus died for your sins, and that God raised him from the dead. You must confess that you accept Him as your lord and savior. And bingo, you are a Christian. The constitution tells how you become a citizen; the Bible tells how you become a Christian."

"Is that all there is to it?"

"Yes, but there are other things you do after becoming a Christian. Just as there are things you do as a citizen of the United States. As a citizen, you obey the laws of the land, pay taxes, vote, and defend the constitution, and the country, if it becomes necessary. But those are not things that make you a citizen. They are things that good citizens do.

As a Christian, you get baptized, take communion, read the Bible, go to church, and obey God's word. Again, those are not things that make you a Christian. They are things that good Christians do. So, would you like to become a Christian, or be sure that you are a Christian?"

"Yes," Alou said. *I can see that I'm not going to get very far with you if I don't, and I really should anyway.*

"Okay, repeat after me, bow you head. Say God, I confess that I am a sinner, and I need a savior. I believe that Jesus died for my sins, and that you raised Him from the dead. Lord Jesus, come into my heart and into my life; I make you my lord and savior. Thank you father, in Jesus' name, amen." Alou repeated the prayer. He opened his eyes and looked at Justice.

"Is that it? I could have done that a long time ago if someone had told me how."

"Yes, that's it. Welcome to the family of God. Now we are brothers and sisters in Christ."

"Justice, I have no desire or intentions of being your brother. I want to become your husband."

"I don't mean naturally, silly, I mean spiritually." She leaned over and kissed him.

"Hey, I like that. Do it again, sister." She giggled and kissed him again. *Just wait till I tell Lela, she will certainly be surprised. And that was so easy.*

Justice walked into the Sunset Medical Center and looked around. Since she was a few minutes early she decided to check the place out. Nice. After checking all of the non-restricted area, she went to the receptionist station and told her that she had an appointment with Dr. Timothy Burkett. He was the doctor who had treated the young lady that accused her client, Jerame, of breaking her arm. The receptionist sent Justice to his assistant on the third floor. Justice was ushered into a room where she would meet with the doctor.

"Good morning, I'm Dr. Burkett, Timothy Burkett," the doctor said as he entered the room and extended his hand to Justice.

"Good morning, I'm Justiana Fullilove." She shook his hand

"How can I help you?" he asked.

Do I detect a bit of hostility from the good doctor? "I'm from the public defender's office and I wanted to ask you a few questions about a criminal case I have. I understand that you were the doctor that treated the victim, Shemika Hoskins."

"I did."

"What type of injury did she sustain?"

"It was a fracture to the right arm, just above the wrist."

"Was it a single fracture?"

"Yes." *So he doesn't intend to be helpful.*

"Were you able to determine what could have caused the fracture?"

"Your client knocked her down and stomped on her arm."

Justice was stunned by the anger that rose up in her. "And you are able to tell not only how the injury occurred ... but who did it ... by what, an x-ray?"

"Yes, I can tell how the injury occurred by the x-ray, and she also had bruises on her arm, and she said he stomped her arm. Does he deny it?"

"Yes, he denies it, but you need to understand your position as a witness. You don't ask me questions about my client. You simply answer the questions I ask you about your medical treatment of the victim in this case. That's what the court will require you to do on the witness stand."

"When is the trial anyway, I may have to work that day." He opened his day planner and began to look through it.

Justice stood up and walked around the doctor's desk. She was so close she almost touched him. "Work," she said slowly and with as much control as she could muster, "is not an option when we subpoena you to come and testify as a witness. If you refuse to come and you are performing an operation, the sheriff will allow the medical center enough time to find someone to replace you, then you will be handcuffed and brought to court. If you are subpoenaed, you *will* come, and you *will* testify, and you *will* tell the truth. If you lie, I will *personally* see that you are prosecuted for perjury. Have I made myself clear, Dr. Burkett?"

He nodded his head and sat there in shock. He had no idea how the conversation got to that point. He tried to stand to show Justice out, but she stopped him with a wave of her hand.

"I can find my way out," she said, as he slumped back in his chair. He was suddenly angry. Angry at what he perceived as an arrogant attorney who thought she could intimidate him, angry with the defendant, the victim, and the hospital. He was angry with his wife because she never seemed to have enough "stuff." He was angry at the court because they could waste his time by making him come to court against his will. He didn't want to be a witness; he didn't want to go to court. He just wanted to be left alone to practice medicine. He loved being a doctor. It was a little like being God, and he loved being able to help patients and ease their suffering and anxieties. He knew that he would not be in this predicament if his wife had not been so caught up in things. He wished he could turn back the hand of time. He did not want to face Justice in court. He felt as if her anger had spilled over to him. He struggled to figure out how the conversation became so explosive. "Get a hold of yourself," he said out loud. "You have patients to see." He counted to 20, walked around the desk four times, took a deep breath and went to see his next patient.

Justice walked to her car and just stood there. *Why? How could you have gone off on the doctor like that? Did he deserve it? Maybe, but do you have a right to get so completely out of control?* She walked around to the driver's side, stopped and looked around the parking lot, sighed and slid into the car. She looked back at the building one last time and drove away. *I should call the man and apologize. No, give it a few days. I'm sure he hopes he never hears from me again in life.*

⌒

A STEADY RAIN had begun when Justice stopped at Dairy Queen to treat herself to a banana split. She decided not to beat up on herself anymore. She would just do better next time. As she pulled out of the Dairy Queen driveway, a garbage truck came across the line and headed straight toward her. She slammed on the brakes, screamed "Jesus help me," and covered her eyes with her hand. A few seconds later her car was still, all was quite, and she was afraid to move her hand from her face. She listened for the noise, there wasn't any. She removed her hand from her face. The truck was not there. She looked in the rear view mirror and the truck was back on the right side of the street and moving along as if nothing had happened. All the cars behind her were sitting still. She placed her hands on the steering wheel and began hyperventilating. The guy behind her blew his horn. She didn't move; he laid on the horn. Suddenly, a policeman pulled up and blocked Justice's car. He turned on his blue flashing light. She was shocked. *How can he give me a ticket, I didn't do anything wrong?* She rolled her window down; she wanted to cry. He got out of the car and walked over to Justice. "Are you okay young lady?" he asked. He reached in the car and touched her shoulder. Justice was so relieved, she started to cry and nodded her head yes. She tried to stop the tears, but they kept coming.

"You just sit right there until you feel better. I'll direct this traffic around you. Are you sure you are okay?"

"Yes, I'm okay," she whispered. And he moved into the street and began directing traffic around her.

WHEN SHE GOT home she threw the banana split in the trash. She no longer had a desire to treat herself. Justice sat on the floor and looked up at her dad's picture on her bedroom dresser. "Dad," she whispered as she scrambled to her feet and moved to the dresser. She picked up her Dad's picture and held it to her chest. She just stood there as tears rolled down her cheek. *How can I still miss my Dad so much after all this time?* She sat on the floor and continued to hold the picture to her chest. She thought of her dad and his faith in God. She could never have that much faith. Justice placed the picture on the bed and got down on her knees.

"God, I could had been killed by that truck. How could this have happened God, for both my mom and dad to die and leave me all alone in the world. I never even had a chance to know my mom, and I had the best dad in the whole world. Why couldn't one of them have been left with me, at least until I was out of law school. My dad would have been so proud of me. Anyway, I guess even you can't change all that now huh? But you can help me now. And I do need help. I guess you saw how I went off on the doctor today? And you remember how I screamed at the prosecutor? Kinda pitiful, huh? I'm sorry I haven't been talking to you lately. I guess I've been kinda angry with you because my mom and dad died and everything seems to be going wrong in my life. My dad always said you didn't take my mom, so I guess he would have said the same thing about himself. So I'm not going to be mad at you anymore. As a matter of fact, I'm going to draw close to you again instead of just going to Church because I know it's the right thing to do. I guess you want to know what I want from you, huh? No point in lying, you know I have ulterior motives, huh? Here's what I'm praying for, I need to find a good Christian psychiatrist. I'm not crazy; I just need some good sound counseling. I really need someone to talk to who can understand how I feel and help me deal with this temper. I can deal with everything else. So, God, please help me to find a good Christian psychiatrist--and soon, Amen."

Justice placed her dad's picture back on the dresser and picked up her mom's picture. Not because she missed her mom the way she missed her dad. She really didn't remember her mom. She felt guilty when she thought of how often she held her dad's picture and not her mom's. She always picked it up as an after thought. Just in case they could see her from Heaven, she didn't want to hurt her mom's feeling.

She felt so much better after talking to God. She knew she would put God back at the center of her life and get control of her temper. She knew that would please her dad. She wondered if he could see her or whether he was aware of how she was doing. She thought about what her dad had taught her about God, and she knew that she would spend eternity in the same place as her parents. Eternity must be a long time she thought as she slipped on her sneakers and a blue jogging suit for a walk in the park. She hoped it wouldn't be too long before she found that psychiatrist to help her deal with her temper. She took her wallet and cell phone from her purse, grabbed her keys, and headed out the door.

SOLOMON WAS ABOUT to get into his car when he realized that he had left his cell phone in the condo. He closed the car door and started back to his unit. He had an irresistible urge to walk all the way around the building. He reached the other side and began running up the steps. He turned his head, just for a second, when he heard a car door slam. When he tried to look where he was going, it was too late. A running female in blue crashed into him and they went tumbling down the steps to the ground. She landed on top of him. They were eyeball to eyeball. Neither could think of anything to say. She spoke first.

"I'm sorry, I didn't see you."

"I'm sorry, I didn't see you either."

"My name is Justiana and I live here."

"My name is Solomon and I live here too," he said, feeling like an idiot repeating after her.

"Are you okay?" she asked.

"If you weren't on top of me, I might be able to tell." Her eyes widen, and then she started to laugh and rolled off of him and onto her back. He began to laugh also and neither could get up. They just lay side by side on the ground laughing. The more ridiculous they felt, the more they laughed. After what seemed like a very long time to Solomon, he was able to pull himself up and help Justice to her feet. They were both a little embarrassed.

"Where are you going in such a hurry?" Solomon asked.

"I was on my way to the park to walk off a little frustration." For some reason, Justice felt real comfortable with this stranger. *After all he is a neighbor, and I have never seen such a beautiful man. I know men are usually not thought of as beautiful, but how do you describe a man whose flawless skin is a dark chocolate and looks like velvet, whose teeth are so white and beautiful they look artificial, and whose smile begins as a sparkle in his eyes, then spread to his lips? He must be at least six feet four. I wonder if this is what the African prince looks like.*

"That wouldn't happen to be Evergreen State Park would it?"

"As a matter fact, that's the one," Justice answered.

"That's where I'm going," Solomon said. "I forgot my cell phone and was running back to get it when I was knocked flat on my back by a beautiful female. Can I give you a lift, I'm coming right back here when I'm done."

"I'll follow you, I'm not sure where I'll go when I finish walking."

☞

"WHY ARE YOU frustrated?" Solomon asked, as they walked around the park.

Justice got right to the point. "Both my parents are dead. I miss my dad a lot even though he's been dead almost three years. I don't really miss my mom because I don't remember her; she died when I was 18 months old. But I miss not having a mother. I don't even think I could make a good mother because I don't know what it takes to be a good mother. But I do know how to be a good father. On top of all that, I feel guilty because I miss my dad more than my mom, and sometimes I think they are looking down on me from Heaven, and my mom's feeling are hurt because I still cry sometimes for my dad. And today I realized for the first time, or I was able to admit it for the first time, that I have been a little angry with God. Is that crazy enough to be frustrated?"

"It is, and I can help you with that."

"What are you, a psychiatrist or something?"

"Yep, as a matter of fact, I am." He reached into his pocket and handed her one of his business cards. Justice looked at the card and stopped in her tracks. She was unable to walk or talk for a few seconds. Solomon looked at her face and asked, "You have something against Psychiatrists?" She shook her head and looked around for a place to sit.

"Are you a Christian?" she asked.

"Yes, I am, why do you ask?" He put his arm around her

shoulder; she looked like she was about to pass out. "What's wrong?"

"I should be happy instead of shocked," Justice mumbled. "I prayed that God would help me find a Christian psychiatrist just before I ran down the steps and into you."

Now it was Solomon's turn to be shocked. "You did what?" Justice merely nodded her head yes. She was no longer able to speak. He took her by the arm and led her to a nearby bench.

When they were seated, she told him about her encounter with Mark, the doctor, and the garbage truck incident.

"When I saw that truck rushing toward me, I knew I could end up in an accident that would take me into eternity. And I knew that was not how I wanted to meet God. I guess it made me realize how foolish it is to be angry with the one who gives you the very breath you breathe."

"So you were angry with God because of the death of your parents?"

"Mostly, but also because so many things have gone wrong in my life. I felt that if Mom or Dad were here, things would be better. I think my temper stems from that anger. Of course I have two good friends, Lela and her husband Ted. I have an aunt and a cousin, but we don't get along. I shouldn't say we don't get along, we just don't have anything to do with each other."

"Why not?" Solomon asked.

"My dad said they assumed that we thought we were better than them. It didn't matter what we did; they were always hostile. At least my cousin was, and my aunt just didn't know how to handle it. So, he finally told me to leave them alone."

"Where do they live?"

"In Augusta, at least that's where they were the last time I heard from them."

"My sister and her family live in Augusta, I visit them often." Solomon was quite for a moment. "You know Justice, my parents are both dead also. They were killed in an automobile accident when I was in my last year of med school. God sent a professor to help me through it. I would never have finish school without his help. He was a real angel. Lela and Ted may be angels in your life, and I may be one as well. I know how you feel, I've been there."

"Were you ever mad at God?"

"Only twice in my life, when my parents died and when I was kicked to the curb by the love of my life."

"So how did you get over your anger?" Justice was beginning to feel better already. She thought she was the only person silly enough to be angry with God.

"It seemed like everything was going wrong for me, too. Then, a day came when I needed help and there was no one to turn to but God. Not that friends and relatives wouldn't help, there was nothing they could do. I had always been close to my aunt Gracie, my mom's sister. But she was as devastated by my parents' death as I was, and my sister . . . well, she was a basket case. I realized that human beings couldn't give me the help I needed, and I couldn't help my little sister. I remembered my grandmother and her prayer closet. I thought that was kind of silly the way she kept a little spot in her closet to pray. We told her that God could hear you anywhere and in any position. Well, I want to tell you I cleaned out a spot in my closet and got down on my knees. I didn't want to debate about when and where God could hear my prayer, I just knew I needed help real quick, and my grandmother always got help when she went into her closet."

"Did you tell Him you were mad at Him?" Justice was beginning to feel so much better just listening to Solomon.

"Yes, that was the first thing I did. You can't really pray to someone you are angry with. After I told Him how sorry I was, I cried ... not just cried, I wept for a whole hour. I was glad I was alone. I would have been really embarrassed for anyone to hear me carry on the way I did. You know, Justice, I never really told Him the problems about which I went in the closet to pray. Somewhere toward the end of all that sobbing and snotting, I realized that He was already aware of the problems and was going to help me. It was the first time I knew for sure that I had heard from God, and there were no words spoken, just a peace and a knowing. There are no words to explain it. But I knew. Things didn't change overnight. But when my attitude changed, the problems just seemed to melt away, and best of all I was back in touch with God." Solomon stood and pulled Justice up. "Let's walk and talk, we didn't come here to mope."

They walked for an hour. Justice was just getting back into walking, and she had a hard time trying to keep up with Solomon, who usually walked for an hour at each workout. She was so happy she had met him. He was wise, humorous, practical, and so easy to talk to. It seemed like they talked about everything. He told her he was a Sunday school teacher and invited her to his class. She promised him that she would come.

Justice told him about Alou and the break up she experienced before she met Alou.

"We have a lot in common. I had a really bad breakup, and my fiancée's name is Juliana. She's an international flight attendant based out of Texas, so we don't get to see each other very often. We take turns flying to meet each other. It's my turn to fly out to Texas for the next holiday. Occasionally I go out on dates with other ladies, but it's just that, a date, and I let them know up front that my heart belongs to Juliana."

"Does she know about these dates?" Justice asked.

"Yes, we have an agreement to always be honest with each other. She goes out occasionally herself. But she never forgets to whom she belongs."

Justice wished she were that strong. She couldn't bear the thought of someone she loved going on a date with another woman.

When they returned to the condo, Solomon insisted that Justice walk him to his door and then he walked her to her door.

"Now you will have no excuse for feeling frustrated when you have a new friend nearby who will listen to your woes and help you come up with a solution to every problem," Solomon said.

Justice felt for the card in her pocket to be sure she still had it. "And how much will I have to pay for this counseling service?"

"No charge for you, as long as it's not between the hours of 9 to 5 weekdays. However, if it's during work hours, call my secretary and she will work it out according to your income."

"I'll keep that in mind. Thanks for the walk, the advice, and being an angel when I needed one the most. Enjoy the rest of the evening,"

"I will, but that's on the condition that you have a wonderful evening yourself."

"I definitely will," she said.

"Then I will too, see you later." Solomon took two steps backwards, stomped the ground twice, saluted, and disappeared around the corner.

Justice just stood there laughing. *Solomon is so dramatic.*

7

Justice's first jury trial was the case of Abdullah Hashid, charged with possession of cocaine. She was angry when she read the police report. She felt that the police officer had fabricated the whole thing. When she talked with Vanessa about it, she simply shrugged and admitted that she sometimes felt the same way.

"But why would a police officer lie on an innocent citizen?" Justice asked.

"Most of the time they report the facts as they see them, but there are officers who are mean or corrupt, or both. Being a police officer gives them a chance to harass or harm far more people than they could otherwise. Guilt or innocence is not something they consider. They just want to see people thrown into jail for as long as possible. But there are corrupt individuals in all professions. Welcome to the real world, Miss Fullilove, and remember what your professors told you in law school: Don't love, don't hate, just apply the law. And let me add to that, at the end of the day, just be sure you have done what's right and best for your client. Then, go home and forget about it, you are not God, you are just a lawyer, and a very new one at that." Vanessa could only hope that Justice didn't become discouraged too quickly; she was just the kind of person needed for people like the prosecutor and judge in courtroom D.

THE FIRST OFFICER to testify was a female. Justice knew she was lying and was happy she had gone to the scene of the alleged crime.

"Your witness counselor," Mark said as he strolled back to his seat.

"Thank you counselor," Justice said as she flipped through her notes. "Officer Tate, you testified that you were driving down Lincoln Parkway, a major thoroughfare, near Memorial Drive, which is a major intersection when you saw the Defendant in the alley.

"Yes."

"And it was approximately 12 noon, on a Friday?"

"Yes."

"And he was in a huddle with 4 or 5 other people?"

"Yes."

"And when you say huddled you mean the group of people were bent forward and facing each other?"

"Yes."

"Did you recognize any one *other than* the Defendant?"

"No."

"Is it true that you were alone in the vehicle?

"Yes."

"Now, you testified that you saw the Defendant pass drugs to one of the people in the huddle."

"Yes."

"Was that person a male or female?"

"I . . . I couldn't tell." The officer seemed surprised by the question.

"You couldn't tell if the person to whom he passed the drugs was male or female? Were you able to tell whether the Defendant was male or female?

"Yes, he's male?"

"And you were able to tell that from looking at him in the huddle."

"Yes."

"But you were not able to determine if the person to whom he allegedly passed the drugs was male or female, and they were all in he same huddle?"

"Because I already knew the Defendant."

"So, you can only tell the difference between a male and a female if you already know the person?"

Even the judge had to laugh.

"No, I can tell if I can see their faces clearly. But they were all bent over in a huddle."

"The fact that they were all bent over in a huddle kept you from seeing everyone's face except the Defendant's? You were able to see his face in spite of the huddle?"

"Well, no I didn't see his face, but I already knew him."

"Was he wearing a uniform?"

"I don't think so, I don't recall seeing a uniform."

"Was he larger than all the other people in the huddle?"

"No."

"Was he smaller than all the other people?"

The officer hesitated. "No, I don't think so." She shifted in her seat and glanced at the jury.

"Isn't it true that the alley in question is approximately 30 feet wide."

"Yes, I guess so."

"Isn't it true that the distance between where you were, which was the opposite side of the median, and where the people were huddled together is approximately 350 feet, roughly the length of a football field?"

"Yes."

"So, let me see if I understand your testimony before this court. Is it your testimony, officer Tate, that you were driving down Lincoln Parkway, a few feet from Memorial, a major intersection, around 12:00 noon, on a Friday, and that you passed an alley that's approximately 30 feet wide, and you did not stop, but continued driving. And, as you drove pass the alley, you looked across the median, down the alley, and saw a group of people huddled together, with their backs to you. You were approximately 350 feet away from them, and you were not only able to see and identify the defendant, without seeing his face, because you knew him. He was not wearing a uniform, no larger or smaller than the other people in the group, and you not only could tell that the Defendant passed something to another person, but you were able to tell that it was drugs. Is that your testimony before this court?"

"No, that wasn't exactly my testimony."

"Then let's see which part I misunderstood. Is the part true about you driving down Lincoln Parkway, near Memorial Drive, which is a major intersection?"

"Yes."

"And was it around 12:00 noon on a Friday?"

"Well . . . yes."

"And is it true that you didn't stop as you passed the alley, but kept . . ."

"Objection," Mark said. "Your Honor those questions have been asked and answered."

"I don't think so, Mr. LaNear," the judge said. "When Miss Fullilove asked the witness if that was her testimony, she said that was not exactly her testimony. I want to know what part of her testimony Miss Fullilove misunderstood, because I apparently misunderstood it as well. I thought that was her testimony."

The Jury nodded their heads to indicate that they had misunderstood as well. The prosecutor sat down, and the officer shifted in her seat.

"Without going through the entire testimony, why don't you tell me which of my statements were not your testimony," Justice said.

"Well, it was all basically my testimony."

"Then point out the statement that I made that was *not* your testimony.

"Well, now that I think about it, I guess that was my testimony."

"Okay, so it's your testimony that you were . . ."

"Objection," Mark said. "Your Honor, again, those questions have been asked and answered."

"That's not true your Honor," Justice said. When I asked ...

"I understand your point, Miss Fullilove, but I think the jury will remember the testimony of the officer and all the facts in the case. Besides, you will have an opportunity to reiterate the facts in your closing arguments. Objection sustained."

⌒

ON DIRECT EXAMINATION, the second officer testified that he saw the Defendant walking along Memorial Drive.

"What happened next?" Mark asked.

"That's when Office Tate told me..."

"Objection, hearsay," Justice said.

"Sustained," the judge said.

"Did the Defendant run when he saw you?" Mark asked.

"No, but Officer Tate said he ..."

"Objection! Hearsay. This officer only saw the Defendant walking along Memorial Drive. Period!"

"Objection sustained," Judge Denver said. "Mr. LaNear, why don't you have this officer testify to the facts as he knows them, rather than trying to have him reiterate the testimony of Officer Tate."

Mark was exasperated. "I have no further questions for this witness, your Honor."

"You may cross examine the witness Miss Fullilove."

Justice stood, flipped through her papers, and turned to look at the witness.

"Is it your testimony, that the only thing you saw the defendant do is walk along Memorial Drive?"

"No, that was not the only thing I saw him do."

"What else did you see him do?" Justice asked.

"Officer Tate said ... "

"I'm only asking you about what *you* saw him do."

"Well, I guess that was all I saw."

"Thank you, I have no further questions for this witness."

"Call your next witness, Mr. LaNear," the judge said.

"Your Honor, the state rests."

Justice called three witnesses: The Subway employee, who testified that the defendant came in, bought a sandwich and ate it there; the defendant's employer, who testified that the defendant left for lunch at approximately 11:30 a.m. and never came back to work, and the defendant who testified that he left work and went directly to Subway, bought a sandwich, ate it there, and was walking along Memorial Drive on his way back to work when the officers stopped him. He had not been in the alley. The Carwash is two blocks south on Memorial Drive, and he would have been back to work on time had he not been stopped by the officers.

The prosecutor did not have any questions for the employer or The Subway employee. The prosecutor had questions for the Defendant. After a few preliminary questions, he asked about prior arrests. The Defendant had never been arrested before.

"Mr. Hashid," Mark said. "How many times have you been arrested on drug cha. . .?"

"Objections!" Justice yelled, stood, and took a few steps toward Mark. "Your Honor, the prosecutor knows that the defendant has never been arrested before, and the defendant did not put his character in issue. The defense motions for a mistrial." She was furious.

Judge Denver denied the motion and said he would give the jury curative instructions.

Justice walked back to the defense table and put her hands on her hips. "I'm sick of this," she said.

Judge Denver leaned toward Justice, allowed his glasses to fall low on his nose and growled, "And just what is the problem Miss Fullilove. What is it you're sick of?"

"I'm sick of this stinking prosecutor, who is consistently trying to send people to prison when he has no evidence against them. He puts lying witnesses on the stand and fabricates evidence by asking question for which he does not have one shred of evidence. I'm sick of these stinking police officers framing people just to increase the number of arrest and convictions. And I'm sick of this stinking Court overruling objections that ought to be sustained, sustaining objections that ought to be overruled, and just so there's no mistake about who the court is, I'm sick of you, your Honor. As a matter of fact you are not an honor you are a dishonor to this courtroom and to the legal profession."

There was complete silence in the courtroom. No one breathed. All eyes were on Justice. It was as if they were afraid to look at the judge. Judge Denver leaned forward slowly and took his gavel. As he did, he felt strong hands go around his throat, and a voice whisper in his right ear.

"This seems like a good time to call for a 30 minute recess. As a matter of fact this is the perfect time."   He knew someone was standing beside him, he heard him, he felt his hands around his throat, but he couldn't see him.

The voice whispered, "I'll loosen my grip just enough for you to call for a recess. If you call for anything other than a recess, it will be your last call today, and forever."

The stranger loosed his grip ever so slightly. Judge Denver realized that no one else was aware of the presence of this guy.

"Do not EVER discuss what just happened in this courtroom with anyone at any time. Are we clear? His hands began to tighten on the judge's throat again.

Judge Denver nodded his head slightly and raised the gavel. He banged his gavel on the bench and said, "Let's take a 30 minute recess. I remind the jury not to discuss the case among yourselves and don't allow anyone to discuss it in your presence."

The jury stood to leave and stopped when Judge Denver practically ran from the courtroom. No one moved, not even

Justice. Everyone was in shock. They stared at the Judge's chair. They seemed to be expecting him to come back and do something that made sense. This last scene certainly hadn't made any sense. The jury liked Justice, but thought she had gone a bit too far. Even for Justice.

Justice just stood there. She felt the presence of her father so strongly that she actually turned around and looked for him. *This is crazy; my dad has been dead almost three years. What's happening to me?*

As she left the courtroom, Justice pulled out her cell phone and dialed Alou's private number.

"This is Alou."

"Hello, this is Justice."

"Is something wrong, you sound" ... Alou couldn't think of the word to describe the sound of Justice's voice. But he knew something was wrong.

"I think I'm going to end up before the displinary committee of the Bar." Justice sounded like she was going to cry. She was not about to tell Alou that she felt the presence of her dad in the courtroom.

"Hey, I'll be right over, where are you?" Alou asked.

"I'm on my way back to the office. I went off on the Judge and called him a name and said he was a dishonor to the legal profession"

"It had to have been his fault. Hasn't he been giving you a hard time every since you've been there?" Alou asked.

Justice simply nodded her head. She knew Alou could not see her but she was unable to speak.

"Justice, have I told you how much I love you lately?"

"No," she mumbled, and he knew she was crying.

"Where are you? I'm coming to get you; we can talk about it then. I bet it's not as bad as you think. The guy must have been out of line; it had to have been his fault. You're such a reasonable person. Tell me where you are."

"No, I have to go back to the office and we only have a 30 minute recess. I'll call you later. I just needed to hear a friendly voice."

"You know that I love you, don't you?" Alou asked.

"Are you sure?"

"Justice, there is nothing you can do to stop me from loving you. Even if you murdered me, I'd come back to life and testify at your trial that it was an accident."

She giggled and clicked the cell phone off.

Alou was relieved. He knew the somehow she would be okay, but she would not allow him to come and comfort her. *I'll just have to get used to that independent spirit.*

THE BAILIFF WALKED up to the jury box without a word and the jury followed him to the jury room. He turned and walked away. They sat and stared at each other in silence.

"Its cold in here," said Mrs. Holiday, feeling a duty to break the silence.

"Yes," echoed the women, happy to have the silence broken. They had not been able to think of anything to say. Their minds were whirling with questions and they didn't know who had the answers.

"What happened," Ms. Lowell finally asked the question that was on everyone's mind. "And why did he let her get away with it?" she continued.

"Who said she got away with it?" asked Mrs. Swanson.

"Well, if she hadn't gotten away with it, he would have said, come back in 30 minutes and show cause why you should not be held in contempt of court," said Mr. Johnson.

"It's still not too late for him to hold her in contempt," said Mrs. Swanson.

"Oh, but it is too late," said Mrs. Jimenez. "If he didn't address it when it first occurred, he waived the right to bring it up later."

"That's not true, he's the judge, he can bring it up whenever he pleases," Mrs. Swanson said.

"I don't think so Mrs. Swanson," Ms. Lowell said. "I believe Mrs. Jimenez is right, he waived that right."

Suddenly the bailiff was at the door and they realized they had spent the entire 30 minutes trying to show each other that they were smart and well versed on the law. They filed silently back into the courtroom. All eyes were on the Judge. They waited for him to tear into Justice. He actually smiled at her. Her mouth fell open. The jury's mouth fell open. The prosecutor stood, looked at Justice, then at the judge. He was in total shock.

"Your Honor, I believe we have a matter to take up out of the presence of the jury," Mark said.

"And just what matter is that Mr. LaNear," asked the judge, looking at Mark as if he were the one crazy. Mark gestured toward Justice but couldn't bring himself to speak. Justice turned and stared at Mark as if she had no idea what he was talking about.

Justice jumped to her feet. "Your Honor, it's obvious that the prosecutor is engaging in his usual delaying tactics. This trial has already lasted longer than it should have. If it pleases the court, the defense is ready to proceed."

"I agree that this trial has already lasted far too long, are you ready to proceed Mr. LaNear?" Now it was Mark's turn to be angry. But he knew he could not get away with what Justice had obviously gotten away with. He wondered if the Judge had lost his mind completely, and why would he allow her to get away with that? The Jury felt sorry for Mark. They thought he was going to cry. He just stood there trying to compose himself with his hands hanging loosely at this side.

The judge just sat there and stared at Mark. He could still feel those fingers around his throat. He was sick of both Mark and Justice. If he could work magic, they would both disappear into oblivion.

Mark's closing argument was brief. He assailed the defense for wasting taxpayers money and the police officer's time.

During her closing argument Justice requested permission to present a demonstration to the jury. Mark objected, but his objection was overruled.

The presentation involved 2 separate groups and 4 kids in each group from My Brother's Keeper at Oaktree Downs. As the kids entered the courtroom, jurors were instructed to close their eyes. Once the kids were huddled together in a circle, the jurors were instructed to open their eyes. Justice explained that this is the position the officer testified that the people in the alley were in when she first saw them. The kids remained in a huddle and exchanged Hershey kisses. Then they turned and hurried from the courtroom. The jury never saw their faces. The second group came, huddled in a group and exchanged lollipops. They hurried from the courtroom. Then they all came back; all mixed up, and stood facing the jury.

"Is there anyone who feels that they can tell me which four students were in the first group?" Justice asked. The jury stared at the group and slowly began to shake their heads.

"Now, you may have been able to determine that they were passing something around, but, is there anyone who can tell me *what* they were passing?" "Don't raise your hand, just answer in your heart." One by one the jurors began to shake their heads.

"Thank you," Justice said to the kids; "I'll contact you later." Indicating that they were dismissed. They quietly left the courtroom. Justice continued with her closing argument.

"If you, sitting *less than 20 feet* from those young people, who were huddled in the same manner as the officer has testified that the defendant was huddled with 4 or 5 other people, and the distance from where the officer testified that she was and where the Defendant was when she saw him is *approximately 350 feet,* and the officer also testified that she was driving a car on a major thoroughfare, a few feet from a major intersection, and she looked down an alley as she passed by on the opposite side of the median and saw the Defendant, who was *already* huddled when she saw him. Now, do you believe the officer could see who was in that huddle and what they were doing? You couldn't, and you were less than 20 feet away, you were not driving on a major thoroughfare, and your view was not limited by the few seconds it takes to pass an alley. Ladies and gentlemen, I submit to you, there is just no way the officer could have seen who was in that huddle, nor could she have seen what they were doing.

If that's not bad enough, consider the fact that the employee at Subway testified that Abdullah had just eaten a sandwich there. She told the officer that when she was questioned on the day of the incident.

And if that's not bad enough, consider the fact that his employer testified that Abdullah left for lunch at 11:30 and was expected back by 12:00 noon. Had he not been stopped and arrested by the officers, he would have been back to work on time. The police report will show that the arrest took place at approximately 12:00 noon, just about the time his employer expected him back at work.

"Now, I ask you, ladies and gentlemen, based on the facts in this case, and the testimony of the defendant, the employer, the Subway employee, and the officers themselves, is it remotely possible that the officer could have determined who was in that huddle and what they were doing?" All twelve jurors were shaking their head. She walked around the podium and moved closer to the jury box. She stared each juror in the eye, looked down, took a few steps backwards, and continued.

"Can you believe the prosecutor actually had the nerve to talk about wasting the police officer's time? Or that he even called those people police officers? Now he was right about wasting the taxpayer's money, and he should have added, wasting your time. But it wasn't the defendant that did the wasting; it was the state, and the police officers. How pitiful. The defendant has been arrested, for the first in his life--for a crime he did not commit. The only crime committed in this case was the arrest of an innocent man--which is a crime against us all. The injustice of it all was taking him from his job and family with full knowledge that he had committed no crime. The defendant will never be able to recoup his time and maybe not even his job, and he will have a criminal history in his file for life. Oh, the file will show that the verdict was not guilty, and I fully expect you to return a verdict of not guilty. But the arrest will remain in his file. How pitiful. The officers did wrong by fabricating a charge against the defendant, and the state did wrong for prosecuting the defendant. You are the only ones who can right those wrongs by returning a verdict of not guilty. And that, ladies and gentlemen, is exactly what I'm asking you to do. Thank you."

When Justice returned to her seat, the judge asked Mark if he had a rebuttal. He shook his head no. He could tell by the look on the juror's faces that anything he said would be useless. The Judge gave the jury the usual post trial instructions, including curative instruction about the prosecutors question regarding the defendant's arrest on drug charges, and they were sent to deliberate. They reached a verdict in two hours. They found the defendant not guilty.

That was the first jury trial in Courtroom D in 11 months. The Defendant kept hugging and thanking Justice who appeared to be calm and laid back, but she was very much aware of the dark cloud and oppressive spirit hanging over the courtroom which seemed to be sitting on her shoulder as Mark glared at her with slits for eyes. As soon as the defendant left, she shivered, gathered up her belongings, and hurried out.

Chapter

Justice did not want to go home alone after her first trial. She felt an urgent need for company. She dialed Alou's private number and got right to the point when he answered.

"Alou, if you don't want to go out to dinner or just have some company, you'd better say so now, because I'm headed your way."

"You picked the right guy, because I want your company, I want to go out to dinner, and I am thrilled that you are headed my way. But tell me, when did you start asking guys for dates?"

"Since I began feeling so overwhelmed by the oppressive spirit in that courtroom. Alou, it's so real I can feel it. It's like the judge and the prosecutor are driven to do all the harm they can do to everyone, the defendants as well as the attorneys. The few defendants who are given probation are ordered to finish high school or get a GED in an unreasonable timeframe and ordered to pay fines and do community service. If they don't have a job and can't pay the fine, or get to the far out places to do community service, they end up in prison anyway. It's like they think of ways to set them up for failure. It's awful. It's like the other attorneys have gotten used to it and it doesn't bother them anymore, and to top it all off, I could swear that someone followed me to the clubhouse at Oaktree Downs . . . I'm sorry Alou, I promise I won't talk about it any more today, and I 'm not going to be a bore at dinner.

"You could never bore me, Justice. But I want to hear more about this. If these guys are so awful, why haven't someone done something about them. Surely they have to go by some kind of rules. Aren't they governed by the Bar like all other attorneys? Do you think they may have someone following you?"

"Yes, they are governed by the Bar," Justice said and sighed. "I guess the attorneys have just grown weary of fighting a losing battle. And I don't have any proof that someone is following me, but I think it's possible and I think it has something to do with either Mark or Judge Denver. They are both creeps. Anyway, I'm changing the subject. Where would you like to eat?"

"Alright, the subject is changed, but I'm adding a footnote. I will find a way to stop those guys. They will not get away with frustrating my baby."

"You don't have a baby, you're not even married."

"Well, I'll just have to see what I can do on both counts . . . Getting back to dinner, why don't I have Shane come over and whip us up something here? There's no better chef in Georgia, and I can have you all to myself." Shane was known as a one-man restaurant whose motto was: I'm available 24/7 to prepare your meals the way you want them on a first-come first-serve basis.

"Sounds good to me," Justice said. "I'll see you in 15 minutes." Justice knew that Alou had Shane come to the office and prepare lunch for his employees at least once a week, and dinner on the evenings when they worked late. She didn't care what they had for dinner; she just wanted to be in the company of someone who cared about her--and away from that oppressive spirit that engulfed her in Courtroom D.

ALOU HAD BEEN working on a report that was due the next day. He placed it in the file cabinet and called Shane.

"Hello, my man," he said when Shane answered the phone. "I am desperately in need of a good chef to whip up a couple of delicious grilled salmon salads and some type of chocolate desert, in my office, pronto. Tell me you can do it."

"Sure, I can do it. Only two people working late tonight?"

"You know what they say about all work and no play. So, this is not work, this is pure pleasure."

"Sounds like *Justice* to me, and I'll put *my foot* in the salad and the desert."

"That's what I wanted to hear. What would I do without you, man?"

"Probably order a couple of hamburgers and large fries." They both chuckled and hung up.

Alou dimmed the lights and turned on soft music. He beat the pillows on the couch in his private lounge and sprayed some fresh pine air freshener into the air. He decided it was too strong and opened the door and tried to fan the fragrance out. Shane arrived before Justice and waved to Alou as he passed his lounge enroute to the kitchen. Alou found a peach blossom fragrance and sprayed a small amount into the air and fanned it with a pillow to help mix the two fragrances. He sniffed the air and smiled. The peach had taken over and the combo was awesome. He turned when Jan stuck her head in the door to let him know that Justice had arrived and that she was leaving for the day. He just stood and stared at Justice as she entered his lounge. He had forgotten how much he loved her. He wanted to take her in his arms and never let her go. He was always a bit frightened by the depth of his love for her. *What if something goes wrong and she walks away for good. I don't even want to think about it.*

"Wow, it smell peachy in here, what fragrance is that?" Justice asked as she sniffed the air.

"A combo of peach and pine. I created it just for you. Peach is your favorite and pine is mine. They make a wonderful combo, just like us. Shane is preparing dinner, and I'll get you a glass of green tea and I want to hear more about your day and those evil guys in your courtroom and the creep that may be following you. And I don't want anyone interrupting us or listening in on our conversation. I'm all ears, and I'm all yours."

"Do you really want to hear about it, you are not just being nice are you?"

"I really want to hear all about it. I may be able to help you come up with a solution to the problem. You know what they say: two heads are better than one. Besides, whatever concerns you concerns me. No matter how small it may seem to you, it's a big thing to me if it causes you any distress. And sometimes it's good just to talk about what concerns you. And I never get tired of listening to you. Never."

"Okay, you asked for it," she said. They sat on the couch and she told him about her day and how she had felt an oppressive spirit from the moment she entered Courtroom D. She had been in other courtrooms, and none were like Courtroom D. Both the judge and the prosecutor seemed desperate to put people in prison. Alou hung onto every word, as he made notes and asked questions. Justice could see that he was really concerned and his questions let her know that he believed her. Alou pointed out some specific things to which she should pay attention, and they agreed to discuss it again in a couple of days. Alou took her hand and kissed it. Then lifted her chin so that he was staring into her eyes.

"Don't ever forget that I love you, and you can talk to me about anything you want, at any time. Nothing is too small or large, and I'm never too busy to talk with you, and it's never too late or too early for you to call me."

"Wow, I don't know what to say. That is so special, Alou. Wow." She was almost moved to tears. Alou leaned over and kissed her on the mouth.

Shane cleared his throat and they looked up. "Dinner is served my lady and my man."

"Let's go eat," Alou said as he grabbed Justice by the hand and pulled her up and toward the kitchen. Shane followed them back into the kitchen. When Alou was sure everything was as he wanted, he turned to Shane and bowed.

"Thank you, my man, I hate to throw you out, but you are no longer needed around here. You may depart in peace."

"You didn't have to be so blunt, I could have taken a hint," Shane said as he gathered up his backpack and disappeared.

After dinner Alou told Justice that he was thinking about trying to find his dad, and that Snaggie Jones, was making some inquiries for him. That name sounded familiar to Justice, but she could not remember where she had heard it before.

Snaggie was a 28-eight-year-old, private investigator. She had been labeled a tomboy when she was a kid. She had liked to hang with the guys and could beat them at almost anything they did. She was tall and slender with large brown yes, dark brown skin, and always wore her hair in a ponytail. She had a reputation as one who could find a needle in a haystack.

After Justice left, Alou made a list of influential people that owed him a favor. He called Snaggie and asked her to pick up the list the next day and to think of ways he could extract favors from his debtors on Justice's behalf. He instructed her to keep up with Justice's court dates and find out who could sit in, inconspicuously, and had enough influence to make the judge sit up straight on the bench. Justice was not to ever know.

"Keep me abreast of each 'sit in'. Once you determine when and who to send in, check with me before you set it up. If you're unable to reach me, use your best judgment, and put forth every effort to make sure each court hearing is covered . . .And assign someone to keep an eye on her. I need to know if anyone follows her, especially when she goes to Oaktree Downs. Better yet, bug the clubhouse at Oaktree Downs, and find a way to put my new tracking device on her car and in her purse. We will have a chance firsthand to see how the device works while I put the patent application together.

"Will do," Snaggie said. "See you first thing in the morning." *I need to meet this Justice lady. She must be the one that Leroy and all the kids at Oaktree Downs talk about all the time.*

Snaggie called Nito and gave him the assignment of following Justice. Nito was six feet two, weighed 225 pounds, and fit as a fiddle. His mom sometimes called him the jolly brown giant. He loved his job. The work was steady and he made more money that he had expected to make. He shut down his computer and headed for his jeep. His dad had given him the jeep for his birthday when he turned 16.

~

NITO SHOOK HIS head when he thought about the events that led up to his getting the job. He had had several arrests for fighting as a juvenile, and was always released to go home with his mom, until his final brush with the law when he was sent to boot camp for 120 days. That experience changed his life. He determined that he would never go down that road again.

He was released from boot camp on a Monday, and he had gone job-hunting every day for two weeks. On Friday, he had responded to an ad by Snaggie Jones for a private investigator. She had made him feel like an idiot for inquiring about the job. Nito told her, as he did all prospective employers, about his arrest record. She frowned and said she had never had an applicant for the position before who had a criminal record. When she asked how many times he had been arrested, and he said four, she laid the pencil down and stared at him. He knew the interview was over. She told him that she would keep his application on file and would give him a call if she had a position that would be right for him. Nito knew she was just being polite. So he thanked her and went his way. *How am I supposed to earn a living when no one will hire me? Is my life over now?*

The second Sunday Nito was home from boot camp he agreed to attend church with his mom just to get her off his back. He slumped down in the pew and determined that he would not pay any attention to anything the preacher said. The pastor introduced the guest preacher, an old man who had apparently traveled all over the world. When the preacher stopped preaching and began pointing out people in the audience and telling them past and future things about their lives, Nito was disgusted because the people clapped and acted as though they believed what he said was true. How can grown people be so dumb? He asked himself. After speaking to about four people, the preacher pointed to Nito. His mom was so happy, Nito thought she was going to faint.

"You in the blue shirt," the preacher said. "Raise your hand so I can be sure you know who I'm talking to." When Nito didn't raise his hand fast enough, his mom reach over and tried to raise it for him. Nito sat there with his hand raised and glared at the preacher. *What lie is he going to tell me?*

"The Lord said that you have just about given up on finding a job. As a matter of fact, when you left the interview Friday, you said that you were not going to waste your time looking for a job any more. But you really wanted that job. He says go back in three days and the job is yours. Three days," the preacher said as he held up three fingers. The people clapped, his mom cried like a baby, and the preacher went back to his sermon.

Nito just sat there in shock. He had not told anyone, not even his mom, that he was so discouraged that he had decided to stop looking for a job. He could never go back to Snaggie Jones about the job as a private investigator. Never.

☙

NITO DIDN'T HEAR anything else the preacher said that day. He just sat there thinking about the man telling him to go back to Snaggie and the job was his. He argued with himself until service was over, and argued with his mom all the way home. She insisted that he go back to see Snaggie in three days because she knew he would get the job. Nito finally agreed to go to get her off his back. He kept thinking about what the preacher said. He wondered if somehow what he said was true. He certainly got it right about him giving up on the job hunting, and he really wanted that job. He thought about his days in Sunday school as a kid. On the night before the third day, Nito got down on his knees beside his bed and said a prayer for the first time in years. "God, if you really spoke to that preacher, and you really help me to get this job, I will pray every day, go to church as often as I can, and I'll never forget what you did for me. Amen."

WHEN NITO WALKED into Snaggie's office, she swiveled her chair around and said into the phone, "never mind, he just walked in the door, thank you very much." She hung the phone up and stood.

"Would you believe that I was just speaking with your mother on the phone?"

"She called you?" Nito was angry with his mom for interfering. *Why couldn't she just stay out of it?*

"No, I called her. I decided to offer you the job if you still want it."

Nito was speechless. He just stood there with his mouth open. His emotions were out of control. He realized that his anger at his mom was unjustified, what the preacher had said was true, and that he had received a blessing that he probably didn't deserve.

"Yes, yes, I still want the job."

"Then it's yours. If you can start tomorrow, I'll hook you up with Big Red, he's my best trainer. He'll teach you everything you need to know."

NITO LIKED BIG Red and concluded that Snaggie had been right about his being a good trainer. He paid attention and took notes. He went to the library and studied on his own. He told his mom that the work was interesting and exciting. He learned that he did not even know the meaning of the word *exciting* until he began following Justice Fullilove.

9

Virgil Boatner, a self-made millionaire, began investing in real estate after dropping out of college during his sophomore year. For years he was a womanizer. Then he fell head over heels in love with Emily, got rid of all the other women and married her. He was devastated when she left him for a man whom he had given a job. He purposed in his heart to kill them with his own hands and watch them die slowly, but they simply disappeared. He searched for them for months before he gave up and worked out his current plan to avenge his hurt. And it was working well until a few months ago.

He frowned as he read the report given to him by his security guard. Someone was interfering with his plans. He sent one of his goons to find out what had gone wrong. He vowed that whoever was impeding his progress in obtaining relief from his sufferings would pay dearly, even if he had to see to it personally. When he found out who was messing up his plans, he began to lay his plan to put an end to the troublemaker.

☞

SNAGGIE WALKED INTO Courtroom D, where the attorneys and defendants sat waiting for the judge, and looked around to see if she could pick out Justice Fullilove. A beautiful young lady stood and moved over to whisper something to the deputy and went back to her seat. Snaggie considered her and decided she was not the one. *Good looking, nice figure, but not his type. She's covered from her neck to below her knees. She leaves everything to the imagination.*

Then she spotted the one she concluded was Justice. She was pretty, shapely and dressed more traditionally. The neckline was plunging, but not too much, the skirt was short enough to show a pair of nice legs, but not too short. Snaggie moved over to her and whispered, "Miss Fullilove?" The woman giggled, shook her head, and pointed to Justice. Snaggie was surprised. She would never have figured she was his type. She moved over to the lady whose dress suggested she could be a prude, and smiled.

"Miss Fullilove?"

"Yes," Justice said.

"I'm Snaggie Jones; I believe you know my nephew, Leroy, who lives in Oaktree Downs. He talks about you all the time."

"Wow," Justice said. "Now, I remember where I heard your name, he gave me one of your cards. Said you were a private investigator who could locate anyone or anything. I'm happy to meet you. They shook hands. Snaggie looked down and spotted Justice's purse. She sat down next to her.

"Hey, I like your purse. I wish I could carry that kind of purse. But I'm so tall; it wouldn't look good on me."

"I bet it would," Justice said. She picked the purse up and handed it to Snaggie. "Try it on and see." Snaggie stood, swung the strap over her shoulder, and took a few steps back. She turned to look at Justice as if to say how does it look on me.

"Go look at yourself, it looks good on you. There's a mirror right inside the ladies room, in the hallway, first door on the left."

"Are you sure?" Snaggie asked. *This is way too easy to be for real.*

"Go on," Justice said as she motioned with her hand to "shoo" her to the ladies room. "Seeing is believing." Snaggie walked into the ladies room and quickly fastened the device inside the flap of the purse. She swung the purse back over her shoulder, and turned around while looking in the mirror. It did look pretty good on her. She hurried back to the courtroom with the purse swinging on her shoulder. Justice looked up and smiled.

"You're right; it does look pretty good on me. I never knew I could carry this kind of purse. Thank you." She handed the purse back to Justice and sat down again.

"You are welcome. Your nephew is such a great kid. He talks about you all the time."

"I hope not as much as he talks about you." Snaggie said. "He told me what kind of car you drive. Said you got rid of a Mercedes and bought a Toyota Avalon. Said he would have kept the Mercedes."

"Smart kid," Justice said. "I just didn't want them making a big fuss over my car every time I went out there. There are a lot of things more important than big cars."

"Well, I will have to check out a Toyota that replaced a Mercedes. It must be an eyeful. Are you driving it today?"

"Yes, if you parked on the first level, you came right pass it. It's the blue Toyota right in front of the elevator. Someone was pulling out just as I drove in. It was raining and I didn't have my umbrella. My angel must have helped that person finish their business just in time."

"No doubt," Snaggie said. "Well, it was nice meeting you, and if your ears begin to burn about 3:30 this afternoon, you will know it's because my nephew is home from school and we are having a little chat about you."

"Thanks, it was nice meeting you too. Say hello to Leroy for me."

"I will." Snaggie went straight to the first level and found Justice's car. She walked around and admired the car in case someone saw her. Then she dropped her book and stooped down to pick it up. She placed the device under the fender. *The lady is much too gullible. I wonder if I should speak to Alou about it. Surely he knows by now.*

☞

Lela and Ted had tried, on several occasions, to persuade Justice to attend a function at the local social club. Justice had refused, stating that she hated clubs that excluded some segment of society for no other reason than the fact that they made $10,000 per year less than those permitted to join. She called it a club for uppity people. Lela was concerned about Justice because she didn't do anything but go to work, Church, meet with the kids in Oaktree Downs, and read. She had finally convinced Ted that Justice was becoming a hermit, and they, as her friends, had a duty to at least try to get her to join the real world.

"Do you consider me and Lela uppity people?" Ted asked.

"No," Justice had to admit. Besides, it had become such a big issue that she and Lela seemed to argue about it all the time. Justice didn't like the fact that Lela always thought she knew what was best for her, but she didn't want to alienate Lela and Ted. They were her security blanket. And so, against her better judgment, she had agreed to attend the Labor Day celebration at The Club.

"Everybody who's anybody will be there. The only affair that has better attendance is the Christmas banquet," Lela said excitedly as she pulled Justice toward the kitchen. She was so happy that Justice was finally going to meet all the right people.

"Yeah, right," Justice said as she rolled her eyes and sighed. "I hope I don't regret this decision. You know how much I hate stuck-up people. You and Ted are such nice people. I can't figure out how you two got involved with people like that."

Lela laughed and pointed Justice to a chair at the kitchen table. "It's not about how much money you make; it's a whole different class of people. They are well rounded, opened minded, and fun to be with. I guarantee you'll love it and regret that you haven't been before. Justice, we used to have so much fun in DC, but you never go anywhere anymore.

You have become a stick in the mud. There has to be some kind of law against a woman becoming a recluse before the age of 30." Lela was secretly hoping to introduce Justice to Robert; a man she thought would be a whole lot better for her than Alou.

"Okay, I said I would go, and I am finished with this conservation. Let's have a cup of tea so I can go home and prepare for work at the *lowly public defender's office*."

LELA, TED, AND Justice moved about sampling the finger food. It was delicious. About a dozen couples were dancing and everyone seemed to be having a great time. Lela was disappointed because Robert was not there. *The one night I convince Justice to come and he doesn't show. I'll kill him*. They turned when they heard someone singing. It was Alou.

"I've got sunshine on a cloudy day. When it's cold outside, I've got the month of May. I guess you say, what can make me feel that way... my girl." He shook Ted's hand and kissed Lela and Justice's hands. I'm so happy to see you guys tonight. It makes me feel like singing and dancing." He stepped back and went into a brief dance routine. They all laughed.

"Whatever you're drinking, give me some," Ted said.

"Me too," Lela said. They all laughed.

Alou turned to Justice. "Could I entice you to go over with me to meet my mother?" Justice turned to look at Lela.

"There's Olivia," Lela said as she turned and looked across the room. "I haven't seen her in ages. I'll be right back." Justice turned and looked at Ted. He simply smiled at her. She turned to Alou.

"Okay," she said. Alou took her by the arm and guided her toward his mother.

Justice wanted to turn and see what Lela was doing, and to see if Ted was watching them, but she decided against it.

She had expected them to protest, she didn't know why. She knew Lela didn't want her to get involved with Alou. *Maybe she has changed her mind.*

Auryola Hambrick, Alou's mother, was a tall beautiful lady. When Alou introduced her to Justice, she refused to shake Justice's hand.

"I understand you are a *public pretender*," his mom said. Her dislike was obvious. Alou was completely taken by surprise.

"No, I'm a public defender," Justice said. "There is no pretense about what I do or the people I represent."

"And I take it you represent criminals," Auryola said, with a look of disdain.

"No," Justice said. "I represent people who have been accused of a crime, criminals are people like you. You just haven't been caught yet. And since I am not a pretender, I won't pretend that it was nice meeting you."

"I didn't send for you, so what makes you think I should be happy to meet you?"

"You shouldn't, but you should be happy that your son thought enough of you to want to allow you in my presence. You don't really qualify to meet people like me, or even to be in my presence. So be grateful to your son, because you don't deserve him either." Justice turned to look at Alou and was shocked by her feelings for him. *He is so handsome, so kind, and such fun to be with, I don't want to be without him, oh... my... God.* It was at that moment that she realized that she had fallen in love with him. She had been so busy trying not to fall in love; she hadn't realized that it had already happened.

"I'm going back to the other side where Ted and Lela are," Justice said as she pointed toward Lela and Ted. She was already scolding herself for the way she had talked to Alou's mom. Alou just stood there for a moment, he was in total shock and speechless.

"I'll walk back with you," he finally stammered.

"That's not necessary."

"But I want to." He put his arm around her shoulder and guided her back toward Lela and Ted. His mom was in a state of shock. She looked around and then moved over to the nearest table and sat down. She had never had anyone respond to her in that fashion before. And to think that her son had walked with her after she had treated his mother so disgracefully. She was mortified. "How dare he," she said out loud.

They kept walking, in silence.

Justice stopped when they were half way across the room. She wanted to be sure that neither Lela, nor Ted, nor Auryola could hear what she had to say. Alou stopped and she turned to face him.

"Alou, I don't even know how to begin to apologize to you for ..."

"No, I should apologize to you for my mother's behavior. You have to know that I had no idea she would act that way. But you have no reason to apologize, she has been asking for that for a long time. She just hasn't run into anyone who had enough nerve to tell her where to go before."

"I didn't tell her where to go. And you should go back to your mom; she will be angry with you for leaving her and because you are with me."

"Then let her be angry. She'll get over it."

"What if she doesn't?"

"That's one of her problems that I can't solve." Alou said as he put his arm around her shoulder and guided her toward Lela and Ted. Lela had rejoined Ted almost as soon as Justice left.

"That was . . ." Lela stopped when she saw the look on Justice's face. Justice was trying to smile, but it was no use. Lela could read her like a book. Justice smiled at Alou, embraced him, and thanked him for introducing her to his mom. She was trying to tell him that she was not angry with him, but she wanted him to go away.

Alou turned to Lela and Ted and explained what had happened. "My mother was quite rude to Justice. I was completely taken by surprise. Especially since she knows that I'm in love with Justice."

Justice just wanted to go home. She didn't want Alou saying that he loved her in front of Lela and Ted. She didn't want to deal with Lela's feelings about Alou and now Alou's mom's obvious dislike for her, and she didn't even want to think about the fact that she had been stupid enough to fall in love with Alou. She just wanted to get away from all of them, but she knew she would stay because it would upset Lela and Ted if she left. *I would have been happier had I gone to Dexter's and had a salad by myself. Next time that's what I'll do.*

Ted put his hand on Alou's shoulder and said, "Alou, you have to realize that you have changed, or at least to me you appear to have changed, since you met Justice. That may have frightened you mother. Most women think no woman is good enough for their sons. That's especially true when he's the only son. And don't let her become divorced or widowed, she holds on to her son for dear life."

He took Justice's arm and moved her from her position of huddling next to Lela and stood her next to Alou.

"Just look at you two," He said as he gestured toward them and turned to look at Lela. "Is there a better looking couple in this place?" They all looked around and everyone shook their head no, except Justice. She was unable to see the other people in the room. She was too busy trying not to cry. She was trying not to disappoint Lela and Ted and she had decided to let Mrs. Hambrick have her son. She was not going to fight over Alou. She wasn't going to fight for any man. As far as she was concerned, any women who wanted Alou, or any other man on this planet, wouldn't have to worry about so much as a glance from her from now until eternity, and beyond. All she wanted to do was go home and cry. It seemed that everything in her life was going wrong. Everything.

"Now, may I have this dance," Ted said as he extended his hand to Justice. She nodded and allowed him to lead her onto the dance floor. She put her head on his shoulder and cried. He knew she would, but he also knew he had to find a way to convince her that The Club was a fun place to go and that there were only a handful of people like Auryola around. He wanted to shake Auryola.

⁓

ALL JUSTICE COULD think about later that night was how she had attacked Alou's mother. She got down on her knees and began to pray. A thought came to her mind that was so strong it seemed like an audible voice. *You prayed to meet a Christian psychiatrist, you met him, and how has it helped you?*

"I'm going to his Sunday School class in the morning," she said out loud. "And I expect to hear something that will change my life. And I will follow it."

⁓

JUSTICE FOUND SOLOMON'S classroom just as he picked up his Bible and moved to the podium.

"Good morning class, I'm happy to see each of you today. Let's pray." They bowed their heads and Solomon prayed.

Solomon opened his Bible, shuffled his notes and moved around to the front of the podium. He noticed Justice and smiled. "Justice, welcome . . . class I want you to welcome my neighbor and good friend, Justice Fullilove. Stand up Justice."

Justice stood and the class clapped. She smiled, nodded, and took her seat. The ladies around her shook her hand and several simply touched her on the back. Justice felt really welcomed. *These people are so friendly.*

"Today, we are going to talk about entering the Kingdom. Turn in your Bible to the third chapter of Saint John." Solomon read verses one through five.

"In this conversation with Nicodemus, Jesus talks about the two levels of the Kingdom. In the first level, you can see the Kingdom. The requirement for this level is the new birth. A person who is not born again can't even see the Kingdom.

That means they don't even know it exists. The new birth gives you eternal life in the hereafter, entering the Kingdom is like a premium version. You gain eternal life plus many benefits in this life that are not available to those who never enter.

"So, salvation is about our attitude, and entering the Kingdom is about our conduct. It's that simple. The entire Sermon on the Mount was to Christians. The multitude is always there, but only a few enter the Kingdom.

"So, how do we enter the Kingdom? We must hear the Word and do it. Jesus said if you want to enter the Kingdom, you must come as a little child; If your right eye cause you to sin, pluck it out; You have heard it said of old, thou shall not kill, but I say unto you don't be angry with your brother; If you want to be great, become a servant.

"The rules of the Kingdom are diametrically opposed to the rules of the world system. Jesus introduced a new order, 'you have heard that it was said; you shall love your neighbor and hate your enemy. But I say to you, love your enemies, bless those that curse you, and do good to those that hate you, and pray for those that spitefully use you and persecute you.' Why? Because it's easy to love people that love you. If that verse makes you tremble, you are not alone. I tremble every time I read it.

"Once you are saved, our teaching is no longer about salvation, it's about conduct. There are three things for which you will be judged as a Christian: 1) How you respond to God; 2) How you treat people; and 3) How you use the talent and resources God gave you. Nothing else.

"The parable about the ten virgins was about conduct, not about their nature. They were all virgins, they all took their lamps, they all went out to meet the bridegroom, they all slumbered and slept, they all heard the cry at midnight that the bridegroom was coming, and they all rose and trimmed their lamps. The only difference between the two groups was the fact that the foolish virgins took no oil. When the five foolish virgin came later and said Lord, Lord, open to us, notice what the Lord said. *I don't even know you.* Jesus said in Luke 6:46, why do you call me Lord, Lord, and do not the things that I say? He explained what happens to people who hear His words and don't do them. He's not talking about salvation; He's talking about entering the Kingdom.

"In conclusion, let me encourage you, by telling you, that whatever God has called you to do, you can do it. It won't always be easy, and there won't always be someone to encourage you, and you will have to **press** your way into the Kingdom, one incident at a time, and one day at a time.

"If you understand the Kingdom, and remember that the King is always with you, you will understand that you cannot fail. So, go out this week and demonstrate the Kingdom, and come back next Sunday and we will talk about the King." Solomon dismissed the class and motioned for Justice to stay.

"Did you like the class?" he asked.

"I think I heard the answer to my problem today, and I promise to come visit again soon. I'm going to apply those principles to my life and overcome my temper. I'm going to make an appointment with you to find out how to **press** my way into the Kingdom. Does that answer your question?"

"It does, and thanks. I'm glad you could come." Solomon gathered his belongings and placed them in his briefcase. Justice asked the question that had been on her mind for a long time.

"Solomon, sometimes I have a thought that is so strong, it seems like an audible voice. Then there are times when I can feel what seems like an oppressive spirit hanging around or sitting on my shoulder, especially when I'm in Courtroom D. How can I know what's going on. What is it?"

"The thought that seems like an audible voice, do you recognize the voice?" She thought about it for a moment and was surprised.

"Yes . . . as a matter of fact it's my voice I hear. I didn't realize that until you asked."

"The oppressive spirit, do you hear a voice or just have a feeling, and awareness that something evil is present?"

"That's a perfect description of it," Justice said. "How did you know?"

"I've experienced both. The thought that seems like an audible voice is the Holy Spirit speaking to you through your spirit. And it comes from the inside of you. When the Holy Spirit speaks to you directly, it's much more authoritative and comes from the outside. For me, it's usually over my left shoulder. I always turn to see who's there. It doesn't happen often, but the voice on the inside happens more often than we ever hear.

"The oppressive spirit is just that, it comes to oppress. There's usually someone near you that that spirit is operating through. The person is usually not aware of the spirit, they are just concentrating on the evil intent they have toward you. And it may not be toward you, he or she might just be a person with an evil spirit. The oppressive spirit makes you want to get away from the place or the person. The Holy Spirit, on the other hand, gives directions, or places choices in front of you. You are free to make the right or wrong choice. It's entirely up to you. Does that make sense?"

"Yes," Justice said. "But let me tell you something that doesn't make sense. I said I would never tell anyone this, but you may have the answer for this as well. One day I insulted the judge in his courtroom, and I felt my father's presence so strongly that I actually turned around and looked for him. The judge called for a recess and never mentioned the incident when we came back. Do you think my father was in that courtroom?"

Solomon laughed. "Probably. I think God allows departed loved ones to come back on rare occasions when they are concerned about us. That kind of behavior would certainly cause your father to be concerned about you. Especially since he decided that you would be a lawyer before you were born. He wouldn't want you to go and lose you license because of your big mouth and hot temper. He probably slapped the judge up side the head a couple of times and threatened his life. Any of this make sense to you?"

"Yes, and you are a sweet and wise man, Solomon Owens."

"Thank you, 'Mam'." Solomon picked up his briefcase, hit the light switch, and they walked out together. Both of them were happy she attended his class.

Chapter

10

"Did something go wrong this weekend, Mr. Hambrick? You have been distracted all morning," his secretary, Jan, asked.

"Nothing that I can't handle," Alou said. "And I guess I had better start by separating non-work functions from work functions. Is it that obvious?"

"Yes, at least it is to me. Anything I can do to help?"

"Not unless you are a psychiatrist."

"That bad huh?"

"Yep, but I'm going to work on that. In the meantime, let's get to office functions. Firstly, I want a cup of steaming hot coffee with one cream and one sugar. Secondly, I want you to call Justice and tell her that I love her." Alou folded his arms and waited for Jan's reaction.

"The first request I can handle, the second ... well I'm not ready to go there yet."

"See, that's the way people are. They see you suffering and ask 'is there anything I can do to help?' when you tell them how they can help, they never do it. So, your offer to help was just empty words, right?"

"But Miss Fullilove already knows that you love her. There's nothing anyone could say that would convince her more. Now ... I'm going to get you some coffee and my offer still stands, if there's something I *can do* to help, you better let me know." Jan paused and placed her hand on her chin. "Suggestion—why don't you knock off early this afternoon and pay her a visit. I'll get Benny to help me finalize the report. Take her out to dinner. After a harrowing weekend and a day in court, I'm sure she could use a good meal and good company."

Jan knew that Benny was the only person Alou would trust to help finalize the report. Benny was the first employee Alou hired, and he knew almost as much about the business as Alou.

"Now, that's the reason I pay you. Anybody can do secretarial work, but you are a lady who gives good advice on occasion. And tonight, I'll take your advice and your offer to ask Benny to help finalize the report--now fetch my coffee." Alou leaned back in his chair and smiled. He was already beginning to look forward to a quiet evening with Justice. *There is no other woman like her on the planet. I can't lose her, no matter what I have to give up. Even if it means my own mother . . . But that's not my choice, it's mother's choice.* He smiled and shivered when he thought about how Justice had put Auryola in her place. She had not encountered anyone who had the nerve to do it before. He was sure Auryola would remember that night for a long time.

☙

JUSTICE GOT HOME at 2:30 p.m. and realized that she had not taken anything out of the freezer to cook. She decided to finish up the story she was reading, have a bowl of cereal, and go to bed early. She had not slept well since she realized that she was in love with Alou. She was distressed because she couldn't see how they could have a good relationship when his mother disliked her so much. Especially since she didn't know the reason, and therefore, couldn't do anything about it. She wasn't even sure if she wanted to. She flopped down on the couch and put her head in her hands. She was disgusted with herself. She had broken a promise to herself to never fall in love again and she was already feeling the pain. *How could this have happened? I honestly didn't see it coming. But I should have. I always had such a good time with him. I think about him all the time, I am always glad to see him. How could I have been so stupid? I'm stupid, stupid, stupid. Lela is going to be so angry with me. Oh God, oh God, oh my God.*

The telephone rang and interrupted Justice's pity party. She quickly moved over to the other side of the couch and lifted the receiver.

"Hello." One part of her hoped it was Alou. She loved his deep voice, it was so steady and calm, and no one could say *Justice* the way he did. The other part of her hoped it wasn't him. She wasn't ready to deal with him about his mom. She realized that she had run up against an insurmountable problem.

"Justiana, this is Auryola Hambrick, and I want to speak with you about my son."

Justice sat up straight and gripped the phone. *Man, she gets right to the point, no preliminaries such as hello and how are you. But she obviously doesn't care, so why pretend.*

"Yes mam," Justice said. "What about your son." She had decided to be nice to her no matter what she said.

"If it's money you want, I'm prepared to offer you ..."

"Stop! Hold up, Mrs. Hambrick. I don't want your money or your son. Why don't you just keep them both? Keep your money in your bank account or stocks and bonds, and keep your son away from me. That would make me very happy, and I hope I never see or hear from you or your son again. Have I made myself clear?"

"Perfectly clear, only I don't believe you, I've seen your kind ...

"Oh, but you are wrong, you haven't seen my kind before, if you had you would never have called to offer me money. But, if you ever call me again, or approach me in any way about your son, you *will* find out what kind of person you are attempting to deal with. No, you have not seen my kind before, and you don't want me to have to show you how I know. So do yourself a favor and forget this phone call, and I'll do the same. If you choose to do otherwise, well, you *will* regret it." Justice slammed the phone down just as the doorbell rang. She rush over and snatched open the door and looked into the smiling face of Alou who was handing her a beautiful bouquet of flowers. All she could do was cry and pray. "Oh God, oh God, oh my God."

"What in the world happened?" Alou asked as he stepped inside and closed the door. Justice took the flowers and tried to stop the tears. She didn't know if she was crying because she loved Alou, or because she has just talked so ugly to his mother, or because he had brought her flowers. She turned and went to look for a vase for the flowers. Alou stood there looking puzzled and wondering why she was crying.

"Alou," she said when she returned and placed the flowers on the table. "I Just finished talking ugly to your mother on the phone."

"You called my mother?" he asked.

"No, she called me. And she offered me money to leave you alone. Of course I told her I would do it for free. Look, I knew this would never work and I'm sorry I took up so much of your time. I should have never allowed it to happen. I am simply not available for a relationship." She sighed and flopped down on the couch. "Even if I were, this thing with your mother would make it impossible."

"Why don't you let me handle my mother? This is not about her; it's about you and me."

"I don't want you to handle your mother; I just want you to go away. I want to be left alone. I am sorry I didn't say it sooner. Again, I apologize for taking up so much of your time; so please forgive me and just go away."

"Is that all I mean to you? One phone call from my mother and you are ready to kick me out of your life. I never expected you to think so small . . ."

She stood and turned to face him. "How do you get the nerve ..." she stopped when she saw the look on his face. All the anger began to drain away. She realized that her anger was misdirected. She just stood there and stared at him. She couldn't believe that anything she said had caused the pain she saw in his eyes. She began to walk slowly toward him.

He just stood there. When she lifted her head, he could see tears in her eyes. He reached out and gently took her into his arms. He didn't know what to say, so he just held her.

"I don't know how this happened, Alou, I never meant to fall in love with you," she whispered as she slipped her arms around his waist and laid her head on his shoulder. He could feel the warm tears seeping through his shirt.

"Someway, somehow, I'll fix this. I know I can fix it if you just give me some time. I promise you I will find a way to completely fix it, I promise." Alou knew he had to fix it, he had to find a way, he had to have a serious talk with his mother, but it was not something he was looking forward to.

"Alou, why don't we just cool it for the time being. Maybe your mom thinks we are moving too fast. Let's just stop seeing each other for a while."

"I would never agree to that. I don't want to be without you. I am going to have a talk with my mother tomorrow, and I will call you later."

Justice didn't know how to handle Alou, so she decided that she would take the coward's way out and refuse to answer her phone when he called.

JUSTICE REACHED FOR the phone to stop the ringing. She couldn't find it. She sat up, turned on the light, and grabbed the phone. "Hello." She turned to look at the clock. It was 2:15 in the morning. "Who is this?"

"Miss Justice, it's me, Big Man. Can you come over here Miss Justice? I'm in trouble."

"What's wrong?" She swung her feet over the side of the bed and rubbed her eyes. She had no desire to get out of bed and go to Oaktree Downs.

"Some men came by and attacked me."

"Attacked you how, you mean they beat you ...where are you?"

"I'm in the clubhouse. No, they didn't beat me they just shoved me around and threaten me."

"Why are you calling me? I'm a lawyer not a police officer, call 911."

"They said they would kill me if I called the police and I can't move, I think my leg is broken."

"I thought you said they didn't beat you."

"They pushed me down and I hurt my leg when . . ." The phone went dead. Justice pushed the button on her phone to get the number from caller ID. Private number was all that showed up. She put her hand to her forehead and tried to think. *Should I call the police and send them out there?* The phone rang just as she was reaching to call the police.

"Miss Justice, please don't call the police. Could you just come to the clubhouse and help me back to my room. My mom doesn't know I'm out here. I snuck out; if the police come they will come back and hurt me and my family. Please Miss Justice!"

"Okay, I'm on my way, stay inside the clubhouse until I get there." She hung up and hurriedly put on her jogging suit and a pair of sneakers. Then got down on her knees and began to pray. "God let your angels encamp round about me and Big Man and protect us from all hurt, harm, and danger, and help me to understand what I'm supposed to be doing and . . . I'll talk to about that later Lord. Just send your angels to protect me now." She grabbed her purse and ran out the door and headed for her car.

Nito sat up when he heard a car door slam. He shook himself and looked around to see who was in the car. He started his motor when he realized that it was the target, Justice Fullilove. He was the investigator assigned by Snaggie to follow Justice. He sat on the street with his lights out until she had pulled out of the parking lot. He didn't want to follow too closely. There wasn't much traffic in Winston that time of morning. He looked at his watch; it was 2:30 a.m. Where in the world could she be going this time of morning he asked himself. He was happy to see two other cars on the street. He slowed and kept her in sight. He finally figured out that she was headed for Oaktree Downs, and it seemed that he was not the only one following her.

The other car finally turned off and disappeared. He relaxed and kept a safe distance. When she turned into the housing project, she dimmed her lights and headed toward the clubhouse. He kept driving and noticed two policemen sitting in a patrol car across the street with their lights out. He pulled around the corner and parked. He ran back and peeked to see what the cops were doing. They had gotten out of the car and were headed toward the clubhouse as well. Nito was suspicious of the cops. *If there is something illegal going on, why didn't they move in before she arrived? I don't like this.*

Nito scaled the fence and ran toward Justice. "Hold up lady, I'm with security. I need to know what you are doing out here this time of night. There shouldn't be anyone in the clubhouse. Do you live here?"

"No," Justice said. "I work with the kids who live here and one of them called me and said he was hurt and in the clubhouse." She didn't want to give him too many details.

"Let's take a look together," Nito said as he placed his hand on her shoulder and they moved toward the clubhouse together. Before he opened the door, he turned slightly to see what the cops were doing. They were moving slowly back toward the patrol car and glancing back over their shoulders.

"What's the kid's name?" Nito whispered as he pushed open the door.

"Big Man, at least that's what everyone calls him," Justice whispered.

"You call him, he's expecting you," Nito said as he turned his flashlight on and shined it around the clubhouse.

"Big Man!" Justice said as the light beamed in on his face. "What happened to you, I thought you said they didn't beat you." His lip was busted, he was sitting on the floor, and she could tell he had been crying. He didn't say anything at first. Then he extended his hand toward Justice.

"They told me to give you this, Miss Justice."

"What is it?" Justice asked as she moved toward him.

Nito held his arm out to block her because the kid was handing her money. "It's money . . . and why did they tell you to give Miss Justice money?"

"I don't know," Big Man said and started to cry. He had known the men did not have good intentions toward Justice, even though they kept telling him that their boss just wanted to give her money to help with her work at Oaktree Downs. He was sure they had meant to harm her when they kept hitting him when he refused to call and wake her up.

"Why can't I just give it to her tomorrow?" he had asked.

"Because our boss wants her to have it tonight," they insisted. When he said no, they had slapped and punched him until he dialed the number and asked her to come. They assured him that nothing would happen to her, and said all he had to do was hand her the money and his family would not get hurt.

Justice moved toward him again and Nito stopped her. "Why don't you go and call the policemen across the street. On second thought, why don't we all go and talk with them."

"Policemen?" Justice asked but kept staring at Big Man. Nito moved over and helped Big Man to his feet, but would not allow Justice to come near him. Justice finally turned and headed out the door.

"Hey!" she said and began to wave her arms as she saw the patrol car pull away from the curb. She started to run toward the car and wave her arms but they sped away. *Why were they here, and why did they leave. I know they saw me. And why would someone ask Big Man to give me money at two o'clock in the morning. If it were legal, why couldn't it wait?* She decided to let it go, Big Man obviously didn't know what was going on and she didn't want to cause him further distress.

Nito called 911 and reported that a kid had been beaten at Oaktree Downs. A patrol car came and they had to wake Big Man's mom. He was not seriously hurt, but his mom was upset, Big Man was terrified, and Justice was beyond frustration. She thanked Nito and told him she didn't know what she would have done if he had not come along. He said it was nothing and that she would have handled it nicely without him. She wanted to go to Alou's house so he could hold her in his arms and make her feel better. She thought of his mom, and decided to go home and cry alone. *Where do people like his mom come from?*

Nito went back to the clubhouse the next day, retrieved the tape, and turned it over to Snaggie. Snaggie reviewed it and provided Alou with a written report. Alou read the report and tried to make sense out of what Justice had told him. He knew he had to find out who the men were and why they wanted to harm Justice. He was sure that these men had no real interest in her work at Oaktree Downs.

11

When Alou talked with his mom, she apologized for the way she treated Justice. She attempted to explain her behavior.

"Alou, when I saw you walking toward me with her, I knew she had not been intimate with you. I can always tell when you have been intimate with a woman when I see you with her. It's the way you relate to her. Well, I knew you had been seeing Justiana for a while, and if you were still seeing her in spite of her refusal to sleep with you, I figured you two would be getting married soon. I guess I just panicked. I don't know what came over me. I was so wrong. Please, please forgive me. After all you are all I have in the world. Sometimes women who are all alone don't know how to respond to their son's girlfriend. But I promise it won't happen again . . . Will you forgive me son?"

Of course I forgive you mother. You will love Justice once you get to know her. She's different from any woman I've ever known. I want to spend the rest of my life with her. It's important to me that the two most important women in my life get along."

"I will certainly do my part," Auryola promised.

"Then it's a done deal," Alou said. "I know Justice will do her part. I'm headed back by the office to pick up some cash a customer left this morning. I don't want to leave it in my desk drawer all weekend. I'll see you later mother." He kissed her on the cheek and left.

⌒

ALOU WHISTLED AS he drove down Woodbury Lane, and it was such a beautiful Saturday morning. He slowed when he saw the sign pointing toward Oaktree Downs. He decided to go by and visit the kids. A large group had already gathered at the clubhouse. Some were playing basketball and others were just milling around. Alou spoke with some of the kids and then spoke with several of the mothers and told them that he would be working with Miss Justice to help keep the kids on the right track. He offered and they accepted his invitation to buy hotdogs, drinks, and chips for everyone. He got permission and took Leroy and Jimmy with him. They were both 11 years old and the oldest boys in the group. He bought hot dogs at Happy House and burgers and fries at Burger Hut. He stopped at the grocery story and bought drinks, ice, napkins, chips, paper plates, and cups. The kids were so excited. He helped them set up the food and appointed two kids to make sure that everything ran smoothly and to let him know if there were any problems. He went to the door of a couple of the mothers to thank them for allowing him to treat the kids to a picnic.

"You don't know what joy it gives me to be able to treat the kids," he said. "I grew up without a dad but I worked hard and now I own my own business. I want to see that every kid here has the opportunity to own his or her own business or get a good job. I will be working with my good friend Miss Justice and helping her in any way that I can."

When Alou was sure all the kids had food, he fixed a plate for himself and sat next to Katrina. He could tell she was in charge.

"What kind of problems are you guys having in the club? Is there any thing that Miss Justice wants to do that she had not been able to do yet?" he asked while keeping his eyes on his plate.

They told him about Amy and Raul not being able to join the club. Alou said he would have a talk with their mothers. He told them that the mothers would probably feel better about allowing their kids to come if they knew there would be two adults supervising the kids in the future.

When Alou finished his hot dog, he went to Mrs. Lawson's apartment to see whether he could persuade her to change her mind. He exhibited his most persuasive smile when she opened the door.

"I'm the new assistant who will be working with Miss Justice and will be helping her supervise the MBK club. I understand that your child has not yet become a member."

"Amy doesn't want to become a member; she has too much homework. Amy is small for her age and the bigger kids are so rough. It's for her safety." Mrs. Lawson explained as she began closing the door. Alou took a roll of money from his pocket and peeled off five $100 dollar bills.

"I'll make you a bet," he said. "If your child comes to the picnic and eats hot dogs and chips today and she has a good time and wants to come again, you win the money. On the other hand, if she says she didn't like it and doesn't want to go again. I get my money back. And I will personally supervise the kids to be sure there's no rough play today. Deal?" Mrs. Lawson called for Amy over her shoulder as she reached for the money.

"Deal," she said as she turned to explain to Amy that Mr. Alou is Miss Justice's assistant and she had agreed to allow her to go to the picnic today.

"Can I go now?" Amy squealed and ran pass Alou and Mrs. Lawson before she could reply.

When Chandra and DeDe saw Amy running toward the clubhouse, they ran to meet her. They hugged each other, "high fived" each other, and jumped up and down.

"Look how much fun you have been keeping from her. You should be ashamed of yourself," Alou said as he turned and headed for Mrs. Romero's apartment where he expected to have the same results. *After all the kids are not out of the mother's sight, she can see everything from her window. Single moms are just too protective. I ought to know.*

Maria Romero would have allowed Raul to attend the club meeting had it not been for her sister's fear. She kept reminding Maria of a Hispanic kid that had been severely beaten by a group of Black kids. "But he goes to school with mostly Black kids," Maria had protested.

"Yes, and there are teachers and grown ups supervising them all the time, and there's a security officer there in case things get rough." Maria had seen the man bringing in food and knew that Raul was in his room watching from his window. As she sat sipping her second cup of hot chocolate, she thought of the time she had pushed Raul's door open to tell him he was too loud. She had stopped short when she saw that he was dancing and singing and pointing to his own chest. He never knew she had opened the door he was singing so loud. "I am somebody, I really am somebody, I've been washed in His blood, I've been filled with His love, and I'm a child of the Most High King."

Maria had closed the door and went to watch the kids from the kitchen window. The kids were standing in rows like a church choir. Miss Justice was standing in front as if directing, and periodically she would point to a particular kid and they would come forward and dance with her. Everyone in the group would point to the chosen kid and say, "You really are somebody." They seemed to be having such a good time. Maria felt a little sad because she could not let Raul participate. She had argued with her sister on the one occasion she had determined that she would allow Raul to participate.

"He will be in my sight all the time; I can see them from my kitchen window. If they got rough, I could be out there in less than a minute," Maria said.

"What happens if someone stabs him?" her sister asked. "You will make it there in time to pick up the dead body of your only son, and you would never forgive yourself." Maria had let it go; Raul was all she had left in the world. *I should have let him go, after all they were singing about God. And the lady, being a lawyer, could have inspired Raul. He wants to be a lawyer. Sometimes it's so hard to know what to do. God where are you?*

Maria was surprised by a knock on the door. When she opened the door Alou got right to the point and gave her the same line he had given Mrs. Lawson. All Maria could do was cry. She knew she had already won that bet. She took the money and carefully dried her eyes before she called Raul to give him the good news.

⌒

THE PICNIC WAS a smashing success. Alou and Katrina organized the kids into groups to make sure they left the area sparkling clean. He personally walked Amy and Raul home and thanked their mom for allowing them to attend. He asked each, in front of their mom, if they had had a good time and would like to attend again sometimes. They both said yes, and asked if they could become members. Alou shrugged his shoulders to let the mother know that he recognized the fact that she had won the bet.

He thanked all the kids for coming and promised that he would come back with Miss Justice as often as he could, always remembering to say something nice about Justice. He smiled as he waved to the kids and headed for his car. He was sure the news about his visit would get around and bring Justice to his office or home very soon.

Katrina called Justice that night and told her about how her new assistant, Mr. Alou, had treated the kids in Oaktree Downs to a picnic.

"When did all this happen?" Justice asked, completely taken by surprise.

"Today. And I think he likes you Miss Justice. He said such nice things about you and said he would come with you to the monthly meetings whenever he could. Guess what else happened Miss Justice, he even got Amy and Raul to come to the picnic."

"Are you kidding?

"No, they really came.

"How did he do that?" Justice asked. She couldn't believe it.

"He just went to the door and talked to their moms. He must have promised them that he could be sure the kids were safe or something, because he walked both of them back to their door after it was over and talked with their moms. It was so much fun Miss Justice. The only thing missing was you, but he said you were working on a trial for next week, and we understood."

"Thank you for calling to tell me Katrina. This is such good news. I'm glad everyone had a good time. I'll be sure to let him know about the next meeting." After a few more questions, Justice said goodbye to Katrina and pressed the hook to get a dial tone and began dialing Alou's number. She stopped and replaced the receiver. She decided to talk with him in person. It would have to wait until Monday. She didn't know whether she was more angry or surprised. *My assistant huh? I need to talk with that man. And how in the world did he ever convince Mrs. Lawson and Mrs. Romero to let their kids come to a picnic?*

⁓

ALOU STARED AT the mound of paper on his desk. He wanted to just throw some of this stuff in the trash and start all over again. Somehow he had to get through this. But his mind wasn't working yet. He buzzed his secretary. "Did you make fresh coffee this afternoon, Jan?"

"Yes"

"Would it be too much to ask you to bring an old man a cup of coffee with a cream and a sugar?"

"Depends on who the old man is."

"It's the old man that pays your salary."

"Oh, that old man," she said and lowered her voice to a whisper, "Miss Fullilove, Miss Fullilove, Miss Fullilove."

"What about her?" Alou whispered, as his heart began to race.

"She's headed this way and she has a machine gun," Jan said lightly. Jan was known for her ability to exaggerate. Alou hung up without another word. He raced to the mirror on the back wall and patted his face. He stared at himself and wished he had taken more care when he shaved. He had nicked his face. He patted the spot again and told himself that he was acting like a silly female. He moved back to his chair and lowered his head as if he were hard at work. Jan opened the door and told Alou that Justice was there to see him. He looked up and feigned surprise. He stood and moved quickly around the desk with an outstretched hand and a broad smile. "Come in, how nice to see you." Justice extended her hand and he clasped it in both of his and pulled her forward.

"Have a seat, have a seat, I can't tell you how happy I am to see you, Justice. Can I get you something to drink?" He knew exactly why she was there.

"I came to talk to you about the kids in Oaktree Downs".

"Is there a problem?" he asked.

"There wasn't, until I learned that you had the nerve to go snooping around Oaktree Downs asking questions about me and telling them that you were my new assistant. Don't you realize that kids expect you to keep your word when you make promises?"

"I wasn't snooping and I didn't ask any questions about you directly, I was just trying to determine how I could help. I really want to help. I have the resources and now for the first time in years, I have a little extra time. Please let me help you. And I intend to keep my promises."

"I would appreciate it if you would stay away from Oaktree Downs."

"Are you asking me not to go to the projects?" Alou asked.

"Not the projects, just Oaktree Downs"

"Okay," Alou said as he threw up his hands and sighed. He walked around and sat on the front of his desk.

"I *admit* that I went there for the purpose of getting you back. But when I began to talk with those kids and interact with them, I realized that the only difference between them and me is where we live. I was raised up without a father just like most of them, but my mom was a nurse. We didn't have to live in the projects. Most of their moms probably don't have any marketable skills. Those who do may be so beat down by the stress of raising kids, dealing with life and trying to make ends meet, that they no longer have any hope for a better life. But the kids deserve a chance. And with your help and encouragement they can have it. I hope that I can play a small part in that. That could have been me in the projects. Maybe I wouldn't have my own business, and I wouldn't have had the opportunity to meet you. How can I *not* help? Besides, I think that both of us together can have a greater impact." Alou stopped and placed his hand on his chest. "And I mean every word. Even if we never get back together, I'll still help with the kids if you will allow me." Alou could tell Justice was touched by his speech. He decided not to mention Amy and Raul if she didn't.

"I don't believe you, but I am curious to know how you managed to get Mrs. Lawson and Mrs. Romero to let the kids come to the picnic? How did you come up with the idea of a picnic anyway?"

"Actually, I was on my way home. I was driving and thinking about a certain young lady, a "do gooder". And I suddenly felt the urge to do a good deed myself. Oaktree Downs came to mind, and the rest is history. Oh . . . I used my charm on the ladies; it seems to work on everyone except you."

"Look, I don't know how this relationship got here. I never intended it to get this far. So, I need a little time. Maybe that's why your mom's so dead set against it. Let's just slow it down. Then I'll be okay, you'll be okay, and maybe she'll be okay."

"Okay, I'll give you three days."

"Three weeks," Justice said.

"One week."

"Okay two weeks."

"One and one half weeks, anything else is to too unreasonable, Justice," Alou said. "Why would you want to torture me that long?"

"Okay, one and one-half weeks," Justice conceded. Somehow she felt that she had gotten the short end of the stick. *Serves you right for falling in love with him.*

Chapter

12

As Justice walked up to the reception's station after lunch to see whether she had any messages, she overheard the conversation between the receptionist and a lady who looked like she was about to cry.

"I know I don't have an appointment," the lady said. "I have been calling her for two days and her voice mailbox is full. I just need to ask her a question about my son and how much time he could get. People keep telling me he could get life in prison."

"I'm sorry," the receptionist said. "Miss Rice said she can't see you today. You need to come back when you have an appointment." The lady stood there for a moment, sighed, turned and began to walk toward the elevator. Justice turned to look at the lady.

"Mam, I'm a public defender," Justice said. "I don't know anything about your son's case, but I may be able to give you some general information that may . . ."

"Please Miss, I would really appreciate that."

"Okay," Justice said. Let's go to my office." The lady followed Justice and kept thanking her. The receptionist looked up as Justice walked her back to the elevator a few minutes later, and the lady looked like a different person. She kept thanking Justice and shaking her hand. As she stepped on the elevator, she ran back to shake Justice's hand one more time. Justice stood there smiling and waving at the lady until the elevator door closed. Then she frowned and headed toward Shannon Rice's office. Justice knocked and before Shannon could answer, she pushed the door open and walked in.

"I wanted to see what was so important that you couldn't take the time to see a client that has been calling you for days and your voice mailbox has been full," Justice said as she walked up to Shannon's desk and folded her arms.

"She didn't have an appointment," Shannon said. "I get sick of these people thinking they can just drop by any time they feel like it. She didn't know what I had on my schedule for today."

"Obviously you didn't have very much on your schedule, because right now you're sitting on your fat butt doing nothing."

"That's not true," Shannon said.

"What's not true?" The part about the fat butt, or doing nothing?"

Shannon looked down at her lap. She almost giggled. She certainly couldn't deny she was sitting on a fat butt, and she couldn't really deny that she was "doing nothing" when she looked at her desk. Suddenly Shannon was angry.

"Who do you think you are? And what gives you the right to storm into my office and tell me what to do?"

Justice unfolded her arms and leaned forward. "How old are you Shannon?"

"I'm twenty-six, what does that have to do ...?"

"That's what I thought. Well, I'm twenty-six and a half." Justice walked over to Shannon's bookcase and picked up her Bible. I'll tell you what gives me the right to tell you what to do. This is what gives me the right to tell you what to do. Unless, of course, you just have it here for decoration. Is this something you believe in?"

"Yes, I believe in the Bible."

Justice opened the Bible and turned to the second chapter of the book of Titus and asked Shannon to read verse 3 and the first seven words of verse 4 out loud. Justice passed the Bible to Shannon. Shannon hesitated, stared at Justice, and then began to read.

"The older women likewise, that they be reverent in behavior, not slanderers, not given to much wine, teachers of good things—That they may teach the young women ..."

"That's enough," Justice said, as she took the Bible from Shannon's hand, closed it, and placed it back in the bookcase.

"That's not talking about someone who is just six months older than somebody," Shannon said.

"The words used were older women and young women. I'm the older woman and you're the young woman in this scenario. Look, Shannon, I'm not trying to correct you. But you shouldn't treat people that way. You're better than that. Especially if you call yourself a Christian. You are on *that* side of the desk today, but tomorrow you may be on *this* side. How would you like it if someone treated your mother like that, or your sister, or your friend? Most of these people come to us because they can't afford a private attorney. Is it okay for us to neglect them because they can't afford to pay? All she wanted to know is whether someone charged with aggravated assault could be sent to prison for life, if he had never been arrested before. How much trouble would it have been for you to answer that question for her? She was worried about her *son*, Shannon . . . and she said your voice mailbox has been full for two days. Do you honestly feel that it's okay to treat people like that?" Shannon just sat and stared at Justice. Justice turned and walked toward to door.

"So, did you answer her question?" Shannon asked.

Justice stopped and turned to face Shannon. "Yes, I gave her general information, but I told her that I would ask you to call her and give her specific information about her son's case."

"Okay, I'll call her when I think she's home," Shannon said. "And Justice . . . thanks older woman."

JUSTICE THOUGHT MAYBE she was a little too hard on Shannon. A few days later, she went to Shannon's office to apologize. She was about to knock on Shannon's door when she heard her name. She stopped and listened to hear what was being said about her. It was Shannon, and Tammy, another public defender.

"Let's go to lunch, why are you fooling with that case, you know Antonio is going to give that case to Justice," Tammy said.

"What do you mean, give it to Justice?" Shannon asked.

"Haven't you noticed; she ends up with all of your impossible cases. And this certainly is one of the most impossible cases you have had in a while."

"I don't know about all that, but let's go to lunch, I'm starving."

Justice could tell that Shannon's feelings were hurt. It was a put down for both Justice and Shannon, and that was just what Tammy meant to do. Justice turned and moved quickly back to her office. She locked her door and walked slowly to her desk. So that's how it is, she said to herself. She began looking through her files, and sure enough she had taken over a number of Shannon's cases. When she thought about it, she realized that Shannon very seldom tried a case. Justice could feel the anger creeping upon her. She stood and walked to the window. "The nerve of Antonio!" She said as she began pacing the floor. She became angrier by the minute. She fingered the badge hanging around her neck. She slowly removed the badge and walked to the door. She closed her eyes and stood there for a second. She opened the door and walked across the hall to Antonio's office. She opened his door and walked in without knocking.

"Hello Justice," Antonio said cheerfully, I was ... he stopped short when he saw the look on her face.

"What's wrong," he asked, standing and moving around the desk.

"Why I am the one who ends up with all of Shannon's impossible cases," she asked sarcastically as she threw her badge on his desk and backed away. I have always done my fair share of work," Justice continued. "I just finished looking through the cases I have handled lately; and I have handled almost all of Shannon's cases. Why?"

Antonio sat on his desk and folded his arms. He could tell that she was angry and was concerned that he would not get a chance to explain his actions. "Please, have a seat, and I will be happy to answer your question."

Justice moved to the chair near the door. She wanted to get as far away from him as possible.

Antonio moved to his file cabinet and opened the drawer. He searched through the file and removed a list of names. He scanned the list and began placing check marks by certain names. He knew she wanted to know what he was doing. He took his time. She folded her arms, crossed her legs, and pretended not to care. He placed his finger on the name of Andy Holmes, the defendant whose case Justice had taken over two months ago. The defendant was a 15 year old who could never understand why he was arrested. He had pushed a boy who was picking on his little niece. He had not intended to hurt the boy, just make him leave his niece alone. It was an accident, the boy had fallen, his head had hit the corner of a table and he had died a few days later.

"Since you have already made up your mind that I am a monster and that you are leaving, would you do me the favor of answering all of my questions and listening to what I have to say?"

"Yes."

"Let's talk about the case of Andy Holmes, where is he now?"

"In boot camp."

"He was charged with murder when it was clearly a freak accident, where do you honestly think he would be if you had not taken over that case?"

110

"I guess he would be in Jackson State Prison," Justice said slowly.

He moved his pencil down to the next checked name.

"Ms. Jones, the mother whose child ate rat poison and almost died, where is she today?"

"At home with her children."

"Can you honestly tell me where you think she would be if you had not *tried* that case?

"Probably in prison, the DA was asking for two years to serve." Justice was beginning to feel a little uncomfortable. She didn't like the way this was turning out. She may have jumped to the wrong conclusion.

"What about Ernesto the guy who tried to strangle his new neighbor. He said the guy was an alien trying to kidnap his family. Where is he now?"

"In a mental hospital, getting the help he needs?"

"Where do you think he would be if Shannon had handled the case?" Both Antonio and Justice were a little uncomfortable using Shannon's name in that fashion. But Antonio had to get his point across. Justice had begun to see that she had misjudged Antonio. She moved to the chair closer to his desk. It was a little cold way over by the door.

"Do I need to go through each one of these cases?" Antonio asked.

"No, I guess not."

"Justice, we are about giving our best service to everyone who comes to the Public Defender's Office. We don't care who handles the case; we just want them to get the best defense possible. Sometimes it means shifting cases around. Shannon is an excellent investigator; her trial skills are not as good as yours. When a person is at risk of losing his life or liberty, shouldn't the best defense possible be our concern rather than who handles the case."

"Yes, I guess so."

"You are full of "guess" today aren't you?"

"Yes, I guess I am." They both laughed because she had used the word again.

Justice stood and moved up to Antonio's desk. She snatched her badge and took a few steps back.

"I hope you don't think you are going to get rid of me that easily," she said as she turned and walked toward the door. She stopped, turned around, and looked at Antonio.

"Antonio, you are a good and fair-minded man, how did I get so mixed up on that? Can we just forget this ever happened?"

"It's already forgotten," Antonio said. "Why don't you take the rest of the afternoon off. You are my hardest working employee. You are probably a little overworked." They laughed.

"Okay," Justice said. "And thanks, I needed that."

"You're welcome, and have a good afternoon," Antonio said as he smiled and moved back to his seat. *Where do people like Justice come from?*

INSTEAD OF GOING home, Justice decided to spend the afternoon at the library. She just wanted to browse. She picked up a stack of magazines, and a couple of books she wanted to scan, and settled in a comfortable chair and placed the magazines and books on the table next to her. She looked at her watch when she finished the last magazine and realized that she had been there nearly three hours. The library was her haven when she wanted to get away from the real world. "Back to the real world, and don't forget to pick up milk for your cereal," she said out loud as she slid into her car.

She paid no attention to the car behind her until it pulled along side her, then pulled in front of her, and stopped abruptly. She slammed on her brakes and sat gripping the steering wheel. Her chest tightened and her breath came in short gasps. The combination of shock and fear numbed her mind. She forgot about the cell phone. She simply sat there and stared as the two men ran to the driver's side of her car and pounded on the window and ordered her to open the door.

When she did not, they placed a device on the door and it opened. She was unable to move. She stared at them and told herself that this was all a dream. A nightmare. Then she felt their hands on her arm as they grabbed her and began to drag her from the car. She wanted to scream or cry but her voice wouldn't work. One of the men threw her to the ground while the other man ran back to the car. He came back with what looked like a sawed-off shotgun. He raised it over his head to strike her and she could see that it was a lead pipe. From somewhere deep down on the inside, she found the strength to resist. She began to struggle and kick and the intended blow missed her. The man on the ground grabbed her shoulders and shook her. He placed one hand in her chest and one on her right knee.

"Hold her legs," the man with the pipe said as he raised the pipe over his head again.

She could feel a scream moving up to her throat. As she opened her mouth, she heard someone yell from a few feet away.

"Freeze, you scumbag!"

All three of them turned toward the voice. A man was crouching and holding a pistol with both hands and pointing it at the man with the pipe. The man, who was holding Justice, yanked her to her feet as he stood. They cowered behind her, then pushed her toward the man with the pistol and ran to their car and sped away. Nito placed the pistol back in its holster and ran over to Justice.

"Are you okay?"

Justice went limp with relief; she fell into his arms, and began to cry. I'm the same lady you rescued less than a month ago at Oaktree Downs Housing Project. Nito held her away from him so that he could look at her.

"Well, I'll be a monkey's uncle," he said. *You just think I don't know who you are.* "Seems like we keep running into each other. We just need to wait for the police. I called them when I saw them pulling you out of your car. Did you recognize either of them?"

"No, I didn't"

"Were they trying to rob you?"

"I don't think so. I think they were trying to break my legs. The one holding the pipe kept saying hold her legs. When I saw the pipe, I finally found the strength to resist. I was frozen at first." She cried as she told him what happened. He wanted to tell her that he had seen it all so she would stop crying. He hated it when women cried.

They turned when they saw the blue flashing lights. A lone officer got out of his patrol car and came over to take the information from Justice. She cried as she told him what happened. Nito wished she would stop crying. When the officer finished his report, he told her that he would escort her home and make sure everything was okay. Realizing that he was not needed any more, Nito touched her arm and mouthed goodbye. She thanked him again and he headed for his car. *Why do women always cry when they talk about something bad that happened to them? Why do we have to put up with women crying all the time?*

Chapter

13

Justice Fullilove was frustrated in her love life, anxious because someone obviously wanted to harm her, and disgusted with the situation in courtroom D. However, when she walked through the courtroom door, she laid all of her own stresses and distractions aside in order to become an effective advocate for her client. It was that determination and fight that gave both Mark and Judge Denver an uneasy feeling and was shifting the tide in Courtroom D.

When she attempted to enter the courtroom after lunch, a man stepped out and blocked her entrance.

"What seems to be the problem?" she asked.

"I just want to ask you a few questions about the trial today." The reporter said as he lifted his microphone and motion for the cameraman standing nearby to begin filming. "Miss Fullilove, what ..."

"Who gave you permission to stick a microphone in my face and point a camera at me?" Justice asked.

"Talk with him." She heard from somewhere over her left shoulder. She turned and no one was there. She turned and looked at the reporter.

"The Winston Journal," he said. "I'm Hercules Cole and I'm doing a story on the trial today. Could you please just answer a few questions, please," he pleaded.

Justice sighed and stared at him. "Okay," she said. "Shoot."

"Rumors have it that this is your fifth trial in this courtroom in seven months and that before you came, there hadn't been a trial in Courtroom D in two years. Is that true?"

"I haven't been in this courtroom two years, so I'm afraid I can't answer your question about the rumors of the history of this courtroom. But this is my fourth trial, not fifth."

"Again, rumors have it that some of the attorneys are complaining that you file too many motions and want to try every case. Is that true?"

"No, that's not true. As an attorney, I am legally and morally bound to advocate zealously for my client. So I can't file too many motions and cases are supposed to be tried. I'm a criminal defense attorney and that's what criminal defense attorneys do. Attorneys who don't want to file motions and try cases shouldn't be practicing criminal law. There are lots of other things they can do."

"What about . . ."

"That's all for today," Justice said and held up her hand. "Maybe we can talk again sometimes when you don't have your camera and microphone. Good day, sir."

"Thank you, thank you very much," the reporter said. He was surprised to get that much from her. He had heard that she was one mean lady. She seamed like a nice lady just doing her job. He handed her one of his cards. She took it, stuck in her purse, and hurried into the courtroom.

Justice was already worked up when she entered the courtroom and both Judge Denver and Mark were worked up at the thought of what unreasonable tactic she would try during the trial. They both wished they had never laid eyes on Justiana Jurisprudence Fullilove. The tension was so obvious, even the spectators could feel it.

Pre-trial motions and objections had been fought to the death in the judge's chambers on Monday morning and the judge had ruled in Mark's favor ninety percent of the time. Justice was completely ticked off. Jury selection had begun Monday afternoon and it seemed that it would take at least the rest of the day on Tuesday. At the end of the day, they had only seated seven jurors, and everyone was worn to a frazzle.

Jury selection was finally completed Wednesday morning around ten o'clock and the Judge wanted to get right to the trial. After a 20-minute break, the jury was seated and he gave them his customary pre-trial instructions. After brief opening statements by both sides, Mark called his first witness, the arresting officer. The security guard, the only witness to the alleged crime could not be located. Justice had asked Mark for a better address and phone number for him, Mark promised he would provide it but had not done so.

When the prosecutor called the police officer, Justice renewed her objection to the witness's testimony.

"Again, Your Honor, I must object to this witness testifying at this trial. This witness is not on the witness list, the prosecutor was aware of the fact that he was not on the list and it's too late to amend the witness list. The jury has been seated, jeopardy has attached, and this is not a proper witness for this trial."

Judge Denver called them to the bench because the jurors were beginning to frown and whisper as Justice began explaining the law and how it was being violated.

"I will allow it this time, but in the future, Mr. LaNear, you must provide opposing counsel with an amended witness list *before* trial date."

As they left the bench, Mark purposely stepped on Justice's heel. She screamed and fell against the table.

"He kicked me your Honor," Justice said as she turned to face the judge then glared at Mark.

"Your Honor, she stopped without warning and perhaps I was walking a little faster than I should have been and my foot accidentally bumped hers. And, as always, she overreacted. It was simply an accident." Mark turned and they stood glaring at each other.

"It's about time for lunch," Judge Denver said calmly. Court will resume at two o'clock. He instructed the jury not to discuss the case and told Mark and Justice that he would see them in his chambers at 1:45.

Judge Denver began before they were seated. "I have had all I'm willing to put up with from you two. Do you think I'm going to allow you to continue acting like two high school students--correction, elementary school students, in my courtroom?"

They both stared at him and waited for the other to answer. He refused to go on. He stared and waited. He was not going to allow them to act as if they didn't know what he meant. Justice spoke first. She was beginning to feel sorry for the way she had conducted herself. Although Judge Denver did not deserve any respect, she knew she had no right to disrespect him in his courtroom.

"I'm sorry, your Honor, it won't happen again".

"I agree," Mark said.

Judge Denver was stunned. He had expected them to blame each other, or at least try to justify their behavior. He sat there for a while. He realized that he expected to have to argue with and scold them. He had wanted a bit of a fight. He was confused, but what could he say.

"Okay, I accept your apology and I don't expect it to happen again."

"It won't," they said in unison.

"Then I'll see you in the courtroom at two o'clock." He nodded his head to let them know they had been dismissed.

When they were in the hallway, Mark pushed Justice in the back. She couldn't believe it. She kept walking. *Just pretend it never happened.* He pushed her again. She stumbled against the door to the witness room. She braced herself, turned around, grabbed his necktie, and yanked him into the witness room. She closed and locked the door, then kicked off her shoes and began to shorten her skirt by rolling it up around her waist.

"I didn't realize this was what you had in mind, Ms. Fullilove," Mark stammered

"Don't flatter yourself," she sneered as she kicked the side of his head with her right foot.

Mark saw stars. She was about to kick him again when she noticed the look on his face. She didn't know if he was going to fall over dead or what. She took a couple of steps backward, in case he went crazy or something. She had never seen that look on anyone's face before.

He stood there for a few seconds before he lunged at her. "Why you little ... She struck his nose with the back of her fist just as his hands were closing around her throat. Blood gushed onto the front of his shirt as well as her blouse. They both stood there looking at the blood on their clothes. Justice took a step back and kicked him in the left jaw with her right foot then her left foot tore into his right side. He held onto the desk to keep from falling. He had turned white, and she could see her foot print on the side of his face. He grabbed her by the shoulders and began to shake her. She yanked on his necktie and kicked him in the shin. He slapped her and she began screaming. He tried to place his hand over her mouth. She broke free of his hold, sat down on the floor, pulled the pin out of her hair, shook her head so that her hair fell over her face, and began screaming again. She opened her briefcase and dumped her papers onto the floor. He bent down and tried to place his hand over her mouth to stop the screaming; she lay flat on the floor and screamed louder. He could hear voices at the door and he desperately wanted to stop the screaming. The more he tried to stop her, the more she screamed.

"What's going on?" he heard the judge asking.

"Sounds like Mr. LaNear is beating up Ms. Fullilove," the deputy answered.

"Help, hel ..." Justice yelled as Mark's hand clamped over her mouth.

"Open the door Mr. LaNear," the deputy yelled. "Open this door or I'll break it down."

"Okay," Mark said as he scrambled to open the door. The judge, deputy, and all 12 of the jurors were standing there staring at Justice. She rolled over onto her side and began to push herself up from the floor. They all scrambled around her to help. They could see the blood on her blouse; no one noticed the blood on Mark's clothing.

"I'll call for an ambulance," the deputy said.

"No, I'm okay," Justice said hastily.

"Are you sure," the judge, deputy and jurors asked in unison.

"Yes," Justice said, as she began picking up her papers and returning them to the briefcase. Several of the jurors ran to help pick up her papers. When Justice had all her papers in her briefcase and the female jurors had helped her straighten her clothing and tuck in her blouse, she slipped on her shoes and everyone turned and stared at the judge.

"This court is adjourned until nine o'clock tomorrow morning," he said and gave the jury the usual warning about not discussing the case.

Justice turned to face the deputy. "Will you walk me to my car?"

"Sure." He put his arm around her shoulder and began to guide her to the elevator. The jurors followed the deputy and Justice to the elevator, and kept asking Justice if she was okay. When she assured them that she was okay, they went to the jury room to collect their belongings and went home.

☞

"WHAT WERE YOU thinking?" Judge Denver asked Mark, when they were alone. "What were you trying to do to her?"

"Has it occurred to anyone to ask what she did to me?" Mark asked. "This is my blood on my shirt, and that was my blood on her blouse." Judge Denver really looked at Mark for the first time since he came into the room. He saw Justice's footprint on Mark's face and how white and pale he looked as he stood there holding onto the desk. Suddenly the judge began to laugh. He couldn't help himself. It seemed that all the pint-up frustration he felt since Justice was assigned to his courtroom and the constant bickering between she and

Mark was unleashed as he stared at Mark and roared with laughter. He looked around for a seat. He was no longer able to stand. He sat in the chair and tried to control his laughter. Mark finally stormed out of the room in disgust, and left Judge Denver sitting there with his shoulders shaking and tears running down his face.

⤚

WHEN JUSTICE GOT into her car, she called Alou. Jan told her that he was on his way home, and advised her to call him on his cell phone.

Alou looked at caller ID and flipped the phone open. "Hello sweetheart, how are you?"

"Alou, do you feel like having company, can I come to your place?"

"Of course you can, where are you?"

"On my way home, I just left the courthouse."

"Why don't you go home and I'll come to you. I'm closer to your place than mine. That way, you won't have to drive home later . . . how bout I pick up some food on the way. If I get there first, I'll wait for you, if you get there first, you wait for me, and don't run off with some other man."

Justice giggled. "You are putting ideas into my head, Alou, but I think I'll wait for you. Over." *There's no way I'm going to tell him about the fight I had with Mark. I'll just change my blouse and pretend it never happened.*

"Good girl, I'll see you in a few minutes, over and out."

One of these days I'm going to kill that judge and that prosecutor. At least she's not crying. When I can get her to laugh, I know she's going to be okay.

⤚

WHEN COURT RESUMED the next morning, Snaggie had arranged to have one of Alou's friends, a law professor, take his class to the courtroom to observe the trial. He showed up and gave his card to the deputy and asked him to let the judge know his class was there to observe an actual courtroom proceeding. Judge Denver looked at the card and turned to smile at the professor and students. After he welcomed them, asked a few questions, and made a few remarks about the trial, Judge Denver turned to mark.

"You may call your first witness, Mr. LaNear."

Mark called the witness and Justice stood as he approached the witness stand.

"Your Honor, I must renew my objection to this witness testifying. He was not on the witness list, the jury has been seated, jeopardy has attached, and it's too late for the State to amend the witness list. Therefore, this witness is not a proper witness for this trial." The professor leaned over and began to explain to the students what was happening in the courtroom. They were asking questions and taking notes. Mark was not concerned. Justice has made the same argument earlier in the judge's chambers and in the courtroom yesterday and the judge had ruled in his favor. When the Judge sustained the objection, Mark was taken by surprise.

"Your Honor, I see no reason why this witness should not be permitted to testify, he was the arresting officer," Mark argued.

"But he was not on the witness list, was he Mr. LaNear?"

"Well . . . no, but it was an oversight, and . . ."

"The objection is sustained," Judge Denver said and advised witness that he was excused. "Call your next witness, Mr. LaNear."

"He's the state's only witness, Your Honor," Mark glared at the judge. He was not accustomed to the judge ruling in Justice's favor. The judge looked at Justice and she stood.

"Your Honor, the defense must move this court to dismiss the shoplifting charge against my client. The state has failed to make out a prime facie case against my client. The state has not proved that my client took any merchandise from the store, or that the Defendant had any stolen items in his possession on the date in question. The state has presented no witnesses and no evidence against my client. When viewed in the light *most favorable* to the Defendant, he is *entitled* to a dismissal as a matter of law."

"Does the state have anything else?" Judge Denver asked. Mark shook his head. He was unable to speak.

"Very well, the motion is granted, and the shoplifting charge against the Defendant is dismissed," the Judge said. He thanked the jury for their time and patience and commended them for their willingness to serve as jurors. He dismissed them and advised them to drive safely and wished them a good evening. Everyone stood while the jury left the courtroom. Judge Denver turned to the professor and students and apologized that they did not get to see a trial, but invited them to come back again. As soon as the invitation was out of his mouth, he regretted it. They thanked him and said they would.

The defendant hugged Justice, shook her hand, thanked her profusely, and hurried from the courtroom. Justice could feel the oppressive spirit; it seemed to be sitting on her shoulder. She sat at the defense table and shuffled through her papers. She did not look at Mark. She knew he was livid. She didn't want to be in the parking lot with him, so she waited and gave him sufficient time to leave the area. She always felt so alone after a trial or hearing in courtroom D. She dialed Alou's private number.

He looked at caller ID, picked up the phone, and said "Justice."

"Alou." They just held the phone for a long time. *He didn't have to say anything; he was connected to her. That was sufficient for the time being. She couldn't speak because she was asking herself. How did I fall in love so deeply with this man? Will I ever get over him? Will I have to?*

"Are you okay?" he asked.

"No."

"Where are you? I'm coming to get you."

"I'm on my way home, I just left the courthouse."

"Go home; I'll meet you there in 20 minutes." He hung up the phone and waved his hand to dismiss the employees. They had been in the middle of a meeting. They picked up their belongings and left without a word. When it came to Justice Fullilove, they knew there was nothing to say. They decided to reconvene in Benny's office and work on the project because their boss had lost his mind over a woman.

Chapter

14

Justice had filed a motion to dismiss a child molestation case. She and Mark were waiting for the judge. The defendant was there but the mother and the alleged victim were not. Mark was standing at his table flipping through his notes. Justice walked up to him and asked, "Mark, why do you hate me so much?"

He turned to look at her. She was standing there staring at him, a bit too close for comfort. He had never even thought of her as a woman before, just opposing counsel. "I don't hate you," he said. *But you are beautiful, and for once in your life you don't seem to be angry.*

Suddenly Mark was back in law school. He was a senior and Sharon was a junior. He hadn't even tried to date her. He didn't have the nerve. She was the most beautiful woman he had ever seen. She had sky blue eyes and long blonde hair, which she wore pulled back behind her ears and hanging down her back. She was shaped like a Coca Cola bottle and always wore outfits to show off every curve. She was an education major and planned to teach school. He was speechless when she approached him one night in the library and asked why he studied all the time, instead of going out and having some fun.

"I'm not allowed to have fun except on the weekend," he said, when he finally found his voice.

"And just what kind of fun do you have on weekends?" she asked, as she smiled and sat next to him.

"Oh, movies, clubs, house parties, stuff like that."

"Why haven't I ever been invited to go to these movies, clubs, house parties and stuff like that? I wouldn't mind having a little fun on the weekend myself."

"I can rectify that in a matter of days," he said. As a matter of fact, I'm going to see a great movie this weekend. I'd be pleased if you would join me."

"What time and where shall I meet you?"

"I'll pick you up at your dorm at 6:45 Saturday night."

"I'll see you then," she said, as she reached over, touched his hand, smiled and headed for the door. He just sat there and stared at her as she left the library. *I guess that was real. I think she talked me into a date.*

From that point on, Mark and Sharon spent every weekend together. Mark was elated. She was beautiful, smart and fun to be with. He had no idea what he had done to deserve such luck. Pretty soon they were making plans for their future. They were married as soon as Mark finished law school. He was hired as a prosecutor before he received his bar results. They were elated when they learned that he had passed the bar the first time around.

Mark saw the first sign of problems when Sharon wanted a wedding that neither his parents nor hers could afford. They borrowed money from relatives and maxed out every credit card, both his and hers. Okay, he thought, you only get married once. We will never do anything so stupid again. Two months after they were married, Sharon wanted to furnish the entire house. Mark pleaded with her to wait and furnish one room at a time. She pouted, refused to talk to him, and began spending weekends with her parents. When Mark finally agreed to buy furniture on credit for the entire house, she was elated. Married life was good for Mark again. Just when he began to relax, Sharon decided she wanted to have a baby. Mark wanted to wait until they paid the furniture bill and made a dent in the student loans. She wouldn't hear of it.

"I want a baby now," she said. "All my friends are either pregnant or already have kids. I'm going to be the laughing stock of my circle." Mark begged Sharon to wait at least a year to have a baby. She told him she would, but immediately stopped taking the pill and was pregnant within two months. She was sick and had to quit work. The bills were piling up. Mark was so unhappy and burdened, but Sharon didn't seem to understand that the bills had to be paid. She charged all sort of things for the baby during her third month. If he was unhappy, that was his problem. She decided that she was going to enjoy her life.

Mark's parents were not able to help them financially. He had really thought that some day he would be able buy all the nice things for his mother that his father had been unable to provide. Instead, he found himself needing to borrow money from them. He refused to ask his parents for money. Then a man approached him in the courthouse parking lot and offered him the opportunity to make some extra money. He agreed, but told himself he would do it for just a few months, just long enough to get his head above water. But that never happened. Sharon's spending was completely out of control. When he asked her to stop buying a new outfit for the baby every week, she cried and said he didn't love his own baby. No matter how he explained their financial situation to her, she ignored him and kept spending.

When Mark finally broke down and talked with his father about Sharon, his dad told him that he and Mark's mother had already figured out what was going on.

"You are fighting a losing battle, son. And I don't know how to help you. There's no way to please a woman like Sharon. All we can do is pray for you. If we had the money, you know we would help, but we never had the opportunity to get a good education like you."

"Would you and mom be hurt and disappointed, if I ended up in divorce court?"

"No, we wouldn't be hurt; maybe disappointed that it had to come to that. But we would trust you to make the right decision; and be sure that you have done everything you could to save the marriage. Divorce is devastating, especially when you have children."

Mark told his father that he was contemplating divorce, but didn't want his mom to know until, and if, he decided to go through with it. He father agreed not to tell her, but Mark could hear the sadness in his voice. Mark had scolded himself repeatedly, *now my parents are unhappy, I'm unhappy, and Sharon will never be happy. It doesn't matter how much she buys; it will never satisfy her. Why couldn't I see that before we married?*

As Mark stood in the courtroom looking into the face of Justice Fullilove, he tried to figure out why she reminded him so much of Sharon. The only thing they have in common was the fact that they were both women, they were both beautiful, and Justice had made his life just as miserable as Sharon had, but she did it for all the right reasons.

Mark realized that Justice had asked him another question and he had been lost in his own thoughts. She turned and started back to the defense table.

"Justice," Mark said. She turned. Mark took a few steps toward her. "I don't hate you." *You are beautiful like Sharon was the day I married her, and you have done everything right. You're a lawyer; you are doing what lawyers are supposed to do, and doing it very well. If Sharon were conducting her life the way you are conducing yours, I would be proud of her, but it would be so nice if you would go away.*

"Okay," Justice said. And they both turned as the judge entered the courtroom. She realized that it didn't really matter anyway. *It seems that half the people in this town hate me. Why? What did I ever do to any of them? I'm going back to DC.*

⁓

ALOU HAD PREPARED a spectacular dinner for Justice. He had taken the afternoon off and Justice arrived five minutes early.

Just like her, he thought as he opened the door and reached to embrace her. He was so happy things were working out for them. He had had a talk with his mother and she understood his feelings for Justice. He didn't expect any more trouble from her.

"Are you ever late for anything?" he asked

"Why should I be?"

"I didn't mean it as a put down, I'm just curious and amazed at you as always."

"Well, I was late for school one day when I was in kindergarten."

"So, you are human after all." He teased.

"Something smells mighty good," she said, turning toward the kitchen.

"If you had given me five more minutes, the table would have been set. Since you are here, you might as well help me set the table."

"No way."

"In that case, come into the kitchen, have a seat and watch me set the table. I promise you this will be the best food your have ever eaten in you entire life."

"This I gotta see," Justice said as she began to look around at the pictures in the spacious living room. "Alou, your home is beautiful. I think I'll take a self-guided tour and look at all the pictures you have in the living room and hallway. I love old black and white pictures."

"Okay, help yourself. But first, let me show you your bathroom."

"My bathroom?"

"Yes." He took her hand and led her to the master bedroom. "That's yours with the symbol of the woman on the door. That's mine on the other side.

"Wow!" Justice said as she glanced around the oversized master suite and sitting room. A double-sided fireplace stood between two beige and white columns. The color scheme was beige, tan, and white. "His and her bathrooms. This is absolutely beautiful," Justice said as she moved toward her bathroom.

"Hey, I'm going back and set the table. Let's eat after you check out his room. I'll show you the rest of the house later. Deal?"

"Deal," she said as she looked around the huge bathroom. The color scheme was peach and white. *My favorite colors. What a coincident.* Justice giggled as she moved into the huge walk-in closet and noticed that the tags were still on a white bathrobe, peach panties, and bra hanging in the corner. They were her size. She was amazed that everything about the bedroom, bathroom and closet seemed to have been built and decorated with her in mind. In fact, everything she had seen so far, was everything she wanted in a home, and more. She realized she had overstayed her five minutes and hurried toward the kitchen.

⌒

ALOU WAS SO happy; he began to hum as he set the table. He went silent when he thought about his mother's visit earlier. Everything about her visit was weird; she showed up unannounced and stayed longer than usual. It almost seemed as if she knew he was preparing dinner for Justice. He couldn't figure out what she wanted. She just made small talk and asked a few questions about Justice. She had looked in the refrigerator and asked when he started drinking green tea and if those were rolls rising on the table.

"It's not just green tea, mother, it's organic green tea. It's good for you and it's Justice's favorite drink. She's coming by after work so I'm fixing dinner. And yes, those are rolls rising on the table. You know I make the best homemade rolls in all of Georgia . . . You ever think about grandkids?" He was surprised by the look on her face. He thought she would be happy, but obviously she was not. He had not entertained the idea of marriage and kids in years.

"Yes, I've thought about it." She said.

"And what do you think about it?"

"We'll talk about it later. I must go; I have a two o'clock appointment not far from here. I'll see you later, and I hope you and Justice have a great time tonight."

"Thanks," Alou said. But he had seen that look on her face when he mentioned grandkids and he knew it had to do with Justice. He didn't know how he was going to deal with his mother, but he knew he had to deal with her about Justice. Alou walked her to the door and kissed her on the cheek. He was not looking forward to this confrontation.

At three o'clock his mom stopped by again. He was surprised. "That was quick, how did your appointment go?"

"Great, like I said, it wasn't far from here. I just had to look at some decorating plans for my ladies club. You know, I read something about green tea last week. Since you have a whole gallon, why don't I taste it, it sounds like something worth trying."

Alou stood and started toward the kitchen, and she waved him away. "I'll pour myself a glass. I promise I'll only take one glass. It must be good because I know you don't care for tea."

"I'm beginning to develop a taste for it. It's really not bad." He hoped she would hurry and leave. He sat there and stared at the TV. He had no idea what was on the screen. His mind was racing. *How do I deal with this? She's going to make it difficult.*

"Well, I won't be back again today," she said as she came over to the couch and kissed him on the forehead. "I'll talk with you later in the week. And don't get up, I'll let myself out."

Auryola had been careful not to say anything negative about Justice. She knew Alou thought Justice was something special, and she knew she had to put an end to this in a hurry. She hoped that he couldn't tell what she was thinking. She was not going to stand by and watch some money-hungry public defender steal her son. Alou was everything she wanted in a son. He was generous with his money and they spent hours talking. She prepared at least two meals for him every week and they spent every holiday together. She was not about to allow Justice to interfere with what was rightfully hers. *I'll break this up if it's the last thing I do.*

Alou shook his head as he remembered his mother's visit. He had not been able to figure out what she wanted. He shrugged his shoulders and decided to forget it. He had fixed grilled salmon, augratin potatoes, creamed corn, a garden salad, and homemade rolls. He had prepared most of the ingredients the night before. He wanted this to be a very special night for Justice. Shane had made a chocolate cream pie. The food was delicious. As they ate, Justice told Alou about her cases. He asked questions and seemed really interested. She loved the fact that Alou always listened to what she had to say. She determined that she would always be available to listen to him when he wanted to talk. They were not able to eat dessert and decided to save it until after the movie.

"I can't believe you went to all this trouble for me," Justice said. "And to make homemade rolls, Alou, you are a sweet man."

"I agree that I'm a sweet man, but it was no trouble preparing a good meal for you. I love doing nice things for you. Because ..." He stepped back and began to dance and sing, "You light up my life, you make me happy..." He grabbed her by the hand and whirled her around, then pulled her into his arms and kissed her lightly on the mouth.

"Can you tell by my behavior that I'm madly in love with you?" he asked.

"Making homemade rolls would probably cause me to stipulate to the fact that enough clear and convincing evidence exist to sustain your allegation."

"Lawyers," Alou said as he rolled his eyes upwards. "Let's go watch a good movie."

As they sat on the couch holding hands, Alou pulled Justice toward him so that her head rested on his shoulder.

"Are you ready for desert now?" he asked.

"No, I'm still full. I simply ate too much."

"If you marry me, I'll cook you good food like that every day."

"I don't believe you. If I did, I'd marry you tonight. No woman in her right mind would turn down an offer like that."

"Well," Alou said. "That may have been a slight exaggeration, but I promise you that you will be a happy wife." He lifted her chin and bent to kiss her on the mouth. She didn't pull away. He was pleased, but wanted to take it real slow. He didn't want to frightened her or make her angry. He knew the last failed relationship was still fresh in her mind.

They were both awaken by the sound of the static from the TV indicating that the movie was over.

"What happened?" Justice asked. "Did they get married?"

"I don't know," Alou said. "I must have dozed off." They both looked at their watch and Justice jumped to her feet.

"It's eight o'clock, I'd better get out of here, I have court tomorrow."

"You wanna take your desert home, or will you come back again tomorrow?"

"I'll pass. Thank you for a delicious meal and a wonderful evening." She put her arms around his neck to give him a good night kiss and it turned into anything but what she had in mind. She kissed him deeply and passionately and was surprised to find herself pressing her body into his. He responded with the same passion and she kept thinking it's time to let this go. But she kept telling herself, one more second and I'll let it go. It was finally Alou who broke away and took both her hands in his. It took all of his will power and he was confused and literally shaking. "We better stop this before we start something we can't finish." He looked into her eyes and saw passion, then confusion, then disappointment, and then anger. She just stood there staring at him, then shook her head as if to clear it. She turned without a word and ran to get her purse.

"Wait Justice . . ." he didn't know what to say. He was confused. He didn't want her to leave. What he wanted was to pull her back into his arms and make love to her. But he had promised himself that he would not go there until they were married. He knew how important that was to her. "Justice, please," he said. But she just held up her hand and backed toward the door. She turned, opened the door, and ran out of the house. He followed her to her car. Neither of them spoke, they didn't know what to say. When she got into her car, he reached inside, locked the door, and closed it. She drove away without waving or looking back. He waited until he felt she was a few blocks away, then got into his car and followed her.

At first Justice was angrier with herself than Alou because the situation had gotten a little out of control. Then she realized that she had been drinking something more than just green tea. She was half way through the red light when she realized what had happen. She slowed down to 25 miles per hours and gripped the steering wheel with both hands. She forgot her anger and began to concentrate on getting home safely. She was thankful that traffic was light. *Oh my God, he put something in my drink. I would have never expected Alou to do such a thing.*

15

Justice was so disappointed and broken hearted. She sat on the couch and cried and cried and cried. Then she began to pray. "God, I'm going to die, I can't stand this pain. I can't rub it or take anything for it because it's inside the core of my being. I can't stand it; you gotta help me. Oh God, oh God, oh God. I gotta have help right now." The phone rang and Justice stopped crying and stared at the phone. She lifted the receiver and listened. When she didn't hear anything, she whispered, "God?"

Solomon hesitated for just a moment because he thought she had said God. Then he decided that he had misunderstood her and said excitedly, "Justice, this is Solomon, and I know it's a little late, but you have got to taste this pizza, and this salad, and this tea. My aunt made dinner for me. You will never taste pizza this good again until you get to Heaven." When he took the first bite of his pizza, he knew he had to share it with Justice. He knew that food that great had to be shared. Justice had to smile in spite of her broken heart. Solomon was always comparing or contrasting Earth and Heaven. Listening to him, one would think he was an expert on what life will be like in Heaven.

"I'm bringing the pizza over now." When she didn't interrupt him, he realized something was wrong.

"Okay," she said softly, trying not to sound as if she had been crying.

"I'm on my way . . . are you decent?" Solomon asked, hoping to make her laugh. He could tell that she had been crying.

"Yes," she whispered as she placed the receiver on the hook and rushed to the bathroom to splash cold water on her face.

Justice opened the door as soon as Solomon rang the doorbell. She had been standing by the door.

"What's wrong?," Solomon asked, as he stepped into the living room, set the food on the table, and took both her hands in his.

"My heart is broken into a million pieces."

"Justice, the human heart is too small to break into a million pieces."

"I'm not talking about my human heart; I'm talking about my spirit heart."

"Now, now kiddo, it's going to be alright," Solomon said as he pulled her into his arms. She began sobbing and saying that her heart was broken. Solomon kept trying to comfort her and get her to stop crying.

Suddenly, Solomon was twenty-two and Tiffany was crying in his arms and telling him that she was in love with one of her professors at school. She was sorry that she would have to break their engagement. He was in shock, he held her close, he was not going to let her go. She had tried to wiggle out of his arms, but Solomon just held her tighter. "No, he said, I won't let you go; you can't do this to me, to us. He heard Justice calling his name and realized she was struggling to get free of his hold. He released her.

"What got into you, Solomon, why were you holding me so tight? I thought you were going to crush my ribs." She was shocked and a bit upset. Solomon allowed his arms to fall and hang loosely at his side. He was shocked because he had gotten carried away and because Justice had felt so good in his arms. He hung his head and began his explanation. He had to appease her anger and comfort her at the same time.

"Justice, I'm so sorry, I guess I just got a little carried away. When you kept saying that your heart was broken, it made me think of the time when I felt that exact same way. But I'm a man and I couldn't cry. I would have given anything if there had been someone I could have gone to and poured my heart out. When Tiffany told me that she was breaking our engagement because she was in love with one of her professors, our professor, I was devastated and humiliated. I wish there had been one person to pat me on the back and say, Sol, it's going to be okay." He reached his right hand up and patted himself on the back. "I wish I had had one person to pat me on the knee and say, Sol, you are going to get through this." He reached down and patted himself on the knee. "If only there had been one person to put their arms around me and say, Sol, I don't know how to fix this, but I'm here for you." He folded his arms across his chest and hugged himself. "There was no one I could turn to. I didn't have any hope; I thought I was going to die. So I know exactly how you feel." He raised his head just a tad to see if he had effectively appeased her. She had tears in her eyes. She ran to him and threw her arms around him.

"Oh, Solomon, if I had been there I would have patted you on the back, and on the knee and put my arms around you and told you I was there for you. And I would have kicked that professor's behind, and told Tiffany that she was an idiot. What was she thinking?"

Solomon disentangled himself from Justice and lifted her chin. "Hey, let's make a deal, let's not think about anything negative for the rest of the night. I have a good friend here, delicious pizza, a crisp salad, and sweet tea; can we let that be enough for right now?"

"Yes," Justice whispered. "Let's eat before the pizza gets cold." They were both in deep thought as they walked into the kitchen.

"You know, you're right, this pizza is delicious. Thank you for sharing it with me."

"It's too good not to share."

"How long did it take you to get over Tiffany?"

"Well, I had pictures of her on the refrigerator, on my bathroom mirror, on the nightstand by my bed, almost everywhere. I removed all of her pictures. I kept them in a bag in the back of the closet for a while, in case she changed her mind. Then, after about two months, I realized that I didn't want her back even if she changed her mind, so I burned the pictures. At that time I was in the habit of changing the oil in my car myself. So, about three months after we broke up, I got on the dolly and slid under my car to change the oil. And there was a picture of her taped to the bottom of the car that I had forgotten to remove. At first I just stared . . ."

"What happened, what did you do?" Justice asked. Solomon turned to face Justice and took her by the hand. He wanted her to get the full impact of what he was about to say. She placed her pizza in the plate and gave him her undivided attention.

"You know, Justice . . . honestly, at that moment, I couldn't even remember her name. She was history."

"Three months, that's all it took?" she asked excitedly. "You think I'll get over Alou in three months."

"Well, the Bible says, as a man thinketh in his heart, so is he. If you continue to think about Alou and talk about him, it will take a long time to get over him. It's not easy to stop thinking about someone you love. But it can be done, and the sooner you stop talking about them, the sooner you can get over them." Justice decided that she would not talk or think about Alou any more. She found out that very night that it was easier said than done.

⌒

ALOU HAD FOLLOWED Justice home and watched her living room from across the street until he saw the light turned on. He dialed her number but she didn't answer. He didn't expect her to; he just wanted her to know he was thinking about her. As he drove home, he thought about the car he had barely missed when he went through a stop sign while following Justice. He thought about her behavior. It was also a bit unusual. He knew something was wrong. He decided to check out the green tea. He sniffed it and detected the smell of alcohol, but there was something else. He wondered if it was the raspberry. He poured some in a small bottle and placed it beside his briefcase. He knew he had to find out for sure what was in that tea; he already knew how it got there.

Alou dropped the bottle of tea off at the lab of one of his friends on his way to work. When he picked up the report that afternoon, he went to see his mother.

"Why?" he asked when she opened the door.

"Why what?" she asked.

"Why did you put *alcohol and aphrodisiac*, of all things, in my green tea yesterday?"

"Have a seat, Alou."

"I don't want to sit, I want an explanation!" He shoved the report into her hands.

"I don't know what you are talking about," she said as she glanced at the report.

Alou folded his arms and leaned against the door. "I'm not leaving until you tell me why you spiked my tea."

"Suit yourself, but I don't know what you are talking about."

Alou walked over to his mother and gently took the report from her hand; he turned and walked out the door without another word. He knew he was not going to get an answer from her. He knew she had spiked the drink and could have caused Justice to have an accident and him to break a promise he had made to himself. He didn't like what he was feeling. He was having thoughts about his mother that he never thought were possible. And he knew it would only get worse.

16

Jerame's trial had been postponed several times, but both attorneys finally answered ready when the case was called on Monday, October 24, 2006. Both Justice and Mark were ready to get on with the trial. Mark had actually had to do trial preparations. He was so sick of Justice Fullilove. She had changed his courtroom and caused what had become an easy job to become difficult for him. Now other defense attorneys were beginning to try more cases. He wished there was something he could do to get rid of her once and for all.

Dr. Burkett and Shemika were the two state witnesses. Half way through the doctor's testimony, the Attorney General entered the courtroom. Snaggie had made contact with him two days earlier. He passed a card to the deputy and asked him to give it to the judge. "Tell him not to mind me; the father of one of the attorneys is a good friend of mine. I just wanted to observe a few moments and I'll be on my way." Neither Mark nor Justice knew he was there.

After the doctor finished his testimony, Mark turned and looked at Justice with a smirk, "Your witness counselor."

"Thank you, counselor," Justice said as she moved to the podium. She took her time arranging her papers. Then she moved around in front of the podium and folded her arms.

"Dr. Burkett, you testified that you were able to tell how the fracture to Ms. Hoskins' arm occurred by the x-rays, is that correct?"

"That's correct."

"If you can look at Ms. Hoskins's x-rays and tell how the fracture occurred, then you can look at the x-ray for any fracture, of a person's arm or even a leg, and tell how the fracture occurred, it that correct?"

"Yes." He didn't like Justice.

"Your Honor," Justice said as she turned to the Judge. "I would like to have this witness step down and call Ms. Kelly to the stand before I continue with his testimony.

Mark was on his feet immediately, "Objection!"

"To what?" the judge asked. Mark stood there and stared at the judge. He was not accustomed to the judge asking any questions, he almost always sustained Mark's objections.

"To interrupting this witness's testimony to call another witness, why can't she finish with this witness and let him go. He's a doctor, he has patients to see."

"Objection overruled, Ms. Kelly will take the stand and Dr. Burkett, you have not been excused, you will wait in the hallway and we will let you know when you are to return to the stand." Ms. Kelly moved to the witness stand and was sworn in by the deputy.

Justice moved back behind the podium. She arranged her exhibits in the order she planned to present them and handed the first exhibit to the judge as Mark moved forward. "Your Honor, I would like this record to be entered as evidence." Judge Denver scanned the record and handed it to Mark. The record was a medical file for the victim, Shemika Hoskins.

"Your Honor, I must object to this record being entered as evidence, there is no question as to whether or not the victim's arm was broken," Mark said.

"Your Honor," Justice said. "We will use this record to prove our point; it will only take a few minutes for the court to see why we are introducing this evidence."

"I'll allow it," Judge Denver said.

Mark passed the exhibit to the clerk. The clerk marked the exhibit and returned it to Justice. Justice walked over to the witness and handed the exhibit to her.

"Ms. Kelly, I handed you a document marked as exhibit 1, do you recognize that document?"

"Yes."

"Would you tell the jury what it is?"

"It's the medical record of a patient by the name of Shemika Hoskins, who was treated in the emergency room of Sunset Medical Center for a broken arm by Dr. Timothy Burkett in September of 2005."

"Would you pull the manila envelope from that file and tell the jury what it is."

Ms. Kelly pulled out the envelope containing the x-ray films. "It's the x-ray films of Ms. Hoskins' arm."

"Was this patient seen by any other doctor during this visit?"

"No."

"Did this patient return to the medical center for follow-up care?"

"Yes, she did."

"Who did the patient see for follow-up care?"

"Dr. Burkett.""

"Now, Ms. Kelly, is there a narrative in the file prescribing treatment for the patient following the x-ray report written by the radiologist.

"Yes."

"And who wrote the narrative?"

"Objections," Mark yelled. "How can Ms. Kelly testify as to who wrote the narrative?"

"I'll rephrase the question . . . The narrative following the x-ray report, was it signed by a doctor?"

"Yes, it was."

"Do you recognize the signature on that document?"

"Yes."

"And whose signature is it?"

"Dr. Timothy Burkett."

"Is it customary for the doctor who wrote the narrative to sign it, or can any doctor sign it? To put it another way, if

Dr. Burkett signed the narrative, does it means that he also wrote the narrative?"

"Yes, it does."

Justice asked the court to admit exhibit two into evidence and moved over to the witness.

"Now Ms. Kelly, I am handing you a document marked exhibit two, do you recognize this document?"

"Yes."

"Would you tell the jury what it is?"

"It's a medical record for the same patient, Shemika Hoskins. She was seen for a broken leg in March of 2005 by Dr. Burkett."

"Your Honor, I object," Mark said. "The defendant is not on trial for breaking Ms. Hoskins' leg."

"Again, your Honor, this evidence is relevant and it will only take a few minutes for the court to see why we are introducing it," Justice said.

"I think we can spare a few minutes to see how it's connected to this charge, Mr. LaNear," Judge Denver said. Mark was exasperated and Justice was delighted. They both wondered what had happen to the judge. In the past, the judge had always ruled in Mark's favor and against Justice.

Justice continued her examination of the witness. "Was this patient seen by any other doctor during this visit?"

"No."

"Did this patient return to the medical center for follow-up care?"

"Yes."

"Who did the patient see for follow-up care?"

"Dr. Burkett."

"Did she see any other doctor for follow-up care?"

"No."

"Thank you, Ms. Kelly." Justice turned to the judge. "Your Honor, I have no further questions for this witness at this time. I would like to excuse her with the understanding that we may need to recall her."

Mark stood, "Objection, Your Honor, these people are busy, they are trying to help sick and injured people, we shouldn't have them spending days down ..."

"Your Honor," Justice said. "The defendant is accused of a very serious crime, and he is entitled to have every witness available to testify on his behalf, and for as long ...

"I don't need a long dissertation from either of you," Judge Denver said as he turned to the witness. "The witness is on notice that she is excused with the understanding that she may be called back to the witness stand. You may step down."

"At this time, Your Honor, I would like to continue my cross examination of Dr. Burkett," Justice said as she leaned on the podium and glared at Mark. The judge turned to the deputy who was already moving to the back to bring Dr. Burkett back to the stand. Dr. Burkett was reminded that he was still under oath and Justice resumed her cross-examination.

"Dr. Burkett, Isn't it true that almost all injuries to the arm that result in a broken bone are caused by either direct trauma or a fall?"

"Yes."

"Isn't it true that X-rays are typically the test used to assess for broken bones?"

"Yes."

"And at least two views of the bone are taken initially?"

"Yes."

"Isn't it also true that some fractures are not visible on the first set of x-rays?"

"Yes."

"Tell me doctor if this statement is correct: If there is no evidence of a fracture from the first x-rays, there is an assumption that the bone is not broken and the patient is sent home with pain medicine, and basic instruction on how to care for the injury."

"Yes, that's correct."

"I understand that there is a term in medicine call the 'National Standard of Care,' would you tell the jury what that means."

"Well, it basically means that all doctors in the nation are held to the same standard of care when treating a patient."

"So, if one doctor is required to leave a cast on a broken arm for six weeks, you would be required to leave it on for six weeks as well. Is that correct?"

"Yes," the doctor whispered.

"In this case, I believe the record shows that you removed Miss Hoskins' cast after only two weeks. Why?"

"She insisted that I take it off, she's a single parent and had a chance to get a good job. If she had reported to work with the cast, she would have lost the opportunity . . ."

"Are you in the habit of allowing patients to make medical decisions about when a cast should be removed based on their financial needs doctor?"

"Objections!" Marked yelled. "Argumentative."

"I want to hear the answer," Judge Denver said. "Answer the question doctor."

Dr. Burkett shook his head no. "Please answer so that the court reporter can record your answer. It's difficult to record head movement," the judge said.

"No," the doctor whispered.

"So, if a patient leaves the emergency room with a cast on her arm, that would mean that the bone was broken as evidenced by the x-rays taken upon her arrival in the emergency room. Is that correct?"

"Yes."

"Let's take the facts of your testimony and apply them to the case before this court today . . . If there had there been no evidence of a fracture of Miss Hoskins' arm, as evidenced by the x-rays taken upon her arrival in the emergency room, you would have sent her home with pain medication, and basic instruction on how to care for the injury. Is that correct?"

"Objection, irrelevant," Mark said and glared at Justice. "Your Honor, we are not here to give the jury a crash course in how to care for a broken bone, we just want to ..."

"Your Honor, the doctor is here as an expert witness, and how he treated the patient in the case before this court, in light of his ..."

"Objection overruled, the witness will answer the question." Judge Denver wondered where Justice was going with this. He didn't like the sound of it, especially from Justice Fullilove.

"Yes," Dr. Burkett said and squirmed in his seat. A sick feeling was gnawing at the pit of his stomach. Justice walked over to the table and picked up the exhibits. She handed him the document marked exhibit two. "Dr. Burkett, I handed you a document marked exhibit two, do you recognize that document?" She deliberately gave him the exhibit showing the x-rays of the leg first.

"Yes."

"Will you tell the jury what it is."

Dr. Burkett looked at the record and said, "It's the x-rays of Miss Hoskins' leg."

"I now give you exhibit 1, do you recognize it?"

"Yes."

"Would you tell the jury what it is."

"It's an x-rays of Ms. Hoskins' arm."

"And you viewed both set of x-rays for Ms. Hoskins, the arm and the leg, and prescribed treatment based on those x-rays, is that correct?"

"Yes."

"Would you please remove the x-rays from the file that show her broken leg and place it on the lighted board for the jury to see."

Dr. Burkett placed Exhibit #2 on the counter, removed the x-rays from the envelope, walked over and placed them on the magnetic lighted board and started back to the witness stand.

"Just a minute, Dr. Burkett," Justice said as she picked up the pointer and handed it to him. "Would you use the pointer and show the jury where the bone was broken in Ms. Hoskins' leg."

"Here." Dr. Burkett said as he pointed to the red line on the x-rays that indicated a fracture.

"Thank you Doctor, now would you remove the x-rays from the file that shows the broken arm and place them on the board next to the first x-rays." Dr. Burkett removed the x-rays and placed them on the board next to the x-rays of Ms. Hoskins' leg.

"Objection your Honor," Mark yelled. The questions have been asked and answered, all of those records were identified by the other witness."

"I have only a few more questions for this witness, your Honor," Justice said as she turned to stare at Mark. She was thankful that she had gotten that far. Ordinarily the judge would have sustained almost all of Mark's objections.

"Objection overruled, you may proceed Ms. Fullilove," the judge said as he glared at Mark. Mark was in shock.

"Now, Dr. Burkett, would you use the pointer to show the jury where the fracture is on Ms. Hoskins' arm." It was obvious that there was no red line on the x-rays of Ms. Hoskins' arm to indicate a fracture.

The doctor simply hung his head and remained silent. Justice folded her arms and stood there staring at the doctor. After a long pause, the judge said, "Dr. Burkett, would you point to the fracture." The doctor never lifted his head. For just a moment there was complete silence in the courtroom as everyone stared at the x-rays.

"No more questions," Justice said and walked back to the defense table. Suddenly everyone was talking at once. The jurors as well as the spectators were murmuring and Ms. Hoskins stood, screamed at the doctor, and began to move toward him. Some of the spectators began to yell; the Judge banged his gavel on the bench and called for order. When the deputy began to move toward Ms. Hoskins, Justice stepped in her chair and then upon the defense table and yelled.

"**GOD** is on His holy throne let **ALL THE EARTH** keep silent before Him." There was an immediate hush in the courtroom. Members of the jury bowed their head. Some of the spectators bowed their head and some placed their hand over their heart. Justice looked at the judge. The prosecutor looked at the judge. The judge glared at Justice. She shrugged her shoulders, climbed down from the table, whispered "Amen", and took her seat. The prosecutor was the only one left standing and staring at the judge.

"Amen," the judge said as he looked at the prosecutor. "Redirect, counsel?"

"Yes," said Mark, out of sheer habit. He had no idea what he had planned to ask the witness and at that moment he really didn't care. His notes were out of order and so was his mind, but then so is this courtroom he thought to himself. Mark tried his best to rehabilitate the witness. But the doctor simply sat there and stared at his feet.

"Your Honor, I would ask the court to grant us a brief recess," Mark said.

"It's about time for a break," the judge said. "Court will resume in 20 minutes, I remind the jury not to discuss the case, and don't allow anyone to discuss it in your presence." The attorney general hurried out, he knew that Justice was not supposed to know he was there. He would sneak back in after recess. The case was becoming quite interesting.

When court resumed, Mark informed the court that he had no further questions for the doctor and the judge asked Mark to call his next witness.

"Your Honor, the state rests," Mark said.

"Your Honor, I would like to make a motion out of the presence of the jury," Justice said.

"Very well, the jury may retire to the jury room."

"Your Honor," Justice said after the jury left the courtroom. "We are asking the court to direct a verdict of not guilty because the indictment alleges that the defendant broke Ms. Hoskins' arm by knocking her down and stomping on her arm. The evidence has clearly shown that the victim's arm was not broken. Therefore, the indictment is invalid, and my client is entitled to a directed verdict of not guilty as a matter of law."

"I believe you are right, Ms. Fullilove," the judge said, and then turned to Mark, "Unless you have some basis for objecting to Ms. Fullilove's motion." Mark stood, moved around the table and took a step toward the bench, shook his head no, moved back and sat down. The attorney general gave a slight nod to the judge and took his leave. Both Mark and Justice had been so caught up in the trial that they were not aware he had been in the courtroom.

"Based on the evidence presented to this court, I'm going to grant the motion; this court enters a directed verdict of not guilty, and orders the defendant's immediate release from custody."

Jerame grabbed Justice and hugged her. "You are the best attorney in the whole wide world, I had no idea a public defender could be such a good attorney. Thank you, thank you, thank you." He was given a brief moment with his family before he was returned to jail to be processed out.

Both Mark and Justice were in a daze. Neither had an explanation for what had just happened; they just knew it was the exact opposite of what they had expected. Justice took her time gathering up her belongings. She wanted to give Mark enough time to clear the parking lot before she left. She knew he was highly ticked off. *Don't fuel the fire. Where there is no wood, the fire will go out.*

17

Alou was waiting for Justice when she left the courtroom. She refused to talk to him. He walked with her to her car and she never said one word to him; simply got in her car and drove away.

"I am not going to give him the opportunity to persuade me to allow him into my life again. I may have a broken heart, but my mind is not broken and I am going to stay as far away for that man as I can. I am going to get over him if it's the last thing I do," Justice said as she drove away. She did not notice that a blue Buick Rivera was following her.

The Rivera slowed as she turned into her condo complex, and then sped away. Alou saw the car as he turned into Justice's condo visitor's space and noted that he had seen the same man when he entered the courthouse parking lot and the man had gotten into his car when he and Justice walked into the parking lot. He tried to get the license number, but he sped away too quickly.

Justice kicked off her shoes and threw her jacket on a chair in the living room and headed for the kitchen to heat water for tea. The doorbell rang.

"I'm coming," Justice said as the doorbell continued to ring. She opened the door and Alou was standing there. She tried to close the door and he stuck one foot in.

"You can't turn me away," he said.

"Why not?" Justice asked.

"The Bible."

"What does the Bible have to do with you trying to push your way into my home?"

"It clearly states, I was hungry and you didn't feed me, sick and you didn't come to see about me, in prison and you didn't visit me."

"Would you please leave, Alou, you are not hungry, you are not sick, and you are not in prison."

"It also says, I was naked and you didn't clothe me."

"And you are not nak..." she began, but stopped and stared at him when he began taking his clothes off.

Alou took off his coat and threw it on the floor; he unbuckled his belt, pulled it from his pants, and threw it on the floor. He began to unbutton his shirt. Justice stepped out on the porch and looked around to be sure the neighbors were not looking. She grabbed Alou and yanked him into the living room, picked up his clothing, and closed the door.

"Are you crazy?" she asked. "Do you want to get arrested for indecent exposure in front of my apartment?" She piled his belongings on the love seat and turned to face him. He could tell she was angry.

"It may be a good idea for the police to come here. It seems that I am not the only one that followed you home today."

"Just what is that supposed to mean?" she asked.

"Did you notice the man with the bright orange shirt and jeans standing by the blue Buick when we walked to your car?"

"No, but I am not in the habit of noticing every man who stand by a car in the parking lot. There's nothing unusual about people standing by cars in parking lots."

Oh, but there was something unusual about this one. He was standing there when I arrived and was still there when we walked to your car. He left as soon as you did and followed you to your apartment, I saw him speeding away as I drove up."

"Are you sure it was the same guy?" she asked, becoming a bit concerned.

"Absolutely, I couldn't miss that bright orange shirt."

"Okay, I'll be extra careful, now would you please leave. I have to prepare for court tomorrow."

Alou sat on the couch and folded his arms. "I'm not leaving until you allow me to explain what happened the night I invited you over for dinner, and why."

"Okay, shoot," Justice said as she took a seat at the other end of the couch.

"First, let me say that I love you. I will always love you. And I'll never get over you because ..."

"Get to the point, Alou; this was supposed to be about why you spiked my drink."

Alou sighed, swallowed, and squirmed around on the couch. He looked at Justice and she seemed so cold and distant. Alou stood and turned to face Justice, then turned and walked toward to the door. He turned around and sighed.

"I didn't spike your drink, I would never do *anything* to harm you or make your angry." He took a step toward her and she held up a hand.

"I don't appreciate your pushing your way into my home, attempting to frighten me by suggesting that someone is following me. I am not going to allow you to continue to abuse me. Leave, don't make me call the police."

"If I could tell you in a very few words what happened that night, would you at least listen to me?"

"You know, it doesn't even matter any more. Please, just go."

Alou turned around and walked slowly out the door. He looked like a different person than the one that entered a few minutes earlier. She felt the tears running down her face as she stared at his back. He closed the door slowly and she ran to the door to listen to his footsteps as he went down the stairs. She fell against the door, slid to the floor, and began to sob. Alou could hear her crying and he knew she was down on the floor. He stopped and gripped the rail. He turned to look at the door and thought of busting the door in and shaking some sense into her, or grabbing her and kissing her until she understood how much he loved her, or just getting down on the floor and crying with her, but he knew she wouldn't let him. So he turned, ran down the steps, and headed for his car.

ALOU WALKED INTO his kitchen and sat at the table without turning on the light. Two hours later, he was still sitting in the dark. He tried to remember every woman he had ever dated. None of them had gotten into his heart the way Justice had. His mind went to Dimples. He couldn't even remember her real name. Everyone called her Dimples because she had such beautiful dimples. She was always smiling, and he was sure he was in love with her. He thought of the day she had joined him and his mother for lunch. She had been a bit nervous about meeting his mother. He kept assuring her she had nothing to worry about because his mother was such a nice person and so easy to get along with. He was in for a rude awakening. He saw a side of his mother that he did not know existed. While she wasn't exactly rude to Dimples, she obviously intended to make her feel uncomfortable. Auryola had quizzed Dimples about her family and made remarks that were obviously meant to be a put down. Dimples felt uncomfortable and didn't quite know how to deal with Auryola. She had glanced at Alou, who obviously didn't know how to deal with her either. He just sat there looking miserable. Dimples had finally said she had a headache and wanted to leave, Alou grabbed her hand and they practically ran from the restaurant. They had never talked about that day and had only a few dates after that.

Alou had had lots of dates since Dimples, but only one other serious relationship. Her name was Charlotte. She was pretty, smart, energetic, and his second love. He had waited before introducing her to his mother. He tried to prepare her in case things didn't go just right at the meeting. Things didn't go right. Charlotte had refused to date Alou again after the meeting with his mother, and Alou had never allowed himself to fall for another woman. He had never been able to deal with the conflict. He knew his mother was a nice caring person, and yet she was mean-spirited toward any woman in which he showed an interest. He could come up with no explanation for her behavior and had no one to discuss it with, so he decided to stop thinking about it.

He had dated a lot of women since Dimples and Charlotte—more than he cared to remember. Most of the time the relationship was mutual. He had no real interest in them and they had none in him. To him it was just the normal thing to do. To most of the women, it was an opportunity to go to The Club.

The Club was an auxiliary of the social club that had been formed 12 years earlier by a group of realtors who were just breaking into the scene as Winston began to develop and grow. It started as a networking club for African American realtors, and was held in the home of the founder. It was so successful that others professionals sought to join. Eventually, a committee was formed to screen applications for membership. The social club had several different auxiliaries that operated daily, but The Club was only open on Friday and Saturday nights. They hired the best chefs and musicians.

Members were always free to bring a guest, and the annual membership fee escalated to $2,000. Alou got a kick out of taking women there who would not otherwise have been admitted. He loved violating the unwritten, unspoken rules—date people who are members of the The Club, marry people who are members of the The Club, hang with people who are members of the The Club. He loved going to functions at The Club. He loved the food, music, and the people. Of course there were always the snotty members, but they were few and far between.

Alou had never thought of his mother as a snotty person until the night she attacked Justice. He had no idea what he would have done that night had Justice not responded to his mother the way she did. He would always be grateful to Justice for the fight in her. It's what gave him the courage to walk away with her and leave his mother standing there fuming.

As he sat staring into the darkness, he knew that it was the fight in Justice that gave him the courage he needed to begin living his life on his own terms rather than his mother's.

"I may never get Justice back," he said out loud. "But I will always love her and I will always be grateful to her, and my mother will never control my life again."

He finally kicked off his shoes and tumbled into bed fully dressed. When he didn't show up at the office the next day and didn't answer his phone, Jan, his secretary, showed up at his door and wouldn't go away. When he finally let her in, he wanted to be angry with her.

"You are my secretary, not my mother or my boss or my keeper," he said as he stood staring at her with his arms folded across his chest.

"If you took one look at yourself in the mirror, you would see why I'm worried about you. Not that I care about you, I just don't want the company to fold. I need my job. That's my only reason for coming out here," she said as she turned and headed toward the door.

"I'm sorry Jan; even I know that's not true. I'm an ingrate. Look, why don't you fix me some breakfast...since you're here."

"I'm not your wife, I'm not your mother, and I'm not your maid. So, why should I fix your breakfast?"

"Because you are still on my payroll . . . and you are in my heart," Alou said as he placed his hand on his chest.

"Okay," she said as she turned and went into the kitchen. "Men!"

Alou followed her into the kitchen. "I guess you have already figured out what happened, right?"

"Yeah, Miss Fullilove kicked you to the curb. But you know she cares about you, she'll come around. You want me to go have a talk with her." Alou had to laugh at that. Justice wouldn't listen to anyone. She was so afraid of having her heart broken that she was breaking it herself and grinding his up in the process. He simply sighed and shook his head no. When Jan placed the homemade pancakes, grits and eggs before him, Alou felt as if he hadn't eaten in days. Jan drank a cup of tea and watched him eat. They were silent the entire time, both lost in their own thoughts. When he finished he looked at Jan and smiled.

"Thanks, Jan, that was delicious. Now, do you want to go back to work, especially since you are still on the clock, or do you want to sit here and mind my personal business?"

"I'm going back to work, I know how to be a secretary, but I don't know what to do about two pigheaded people." After Jan left, Alou called Justice on her cell phone. She didn't answer, so he left a message and went back to bed. *I really need some rest; I have been working too hard. This is not about a woman. No way.*

~

JUDGE DENVER RECEIVED an inquiry from the Bar regarding Justiana Fullilove. The Bar attached a copy of the letter from a third party that complained of Justice's conduct and expressed concern for the judge's safety. The letter stated that the Bar did not investigate complaints of uninvolved third parties, but they were forwarding the letter to him because of the complainant's concern for his safety. The letter stated that it did not require a response. Judge Denver decided to respond, but decided to meet with Justice before doing so. When she was called into the judge's chambers, she did not know what to expect.

"Have a seat Miss Fullilove. I have a letter I want to show you, but first, I want to apologize to you for my conduct since your assignment to Courtroom D. When I received this letter from the Bar, I realized that I had provoked you by my action, and I am asking you to forgive me." Justice was speechless. She just sat there with her mouth open. He handed her the letter from the Bar. After she read it, he handed her the letter from the third party. Justice couldn't think of anything to say.

"So, will you accept my apology for provoking you, it really wasn't your fault. And I take full responsibility for my behavior."

"Yes," Justice said and just sat there and stared at him.

"Well, that's all I have, unless you have some question or comment."

"No, I don't . . . good night, your Honor," she said as she stood and left his office. She didn't know what to make of it. She knew Judge Denver wasn't sorry for his actions, but something about that letter from the Bar frightened him, and enough to make him apologize to her. She wondered what the real deal was. *This is one of those things that I'm not going to try and figure out; I'll just let it play itself out. And I'm sure it will in due time.*

Judge Denver wrote a letter stating that he and Justice had had a run in, and that it was mostly his fault. He stated that they had apologized to each other and forgotten the matter. He did not want the Bar investigating his courtroom or Justice Fullilove. After writing the letter, he held it in his hand as he paced around the room. He considered tearing it up, but he wanted this file closed and filed away. He tried to remember the time when he was like Justice, young, excited about the law, and convinced that the legal system worked as it should. Then corruption had crept in and took over his life. He was introduced to gambling by an older judge early in his career. He was hooked almost immediately. The old man soon tired of the foolishness, but he never did. He couldn't, it became his life. When he became a judge, he sat on the bench and contemplated ways to gamble. He went to Alabama to the dog races, he sent money by friends who were going to Florida, and he called people in other cities to place bets for him.

He thought he would die from excitement when the lottery came to Georgia. He promised himself that he would only gamble in Georgia. He was determined to gain control over his life and put gambling on the back burner. It never happened. His habit grew stronger. He contacted more people and sought more ways to gamble. He flew to Las Vegas as often as he could. He loved nothing better than the slot machines. He loved the sound of money clinging in the bowl. It didn't matter that he didn't keep any of it; he just wanted to continue hearing that sound.

His wife had left him and taken the kids to California to live with her parents several times. Each time he had gone out to bring his family home. He pleaded and promised that he would never gamble again. He was able to devote his time to his family for a few weeks, and then the gambling demon was on his back again. The last time he went to her parent's house, neither his wife, nor her parents, nor his kids would speak to him. He was a broken man, but gambling did not loosen its grip on him. He was having a difficult time trying to balance his child support payments and his gambling career. Instead of going to restaurants for dinner, he had been reduced to fast food joints. One night as he moved through the drive through at Dexter's, a man tapped on his window and asked if he was interested in making some extra money.

"Depends on what I have to do," he said. He had wanted to scream yes, yes, yes. But he knew this man was aware that he was a judge, so he had to exercise a degree of caution and pretend to first give it some thought.

"Why don't we meet for dinner at the Winston Deli on Del Ray tomorrow at six o'clock and talk about it. Treat's on me."

"Sounds good," Judge Denver said and looked around to see if anyone was watching. He felt nervous because he knew this couldn't be on the up and up. *Why would he sneak up to me at a drive-through if it were legit?* Legit or not, he certainly needed to make some extra money. When he met with the man and learned what was involved, he agreed to do it and promised himself that he would only be involved for a few months. He would make as much money as possible and get out quickly. His child support obligations would end in a couple of years and he would be free. This could be just the opportunity to get him back on course. But then he still had to deal with Justice Fullilove. *Why is trouble always waiting for you when you try to climb out of a hole?*

18

O n her way home from the monthly meeting at Oaktree Downs, Justice was thinking about the meeting with Judge Denver and the letter from the Bar. *Who could have written the letter? It had to be Mark. Who else would have wanted to get me in trouble with the Bar? The jurors certainly wouldn't have written the letter. They knew I would never harm the judge. So does Mark, but it had to have been him, who else could it have been?*

She heard a train whistle and looked to her right as she approached the train tracks. She sped up, even though she had plenty of time to get across. Suddenly a pickup truck pulled out of the alley and stopped, it backed up and hit the front of her car. She was stuck on the track and in the direct path of the train. The force of the air bag penned her to the seat, struck her head and she was disoriented. She could hear the train whistle and could see the lights. She thought of opening the door and getting out of the car. Her hand would not move. She wanted to turn her head to see how close the train was, but her body would not obey her commands. She closed her eyes and sighed. The door opened and she tried to turn her head. She felt hands pulling her from the car. She tried to fight, but he was too strong. Fear overtook her and she went limp in his arms.

THE TRAIN SMASHED into her car just as Nito cleared the tracks with Justice in his arms. He had called 911 when the truck backed into her. He put her in his car and sped away. He wanted to put some distance between them and the truck. When he turned the corner, he saw the truck speeding toward him. *How did they get around here so fast?*

He played chicken and sped toward them. They turned before he did and he turned down the alley and crossed over to the next street. He pulled into an empty garage of a house with a for-sale sign in the yard and turned off the motor and lights. Justice opened her eyes, saw him, and started to scream. He clamped his hand over her mouth and she began to weep.

"Hey, it's me, Nito. I'm on your side. Those men are looking for us. Please don't scream. She closed her eyes and continued to weep. Nito dialed 911 and tried to give them his location. Then he called Snaggie and told her what happened and that he had the target with him. Justice was convinced that he was in on the plot and was letting them know that he had captured her. Target did not sound like a harmless word, and why was he always around when someone tried to kill her.

"I'm going to get out of the car, and see if I see them. You are not going to scream are you?" She shook her head no. He removed his weapon and eased out of the car. He looked both ways and then he heard the car door open. He turned and saw Justice get out of the car and run toward the door that leads to the porch. He ran after her. The door was locked. She whirled around and he saw fear in her eyes; she was shaking and staring at the pistol. He placed it in his holster, took her by the arm, and led her back to the car.

"Look," he said. "You need to get a hold of yourself before you get us both killed. I'm not going to hurt you, but those men are playing for keeps. Don't try that again. What makes you think I want to hurt you?"

She didn't answer. She got in the car and sat there. She looked so dejected. He wanted to pat her on the shoulder or something. But he knew better. "I'm not going to hurt you," he said again. She just sat there and decided that she didn't even care any more. Nito saw the blue flashing lights coming down the alley and ran out to meet them. *What a welcome sight.*

He explained what happened as he walked back to the car and opened the door. Justice got out and looked from the officers to Nito. They seemed to know him.

"Are you okay, Mam?" one of the officers asked. She nodded yes. "Your car doesn't exist anymore, not enough left for junk. You're in good hands with Nito." He turned to Nito. "You giving her a ride home?"

"Be happy to," Nito said and turned to look at Justice. "That okay with you?"

She nodded yes. The officers got all the information for their report and got into their car and pulled into the alley to allow Nito to drive out. They followed him about five blocks and then sped along side of him and honked their horn. They waved and then sped away. Justice began to weep quietly again. Nito raced toward her condo. He hated it when women cried. *Why do they have to cry all the time?*

As soon as Justice got inside, she called Solomon. He came over and she cried and cried and cried. All he could do was hold her and tell her that it was going to be okay.

"I could kick myself because I really want to call Alou and tell him what happened."

"Why don't you just call him?" Solomon asked.

"Because I hate him, and I never want to see him again . . . Why couldn't I have fallen in love with you Solomon, answer that for me Solomon. And why couldn't you have fallen in love with me? Why did you have to fall in love with someone that would fly around all over the world? And why did I have to fall in love with someone who would constantly break my heart? Can you answer that question for me Solomon?"

Solomon put his hand on his chin and frowned. He furrowed his brow and narrowed his eyes. "Well," he said. "Weren't we already in love with those someone's when we met each other? Besides, I guess we are just dumb, Justice. I guess we just didn't know any better . . . Hey I'm going to Augusta this weekend, are you going to be okay."

"Yeah, I'll be okay. When will you be back?"

"Sunday afternoon. I'll call you when I get back. Can I go now?" he raised his hand as if requesting permission from a teacher.

She giggled. "Yes, you may go now. I think I can make it from here."

ALOU WAS SURPRISED to get a call from Solomon.

"Solomon, is everything okay?"

"I'm not sure," Solomon said. He told Alou about the train incident. "And Justice is terrified of a certain young man that has been following her. It seems that every time something bad happens to her, he's there. She tried to get away from him tonight and he had to chase her down. Probably put them both in jeopardy. You wouldn't happen to know why he's following her would you?"

"Yes, and I think you already know the answer. I'll tell her. She is going to be ticked off. I'll call her right now."

"Alou, if I ever stick my nose too far into your business, let me know, will you?"

"Yes," Alou said. "Yes, I will, and I appreciate the call. I needed to know that." He wasn't looking forward to telling Justice, but he knew he had to let her know that he hired Nito to follow her. He didn't want her to be afraid of the person who was trying to protect her.

IT WAS FRIDAY afternoon and Justice was thankful that she had made it through another week. She kicked off her shoes and flopped on the bed in one motion; each shoe landed right side up and side-by-side. She giggled, pulled a pillow to the middle of the bed, laid back and closed her eyes. She told herself that she would put Alou completely out of her mind and her heart. She began to analyze her day, then her week.

Successes. Failures. Half success, half failure. Was there any such thing? She rolled over on her stomach and looked at the clock. Four thirty-seven on a beautiful Friday afternoon. She began talking to herself, "I'm tired of being strait laced and sensible. This weekend I want to do something that makes no sense at all. But I want it to be safe and almost sane," she added quickly. "Not something as wild as robbing a bank or stealing a car. Well, you know, within the law, and morally okay. I just feel blah. I don't usually go by me feelings. But today, I'm going to be completely different. I'm going to be daring, dangerous, deliberate, and dishonest. Well, maybe not dishonest." She turned onto her side and pulled her knees up to her chin. "Lord, I guess I sound pretty crazy huh? Bet you never thought you would hear me talk such nonsense. To tell you the truth, neither did I. I can't understand this crazy feeling." She sat up and cocked her head to listen. Could that possible be my doorbell ringing, she wondered. She decided she was hearing things, but just as her head touched the pillow she heard it again. She rolled out of bed and moved quickly into the living room and toward the door as she whispered to herself, "Right about now, I would be happy to talk with anybody. It's better than sitting here alone and having crazy thoughts."

She went to the door, fully expecting to see someone selling something or asking for a donation, and was surprised to see Solomon standing there. He had come to ask her to go with him to visit his sister in Augusta. Solomon knew it didn't make sense to ask her to go to Augusta with him, but he didn't want to leave her home alone to mope all weekend.

"Hi." Justice said as she swung the door open.

"Hi."

"Well." She had intended to say come in. But well was all that came out. "Are you okay?" she finally asked as she stepped back to allow him to come in. That question was what made them both remember their first meeting and they both began to laugh. Suddenly they were both laughing uncontrollably. Justice reached out and snatched Solomon into the living room and closed the door before the neighbors could see him. She staggered to the love seat and he stumbled to the couch. They laughed as tears ran down their cheeks. As they tried to say what was so funny, they laughed even more. After about 10 minutes, they recovered and sat shaking their heads.

"I don't think we will ever forget our first meeting," Justice said.

"I agree," Solomon said. "By the way, I came to ask you to go to Augusta with me to visit my sister. I don't want to leave you here to mope alone all weekend."

"Okay," Justice said, surprised to hear her own voice.

"Pack your suitcase; we'll come back Sunday afternoon."

"Okay," Justice said again. "It'll only take me a second." Solomon thumbed through a magazine while he waited. He didn't really believe she was going. She didn't really believe she was going, but she went to pack anyway.

"Okay, I'm ready," she said 15 minutes later, as she walked into the living room with her suitcase in hand.

"I'll carry that," Solomon said as he walked over and took the suitcase. They walked to the car in silence.

"I'm glad you decided to come with me, I know you are going to love my family, and they will love you."

"I'm glad you asked me." Justice said. "I didn't have any sensible plans for this weekend."

They rode in silence the first few minutes; lost in their own thoughts. They had no idea Nito was following them. Justice turned to Solomon and asked, "remember the professor that you said helped you after your parent's death; what was it he said that helped you?"

"It wasn't so much what he said as what he did. It was the strangest thing, well, it was strange at the time, but later I realized it was God. I would sit in class on a bad day and say to myself, 'I'm not coming back. I don't need this without my parents; I don't want this without my parents.'

I would walk out of the classroom with no intention of ever coming back, and he would come walking up to me and say, 'Solomon, my boy, would you humor an old man and have lunch with him. I need someone to talk to.' What could I say; he had always been very kind to me. My parents didn't want me to work while in college or med school. It was a real struggle for them financially. Somehow he must have figured that out. He bought most of my books every semester. A few days after I registered for the next semester, he would call me and ask me to come by his office and see if I could use some of the book he had come across. Invariably I could use all of them except one or two, and I would have to buy one or two. I figured out later that he bought the books and the extras he had was for some other unfortunate soul who needed them, because they were always new. At the time I wondered how he always came across most of the books I needed. The fact that I never figured that out at the time, tells you that I was probably too dumb to be in med school.

"Sometimes he would tell me about cases he had and how he helped the people. Some of the cases were so simple and people had suffered so much without relief that they felt the need to see a psychiatrist.

"What kind of cases?" Justice asked.

"Well, there was a mother whose kids argued every day about cleaning the bathtub. So, on Professor Long's advice, she sat the kids down and had a nice talk with them. She told them that she would do anything to see that they were able to get along like brothers and sisters. So she worked out a plan with them that would solve the problem. She decided that she would clean the tub. So she told them to let her know immediately when they got out of the tub. So, when the girl got out of the tub the next day, she told her mom and she came and cleaned the tub and straightened up their bathroom. When the boy got out, he told his mom and she cleaned the tub. After that first day, she never heard any more arguing about who would clean the bathtub and they never told her again when they got out of the tub.

"Then there was the case of the little boy who was nine when his parents adopted a three-year-old girl. He felt that they were giving her more attention than him. He told his parents that they shouldn't make any difference in them. His mom tried to explain that she was a little girl, she was younger, and she had just come into the family. But he insisted that they should be treated the same. So, at Professor Long's suggestion, the mom called the little girl in to take her usual afternoon nap. After she put the little girl down for her nap, she went to the door and called the little boy in for his nap. All the kids playing in the street roared with laughter. He came in, got in bed and lay there for about two minutes. Then he got up and told his mom all the things that she had tried to tell him about the differences between them. When she was assured that he really didn't want to be treated exactly like his little sister, he was permitted to go back outside and play. He never asked to be treated like his little sister again."

Justice rested her head on the headrest and asked the question that had been playing in her mind since she left Winston. "So, what do you think about my fiasco with Alou? And am I crazy because I still think about him?"

"No, you are not crazy because you think about Alou. That's natural. Now, let me tell you what I think about Alou. To want to make love to someone you are in love with, is the most natural thing in the world. We didn't think up sex, God did. God gave us sex for a purpose, and he gave us the rules for engaging in sex. We can't violate those rules without someone paying the price. Sex is just like gravity. If you jump off a building, you could get hurt, or kill, depending on the height of the building. If you engage in illicit sex, you could get hurt, or killed, depending of the infections of your sexual partner and how emotionally attached you are. HIV and AIDS are not just ugly words; they represent deadly diseases. And our emotions are not something we can turn on and off like a faucet.

"But . . . I find it hard to believe, that Alou would spike your drink with alcohol in order to try and seduce you, and then allow you to drive home alone. No, I don't think so. I don't know what happened, but there has to be some other explanation. As to his desire to make love to you, I'm sure that's been on his mind a long time."

"How do I tell Lela that I'm in love with Alou?"

"What could Lela do that would make you really, really angry with her?"

"I guess it would be divorcing Ted."

"Would you terminate your friendship with her because she divorced Ted?"

"No!"

"How would she tell you, would she just call you on the phone, or would she come to tell you in person?"

"She would come and look me in the face and tell me."

"There you go," Solomon said, with smug satisfaction. "Go tell her."

⤾

WHEN SOLOMON AND Justice arrived at his sister's house, Justice remembered that she was supposed to take five kids from Oaktree Downs to church on Sunday. She called Shannon and she agreed to take them for her. She called Katrina and asked her to let the other kids know that Shannon would pick them up for church on Sunday.

Justice loved Solomon's family and they loved her. They made her promise that she would come to visit them again. She was sure she would. Justice was impressed with Solomon's sister, Esther, and her husband, Daniel. They had constructed a robot that could walk and talk. His name was Skip. He sat at the table and talked with the family while they ate. Of course, his conversation was off, but he joined in the conversation anyway. Their two children, Ruth and Isaac, ages three and five respectively, were fascinated with the robot. Justice wondered if they thought he was human.

Justice sat in the guest room that night and thought about Alou. She was angry with herself because she couldn't seem to get him off her mind. She wanted to go someplace, but there was no place to go. She wanted to tell someone how she felt, but she couldn't let anyone know she was so stupid. She flopped down on the bed and cried. When she didn't feel any better, she got down on the floor and cried.

"Are you okay," the robot asked. Justice screamed and turned to see who was in the room. She was angry with the robot.

"You silly robot, you should know better than to sneak up on a human being like that." She sat there staring at the robot with her hand on her chest and shaking. The robot's smiling mouth turned upside down into a frown and he turned and began to walk slowly back to the flap in the wall where he had entered the room. He seemed to drop his head and shuffle his feet.

Justice was mortified. "Wait," she said. I'm sorry; I didn't know you had feelings." She was angry with the Martins. *What have they done, they made a robot with feelings. That's cruel. What were they thinking?* The robot stopped with his right foot in midair. He finally placed the foot on the floor and turned. His mouth was now a straight line.

"I'm okay," Justice said. "Thank you for asking. Good night." His mouth turned to a smiling face again.

"Good night," he said, turned, and walked through the flap in the wall. Justice was still staring at the flap when she heard a knock on the door.

"Come in."

"I thought I heard a scream," Solomon said. "Are you okay?" He could tell she had been crying.

"Yes, Skip scared me. Solomon, did you know he had feelings. I screamed at him and his feelings were hurt."

Solomon laughed. "Justice, he is tin and wires. He doesn't have any feelings. My sister and her husband are scientists, but they are not God. But . . . he always knows when someone is crying. Watch this." Solomon made a noise as if crying. Skip came through the flap in the wall and walked up to him and asked if he was okay.

"Yes," Solomon said sweetly. "Thank you, you little ugly, snot nose, bug-eyed, stupid idiot. I hate your guts and hope you brake you neck when you go back to the junkyard where you belong." Skip stood there with the smiling face in place. Solomon assured him he was okay and bade him good night. He said good night and went back through the flap in the wall.

"See, he responds to the tone of your voice, not necessarily what you say. He's programmed to respond to certain phrase–such as, good night and to ask if you are okay if you are crying. So, why were you crying, and remember, I'm not programmed to ask."

"Because I hate Alou, and I never want to see him or his mother again."

"Now, do you want me to go through the flap in the wall and believe that you are okay, or are you going to tell me why you were crying? I'm flesh and blood, not tin and wires, and I have never known anyone to cry because they *hated* someone."

Well, I'm as okay as I'm going to be for right now. So can we talk about it later?"

"Sure, let's play a game of checkers." They played checkers until midnight. Solomon kept trying to cheat and Justice kept scolding him. During the games, Solomon told her about the Martins and their work, and how they came up with the idea of the robot. Justice thought they were the most interesting people she had ever met. By the time they decided to call it a night, she was no longer thinking about Alou. Solomon was pleased that she was laughing. T*hat should keep her until morning.*

☞

As they prepared to leave after lunch on Sunday, Esther fixed food for them to take with them on the return trip home. They all wanted to know when Justice was coming back. Justice was moved to tears. She promised them that she would be back real soon.

They were careful not to mention Alou during the drive back to Winston. When Solomon walked Justice to her door, he placed the suitcase inside the door, took both her hands in his and thanked her for going with him.

"Words can't express what this weekend has meant to me. It has literally changed my life, my outlook on life. I feel really alive for the first time in months. You are a gift to me, and you can tell Alou I said so. If he breaks your heart, he will have to answer to me. And he won't like it." He let her hands go and said on a more serious note, "Justice, there always seems to be some pain in love. I don't know why. That's just the way it is. But the pleasure, the happiness and good times far outweigh the pain and bad times when two people really love each other. You know the old saying, it's better to have loved and lost than never to have loved at all?"

Justice nodded yes. She had never seen Solomon so emotional. She wanted to hug him or say something, but she didn't know what to say.

"Well I never believed it until this weekend. Now I know that's true because I had a door opened in my heart this weekend that I thought would never open again. Watching my sister and her family and remembering the battles they have fought was life changing. I think I'll write a book. You know what I figured out this weekend?

"What?" Justice asked.

"When two people love each, truly love each other, and come to a fork in the road where they see the road of their love and all the seemingly insurmountable problems down that road, and on the other road they don't see any problems, they should choose the love road. You know why?"

"Why?"

"Because as soon as they get on the *no love road*, seemingly insurmountable problems appear. They come out of nowhere. They always do. They are not insurmountable on either road. If you get through them on the *no love road*, you could have gotten thorough them on the *love road*. And wouldn't that have been better?"

Justice tiptoed and kissed him on the cheek. "You are a sweet man, Solomon Owens. You are a gift to me. If you were not a rich man, I'd pay you for inviting me to spend this weekend with you and your wonderful family. Can you tell from that that I had a wonderful time, and that I thank you?"

"Yes, I can," he said. Then he took two steps backward, stomped the ground three times, saluted and disappeared around the corner. Justice laughed, stepped into her condo, and closed the door. She leaned against the door and smiled. *Where do people like Solomon come from? Heaven, I suppose.*

19

Justice picked up the phone and tried to decide if she should call Alou or Lela first. She decided to call Alou because Lela would want to hear every detail of her week end trip with Solomon and his family. She had also decided to tell Lela that she had fallen in love with Alou, and she was not looking forward to that. *Call them both and get it over with and go on with life.*

SHE CALLED ALOU at the office. She knew he had been working Sundays on the new project. When she got the recording, she left a message that she would call him later on his private number or leave a message for him at home. She decided to leave a message at his home.

"Hello." A sleepy sounding female answered on the second ring.

"I'm sorry, I have the wrong number." Justice stammered.

"Are you trying to reach Alou?"

"Yes, "Justice said.

"Let me see if he's awake," the female said. "Wake up sleepy head, you have a phone call . . . Well, she didn't give me a name, do you want me to ask her name, or do you want to take the call?"

Justice couldn't hear the reply, and she was crushed by the lady's response when she came back on the line.

"He wants to know who's calling," Ericka said. Then she whispered, "He's a little hungover. This is Ericka and we are celebrating our engagement. We are going to announce it at The Club in two weeks. I hope you can come, what did you say your name was?"

"It's Miss Fullilove," Justice said. "I didn't realize he had company, I'll call him later." She hung up before the woman could reply. *I am not going to cry, I am never going to cry over Alou again. I'll die before I cry over him again.*

Justice had seen Ericka on several occasions. She knew that Alou had dated Ericka before she met him. But he had dated other women since he and Ericka broke up. Justice thought of calling back and insisting that Alou come to the phone. *And what good would that do?* She paced around the living room and stared at the phone. She wanted to call Lela, but couldn't force herself to pick up the phone. After 10 minutes of pacing, she sat down, picked up the phone, and dialed Lela's number.

"Hello." Lela answered on the first ring.

"Lela, this is Justice, can I come over?"

"Since when did you start *asking* if you can come over?"

"I have to talk with you and I need you to promise me that you won't be angry with me."

"Why, what's wrong?"

"I'll tell you when I get there; you are going to be home?"

"Can't you at least tell me what it's about?"

"Lela, please ... I'll be there in 10 minutes."

"Okay," Lela said and hung up the phone. She immediately dialed Ted at work.

"This is Ted."

"Ted, Justice just called me and *asked* if she could come over."

"So, did you tell her no, or something?" Ted didn't get it.

"Why in the world would I tell her that she couldn't come over?"

"So … what's the problem?"

"The fact that she felt she had to *ask* to come to our house, you don't see that as a problem?" She was angry with Ted. *Why are men so weird sometimes?*

"Oh, sweetheart, I'm a knucklehead. There must be something bothering Justice or she wouldn't be *asking* if she could come over. I get it now. As I said, I'm a knucklehead. What do you think could be wrong?" *Women. I'm supposed to read her mind.*

"I bet you money it's about Alou. I bet he seduced Justice."

"Lela, don't go there. Justice is a grown woman. And you are just speculating. Even if he did, what can you do about it, except be a friend to Justice?"

"I can kill him."

Ted was silent for a moment. "Why do you do this to me? Just when I relax and think to myself, rest easy old soul, you have a beautiful wife; and you are going to have two beautiful children soon; you call me on the phone and tell me you are going to kill some guy because you suspect that he has seduced a women who is obviously in love with him. Not only are you going to prison for life; you are taking away my opportunity to father those two beautiful children, depriving me of yourself and our children."

Lela felt like an idiot. "Ted, I'm sorry, you know I'm not really going to kill Alou. And what did you mean about Justice obviously being in love with him?"

"You can't see that, haven't you notice the way she looks at him?"

"No, I guess I haven't." Lela felt as if all the air had been knocked out of her. "I love you Ted Bolton, and I'll see you when you get home tonight." *I probably don't deserve a husband like Ted; I probably deserve someone like Alou.*

"I love you too, Lela Bolton, and I'll see you when I get home tonight."

☞

ALOU AND BENNY were finishing up the assignment details of their most impressive contract when Jan stuck her head in the door to say goodnight. Alou stood and went over to hug her.

"I can't tell you and Benny how much I appreciate you for spending your whole day on Sunday working with me on the project. You will be adequately compensated with bonuses and hugs and kisses." Alou laughed as they both turned to look at Benny who was groaning and covering his face with both hands.

"Speaking of hugs and kisses," Jan said as she smiled at Alou. "How is Miss Fullilove today?"

"I don't know," Alou said as he turned to stare at Jan. "I haven't spoken with her today."

"Didn't she call you on your private number?" Jan asked. "She called around two o'clock and left a message that she would call you on your private number later, or leave a message for you at home. I should have told you sooner," Jan stammered when she saw the look on Alou's face.

Alou turned, picked up the phone and dialed Justice's number. "Hello, Justice, Jan told me..." He realized he was talking to a dial tone. He pressed the hook and hit the redial button. "Justice, what's the ..."

Benny stuffed his reports in his briefcase and headed for the door. Jan turned to go to her office and await the outcome of Alou's attempt to reach Justice. Alou placed the receiver back on the hook and turned around.

"Jan, would you divide the food between yourself and Benny. I can't eat another bite."

"Neither can I," Jan said and they both looked at Benny who opened his mouth to protest, but closed it when Alou pointed to the food and gave him a direct order.

"Take it Benny; I don't want rats and roaches coming around here finding food."

Benny, sat his briefcase down, took a plastic container from the cabinet and stuffed the food into it. "Thank you," he said to Alou, nodded to Jan, and scrambled out the door. He had a sick feeling in the pit of his stomach. Although he had no proof, he knew he was the cause of the anguish Alou was experiencing. He thought of how unselfish Alou was. How he always gave them a large bonus when they had to work on Sundays. How he always worked with the employees when they had a problem and never complained when they had to take time off. And even today when he was in such agony, he took the time to make sure he took the food, knowing that he didn't get home cooked food often.

There was a full kitchen in the office and Alou had his chef come and prepare a full meal three or four times a month. He said there were too many single men in construction work and they needed a good meal once in a while

"How many employers would have his chef come to the office and prepare a home cooked meal for his employees on Sunday? "Benny asked out loud. "I can tell you," he answered his own question. "None." *And I had to shoot my big mouth off to Ericka about Alou buying Justice an engagement ring. I know she's behind this. I should kick my own stupid behind, and Ericka's for tricking me into giving her the information. The next time I see her, I will not so much as utter a single word to her, I will simply nod my head in recognition of the fact that she is a human being and give her a half smile and go my way.*

⌒

ALOU SAT IN the office long after Jan and Benny left. He wanted to go and yell at his mother. He wanted her to feel some of the pain he was feeling. He tried to figure out why she didn't want him to have a close relationship with a woman. Every time he dated someone that he really cared about, his mother wouldn't stop until she broke it up. Now she seems to be succeeding in tearing him and Justice apart. But this time he was going to fight. He was not going to give in to her. He knew he couldn't win an argument with her because she would cry and play on his sympathy and his nerves until he just gave in. He decided to take the coward's way out and hide from her whenever he could. Somehow, he had to make

Justice understand what was taking place.

He stretched out on the couch and thought about Justice. He remembered how she felt in his arms; how he wanted to be with her all the time. He sat up; he thought he heard a knock on his private door. He rushed to the door. *Could it possibly by Justice?*

He opened the door and was disappointed to see Snaggie. She had the report Nito had prepared of his weekend surveillance of Justice.

"Just wanted to give you the report for the weekend." She stepped into the office and handed him the report. I was on my way home and saw a light. I figured I could drop this off and sleep in late tomorrow."

"Have a seat, let me glance over it before you go, in case I have some questions." She sat in a chair across from him and watched his face as he read it. She could see his eyes clouding over with anger. He hated the fact that Justice always ran to Solomon whenever they had a problem.

"Do you want us to continue the surveillance on Miss Fullilove?"

"What makes you think I've changed my mind?"

"She spent the weekend with another man. So, I was just wondering . . ."

"Now you listen to me, Snaggie Jones, I don't pay you to wonder, I pay you to do investigative work, not to stick you nose into my personal affairs. Don't you ever attempt to put Justice down again. You don't know anything about her."

"I'm sorry," Snaggie stammered. "I wasn't trying to put her down, and I promise you I won't ask any stupid questions in the future. Snaggie moved toward the door and vowed never to make that mistake again. Alou was one of her biggest clients, and he often paid a large bonus on special projects. She opened the door and turned around.

"Again, I apologize, good night, Mr. Hambrick," she said as she stepped out the door.

"Wait . . . and let me close up, I'll walk you to your car."

"That's not necessary, I'm a private eye, I know how to
. . ."

"You are *still* a woman . . . besides; I want to have the
opportunity to apologize. Look, Snaggie, Justice won't talk
to me. I'm just not thinking straight. Will you forgive me; I
didn't mean to snap at you."

"Of course. I understand." She stepped back inside and
waited. *He has it bad.*

☙

LELA WAS STANDING in the door when Justice pulled into the
driveway. She walked to the edge of the porch to meet her.
"What's the matter with you girl, you look like you've been
crying for days? I've been calling you all weekend, where
were you?"

"Just listen and don't interrupt me. I went to Augusta
with Solomon to visit his family for the weekend. He showed
up at my apartment when I was making plans to rob a bank.
He rescued me and took me to Augusta, as any good friend
would."

"Be serious girl, Ted and I were worried about you."

"I really did go to Augusta with Solomon."

"Solomon is not trying to like you is he?"

"No," Justice said and hung her head. "Lela, I don't know
but one way to say it, I'm an idiot and I'm in love with Alou."

"I ought to slap you; I ought to beat you down." Lela
hadn't wanted to believe Ted when he told her Justice was in
love with Alou.

Justice started to cry. "I'm so sorry Lela, I'm so sorry; I
never meant to fall in love with him. It was too late when I
realized it. And now he has already broken my heart just like
you said. So I don't care if you beat me down."

I'm not going to beat you down, silly. Now stop crying."

I'm going to die; I just know I'm going to die. I can't live
like this."

"Stop it Justice, you are not going to die."

"Oh God, oh God, oh God," Justice moaned as she slid down to the floor.

Lela got down on her knees and hovered over her. "I'm sorry Justice; I didn't mean to be so flip when you are in such pain. Look, we got through this mess before and you didn't die, we can get through it again."

I didn't want to die before; I just wanted to be happy again. Right now I just want to die. You don't understand. Everyone I have ever loved has either left me, or kicked me to the curb except you and Ted. You tried to warn me about Alou. But I didn't mean to fall in love with him, Lela; I'm so sorry, so sorry, so sorry."

"I *know* Alou didn't kick you to the curb. What are you talking about?   He loves you. He has changed since he met you," Lela said. She could feel her blood pressure rising. *What has Alou done? He promised me he would never do anything to hurt Justice. I am going to kill him. He has no idea who he's messing with now.*

"He's engaged to Ericka, and they are going to announce it at the The Club in two weeks." Justice said between sobs.

"I don't believe it." Lela said. "Who told you that?"

"I called his house before I called you, and Ericka answered the phone and said he was asleep. She woke him up and he told her to ask who was calling. I told her who I was like an idiot, and then I hung up before he had a chance to refuse to talk to me. Oh Lela, I told him I didn't want a relationship with him. I mean, I couldn't get over his mom's attitude. But I didn't expect him to just forget me overnight. How could he if he really loved me?"

Lela looked at the clock. "It's three o'clock on a Sunday afternoon, why would Alou be asleep this time of day. Something's wrong with this picture Justice. And I'm sure he hasn't forgotten you. Are you sure you dialed the right number?"

Justice stopped crying, sat up, and frowned. I'm sure I dialed the right number, but maybe Ericka was there and Alou was not. I didn't actually hear his voice. You think Ericka made it up? She could have easily seen it was me on caller ID. Maybe he gave her a key when they were dating, and she didn't give it back." Justice turned to look at Lela.

Lela wanted to cry. She could tell that Justice was hoping that everything would be okay between them again, and Lela felt that she had created that hope by her stupid remark. *And what if it's true? What if he really has gotten engaged to Ericka? I'll kill him; I will not allow him to do this to Justice.*

"I should've *never* allowed you to get involved with Alou. I should have insisted that you not go out with him. Your dad expected me to take care of you. He made you come to Georgia to be with me, and look what I have let happen to you." Tears rolled down Lela's face. Justice began to cry again, too.

"It's not your fault, Lela, you warned me. I should have listened to you." Justice fell back on the floor and wailed. Lela sat on her knees and cried and tried to comfort her friend.

☞

TED HAD BEEN in deep thought since the telephone call from Lela. He leaned against the file cabinet and stared out the window. When Mrs. Okojo waved her hand in front of his face, he turned and smiled. "Did you say something? I'm sorry, I'm in another world."

"Penny for your thought," she said as she shoved a penny into his hand. He laughed, put the penny in his jacket pocket and started toward the back of the pharmacy.

"Oh, no you don't," she said. "I gave up the penny, now you give up the thought. That's the way it works."

"Oh, okay," he said grudgingly. "My wife wants to have a baby, but I have been telling her to wait until we pay off our student loans. It's not like we owe a lot. I just want to be debt free for a change. But . . . she has been 'mothering' one of our friends. She says it's because she's six months older and Justice needs someone to look out for her. Granted, both her parents are dead, but she's an intelligent, sensible woman. You know what I think, Mrs. Okojo, I think my wife needs a baby, and I have been very selfish. I'm gonna have a little talk with her tonight."

Mrs. Okojo looked at the clock and nodded. "I think that will probably require more than just a little talk. Your shift ends at six o'clock. If you leave now, you could probably be working on that by six, don't you think? And I won't take no for an answer. This has been the slowest Sunday we have had at this pharmacy in months. Take advantage of that fact and my good mood. I may never be so generous again. Hurry along," she said as she ushered him to his briefcase and waved him out of the pharmacy.

Ted smiled as he left the hospital. He was thinking of the silly conversation he had had with Lela earlier that day. Justice had *asked* if she could come over. Lela thought that was a big deal. Yes, she needs something to occupy her time he thought. And he knew just what she needed.

Ted whistled as he drove into the garage. He grabbed his briefcase and hurried to unlock the kitchen door. When he stuck the key in the lock, he thought he heard someone crying. No, he heard people crying. He pushed the door open and hurried into the living room. He saw Justice lying flat on the floor and Lela hovering over her, they were both crying.

"What . . ." he looked around to see if there was anyone else in the house. Justice and Lela screamed, huddled against each other, and stared at him as if he were a masked bandit.

"Oh, Ted, you scared me silly," Lela finally said. "What are you doing home in the middle of the day?"

"It's not the middle of the day, it's 3:30 in the afternoon, and whatever it was that made you silly, happened before I got here. Why are you two on the floor crying? Wait, let me help you up." He pulled Lela to her feet, and they both helped Justice up. "Just who did you think would be coming into the house with a key in broad open daylight besides me?"

"I didn't hear you open the door," Lela said.

Ted turned to Justice. "Cat got your tongue?" Lela and Justice giggled. He was trying to change the conversation and the mood. He realized that he didn't want to know why they were crying. At least not yet.

"You still haven't told me why you are home in the middle of the *afternoon.*

"Oh," Ted said as he reached in his pocket and pulled out a Hershey's Kiss. He looked at Lela, as he remembered why he was home. "I wanted to tell you that I love you, wanted to be sure you understood how much you mean to me." She could tell by the look in his eyes that he meant it. She started to cry again. Then Justice began crying again. Ted was flabbergasted. *Women, who can understand them?* After a few minutes, Justice tiptoed and kissed him on the cheek. "Sorry I have to run, but I'm having supper with Solomon. I have just enough time to run home and change. I'll call you Lela."

Lela turned to look at Justice. "Girl, are you sure Solomon is not trying to like you?"

"Solomon is doing what he does best, being a psychiatrist and a good friend." Justice hurried to her car and revved the motor to let them know she was backing out of the driveway. She didn't like lying to Lela, but she knew it would make her feel better if she thought she was spending the rest of the day with Solomon. *I may not be the smartest person in Winston, but I know when two people do not need a third party present. Maybe I'll walk over to Solomon's apartment just to say hello. Then I will not have told a complete lie. And I'm not going to cry. I'm never going to cry about Alou again. Never.*

"Hey kiddo," Solomon said when he opened the door and all Justice could do was cry. She was so angry with herself; she wanted to get down on the floor. But she knew Solomon would not put up with such foolishness.

"Solomon, this is the last time I will ever say this to you. But I am so brokenhearted, and I know I'm not going to die, but I sure feel like it."

"As Christians, we don't go by our feelings. We can't afford to. We go by the Bible, do we not?" She nodded as the tears ran down her face. "Jesus said, 'I came to bind up the wounds and heal the broken hearts.' So, either way you are going to be okay. Unless, of course, you think what Alou has done, and I'm assuming it was Alou, can outweigh what Jesus has done."

"No, it can't."

"Okay . . . Give me the definition of the word vicissitude, break it down to its least common denominator."

"Ups and downs," Justice said.

"Move to the head of the class, kiddo. You know Justice, that's the way life is. Always has been. At least, since Adam and Eve were kicked out of the garden. So, if you can laugh when you are happy, it's okay to cry when you are sad. Just don't cry forever. Think of all the good times you had with Alou. You told me yourself how much money the man spent on you, and how he always put forth a special effort to be sure you had a good time. And whatever he did, or you think he did, consider what the Word says about it. The writer of Proverbs put it this way: Get wisdom, but in all your getting—get understanding. So, whatever it is, get an understanding with Alou. Not with me, not with Lela and Ted, with Alou. That's advice you couldn't pay for, but it will save you a lot of heartache and sorrow, and it's free.

"Why should I go to the person who hurt me?

"Because sometimes they have both the answer and the solution."

"Aren't they one in the same?"

"Not always," Solomon said. "Sometimes the answer may be 'this is why I did what I did' and it will make sense. Other times, the reason they did what they did may be the very reason you should walk away from them and not look back, that's the solution. Then there will be times when you will never know the answer and neither will the other person. That's just the way life is. You'll just have to make a decision based on the information available to you. Feelings should not come into play until you have made the right decision. If you make the right decision, you will be okay, because your feelings will eventually follow your decision. Not sometimes, but every single time.

"If that's true, Solomon, why do people stay in abusive relationships for years and can't seem to get over the abuser?"

"Simple. First, they didn't get an understanding. Second, even if they did get an understanding, they didn't make the right decision. There are no exceptions to that rule."

"Well, if there are no exceptions, I'm going to follow it. And thank you. I think I can live with that rule." She kissed him on the cheek and went home. She knew she had to get an understanding with Alou and she had to do it within the next two weeks. Whatever understanding they came to, she would make her decision based on that understanding, and live with it.

☞

ALOU WAS IN the middle of a staff meeting for the biggest project for which his company had ever been considered. Everyone was excited because they knew they would all receive big bonuses if he won the contract. When Jan knocked on the door and opened it before Alou could answer, everyone turned to stare at her. That was so unlike her. She knew they were working on their biggest project. Jan looked at Alou, placed her hand to the side of her head to indicate a phone call, and mouthed, Miss Fullilove. Without a word, Alou rolled his chair back and grabbed the phone.

"Justice," he said.

"Alou," she said. And they sat and held the phone without another word for what seemed like 10 minutes to Alou. He was trying to think of something to say.

"Have you eaten yet?" she asked.

"No, I haven't eaten yet," Alou said. The employees began to stare at their hands or out the window. Because they, as well as Alou, had just finished a delicious homemade breakfast prepared for them by none other than Alou's favorite chef, Shane.

"Can you get away; I can meet you at IHOP in 20 minutes."

"Which one, the one on Del Rey?"

"Yes, are you free, I'm not interrupting anything am I?"

"Oh no, I'm not busy, I'll see you in 20 minutes." Alou hung up the phone and rolled his chair back to the head of the table. The employees were squirming around and trying to pretend they hadn't heard his conversation.

"Benny, move to my seat and carry on. I'll be back as soon as I can. I know I don't need to remind any of you that this is the biggest contract this company has had a shot at. So give it your best. If we win, you will be handsomely compensated." And with that Alou was out the door without so much as a glance backwards.

Alou made it to IHOP in 15 minutes and was out front looking for Justice when Ericka came walking toward him. She wore a yellow dress that revealed every curve, and was two inches above the knee. Ericka's complexion was what people in Winston called high yellow, and she had slanted, dark brown eyes that gave her an oriental look. Her jet-black hair was highlighted with blonde streaks and her make up was flawless.

As a telephone operator, she had connected with a fellow employee who could route Justice's calls to a line that Ericka had access to, and she had listened in on Justice's call to Alou. She knew Alou had bought Justice an engagement ring, and Auryola had hinted to Ericka that she would rather Alou marry her than Justice. She smiled as she walked up to him, embraced him, and then tried to kiss him.

"Hello Alou, it's so good to see you again," Ericka said. As Alou reach to take her arms from around his neck, he heard Justice gasp as she came around the corner. He shoved Ericka away from him and she fell into the flowerbed. Justice turned and ran and Alou ran after her.

"Justice, wait, it's not what you think." Justice ran right into the arms of a uniformed policeman and the other officer stepped between Justice and Alou and held up his hand.

"Hold it Mister. I don't know what's going on, but let's just stop and sort if out. It seems to me the lady is trying to get away from you," Officer Davis said.

"Yes, she was," Alou said. "But it's only because of a misunderstanding."

"Misunderstanding my foot," Ericka said as she limped around the corner with tears streaming down her face. "He pushed me . . . knocked me down because he didn't want her to see him kissing me," she pointed to Justice, and then glared at Alou. The officers exchanged glances and looked at Alou.

Officer Davis was big and tall with blond hair and gray eyes. Officer Clark was tall and slender with eyes the same color as his light brown hair. They had worked the streets of

Winston a combined total of 25 years, and they considered themselves experts in calming squabbles between family and friends.

"I merely removed her arms from around my neck and pushed her away ..."

"I want him arrested for attempted murder," Ericka said. "He could have killed me. My head could have been crushed by those big rocks. And look at my knee." She lifted her dress and revealed a good view of her thigh; the knee was already exposed. The officers exchanged glances again and Justice let go of Officer Clark and began to hurry toward her car.

"What do you want?" Ericka yelled at Justice.

Justice turned around, "I don't want anything, I'm leaving."

"Justice, I'll walk you to your car," Alou said.

"I'll walk with her," Officer Clark said as he turned and hurried to catch up to Justice.

"He hit me and knocked me down," Ericka said. "What did it matter about his kissing me in a public place in broad open daylight, as many times as we have rolled in the hay together. Justice stopped and turned to stare at Ericka.

Ericka pointed to Justice and sneered. "I can tell you this, she never rolled in the hay with him. Not once. And I know it's a fact because his mother told me." Justice was so embarrassed she wished she could have disappeared. All four of them were staring at her. She looked down, and then at Alou. Officer Clark reached out and touched her arm and asked her if she was okay, but she just stared at Alou.

"What more can you do to me Alou. How else can you humiliate me?"

"Justice, I never told my mother that you wouldn't sleep with me."

"Then how would she know?"

He knew how his mother knew, but he wasn't about to try and explain that in front of the policemen and Ericka. He would tell her later, he would make her understand.

"I want him arrested for attempted murder; he could had seriously injured or killed me. He was showing off in front of her." Ericka glared at Justice. Justice turned and started to her car. Alou started toward her and the officer Clark held up his hand. "I'll walk her to her car; she's going to be okay."

Officer Davis turned to Alou and said, "Would you come with me please?" They walked over to the patrol car and he opened the back door.

"Would you get into the vehicle please."

"Why?" Alou asked. "I haven't broken any law or committed any crime. That lady embraced me and tried to kiss me. I didn't hit her; I simply took her arms from around my neck and pushed her away from me."

"I figured as much," the officer whispered as he took a clipboard from the car and let the window down.

"He's lying. I hope you lock him up and throw away the key," Ericka yelled.

When Alou got into the backseat, the officer closed the door and went to speak with Ericka. "Okay, mam, we'll take it from here. We need you name and address for the record." He propped his foot on the bumper of the car, placed the clipboard on his knee, and prepared to write. Ericka gave him all of her information. He wrote it all down and thanked her.

"Like I said mam, we'll take it from here. You can go on home now."

"Thank you, Officer." She walked to the window and glared at Alou. "Serves you right for trying to show off in front of her. She's no better than I am." Alou was angry with himself for getting involved with someone like Ericka. But he couldn't help but feel a little sorry for her. When he thought of Justice, he wanted to cry. He could tell that she was totally humiliated. He knew he had to find a way to make it up to her.

"Okay, I think I get the picture," Officer Davis said after Ericka left. Your ex-girlfriend shows up just before your present girlfriend, and creates a scene. Tried to kiss you in front of the present girlfriend . . . Did you expect both of them?"

"No, Justice called and asked me to meet her here for breakfast. I have no idea where Ericka came from. I haven't dated her in over a year and haven't seen her in months. But, you know . . . it seemed as if Ericka knew that Justice was coming. She embraced me and tried to kiss me at the exact time that Justice came around the corner. Anyway, am I free to leave now?"

"Yes, but let's just talk a while and be sure the ex has gone."

"Okay," Alou said. "What do you want to talk about?"

"Your girl friend, Justice, is that her name?"

"It's actually Justiana, but everyone calls her Justice."

"Why was she so embarrassed for someone to know that she hadn't slept with you, I thought it was a compliment to her?"

"She's just a very sensitive person, and she knew Ericka meant it as a put down."

"Are you a Christian, sir?

"Yes," Alou said. "But I haven't been going to Church as often as I should. But this type of foolishness makes me realize I need to have my behind in Church every Sunday." Alou was a little shocked to have a uniformed officer ask such a question. *Isn't there something about separation of Church and state? Or is it okay in this case because of the foolishness of it all?*

"That sounds like a good idea, sir. Okay, she's gone; I'm going to find my partner."

Alou got out of the patrol car, and they both turned as Officer Clark came around the corner singing. He stopped singing when he saw them.

"Justice is going home, and she's going to be okay."

"Thanks," Alou said. "I'm sorry we took up your time with this. He shook the officer's hand and watched as they got into the patrol car and drove away. *How did Ericka know Justice was coming and the exact time, something is wrong with this picture. And how did the cops show up just as Justice turned and ran. This is weird stuff. Justice actually called me and Ericka had to show up. I wish I had knocked her teeth out. I better get back to work and make sure I secure that contract. It will make up, in some small measure, for the misery Ericka has caused us.*

WHEN THE TWO officers compared notes, they realized that there was a serious misunderstanding between Justice and Alou. As soon as they got into the patrol car that morning, Officer Clark had turned to Officer Davis and said, "Let's agree before God that we will run into someone today that needs a touch from Him, and that we will be the instruments He uses to touch them."

"Agreed, amen," Office David responded. The officers at the station called them Paul and Silas. Officer Clark had been reprimanded twice for preaching to defendants. He had pleaded with his supervisor, and had been allowed to continue his street duties with Officer Davis on the condition that he never uses the words God, Jesus, or the Bible when talking with people while on duty. He was learning how to witness and encourage people without using those words. When he thought of how his conversion had changed his life, he couldn't imagine not witnessing to people. When Officer Davis learned that Justice thought Alou was engaged to Ericka, he was frustrated. When Officer Clark learned that Alou hadn't dated Ericka in over a year and had no interest in her, he was elated.

"Let's just go and tell her she's mistaken," Officer Clark said.

"I think it would be better to tell him what she's thinking."

"Wait a minute, how do we find them, we didn't get their last names or where they work. What did he say the name of his business was?"

"I don't think he ever said. Or if he did, I don't remember."

"We could call the ex, we have her information," Officer Davis said.

"Not a good idea. She certainly wouldn't want to help, and I am not looking forward to talking with her again . . . . You know, Jim, when we ask God to give us an opportunity to make a difference in someone's life, it doesn't mean that we have to see the end-result of the situation. We just have to do what we can, when we can, and trust Him to do the rest. We are not the only Christians that they will encounter during this situation, and God can use whomever He chooses, Christian or not."

"You are right. Well, let's just agree that we'll run into one of them, or someone who knows them." Officer Davis couldn't let it go.

"Agreed, amen," said Officer Clark. He smiled when he thought about how quickly they would always run into someone who needed help after they agreed in prayer for the opportunity. "I know the outcome is not up to us, or for us to necessarily see, but I certainly would like to see those two get back together. She was so brokenhearted and it was all a mistake. It's a shame we didn't get her last name."

Chapter

21

Josie Willis came to see Justice about filing a wrongful death suit against Hines Cement Company. Her sister had finally convinced her to get another attorney and go forward with the case. Insisting that she owed it to LaQuita because she would never recover from the loss of her twin sister and the untold grief the company had caused the family through their negligence.

"Mrs. Willis, I'm a criminal defense attorney, I have never tried a civil case, and we already know the lawyer handling your case will have to go to trial because the company is not willing to settle," Justice said. "Besides, I'm a government employee, I can't take private cases."

"But I wouldn't trust any other attorney," Josie said. "We have already been sold out once by an attorney . . . . Well, if you can't help me, I'll just have to forget it. I'll just have to do the best I can for LaQuita on my own. I appreciated all your help with Jerame." She stood and walked slowly toward the door.

"Wait," Justice said. "I'll talk with my boss and see if it's possible for me to take the case. I know two other attorneys that may be willing to work with me, and both of them have handled civil cases. I'll call you as soon as I have spoken with them."

I have to do whatever I can to help her. The defendant was clearly negligent, and this may be just what I need to take my mind off Alou.

☞

192

JUSTICE TRIED TO read but couldn't keep her mind on the book. She went into the kitchen to make a peanut butter and jelly sandwich. She decided to eat the peanut butter from the spoon instead. She had a mouth full of peanut butter when the phone rang.

"Hello," she mumbled.

"Justice, this is Alou, please don't hang up, I need to talk with you . . ."

"Why do you insist on tormenting me? Why can't you just leave me alone?"

"Because we need to . . ." She hung up, went back into the living room, and flopped down on the couch. The tears began to roll down her face. She wanted to punch Alou. The phone rang again. She grabbed the phone with the intent of giving Alou a piece of her mind.

"I'm not going to . . ."

"Justice," Lela said. "Is something wrong?" Justice didn't say anything; she was trying not to cry. Just the sound of Lela's voice made her want to cry even more. *I swear, I swear before God, I am not going to cry about Alou again.*

"Lela," Justice said and began to cry.

"I'm on my way over there," Lela said, and hung up the phone before Justice could reply. Justice ran to the bathroom and splashed cold water on her face. She combed her hair and applied fresh lipstick, and then inspected her face in the mirror to see if she looked like she had been crying. Satisfied that she didn't, she went into the living room and fluffed the pillows on the couch, picked up the novel, and flopped down on the couch. She tried to read but the words didn't make sense. She threw the novel on the table and got down on her knees.

"Lord, can you help me with this? I need to get over Alou; I need to get him out of my heart and out of my life. Can you help me to forget him, to stop thinking about him? Can you help me to get back to the life I had before I met him. I just want to practice law, work with the kids in Oaktree Downs, and read a good novel once in a while. Is that too much to ask? Lord, can you help me to get back there?" The doorbell rang and Justice scrambled to her feet and ran to the door to let Lela in.

"What has Alou done now?" Lela asked.

"Lela, I want you to promise me something. If you ever see me talking to another man, or hear me even mention anything about a man, promise me that you will push me off a cliff and put me out of my misery. Promise me, Lela."

"Look, there's no sense in both of us going crazy at the same time. I can't promise that I'll push you off a cliff, but I will make sure you regret it. Now get your purse and let's go have a talk with Alou."

"Are you kidding? I never want to see Alou again, and he obviously doesn't want to see me again either?"

"Justice, will you go for me? Just this once and I promise I'll never ask you to do anything like this again. I just want to find out what happened. Then we will leave and I will never mention Alou to you again, and I will shoot you if you ever mention him to me again. Let's just get the facts from him, and be done with this once and for all."

"What if he refuses to see us? I told him I didn't want to see him again. What if he asks me to leave?"

"He wouldn't do that," Lela said. "Whatever else he is, he is not a mean callus person, and I don't think he would do anything to deliberately hurt you. But if he would, you need to know that, too. So let's go, and tomorrow by this time, we may both be able to forget that Alou exist on this planet. Wouldn't that be better than your crying and wondering where you stand with him?"

"Yes," Justice said and picked up her purse. "Let go and get it over with."

⌒

TED WAS IN a good mood. He had been humming and teasing the other employees all day. Mrs. Okojo asked him about the baby. "Did you two make the baby yet?"

"I hope so," Ted lied. He found a reason to hurry away. He didn't want to tell Mrs. Okojo that he had lost his nerve and decided to wait a little longer before they had a baby. I really want to get those students loans paid off he had reasoned with himself. He was happy he had not mentioned the idea of having a baby now to Lela. She would have never let him have any peace until he agreed. Lela only worked three days a week, Tuesday, Wednesday, and Friday. Ted didn't want her to work at all when she became pregnant, or after the baby came. She wouldn't hear of it.

"I hope you don't think I went to school all those years to sit home and do nothing for the rest of my life," she said when Ted revealed his plans.

"As a wife and mother, you will have plenty to do."

"Ted, I love being a pharmacist. I like the interaction with people, and answering their questions and giving them advice. I don't want to work full time, just a few days a week. I don't think I could stay home all day."

"You mean to tell me that you would rather work with people than devote you full time to taking care of your husband and baby!" Ted said as he placed his hand on his chest and put a little distance between himself and Lela.

"Okay, let me put it this way," Lela said, as she folded her arms and leaned against the kitchen sink. "I'm a pharmacist just like you, so why don't you stay home and take care of the baby, and I'll work full time. I'll get two jobs if necessary. Better yet, why don't I take care of the baby the first six months, then you take care of her six months. We can alternate every six month, or would you rather take yearly turns?"

Ted just stood there. He couldn't say a word. He was begnning to see how selfish his thinking had been. He couldn't imagine not working as a pharmacist. He would be miserable.

"I'm sorry Lela, I was being completely selfish." He walked over and put his arms around her. "You sure know how to put a man in his place."

"As long as it's my man, I think I have earned the right to do so." Lela had won this round, but the war was still raging. She would have to continue to work on his silly idea about waiting until they paid off their student loans before having a baby.

☞

ALOU WAS DRIVING along Memorial Drive when he heard the siren and saw the blue, flashing lights. He slowed and began to move to the right side of the street along with all the other traffic. The flashing light came closer and closer to his car. Other cars began to move out of the way as they made their way closer to him. He came to a complete stop. He was surprised when the patrol car pulled right behind him and stopped. Both officers jumped out of the car and rushed to the driver's side of his car. Alou was confused; he had expected one to remain in the car and call to check his record. *I'm sure they have me mixed up with someone else. I was not speeding, I don't have any outstanding warrants, I have not committed any crime, what could they possibly want with me?*

"Hey man, we have been looking for you for weeks," Officer Davis said.

Alou looked up. The officers were smiling. He couldn't figure out what was going on. They could tell that he didn't recognize them.

"Your girl friend, Justice, did you two get back together?" Alou went limp with relief. He opened the door and jumped out of the car. They were shaking hands and grinning. Alou wanted to hug them.

"No, not yet," he said. The smile left his face when he thought about Justice.

"Did you know that she thinks that you are engaged to Ericka?" Officer Clark asked.

"No, I didn't," Alou said. "Why would she think something like that?"

"Ericka told her, she spoke with her on the phone. Ericka told her that she was at your house and that you were asleep." Alou was speechless. Why would Ericka do something like that? How could she be so cruel, and for what reason. I hate to think that my mother put her up to that, but there is no other explanation.

Officer Davis explained to Alou how they would agree together in prayer on rare occasions, only when they felt led, for God to use them to touch someone who needed a touch from Him that day. They had prayed such a prayer before they ran into him and Justice. He was trying to let Alou know that God answers prayer and things don't happen in people's lives just by chance. Alou got it. They had answered his question about how they showed up at just the moment Justice turned and ran toward the parking lot.

"That's why we were so frustrated when we compared notes and learned that you hadn't dated Ericka in over a year, and Justice thought you were engaged to her. We agreed again that we would run into you, or Justice, or someone who knew you. Imagine our delight when we saw you driving down Memorial Drive. We couldn't resist the opportunity to pull you over and shake you up a bit," Officer Davis said.

"You certainly shook me up. I was already beginning to see myself in that ugly orange jumpsuit . . . now that I know what the problem is, I'm sure I can fix it. You know, if you guys weren't fully dressed in your uniforms, and we weren't standing on a busy street in broad open daylight, I would hug and kiss both of you. Come to think of it, I still might do it."

They turned, ran back to the patrol car, hopped in and used the siren and flashing lights to make a U turn, and then sped away in the opposite direction. Alou stood there laughing so hard that tears ran down his face. He felt relief, happiness, and then anger. He would have another talk with his mother, and this time she would understand where he was coming from. He couldn't even be angry with Ericka; she was just an idiot being used by his mother.

ALOU GOT IN his car and headed to his mother's house. He wanted to try one last time to maintain a relationship with her. It was becoming more impossible, but he felt he had to try. He hated any confrontation with his mother because she always won in the end. Even when he knew he was absolutely right, she would not let it go until she pushed him to the point that he just gave in to her desires. Sometimes he won a small battle, but she would revisit the issue at a later date and do whatever she had to do to wear him down. But the fight was over Justice Fullilove this time, and the rules had changed. He was determined to win. He would not lose Justice, no matter what the cost. This time he would win the battle and the war.

"Well," Auryola said as she stepped back to allow Alou to enter her living room. "Come in and sit down, what brings you here in the middle of the day?"

"Mother, I need to talk with you . . . and I need you to listen to me, to try and understand how I feel."

"I hope we are not arguing about *that girl* again."

"We are not arguing, mother, and her name is Justiana. I am simply trying to tell you how important she is to me. You don't like her because you don't know her, you haven't even . . ."

"Alou, you can't push your women on me. I am not required to like every woman you take up with . . ."

"I know you are not required to understand what's important to me, but as my mother couldn't you try. Just for once, mother, couldn't you try to understand what I want?"

"You don't know what you want, Alou, you are confused."

"I know I want Justice . . . if you can't accept that, then there is no point in continuing this conversation." He stared at his mother, sighed, then turned and walked out the door. He felt sad because he knew he had to let his mother go, or rather she had decided to let herself go. He called Justice on his cell phone as he headed back to the office. When he couldn't reach her, he headed to the liquor store. He was not sure why. He didn't want a drink but be felt the need to go to the liquor store. He got out of his car and headed into the store without any idea what he would buy. As soon as he saw Moses Hatch leaving the store, he knew why he was there.

"Alou, my boy, how are things going? Are you engaged or married yet?" Moses asked. He had not seen Alou in over a year.

"No," Alou said. "But I'm trying. My lady won't talk to me because a woman I dated a year ago, called and told her that she and I had gotten engaged . . . and I believe my mother is behind it all. She was one of the few people that I told I bought justice an engagement ring. *Why am I telling this man all my business?*

"I take it your mother doesn't like your girlfriend."

"She doesn't even know her. She doesn't like the idea that I am serious about a woman. I introduced two women to her in the past, and she drove them both away. She attacked Justice in a more vicious way then she did them. But Justice stood her ground and told her where to go. She is not intimidated by my mother, but I'm the one who suffers each time my mother confronts her."

"You can always divorce your mother as I did my daughter. But you really have to have the stomach for it. It's not at all easy. And once you start, you can't turn back. So, you have to ask yourself if you can go on with your life and be happy without any real contact with your mother."

"I guess I need advice on how to proceed," Alou said. "Is the process the same for divorcing your mother as when you divorced your daughter?"

"It can be easier and cheaper for you. We both paid attorney fees and they both knew it was all foolishness. They made some money and probably had a few laughs. But I got what I wanted and needed: a well-thought-out plan as to how my relationship with my daughter would be conducted in the future. And I followed it to the letter. My daughter was determined to get me and Barbara back together. Barbara and I were just as determined to go on with our lives without interference from her. But you don't need a lawyer or to file any papers in court. Just have your secretary draw up a final judgment and decree and you sign it. That's the document that contains all the terms you want to live by. And have it notarized. That makes it look more official. Make sure it says just what you want, and what you can live with. But . . don't do it unless you can stick with it. I can't emphasize that too much."

"Thanks, Mr. Hatch, that's exactly what I needed to know." They make small talk as Moses walked Alou to his car. They shook hands and Moses watched Alou get into his car and drive away. He couldn't help but pity the poor boy, he looked so unhappy.

Chapter

Alou went to see his mother again. He had to make her listen to him and understand how he felt about Justice, before he divorced her. Try again, he told himself. Try one more time. Once he signed the decree, he knew there would be no turning back.

"Hello again, Alou," Auryola said. "Come into the kitchen, I have your favorite desert, peach cobbler, cooking in the oven. I had planned to surprise you and bring it to you later today." She took him by the hand and started toward the kitchen. Alou could smell the peach cobbler cooking. He refused to be led into the kitchen, and took his hand out of hers.

"I don't want any peach cobbler. I just want you to listen to me and consider what I'm feeling. I want you to try to get to know Justice. I love her, mother; I want you to be happy for me."

"I can't understand why you won't listen to me anymore. You know I have your best interest at heart."

"My best interest is Justiana Fullilove. If you don't want me to have her, you can't have my best interest at heart. I love her more than anything or anybody on this planet."

"Don't be ridiculous, Alou. You have lost your mind over that girl. Who does she think she is, and why is she too good to have sex with you. She's no better than ... "

"Hold up! Mother," Alou said as he held up both hands. "Don't ever go there again, you have gone too far. My sex life, or lack of a sex life, is none of your business." He tried to calm himself. He was trembling. He felt anger bubbling up on the inside. He could barely breathe. *This is not about*

Justice; this is about mother and her intent to control me for her own purposes. She needs to get me away from Justice just as she had to get me away from my dad. She wants complete control of me, forever.

"I can't believe you have turned against me this way, and over some . . ."

"Then I'm through talking with you about this. This is our last conversation about Justice."

"Alou, have you lost your mind completely?"

He didn't even answer. He had come with the hope of having a heart to heart talk with her. He wanted to try one more time. But she gave him what she had always given him when he refused to comply with her wishes. He just left. There was nothing else to say.

☞

As soon as Alou left, Auryola call Ericka and they devised a scheme they felt would end the relationship between Alou and Justice once and for all. Auryola was the primary planner, but attempted to make sure that Ericka would be the one to take all the risks of being caught or arrested for criminal trespass. Ericka was so happy to think that Auryola has chosen her over Justice, that she didn't even think that what she was doing might be a crime. Ericka made all the contacts and Auryola gave her cash to pay the men for their services. When everything was in place, Auryola took Ericka to dinner and they celebrated the demise of Justice and Alou as an item. Ericka was quite pleased with herself. She knew Mrs. Hambrick had never approved of Alou dating her, but apparently preferred her to Justice. She knew that when all was said and done, Alou would *always* do what his mother wanted. And his mother wanted him to have her instead of Justice. She could hardly wait to see how Justice would handle the turn of events.

☞

"GET JUSTICE ON the phone, Jan, and don't let her hang up, make sure I have a chance to speak with her," Alou said.

"You're asking me to do the impossible, I can get her on the phone, but I can't make sure she speaks with you."

"You have done impossible things before," he said. "And I'm not taking no for an answer. I want to talk with Justice; I know you can arrange it."

"Consider it done, sir." Jan called Justice several times and did not get an answer. She did not leave a message. Her mouth fell open when Justice and Lela walked into the office and smiled at her. Justice seemed nervous and Lela seemed to be pulling her along. Jan ran up to them and put her hand up to her mouth to shush them. "Mr. Hambrick just demanded that I get you on the phone and make sure he had an opportunity to speak with you. He threatened me. So please talk to him, Miss Fullilove."

"Okay," Justice said and glanced at Lela.

"See, I told you the man loves you." Lela said.

"I hope you didn't *think* that Mr. Hambrick doesn't love you, Miss Fullilove. When it comes to you everything and everybody else takes a backseat. Did you know that the morning he met you at IHOP," Jan leaned in and whispered in a conspiratory voice; Justice and Lela leaned in to listen. "He was in the middle of finishing up the Bismarck Project . . .*and* we had all *just finished* a delicious breakfast prepared by Shane. He just got up, told the guys to make sure the plans were perfected, and walked away. You talk about sweating. Man those guys were scared, but they got it right and we won the project. C'mon, I'll let him know you are here."

Justice and Lela exchanged glances and followed Jan to the door. She opened the door and stepped into the office and stared at Alou. Then she turned and gestured toward the door.

"Mrs. Bolton is here to see you, Mr. Hambrick."

"Lela's here?" Alou rose from his seat and took a step toward the door.

"Yes, and so is Miss Fullilove."

Alou frowned and sat back down. "Jan, please, I'm not in the mood for pranks today."

"Come in ladies," Jan said as she stepped back and held the door open. Justice and Lela moved into the office and Alou looked up. He stood and began to walk toward them.

"Hello Lela," he said. Lela spoke and then he turned to look at Justice.

"Justice," he said and moved toward her.

"Alou," she whispered and just stood there. Jan looked at Lela, turned, and went back to the reception area. Lela stood there and looked at them. She realized that they were not aware of her presence. She wanted to ask him about Ericka and the engagement, but realized that it didn't really matter any more. She turned and went back into the reception area to wait with Jan.

"How are you?" Alou asked.

"Fine, how are you?"

"Fine. I've missed you. I'm happy to see you again. Whatever I did wrong, will you forgive me?"

"Are you engaged to Ericka?" she asked.

"No, but I'm trying to get engaged to you . . . " Alou moved over and took the engagement ring out of his desk drawer, got down on his knees, took her hand in his and placed the ring on her finger. "Will you marry me, Justice?"

Justice got down on her knees and stared into his face. "Yes," she whispered as the tears began to run down her face.

"Why are you crying, sweetheart?"

"I don't know, I guess I'm relieved that you are not engaged to Ericka . . . Oh Alou, there's no way I can tell you how devastated I was when she told me that. I thought I was going to die."

"Don't make me go and strangle Ericka now."

"It's okay, I'm over it now. I was just trying to explain why I was crying."

"You are crying because you are a big cry baby."

She giggled, got up off the floor, and pulled him up. "Now you may kiss the engagee."

"Lawyers," Alou said, and rolled his eyes upwards. "But don't ever let anyone make you think that I don't love you again. There will never be a time when I don't love you." He pulled her into his arms and kissed her. Then he just held her. *That's what I'm talking about.*

"What do you think they are doing in there?" Jan asked Lela.

"Staring at each other like two crazy people. I believe they think the whole world stands still just to hear them call each other's name. They are idiots."

"Guess what?" Jan asked as she leaned forward to let Lela know she was in a gossiping mode.

"What?" Lela asked as she leaned forward to let Jan know that she didn't mind a little gossip.

"He bought her an engagement ring, and the diamond is so big she's going to need someone to help her carry it around."

"You're kidding."

"No, and I bet he's down on his knees right now proposing. What do you think she will do?" Jan asked.

"Being a woman who neither understands nor care about protocol, she will get down on her knees too and say yes. Then the tears will begin to flow. What do you think he will say to that?"

"He'll kiss the tears away," Jan said. Then he'll threaten to strangle anyone who ever causes her to cry again. When he can get her to smile and appear as if she has not been crying, he will bring her out here to show you the ring."

Lela walked over to the window, and then turned to look at Jan. "What would Alou say if Justice wanted a baby? Let's say they were newly married and he was making a change in his business and wanted to wait a few years, but she told him she wanted a baby right away?"

"First he would call her name and stand and stare at her for about 10 minutes. Then he would walk over to her and kiss both her hands, then he would pull her into his arms and whisper in her ear, 'do you want to make the baby now, or wait until after supper?' and whichever she chooses, that's what it'll be. I tell you Mrs. Bolton, that man loves him some Justice Fullilove. And what she wants, she gets. And if . . ."

Justice and Alou came into the reception area and Justice held out her hand to Lela and Jan.

"Look," she said. "We're engaged."

Lela and Jan gathered around Justice and acted the way women are supposed to act when one of them gets engaged. Alou finally cleared his throat and they all looked at him. He turned to Lela. "Do you mind if I drive Justice home?"

Lela was all set to say she didn't mind, but she turned to look at Justice and saw how she was looking at Alou and Alou was now staring at Justice as if she was a bowl of delicious desert.

"Yes, I do mind," Lela said. "My mother always said, 'when you pick someone up and take them someplace, be sure you take them back home, unless an emergency prevents you from doing so.' And I don't think getting engaged qualifies as an emergency."

"Okay," Alou said. "It was worth a try. We'll be right back, I'm going to show Justice where I keep the peach sodas." He took Justice by the hand and they disappeared into his office. "Can I sneak over later tonight?" Alou asked. Justice giggled and nodded. He pulled her into his arms and kissed her, and then he just held her. *This will have to do until I can get her away from Lela Bolton.*

☙

"Hello," Lela said after fishing the ringing cell phone from her purse.

It was Ted. "Where are you sweetheart, I'm home and missing you."

"I'm at Alou's office with Justice. They just got engaged."

"They got engaged without letting the grandfather know?"

"It's not grandfather knucklehead, it's godfather," Lela said. And suddenly she was overcome with emotions. Already Ted was giving his blessing for Justice to have a baby so that he could become a godfather, and she had been married to him over two years and he was still telling her to wait . . . And Jan was right, Alou would allow Justice to have a baby whenever she wanted. But she had to wait and wait and wait.

"Godfather, grandfather, what's the difference. It all refers to an old man. And I feel like an old man tonight. Let's not have leftovers tonight; let's go out to dinner. We can celebrate the engagement."

Lela didn't answer. The tears were rolling down her face. She hung up on Ted, clicked the cell phone off, and moved toward the door. "Tell Justice I'll be in the car."

Jan looked up because it sounded like Lela was crying. "Is something wrong, Mrs. Bolton?"

Lela shook her head no, went out the door, and headed for the parking lot.

"Wait!" Jan yelled. "I'll bring your purse." Lela stopped but did not turn around.

The office phone rang and Jan stopped to answer it. "Homes by Hambrick . . . Yes, Mr. Bolton, she's right outside the door, just a minute." Jan picked up Lela's purse and took it to her. "Here you go, Mrs. Bolton, and your husband is on the phone, he said your cell phone is going straight to voicemail."

Lela held up her hand without turning completely around to let Jan know that she was not going to take the call. Jan wasn't sure what to do and Lela hated to get her involved in her drama. But she could not talk with Ted just yet; she knew she would lose control if she did. Jan gave Lela her purse.

"Thank you," Lela whispered and began to walk slowly to the car as the tears ran down her face. *God, you know I'm happy for Justice. I'm just so sad for me. But I can do something about that. When I get home, I'm gonna throw those birth control pills down the toilet and Ted, and Alou, and Jan, and Justice can all take a slow boat to China. And if I end up divorced because of it, then you will know that a divorce was not what I wanted.*

Jan didn't know how to tell Ted that Lela would not talk with him, so she went to get Justice and asked her if she would talk with him.

"What's wrong?" Justice asked. "Where's Lela?"

"Well, Mr. Bolton called her on her cell phone and it seems that she hung up on him and then she started crying, and she wouldn't answer when he called back. She told me to tell you that she would wait for you in the car."

"So, what am I supposed to tell Ted, and why couldn't you tell him?" Justice asked as she turned to look at Alou.

"You want me to talk with him?" Alou asked.

"Yes," they both said. They were relieved.

They moved into the front office and Alou picked up the phone, "Ted, this is Alou, how are you, my man?"

"I was fine until my wife hung up on me and I have not been able to reach her on her cell phone. Do you know what's going on, Alou?"

"No, but I promise I'll find out and call you back. Stay by the phone, over."

"Roger, over and out"

"Oh, Alou, you are such a sweet man," Justice said. Let's go find out what's wrong with Lela."

Jan didn't say another word. She tried to fade into the background. Married people who had problems made her nervous. She sat at her computer and began to type. She had a final divorce decree to prepare, and she was not looking forward to the phone call she knew she would get from Auryola Hambrick after it was delivered to her.

When Justice and Alou saw Lela sitting in her car they ran to her and tried to find out why she was sobbing. Lela was inconsolable. Alou was beginning to wonder if he would be able to keep his promise to find out what the problem was. After about 10 minutes of Justice crying herself and begging Lela to stop crying and Alou standing there feeling helpless, Lela dried her eyes and sat up straight. She tried to think of a good lie. She couldn't. So she said the best thing she could think of.

"I guess I'm just overly sentimental and happy about your engagement. You know how much I love weddings, Justice. And I always cry at weddings."

Justice believed her; Alou did not. He stood there wondering why she was really crying and what he was going to tell Ted. Then he decided to tell him just what she had said. Justice believed her; maybe Ted would too. At any rate, he would tell Ted what he had been told. If that didn't satisfy him, he could to take it up with his wife.

"Let me see your faces," Alou said to them. "I want to be sure you two are okay."

They both giggled and turned their faces toward him. He stared at them and said, "Well, I guess you pass the test. I'll call Ted and tell him his wife is okay." *Women, God couldn't you have created something easier to figure out.*

"Thank you," Lela said. Alou wondered why she couldn't call and tell him herself. But he was not about to ask. He stood and watched the car until it was out of sight, then he went back to his office to call Ted.

❧

LELA PULLED INTO the visitor's parking area at Justice's condo and shut off the motor. She turned to Justice and sighed. "I want to explain why I insisted on bringing you back home. It's because of something horrible that happened to me after I got engaged to Ted, and we agreed never to tell anyone about it. I think Ted has forgotten it, but I have not. I don't think of it as often as I did at first, but when I saw you grinning at Alou like a "Cheshire cat", I knew you were feeling all mushy inside. When I saw him looking at you like you were a bowl of delicious desert, I knew I had to bring you back home and tell you what happened to me."

"What could have happened to you that was so horrible?"

"I was not a virgin when we got married."

"You were not. What happened? Were you raped or something?"

"No, I was not raped, and it was Ted. We had just gotten engaged the day before and I went to his apartment with him after a movie and I initiated the whole thing. That wasn't what I intended to do, but that's what I did. Afterwards I cried so hard that Ted cried. We knew that sex outside of marriage was wrong, but I had never told him how much I wanted to be a virgin when we got married. So my behavior led him to believe that I loved him and was ready for sex. After all, we were going to be married in a few months. It seemed okay to him. If I had told him how important is was for me to remain a virgin until I was married and the promise I had made to my mom, it wouldn't have happened. He was so disappointed when he learned what was in my heart, and that I never shared it with him. That's why you have to tell Alou how you feel about him and how important it is for you to remain a virgin until you are married . . . We both promised my Mom that we would remain virgins until we got married. I couldn't bear the thought that neither one of us lived up to our promise."

"I think Alou already knows that part; I told him about Ocie and why we broke up. But I didn't really tell him how important it is to me. And I'm afraid to tell him how much I love him."

"Why?"

"He might try to make me do something I don't want to do."

"I hope you are not talking about sex."

"That, too."

"Look, Justice, if Alou wanted to seduce you he could have done it a long time ago. You are probably one of the most seducible women in Winston, you just don't know it, and I want to be sure you don't initiate something without intending to."

"Lela, how could you say such a thing about me?"

"It's not meant as a put down, sweetie, it's just a fact. That's what made me realize how wrong I was about Alou. That was the main reasons I didn't want you to get involved with him. I was afraid he would seduce you. Justice, he's older than you, he's had more experience with the opposite sex than you, and he just knows more about what's going on in the real world than you. Look, you're in love with the man, and he knows how to push all the right buttons."

"So, you are saying that I'm an idiot and a street woman. And, if Alou wanted to sleep with me he could?"

"Justice, I'm saying all the wrong things, but I'm saying them for the right reason. I don't want to see you go through what I went through--due to ignorance and an attempt to be smarter than you are. And you still have a chance to keep your promise to my mom. I wish I did. Look, trust me as a friend—tell the man how much you love him, but let him know how important it is for you to wait until you are married to engage in sex. He needs to know. Let's just talk about this some other time, I have a headache, and I'm going home and go to bed."

"Okay, I'll tell Alou everything the first chance I get . . . Lela, you shouldn't still be crying because you were not a virgin when you got married. We don't become perfect when we become Christians. Let me remind you that Christianity..."

"Are you kidding? Do you know how many years I have been a Christian? And I have never been mad at God."

"Okay, so I've been mad at God, but I got that straight and learned a lot in the process. You remember that verse in St.

John that says, 'If we confess our sin, He is faithful and just to forgive us and cleanse us from all unrighteousness.' I came to understand that God forgives us as soon as we confess our sin, and He forgets. When we continue to confess the same sin over and over, He has no idea what we are talking about. The word says that He casts it into the sea of forgetfulness and remembers it no more. Now if John 3:16 is true, that's true also. I accepted that, and I know He doesn't remember my foolishness any more. So you need to forget about the fact that you were not a virgin when you got married. He has. Otherwise, we are making light of Jesus dying for our sin if we don't accept forgiveness. And if He has forgiven your sin, why don't you forgive yourself? Besides, it's the Devil who reminds us of our sins and shortcomings. Why would you listen to him?"

"Okay," Lela said, as they climbed out of the car. "I'm going to take the advice of my scripture quoting friend, and I think you may be right for once in your life. I'll walk you to your door."

"Then who's going to walk you back to your car?" They finally devised a plan for Lela to walk half way to the apartment and then Justice would run to the apartment and Lela would run back to her car. They would both check to see if the other made it into their intended shelter. They laughed when they realized that they had made the whole thing scarier than it needed to be. Lela called Justice on her cell phone as she drove out of the parking lot. They both agreed that they had had enough drama for one day.

As she drove home from work, Justice was watching the beautiful sunset and thought of the times she had watched the sunset with Alou. Those were some of her most vivid memories of their time together. She thought she heard a gunshot. She turned her radio down and began to look around. She glanced in the rear view mirror and saw a big black car speeding toward her. She decided to pull over and see if it would pass. She heard a bullet hit the back of her car. *No point in trying to outrun them, and I'm not going to get into a high-speed chase. If I die, it won't be because I killed myself and a lot of innocent people in the process.* She slowed down and made a right turn, then stopped. They turned also and pulled right up behind her. She was tired, frightened, frustrated, and angry. *Why are these people trying to kill me? What did I ever do to anyone to make them hate me so much?*

They were trying to decide what to do. They were supposed to shoot out the tires and cause her to run off the road. It was supposed to look like an accident. They saw Nito's jeep make the right turn and they pulled around her and drove away. She just sat there as the tears rolled down her face. She jumped when Nito knocked on her window. She got out of the car and began to tell him what had happened. He patted her on the back and tried to get her to stop crying.

"Hey, they are gone now. I called the police when I heard the shot. You may have saved yourself by stopping. I think they were trying to shoot out your tires."

"Why?" Justice asked. "Who are they and why do they want to kill me?"

"They may just be trying to frighten you. Have you received any threats? Anyone telling you to stop doing something? You think someone doesn't want you going to Oaktree Downs?"

"No, I don't think that's it," Justice said. She felt sure it had something to do with Mark, Auryola, or Judge Denver. She was not about to say that to Nito.

The patrol car arrived and Nito gave the officer his information. A second patrol car with two officers arrived as the first officer was wrapping up his report. She began to cry as she told them what happened. He could tell that the last two officers knew her personally. They hugged her and "carried on" over her. Their comments made her cry even more. He wanted to tell them what happened so she could stop crying. Nito had given the first officer all the information needed from him as a witness. When he determined that they did not need anything else from him, he waved to her and practically ran to his car. *Crying women.*

The officers asked Justice if she wanted them to drive her to Alou's house. She was obviously shook up and scared. She said yes, and they took her to Alou's house. Officer Davis drove the patrol car and Officer Clark drove Justice's car and she rode with him. Officer Davis went to ring the doorbell. Alou peeked out and saw Officer Davis. He opened the door and then saw Officer Clark and Justice. He could tell she had been crying.

"What's wrong," Alou asked as he pulled Justice into his arms. She started crying again as she told him what happened. The officers stood near the door and looked on. Officer Davis cleared his throat and both Alou and Justice turned to look at him.

"We didn't think it would be a good idea for her to go home alone tonight. But if you want to go home, we'll drive you."

"Thank you guys for driving her here, but she's staying here tonight," Alou said.

"You're welcome. Then we had better head back to the beat."

"C'mon," Alou said to Justice, you can sleep in the guest room. They walked to the hall and he pointed to the room at the end of the hallway.

"Way down there?" Justice asked as she walked down the hall and peeked into a room nearby. "This room has two beds, why can't we both sleep in here."

"My room is just at the other end of the hallway."

"Please, Alou, I'll be so scared all the way down there by myself. I don't snore or sleepwalk. Please, Alou."

Officer Davis cleared his throat and they turned to stare at him. They thought the officers had left. But they had stopped when they heard Justice say, way down there.

"We just wanted you to know that we will be patrolling the area, and you can call our cell phone if you hear any noise. We'll be close by."

"Thank you, my man," Alou said and turned to Justice. "You are a special lady and you are getting first class service tonight. With these two guys looking out for you, you have no reason to be afraid."

Both Alou and Justice thanked the officers again and they left. As they walked to the car, they realized that they had not asked Justice if she wanted to come to Alou's house; they had just taken it upon themselves to volunteer to drive her there. Now they were worried about them sleeping in the same room.

"We should have let her decide where she wanted to go. She may have gone to a girlfriend's house. If she's not still a virgin in the morning, it's your fault. You were the one that suggested we bring her to Alou," Officer Davis said.

"Well, you could have taken her home with you and slept in a bunk bed next to her and protected her."

"Yeah, I didn't think of that," Officer Davis said. He stopped, turned around and looked at the house. "Let's go back and get her." Officer Clark grabbed him, turned him around, and gave him a shove toward the car. He started to run and said, "Beat you to the car." And the race was on. Officer Davis won.

"That's not fair, you had a head start." Officer Clark said. They got in the car and rode in silence. They were both lost in their own thoughts and wondering how they got so caught up in those people's lives.

⤳

JUSTICE KNEW SHE wanted to get married and have children. But the idea made her sad because she knew their kids would not have one grandparent in their life if Alou's dad did not like her. She had no idea why Mrs. Hambrick hated her so much. As they sat on the couch holding hands, she turned to Alou and asked.

"Alou, do you think your mom will ever like me or accept me?"

"Yes, I'm positive she will. Look, don't worry about it now; it will work itself out in time."

"Do you miss her a lot? Do you grieve about the strain in your relationship?"

Alou pulled her into his arms so she couldn't see his face. He was not about to tell her how much he missed his mother. She was really a very good mother before she became a stranger to him. "The one thing that makes me happy is you. I have you in my arms tonight. Let's not concern ourselves with anything else."

She sighed and laid her head on his shoulder. "Alou, I know we are not supposed to be spending the night together. People who don't know us may get the wrong idea, but I don't know how I could have gotten through this night without you. I need to know that you are close by tonight."

"Stop it baby, don't do this to me."

Justice giggled. "You don't have a baby, you are not even married."

"That's why I love you so much. You're irrational." They both laughed.

"Hey," Alou said. "Wanna watch a movie?"

"Tonight, I just want you to hold me close."

"Okay," he said, as he pulled her close. *There are times when there is no need for words. This is one of those times.*

Alou and Justice ended up sleeping in the same room. Justice was still trying to figure out why the officers had come back after stepping outside the door. She was sure she had seen them go out the door. Why did they come back, she wondered. Alou knew why. They said good night and got into their respective beds. After about 30 minutes, Alou was about to drift off to sleep when Justice kneeled beside his bed.

"Are you asleep, Alou?"

"No, is something wrong?"

"No, I just wanted to tell you that I figured out why the officers came back. They must have heard me say I would be scared to sleep in the guest room by myself. I think they are worried that I would get scared and crawl into bed with you and we would get carried away and I would lose my virginity. I wish Ericka hadn't shot her big mouth off in front of them about my being a virgin. But I'm absolutely sure that's what they were thinking."

"Thank you, sweetheart. I would never have figured that out."

"You are welcome. Well, I just wanted you to know." She said good night and ran back to her bed. She was snoring in less than five minutes. Alou lay there and stared into the darkness. He tried to remember the color of the ceiling. Then he counted sheep, then goats, and then cows. He rolled over onto his stomach and counted some more sheep.

⌒

LELA AND JUSTICE had lunch at Dexter's Saturday afternoon. Lela knew that Justice was still shaken by the fact that someone was trying to harm her. They were both silent a few minutes, and Lela tried to think of a way to tell Justice what was on her mind.

"You know Justice, I think Alou's mom is behind all this. Think about it. Every time you have an encounter with her, a few weeks later, someone tries to kill you or harm you in some way. I think she waits a little while on purpose. And don't you ever tell Alou I said that."

"I must admit, I've thought the same thing. But I think it's Mark. He has more to lose than Mrs. Hambrick. I think his reputation is at stake, unless he gets off his lazy behind and prepares for trial."

"No, he can get another job, Auryola can't get another son."

"But I'm not trying to kill her son, Lela, we are just dating."

"What about the judge, why is he always on your case?"

"I think most judges are just pro prosecution," Justice said.

"Well, whoever it is, and whatever their reason, I wish they . . ."

They were interrupted by a lady who walked up to Lela and gave her a compliment. "You look so pretty and radiant. That's just the way my daughter looked when she was pregnant with her first child. When is your baby due?"

"Baby!" Lela and Justice said at the same time.

"Yes," the lady said. "You do know you're pregnant don't you?"

"Well, no," Lela said and both she and Justice stared at her stomach.

The woman laughed and advised them to go across the street to the drug store and buy a pregnancy test kit. They were no longer hungry. They went to the drug store and rushed home to do the test. When the test proved positive, Justice helped Lela to the couch.

"I'm calling Ted," Justice said.

"No, wait. I have to think of what I want to say to him first. You know this will be a shock to him. I hope he's not too upset.

"Don't be silly, you didn't make the baby by yourself. And Ted is always talking about his two little girls."

"I know, but I wish I had told him that I had stopped taking the pill. I feel guilty for having deceived him."

"Is that really deception? You didn't really lie to him, you just didn't tell him."

"Yes, it is. Deception has to do with your intent, and …"

The doorbell rang and they both jumped. Justice put her arm around Lela and pushed her gently down on the couch before she went to answer the door. Lela sat up, closed her eyes, and began to pray, "Lord, don't let it be Ted, I need time to think."

"Hello, Justice," Olivia said as she pushed pass Justice and entered the living room. Justice wanted to leave, but she knew she could not leave Lela now. When Lela heard Olivia, she fell back on the couch and groaned.

"Hey, Lela, what's the matter, you not feeling well?"

"I'm pregnant, and Ted doesn't know yet," Lela said. "If I didn't know you would find out sooner or later, I would never tell you."

"You better be careful how you talk to me, you may need a place to stay when he finds out. I have another friend who deceived her husband like that and he kicked her behind out. She had to go back home to her mother, who was not too happy to have two more mouths to feed."

"Ted would never kick Lela out. He loves her too much, and it's his baby too," Justice said. "I'm looking forward to the day when you don't bring a negative pessimistic report."

"Yeah, well my other friend's husband loved her, too, but men don't take too kindly to that kind of deception. Having a baby is a decision both spouses should make. Not one sneaking and doing it behind the other spouse's back."

Justice turned to look at Lela. She had turned pale and looked like she was going to cry. She turned to Olivia.

"She didn't sneak and do anything behind his back. And you can leave now, Olivia. I'm not going to stand by and watch you upset Lela. You know women should not be upset during the first three months of pregnancy."

Justice walked to the door and opened it. "Tell her to leave, Lela. We do not need her here at a time like this. This is a time when you need true friends and not a big fat jealous bimbo."

"Ah," Olivia gasped, and turned to Lela.

"Go, Olivia," Lela said and waved her away.

"Don't call me when you end up in the welfare line. My other friend was so sick, she wasn't even able to work, and her husband never forgave her for her trickery. She ended up losing *everything. Everything.*" Olivia said.

"If she lost everything, it's because she was silly enough to be your friend," Justice said. "Ted is a real man, not some wimp that's scared of a little baby. Look Olivia, don't put us in the category of your kind of people. We are not like you. So go away."

"You're going to regret this," Olivia said and stormed out the door. She gave Justice a dirty look as she passed. Justice slammed the door and rushed over to console the sobbing mother-to-be.

"Lela, I hope you are not paying any attention to that crazy girl. She doesn't know anything about the kind of person Ted is. He would never do anything to hurt you. Now stop crying, before you make me cry." Lela could not stop crying, so Justice sat on the couch and put her arm around Lela. Lela was trying to figure out how she would take care of herself if she were not able to work. She would not beg Ted to allow her to stay with him.

"Justice, I could stay with you until the baby comes couldn't I? I'll pay you back every penny, I . . ."

"Lela, don't go there. Surely you are not going to listen to a pessimistic idiot like Olivia. You know Ted would never kick you out. What's the matter with you? I know pregnant women sometimes go a little crazy . . ."

"Honey, I'm home," Ted said as he walked into the living room. Lela began to cry again. Justice stood and looked from Ted to Lela. She was waiting for Lela to tell Ted she was pregnant.

Ted rushed over to Lela. "What wrong, honey?"

"I'm pregnant."

"Are you sure?" he whispered as he took both her hands into his.

"Yes, I'm pretty sure. We did the home pregnancy test and it was positive."

"They're pretty accurate," he said. "Is it a boy or girl?' He placed his hand gently on her stomach.

"I don't know yet." *What's the matter with him, how would I know so soon?*

"I know I said I wanted a little girl, but if it's a boy, it's okay too."

"You're not angry with me?"

"Of course not, honey. This is not something you did by yourself. This is our baby. Girl or boy, I don't care. It's a little you--and me. Now, help me to understand why you are crying."

She was angry with herself for listening to an idiot like Olivia. *What was I thinking? Ted would never kick me out. I wish I had punched Olivia.*

"I was crying because Olivia said you would kick me out and I would end up on welfare because I would be too sick to work."

Ted swung Lela's leg around to make room for himself on the couch. He sat, then pulled her into his arms. "And you listened to an idiot like Olivia. What have I ever done that would make you think I would kick you out. This is our home, not mine. How could you have believed such a thing?" Ted was hurt and disappointed.

"Hey, I tried to tell her better, but pregnant women are a little crazy. She'll be okay," Justice said. "Lela, I'll stop by tomorrow after work. Good night guys, I'm going home."

Ted said good night and Lela stood and walked Justice to the door. "Justice, I'm going to get even with Olivia if it's the last thing I do."

"She's not worth it, Lela. Let it go. She was wrong, and you were wrong for listening to her. Go make Ted happy."

"Okay, you go home and call Alou. And let's not ever forget who the real idiot is." They giggled and said good night.

24

Lela had organized a group of eight women who would meet every second Sunday after church and develop plans to help raise the self-esteem of the young women in the church. Too many of them were in abusive relationships and unwed mothers. Justice was running late for the meeting because she had to drop off the kids she had taken to church from Oaktree Downs. She had not wanted to participate because Olivia was a member and always had something negative to say about her. Lela insisted that she would keep things in check and that Olivia would never act ugly in front of the other women. Olivia convinced Lela that she had changed and wanted to work with the young ladies. Justice agreed to participate because she felt it was a really worthwhile project.

"Well," Olivia said when Justice entered the dining room. "Important people always come to meetings late."

"Don't start, Olivia," Lela said, and gave her a dirty look. Justice ignored her and took her seat.

"Aren't you engaged to Alou Hambrick?" Olivia's friend, Lottie, asked Justice.

"Yes," Justice said.

"Have you guys set a . . .?"

Lela interrupted Lottie, "Instead of setting the table, why don't we all go to the kitchen and fix our plate and bring it back in here."

"How did you manage to snag him in the first place?" Lottie asked as they walked to the kitchen.

"I didn't realize he had been snagged," Justice said.

"Oh, you can tell he's snagged by the way he looks at you. He played hard and fast until you blew into town. Now he only has eyes for you. What type of black magic do you use?"

"I didn't realize this was supposed to be a meeting about Alou Hambrick," Justice said.

"It's not, leave her alone, Lottie," Lela said. She realized Lottie was speaking for Olivia. Lela was beginning to wonder if this was going to work. She hadn't expected Olivia to go that far.

"What do you guys think about all those prophecies given today?" Jeanette asked. "I received almost every one of them for myself."

"I received the one about the three houses and three cars. The lady he gave that prophecy to was blown away," Cassie said.

"I received the one about meeting a husband in seven days, and going to Hawaii on our honeymoon, and the Rolls Royce," Olivia said. "I would hate to have to drive a Toyota."

Justice knew that was meant as a put down for her because she drove a Toyota. It suddenly dawned on her that she was the only woman in the group that didn't drive a luxury car, and she realized she did not belong with this group. She placed her plate on the counter top and looked at the women.

"You know what, you guys make me sick. Every time some preacher starts prophesying about a bigger house, or bigger car, a husband or boyfriend, or better looking husband or boyfriend, of some material thing you all lap it up. You guys already have big houses and big cars, and a husband or a boyfriend. I've never heard any of you say anything about helping the poor. People are starving in Sudan, and Uganda, and kids right here in Winston don't have decent clothes to wear to school. And you guys only get excited when someone says you are going to get bigger and better stuff. You know, it makes me wonder how effective this group can be in ministering to the young girls we're supposed to reach. What are we going to do for their self esteem when it seems that our self esteem only comes from owning stuff?"

"We can't help it if we all have nice cars and you have a Toyota," Olivia said. "You're a lawyer; can't you get a better job than a public defender?"

"I'm doing exactly what I'm supposed to be doing, and what I want to do. And I don't belong here, so I'm leaving. And when you get your husband and Rolls Royce and go to Hawaii, I hope he chokes you and throws your fat butt in the ocean." Justice turned and walked through the living room and toward the door.

"Justice, wait," Lela said. Justice turned, held up her hand, shook her head, and walked out. She was just a little ticked off at Lela, but more angry with herself. *Why did I allow Lela to convince me to come to anything with Olivia? We have never been near each other and she didn't try to insult me. What was I thinking?*

"You know, Olivia, that was so unnecessary," Recy said. "I understand exactly how Justice feels. "If we treat members of our team like that, how are we going to minister to the young ladies who already have low self-esteem?

"I'm sick of her, always thinking we should cater to her because she lives in a condo and drives a Toyota. Let her stay at Oaktree Downs with the project kids," Olivia said.

"I've lost my appetite, and I don't think I can work with this group," Recy said.

"Ditto for me," Jeanette said. They picked up their purses and headed for the door.

"Wait," Lela said to Recy and Jeanette. "Before you go let me make a statement: Just for the record, let me inform you that Justice's father was a very successful criminal defense attorney in DC, and he left her more money than all of us have put together. She gave up her Mercedes for a Toyota because she doesn't want the kids in Oaktree Downs to be carried away by a big car. She could pay cash for a house big enough for all of us to live in and still not have to work another day in her life. She is the most unselfish person I know. So, Olivia you and Lottie get your purses and go. I should have never agreed to include you. She turned to the other two ladies who seemed to be in shock.

"I hope you ladies will stay. I promise you I will get the group back together, minus those two, and it will be effective. I owe Justice an apology. She didn't want to come because she knew Olivia would be here. I convinced her to come, because I didn't expect that from Olivia." Lela was angry with herself for allowing Olivia to talk her into including her and Lottie. *What was I thinking?*

Olivia and Lottie went off in a huff, Recy and Jeanette left, the other two ladies stayed and the three of them were able to formulate some concrete plans for the group. They were sure they would be able to convince the other ladies to come back.

⁀

JUSTICE WAS CRYING so hard that she had to pull over and stop the car. "God, I'm a useless, worthless idiot. I have upset my best friend and that entire group of women. Why couldn't I have just kept my big mouth shut? It's not my business if they love material things. What reason do I have to remain upon this earth? Who can I help with this lousy temper?" She laid her head on the stern wheel and wept.

A car passed and stopped. A young man got out and hurried back to see if Justice was okay.

He knocked on the window and she jumped. "Are you okay, mam?"

"Yes," Justice said as she rolled the window down. "I was just . . ." She realized that she couldn't tell him why she was crying. "Yes, I'm okay. I just needed to stop for a minute." She put the car in gear and he stepped back.

"Well, okay," he said as he waited for her to drive away. She smiled, waved to him, and drove away. *That was so silly of me to stop on the road like that and upset innocent people passing by. How do I handle this in the Kingdom? I need to apologize to Lela and that entire group of women, and learn to keep my opinions to myself.*

☞

THE DOORBELL RANG and Justice looked out the peephole and saw Lela and Ted. Lela had brought Justice a dinner plate. She opened the door and invited them in.

"I've been calling you all afternoon, why didn't you answer your phone, girl? Ted and I were worried about you. I brought you some food."

"Thank you, you saved me a trip to your house tomorrow. I want to apologize for my . . ."

"Hey, I'm the one who owe you an apology. I should have known better, but we'll talk about it later".

"I'm glad you're okay," Ted said. He hugged Justice and turned to Lela. "Since she's okay, let's get out of here and let her eat her food in peace. I may be able to get home in time to catch the last of the ball game."

"Okay," Lela said, and turned to Justice. "Are you sure you're okay? Girl, I'm so happy you are not crying your eyes out."

"I'm sure, but can't you guys stay a while?"

"Well, Mr. Sportsman can't stand to miss his ball game. But you're okay, we're okay, so we're going home," Lela said. "We'll talk later."

☞

LELA WAS QUIET as they drove home. She thought about Justice and why Olivia was always attacking her. It had to be because she was jealous of Alou's obvious love for Justice. Olivia was always in a relationship, but it never lasted. She thought about how someone or something was always coming against Alou and Justice, and how he always said yes whenever Justice asked him to do something, and how

227

Ted said no to her lots of times. She glanced at Ted and tears began to well up in her eyes. *He loves the ball game move than he loves me. If someone loved me as much as Alou loves Justice, I would always fight for him.*

Ted reached over and took Lela's hand in his. "Why are you so quiet, honey? What are you thinking?" Lela began to sob. Ted pulled over, stopped the car, and rolled the window down a few inches.

"What's the matter, sweetheart? Did I say or do something wrong? Are you worried about Justice? What is it?" Lela could not stop crying. Ted just held her and wondered what in the world was wrong.

"Why do you always say no to me, and Alou always say yes to Justice, no matter what she asks?"

"In the first place, I don't always say no to you, honey . . . But Alou always says yes to Justice because he's afraid she'll be angry if he says no. Our relationship is not based on fear. If Justice asked him to climb up on Stone Mountain with her and jump off, he would say 'okay.' But he would try to find a way to change her mind before it happened. I would suggest that we jump over an anthill in the back yard instead. And I wouldn't be afraid that you would kick me to the curb because I didn't say yes. Look, Lela, I may get angry with you, and you may make me so angry that I beat you down one day, but I'm *never* going to kick you to the curb. That's not an option for us. I'm not going to always say yes to your request, but I'm always going to listen, and I will always care about how you feel. And I hope you feel the same way about me.

"Always saying yes isn't proof of how much you love someone. But I want you to always remember this . . . It will take Alou ten years to *learn* to love Justice, the way I love you."

Lela was overcome. She began to sob again. She wanted to tell Ted how much she loved him and how sorry she was for being such an idiot. But she could only sob and hold his hand.

They both jumped when a uniformed policeman knocked on the window. "Is there a problem?" the officer asked. The second officer came up on the passenger side and stared at Lela. He motioned for her to roll her window down.

"Are you okay, mam?"

Lela nodded. She was unable to speak.

"And your name, sir?" the officer asked.

"Edward Bolton."

"Is this your husband, Mam?"

She nodded again. Lela tried to stop the tears, but they continued to roll down her face.

"Would you two mind stepping out of the car for just a moment." One of the officers talked with Lela and the other with Ted.

"Why are you crying?" The officer asked Lela.

"We just left a friend's house, and a lot of bad things have happened to her lately. So, I'm worried about her." She was not about to tell him why she was really crying.

"What's the friend's name?"

"Justice . . . Justiana."

"Justice Fullilove!" the officer asked.

"Yes," Lela said and stared at him. "Do you know her?"

"Yes, and you wouldn't happen to be Lela . . . of course Edward would be Ted, Lela and Ted." He turned to Officer Clark and said, "Hey man, it's Lela and Ted, Justice's friends."

"Then you must be Officer Davis and Officer Clark," Lela said.

They began to laugh and shake each other's hand and talk about how they already felt like they knew each other.

As the officers drove away, they looked at each other and shook their heads. "Somehow our lives seem to be tied up with Alou and Justice. I wonder what that's all about," Officer Davis said.

"Heaven only knows," Officer Clark said. "And God, don't let us miss you."

"Amen and amen."

Chapter

Justice received a message from Pastor Hopewell asking her not to bring the kids from Oaktree Downs back to the church. A church member had accused one of them of stealing her umbrella the Sunday when Justice was out of town and Shannon had taken them to church. After morning worship service, Justice went to talk with the pastor. She was frustrated because it was such a big deal to get to him.

After the preliminaries, she got right to the point. "Pastor, if one of the kids did something wrong, why are the other four kids not permitted to come back to church? And we are not sure he took the umbrella. Why can't they all come back while we investigate this incident?"

"There's not going to be any investigation. If Sister Tipton said he took her umbrella, he took it. Besides, those kids would feel more comfortable going to a church in their own neighborhood."

Justice frowned. "In their own neighborhood . . .? The kids are quite happy coming to church here. What's the real problem? Are they too poor, is that it pastor?"

"Be careful how you talk to the man of God, young lady."

"If there's a man of God in this room, I wish you would point him out to me, because I sure don't see one." Justice stood, moved toward the door, and turned to stare at the pastor. "And don't bother about asking security to show me out, I'm leaving. And you don't have to ask them to keep me off campus, because I have no intentions of coming back. You know what I'm glad about pastor—that I don't serve the same God you serve, and we won't have to be bothered with each other in eternity. I hope you have a lousy afternoon and all your teeth fall out." She walked out and closed the door gently. *I can't believe he said that, in their own neighborhood.*

Pastor Hopewell summoned his special deacon to his office and told him to contact security to be sure Justice was not allowed back on the premises.

"Justiana Fullilove? Are you sure?" the deacon asked.

"Yes, she insulted me. She has a smart mouth for a young woman. I have been in this business too long to have a young upstart like her talk to me the way she did. And she challenged Sister Tipton, wanting to investigate her claim that one of the kids stole her umbrella."

"Have you seen her tithing record?"

"No, but she's public defender, isn't she?"

"Yes, but I think you need to take a look at her tithing record before we go any further with this."

"Okay, I will," the pastor said as he moved over to the computer, entered his password and typed in Justice's name. When he saw her tithing record he whistled. "Hold the phone a minute; she doesn't make that kind of money as a public defender. What else does she do?"

"I don't know but she's dating that Homes by Hambrick guy. And he came here with her. So, if she goes I'm pretty sure he goes, too."

Pastor Hopewell was already familiar with Alou's tithing record. "Well now, Sister Tipton is a nice lady and all, but she's on social security. We can't run this great ministry on tithes and offerings from social security. Have we given Sister Fullilove and Brother Hambrick stickers for the special parking lot?"

"I don't think so. Neither of them has ever asked about a sticker or anything."

"They shouldn't have to. That's our job to see that those who dig deep in their pockets to support this ministry receive what little special benefits we have to offer. Be sure they get stickers to park in that lot, and when they come in on Sunday morning, usher them right down front. They sacrifice for the ministry; let's show our appreciation."

"Okay, so Sister Fullilove is not banned from the premises?"

"Of course not, man. We are not in the business of excluding people. Jesus said 'whosoever will, let him come'."

"Okay," the deacon said. "I'll get right on it."

☪

WHEN ALOU ARRIVED to take Justice out to lunch, he could tell she was upset. "What's wrong?" he asked.

"I smart mouthed the pastor today. He told me not to bring the kids from Oaktree Downs back to church. One of the ladies claimed Quinton stole her umbrella. One child is accused of doing something wrong, and he bans all five of the kids from church. How can you kick someone out of church for stealing an umbrella? We can replace a stupid umbrella. He said they would be *more comfortable* going to a church in their own neighborhood. I think he doesn't want them there because they live in the projects."

Alou shook his head. "If that's the way he feels about the kids from Oaktree Downs, I don't want to go to a church like that. He shouldn't even call it a church; it's just like The Club."

"Thank you, Alou. And I don't have any desire to apologize to the pastor, even though I will never speak that way to a pastor or church leader again. Now I understand how you felt about church. So what do we do now? I am certainly not going back there."

"There are still good churches out there. And God is still God. Let's just go visit different churches for a while. Let's take our time about . . ."

The phone interrupted them. Justice reached for the phone and glanced at the caller ID. She stopped short when

232

she noticed the call was from Mt. Zion Christian Center. *I bet it's Pastor Hopewell, what could he possibly want with me. I'm not going to answer.* "Look," she said. "It's the pastor calling, and I'm not going to answer. Let's go turn the answering machine up and see what he has to say." They hurried into her study and listened to the answering machine.

"Hello, Sister Fullilove, this is Pastor Hopewell. I just wanted to talk with you about the little misunderstanding we had this afternoon. Why don't you come by after church on Sunday so we can talk about it, or maybe I can meet you some place for lunch next week. Please, give me a call. Have a good afternoon. This is Pastor Hopewell."

Justice and Alou just stood there. They were both in shock. "Now what do you suppose that was all about?" Justice asked.

"Maybe he wants you to come back to church so he can embarrass you in front of the congregation. Maybe he thought about it and wants to get even. At any rate, you shouldn't respond to him at all. Just be done with it. We may never know what that's about." Alou pulled Justice into his arms and held her. "Are you ready to go eat?"

"Yes, and I get to spend the afternoon with you. That will make up for the disappointment I feel for being in a squabble with a pastor."

"Let it go before you make me go and strangle the pastor."

When Alou opened the door, he and Justice stopped short because a man was reaching to ring the doorbell.

"Brother Hambrick, this must be my lucky day. I didn't expect to see you, but I have something for you and Sister Fullilove. Pastor Hopewell wanted me to give you guys these special parking stickers. That way you can park in the special lot right behind the church."

"Why?" Justice asked as she turned to look at Alou.

"He wants you to come by and he will explain it to you. Can you stop by and speak with him Sunday after church?"

"I made it clear to Pastor Hopewell when I left today, that I had no intentions of coming back. So, tell him that I appreciate it, but I don't think I would be comfortable there anymore."

"Well, what about you Brother Hambrick, can I leave this sticker with you?"

"No, I won't be coming back either. Tell Pastor Hopewell I appreciate the offer."

"Can't you at least ..." Justice held up her hand, and the deacon fell silent.

"Would you let the pastor know we appreciate the offer," Alou said.

"Yes, I'll let him know." The deacon turned and headed for his car.

"Alou, what do you think they want. Why would they want to give us a special parking sticker, we are not in any of the ministries, and why would he have a sticker for you when he came by my place. Do you think he's that determined to get even with me that he would drag you into it?"

Alou pulled Justice into his arms and closed the door. "Let's not waste any time trying to figure out what they want and why. Let's just forget them. Okay?"

"Okay

"I'm hungry, let's go eat."

꒜

WHEN JUSTICE AND Alou returned from lunch, there was a message from the church secretary asking Justice to call her so she could schedule an appointment for her to meet with Pastor Hopewell. Justice was a little ticked off. "They need to let it go while I still have my composure."

"Just don't respond to them, and they will go away. They can't make you come back. Let's just forget about it, Justice, and pretend they didn't call."

"Okay, let's look in the phone book and find some churches to visit. Let's try a different denomination. What about Catholic or Lutheran?"

"What about Solomon's church? I like that kingdom stuff you told me about. That sounds like the way to go."

"Alou, you are a sweet man. And I love you too much." She tossed to phone book into the closet and slipped her arms around his waist. "You are going to love Solomon's church."

By the time Alou left, they had decided that they would visit several churches before they joined, and they would not respond in any way to the people from Mt. Zion. Justice knew she would have to tell Lela about what happened. But that could wait.

⌒

JUSTICE AND LELA had spent the July 4th weekend at Lela parent's house in Tampa every year since Harold Fullilove's death. Lela convinced Justice and Justice convinced Alou to join them for the July 4th holiday weekend in 2007. Justice thought Alou would have some reservations about going. He did not. Justice was worried that Alou would be sad about not spending the holiday with his mom. She was also worried because she felt that she had come between Alou and his mom. She was looking forward to talking with Lela's mom about her concerns. She was sure Miss Mary would know what she should do. Alou was hoping for an opportunity to talk with Lela's dad about his mother. He was sure the older man could point him in the right direction.

From the moment their plane landed, everything was funny to Justice and Alou. They couldn't stop laughing. The others got caught up in it and pretty soon everyone was laughing about everything. After dinner, they told stories about Lela and Justice's childhood days, sang songs, popped popcorn, and played a game called happy hunting, well into the night. Everyone made a fuss over Lela, and she was the perfect mother-to-be.

They had a big breakfast prepared by Miss Mary and Mr. Alvin that Sunday morning. Justice and Alou insisted on washing dishes and blew bubbles from the dishwater all over the kitchen. They all wanted to play happy hunting again. It was the funniest game they had ever played.

When dinner was ready, Miss Mary had to take the game away to get them to come to dinner. After dinner she confiscated the game and insisted that they take the time to visit and catch up on each other's news. After they all had a time to share their news, Lela's dad asked Alou to go for a walk with him, and Justice went to help Miss Mary clean the kitchen. Lela and Ted went to take a nap.

"My time is limited so I'll get right to the point," Mr. Alvin said to Alou. "Lela told me that you mom doesn't like Justice."

The man was so blunt; Alou was a little embarrassed. "Yes, that's true."

"I'd like to give you some advice. Wanna hear it?"

"Yes."

"Continue to visit your mother by yourself. You can't force her to like Justice, and you shouldn't stop visiting or calling her because she doesn't like Justice. You don't have to stay long, just let her know that you care, and you want her to be a part of your life. As long as she is not abusive, you should continue to call or visit her until you feel that you have given her ample time and every opportunity to realize how much you want her to get to know Justice. If she still refuses, then she will have made the choice to shut you out of her life by trying to control you. It will not be about choosing between her and Justice, because you will have shown her that you want both her and Justice in your life, it will be about her trying to control you. Nothing else. Any questions?"

"Not that I can think of," Alou said. "That makes perfect sense. I don't know why I didn't think of it myself."

"Experience, my boy. Now let's go back in and see if we can play some more happy hunting."

"HEAR YOU GOT would-be mother-in-law trouble." Miss Mary said to Justice.

"Yes," Justice said, happy to have her bring it up. *Thank you Lela.*

"Don't fight it. Don't try to be a part of her life. No woman can have a son like Alou and not love him. And I'm sure he loves his mother. Only time can work that out. The way I see it, she's operating in the fear of losing something. It could be Alou's affection, his money, or both. Either way, you are going to have to have patience, but it will work itself out, and one day she will love you like a daughter. If she doesn't, it will be her loss. You are too precious for anyone to not love you. And remember, you always have listening ears and a warm bed here in Tampa. Can you wait it out?"

"Yes, I love Alou too much to give up."

"Good," she said and turned toward the living room. "I don't believe it; they are playing that game again. Well, we might as well join them. They were laughing so loud, Lela and Ted said they couldn't sleep and came back to join them. They had never played a game that was so much fun before.

When they headed back to the airport, they all agreed that this was the most fun they had had in a long time. Alou had not even missed his mother. When they got to the airport, Justice urged him to call her. Auryola was surprised to hear that he was in Florida. Alou told her that he just wanted to wish her a happy holiday and let her know he was thinking about her. He was determined to follow the advice that he had been given and felt that it would change his life. He loved his mother, but he was not going to allow her to control him.

When they got on the plane, Lela asked Ted if he would exchange seat with Justice. Justice knew Lela wanted to know why she had not seen her at church.

"Okay, lady, are you a backslider or what?"

"I'm currently attending Solomon's church. I'm not coming back to Mr. Zion, and neither is Alou."

"Why?"

Justice told her about the encounter with the pastor, the deacon and the call from the secretary, and why she felt they wanted her to come back.

Lela was surprised and baffled. "I admit they acted strange. But I can't imagine he would try to embarrass you in front of the congregation. The members wouldn't like that. I'm going to ask Ted about it. I guarantee you he can figure it out."

ALOU HAD LEFT his car at the airport. He dropped Lela and Ted off and he and Justice went to her condo. When Justice listened to her messages, there was a call from Katrina stating that the Pastor had called and said the lady found her umbrella and they could come back to church. He said the lady was very sorry. Alou walk into the study and stared at Justice because she kept playing the message over and over.

"Do I need to tie you down or sedate you or what?"

"Did he do what I think he did? Did he actually locate Katrina and call her? Why would he go to all that trouble? We already know he doesn't care about the kids. Could he possible want to get even with me that bad? What is this, Alou?"

"I don't know, but I'm going to stop it." Alou picked up the phone and hit the button to view the incoming call numbers. He dialed the number to the church and motioned for Justice to leave the room while he waited for an answer. "I need to speak with Pastor Hopewell."

"May I tell him who's calling?"

"Yes, it's Alou Hambrick."

"Okay, hold on Brother Hambrick, I'll get him for you."

The next voice he heard was Pastor Hopewell. "Thank you for calling me Brother Hambrick, you are just . . ."

"Don't thank me, just listen. Do not call Miss Fullilove again. If you, or anyone from your church contact either of us again, I will personally break your neck and have your flunkies arrested for harassment. Let me be clear, all we want you to do is leave us alone. And don't contact the kids from Oaktree Downs again. If you do, we will go to the media, and we will file charges against you for cruelty to children. We are not angry; we just don't ever want to hear from you or your deacon again. Good bye Pastor Hopewell." Alou could hear the pastor stuttering as the replaced the receiver. Justice had moved back to the door. She ran to him and slipped her arms around his waist. Neither could think of anything to say. Alou shook his head and held her close. *How did we get into a conflict with the church? What are we doing wrong? Hopefully they will leave us alone now. I didn't want to go there.*

Alou called Justice an hour before she was supposed to leave for the monthly meeting at Oaktree Downs, and told her that he had found some backpacks on sale and purchased them for the kids. Justice was touched by his thoughtfulness. She was happy because she realized that he really had developed an interest in the kids. She told him what time the meeting would start. He really didn't want her to drive home alone. He knew the men that attacked her were still out there somewhere.

"Why don't I come by and drive you over. That way we can talk on the way home. I won't get a word in edgewise with the kids around. You know how they monopolize your time."

"You wouldn't by any chance be jealous of little kids would you?"

"Yes, I'm jealous of anyone who takes up your time. I want you all to myself. I'm an honest man. I won't pretend it's okay. But, what's important to you is important to me. So, I'll put up with the kids taking up a certain amount of your time because it's for a good purpose. Besides, they are pretty cool kids."

"You have forty-five minutes to get here."

"I'll be there in thirty minutes. Don't leave without me."

Alou arrived in exactly thirty minutes. And Justice wanted to see the backpacks. Alou opened the truck and she was blown away by the variety of color combinations. He had more than enough for every kid. That earned Alou a hug, a kiss, and a declaration that he was a sweet man. He ate it up.

Everyone had a wonderful time. They had a dance contest and Leroy and Miss Justice won the contest. Word got around and kids who were not a part of the club came and were given backpacks. Alou had bought enough extras for every kid in the housing project to have one. Justice was overjoyed and Alou was quite pleased with himself.

As they were saying their good-byes, Brittany told Justice that she wanted to be a virgin just like her when she got engaged. Several of the other girls said they did, too. Justice was shocked. She turned to look at Alou. He shrugged his shoulders to let her know he had no idea how they knew she was a virgin. Justice was embarrassed and frustrated. *There has to be something in this town for people to be concerned about besides my virginity.*

"Miss Mandy told us you were a virgin," Katrina said. "Said she could tell by the way Mr. Alou always touches you above the waist. She said men touch women below the waist when they are no longer virgins." She could tell that Justice wondered how they knew.

"Well," Alou said. "I'm not a virgin, but I sure wish I were. That's one of the biggest regrets of my life. I wish I had waited until I got married to Miss Justice. But you guys can learn from my mistake. You have a chance to make the right choice. I promise you, you won't regret it if you wait." The kids said they would wait, and Alou hoped that somehow that made Justice feel better. *No one likes to have their business in the streets, but she is a bit too sensitive about people knowing she's a virgin.*

⌒

ALOU HAD KICKED off his shoes and was reaching for the remote when the doorbell rang. He looked at the clock. It was only nine o'clock, but he wasn't expecting anyone. He opened the door and was surprised to see Justice standing there.

"Come in," he said. He wasn't sure what to expect. But he could tell that she was still angry about the lady telling the kids she was a virgin.

"There must be something more important to people in this town than my virginity," she said. He could hear the anger in her voice. "Young men and women are dying in Iraq, people are starving in Sudan, kids are being killed on the streets in our cities, young men are being thrown into prison in record numbers in this nation, and a whole town is sitting around worrying about the virginity of one little woman. How crazy is that? But we can fix that right now; we can take that issue off the table."

She took off her blouse and threw it on the couch, and then she unbuttoned her skirt in the back and allowed it to fall to the floor. She stepped out of it and threw it on the couch. She yanked her slip over her head and was throwing it on the couch when Alou grabbed her hands. He had just stood there and stared at first because he was in shock, then he waited because he told himself that he wanted to see how far she would go, and then he waited because he wanted to get a look at what she seemed determined to show him.

"Just what do you think you are doing?" he asked.

"We are going for a roll in the hay."

"We are not doing any such thing."

"You rolled in the hay with Ericka."

Alou pulled her hands up to his chest, cleared his throat, swallowed, and looked into her eyes. "Yes, I did . . . and I can't tell you how much I have come to regret it. I don't want any more regrets about rolling in the hay. I want to remember the first time we make love as something special and precious and wonderful, not with you in anger and frustration. You're better than that, Justice. You are not someone I'm just looking to roll in the hay with; I want to spend the rest of my life with you."

She wanted to cry. She loved Alou more at that moment that she thought possible. She wanted to hug him and tell him tell him how much she loved him. She just stood there as he released her hands and nodded to her clothes. "You need to get dressed before you make me forget my promise. I'm only a man, Justice, even you can push me too far."

She grabbed her clothes and ran to the bathroom to get dressed. She felt like an idiot. *How did I get to be so stupid? My dad didn't raise me to be an idiot. How did I get here?*

Justice came back into the living room and Alou stood up. He reached out and took her hand in his, then pulled her over to the couch, and they sat holding hands.

"Can you stay a while?"

"Yes, and there's something I need to tell you, Alou." She sighed and he just sat and listened. She remembered her promise to Lela.

"I love you more than I can ever tell you, and I want to apologize for my behavior tonight. There's no way I can tell you how important it is for me to be a virgin when we get married. I don't know what got into me. I promise you I will never do anything like that again." She thought about what happened to Lela, and the promise they made to her mom; she wanted to cry.

"Justice, if you love me that much, why are you always trying to get rid of me? Why are you always telling me to leave and not come back?"

"I never want you to leave. It's just that . . . when someone or something threatens to tear us apart, I feel like I'm going to die. I tell you to leave because that seems like the only way I can go on living. When you leave, I always run to the door and listen to your footsteps as you go down the steps, because I don't know if I'm going to ever hear them again. Then I run to the window to see if I can see you getting into your car. Sometimes you take off your tie and throw it in the car and just drive away. Other times you look back toward my condo, then stare at the ground a while before you go. When you do that I keep hoping you will come back and ring the doorbell."

"And if I had come back, what would you have done?"

"I would have opened the door, fell into your arms, and begged you not to leave."

Alou pulled her into his arms and held her; he wanted to cry. He wanted to strangle Ericka and his mother--but mostly his mother. They had made him and Justice miserable so many times, and for no reason. He vowed that he would not let any one tear them apart, and he would find a way to deal with his mother.

⌒

AURYOLA HAD KEYS to Alou's home. She drove around and dropped Ericka off in front of Alou's house. She gave her the key and security code, and told her to come out front and walk to the corner after she retrieved the tape. Ericka was giddy with delight. She was already dreaming that this would be her home someday and she would be the envy of half the women in Winston, especially Justice Fullilove. Ericka removed the videotape, slid in a blank one, reset the alarm, and hurried out the door and down to the corner. Auryola was there to pick her up almost immediately. They were giggling and chatting like old friends as they headed to Auryola's house to watch the video.

They were both in shock as they viewed the video. They hadn't known what to expect, but it certainly was not what they saw.

"What in the world is she doing?" Ericka asked when she saw Justice taking off her clothes. Then she was furious when Alou stopped her.

"Oh, so he thinks she's too good for a roll in the hay. If that had been me he would have been all over me. Every time we got together, we rolled in the hay, and he has spent all this time with her and when she offers to roll in the hay with him, he says they should wait. Men make me sick. He never said one time that he wanted to spend the rest of his life with me, not even the rest of the night. And I can't believe she had the nerve to bring my name . . ."

"Ericka, you decide how far you want to go with a man. Or men, I should say. Alou wasn't the only man you slept with, was he?" Auryola was having a difficult time hiding her dislike for Ericka.

"Well, no, he wasn't," Ericka said as she turned to stare at Auryola. She couldn't miss the disdain in her voice. "But he knew I had slept with other men before we began dating. He never acted like it was a problem for him. Besides, he had slept with other women." *I don't want to watch any more of this.*

Did he ever indicate that he wanted to marry you?" She was not worried about hurting Ericka's feelings. She stood and walked into the kitchen. She wanted to put a little distance between herself and this idiot. *What would make her think that Alou would marry her?*

It all became clear to Ericka that she was a pawn used to get information to be used against Justice. And that Auryola cared even less for her than she did Justice. Disappointment, rejection, and anger washed over her like steam. She couldn't bear to look at Auryola. *What was I thinking? What would make me think this woman would ever accept me if she didn't accept Justice? Justice is beautiful, a virgin, and a lawyer. I'm pretty, but just a telephone operator, and probably everyone in Winston knows that I have slept around. Get up now and go home.*

Ericka stood and walked to the door without a word. Auryola simply stared at her. She had what she wanted, and had no further use for Ericka. She was happy Ericka was not making a fuss and she didn't feel one bit of sympathy for her. Auryola was sure she had information that she could use to end the relationship between Justice and Alou.

"**H**ello," Justice said into the phone without taking her eyes off the book she was reading.

"Justiana," Auryola said. "I just want you to know that the next time you undress and strip down to you lacy peach panties and bra in front of my son, I'm going to have you arrested for indecent exposure and sexual harassment. He tried to treat you like a lady, but you acted like a street woman. Did you have *any* home training?"

Justice was speechless. She had never experienced such pain. Her mind was so torn that she couldn't even feel anger. She tried to speak, but no words came out. She held the phone and willed herself to continue breathing. *Alou would never have betrayed me like that. And yet no one else knew about my little indiscretion. Why would he tell his mother, of all people? But he wouldn't do that to me. Then how could she have known? She must have forced him to tell her . . . Think of something ugly to say to her. Don't let her hang up the phone and be happy. Take away her peace and make her sorry she called.*

"Mrs. Hambrick, I was only trying to help your son. I knew nothing would happen sexually, because Alou is impotent."

"You're lying; Ericka never said anything about him being impotent."

"I overestimated you. You are assuming that Ericka would have sense enough to figure that out. He's your son, don't take my word for it, ask him." Auryola slammed the phone down. Even though Justice knew she had shocked Auryola, it did not ease her pain. She had to go see Alou; she had to know why he betrayed her. She hadn't even told Lela, and he had told her worse enemy. Why? She grabbed her purse and headed for his office.

⌒

ALOU HEARD HIS private door open and he and all the employees turned as Justice stepped into the office. She just stood there and stared. She had expected him to be alone.

"I'm sorry," she said. I didn't know ..."

"It's okay," he said as he stood and hurried over to take her hands in his. "Meeting's over guys. And don't continue it down the hall. It won't hurt us to take this one up in the morning."

"Alou, please," Justice said. "I didn't . . ."

"I said it's okay." He could hear the employees gathering up their belongings. He finally turned to look at them. "Why don't you guys knock off for the day. And don't take all afternoon to get your stuff and hit the highway. Good night."

They said good night and scrambled out the door. Most of them headed straight for their cars.

"What's wrong, Sweetheart?" Alou could tell by the look on her face that he could not afford to let her leave without finding out what Auryola had done. If he did, he knew he would probable never be able to fix it this time.

"You know," Justice said and sighed. "It doesn't really matter. I'm not going to even ask you about it. I'm really sorry about busting in on your meeting, I wasn't thinking clearly. Will you forgive me?"

"Only if you tell me what's wrong."

"Don't put any conditions on forgiving me, Alou, please."

"Okay, I forgive you. Now, will you please tell me what's wrong?"

"Maybe later," she said and hurried toward the door. "I'll call you later." She stopped and turned to look at him when she heard the door lock. He was standing there with the remote—one of his many inventions—in his hand. She looked toward the other door.

"They are all locked," he said. "The whole place is on lock down. Just like in prison, and you are the inmate. And you have two choices, you can tell me what's wrong, or we can go into my private lounge and make a baby."

"Make a baby?" she asked.

"Yes," he said. "You do know how babies are made?" While she stood there trying to figure out if he was kidding, he walked over, picked her up, took her into his private lounge, and laid her on the couch. He stepped back and began to take off his tie.

"Are you going to take off your clothes, or you need me to do it for you?"

"Alou, have you lost your mind?" she asked.

"Absolutely not. You came into my office and interrupted my meeting, and I don't mind you interrupting my meeting. There won't ever be a meeting more important than you, but I do mind you refusing to tell me what's bothering you. You have only two options Justice Fullilove, and I'll take either one. Now, are you going to tell me what's wrong, or shall we make the baby?" He walked over to her and pulled her up into a sitting position and began to unbutton her blouse.

"I'll tell you," she whispered. He sat on the couch next to her, and she told him what Auryola had said. She promised herself that she wouldn't cry, but the tears ran down her face anyway.

"And you think I would tell her something like that?"

"I didn't know what to think. I couldn't believe you would betray me like that, but we were the only two people there. How else could she have known? She described everything, down to the color of my underwear."

"We are going to find out. We'll just go and ask her."

"I'm not going to your mother's house. You know she would be furious if you brought me to her house."

"Then we are back to square one. We're going to have to make that baby."

"Alou, don't treat me like this," she pleaded.

"We have to know what happened. And it wouldn't make any sense for me to go and find out and come back and try to tell you. You have to hear what happened for yourself. I don't like this any more than you do, but we have to deal with this now. So, tell me, do we go see my mother, or do we make the baby?"

"We go see your mom," she said. She was thoroughly frustrated.

☞

AURYOLA EXPECTED ALOU. She had not expected Justice. She had her story ready for Alou.

"Alou," she said when she opened the door, and then frowned when she saw Justice. "I know you didn't bring *that girl* to my house."

Alou felt his hand moving upwards and connecting to his mother's face. He felt the slap and heard her gasp. He saw her stagger back and put her hand to her face. Then he heard his own voice. "Don't *ever* refer to her that way again." He felt as if he had stepped outside his body and was watching everything in slow motion.

Justice screamed and grabbed his arm. "Alou, please," she said and clung to his arm. She turned to stare at Auryola, who just stood there with her hand on her face and stared at Alou. She was unable to move or speak. She saw the look in his eyes and realized that she had only been concerned about ending the relationship between him and Justice. It never occurred to her that she could lose his love.

"Where did you get that information?" he asked and took a step toward her. She could feel the anger. "I asked you a question, Mother."

"Ericka got it," she said. "She put an audio-video camera in your living room." She expected his anger to shift to Ericka.

249

"And how did Ericka get a key to my house and my security code? He wanted her to tell him. He already knew the answer. She simply dropped her head. He walked over to the table and picked up her key chain. He removed his keys and placed the key chain back on the table. He took his keys out of his pocket, removed her door key from his key chain and placed it on the table. He turned and stared at her as if she were a stranger. In fact, she had become a stranger to him. He had no idea what had become of his mother, and it made him very sad.

"Alou, please, let's go," Justice pleaded as she pulled him by the arm and turned to stare at Auryola. Justice begged Auryola, with her eyes, to tell her that she was okay. Auryola finally gave a slight nod of her head, and Justice pulled Alou out the door.

Auryola was a little surprised that she had responded to Justice. But she was also surprised that Justice had shown concern for her after what she had done to her. She was bewildered. Her own son had actually slapped her. Her plan had backfired. Her hope of blaming it all on Ericka had not worked, and she was not sure if Alou would ever speak to her again.

Alou held Justice's hand as they walked to his car. They walked in silence. When he walked around to open the door for her, she just turned and stared at him. He took her in his arms and held her close.

"You okay?" he finally asked. She nodded her head yes, and got into the car. As he walked slowly around to the driver's side, he considered going back to apologize to his mother. He decided against it. *Not yet. She could have destroyed my relationship with Justice. In fact, that was exactly what she had intended to do.*

"We'll go back to my office and get your car. I'll follow you home. You hungry?" he asked.

"No, how about you?"

"Not really, but let's stop and get something on the way. We may get hungry later. Can I stay awhile?"

She said he could and they went by Goody Foods and picked up a salad, chicken, steamed vegetables, and a chocolate cake. When they reached her condo, they just sat on the couch holding hands. They were lost in their own thoughts. Alou couldn't really believe he had actually slapped his mother, and neither could Justice. They ate, watched a movie, and tried to figure out why things kept going wrong for them.

"Do you think maybe we are not supposed to be together?" Justice asked.

"No, I know that's not it. Think about it. How likely is it that we would have met if it had not been the plan of God? According to Lela, and you confirmed it, you only went to church and court before we met. And for you to be standing on that sidewalk at the exact moment I opened that garage door is proof of divine intervention. Ten minutes earlier, I would have missed you. Or ten minutes later, you would have passed by. Besides, I prayed for a girl like you when I was a kid in Sunday school. When I didn't find you right away, I forgot about it. Now that I have you, I'm not letting you go. So don't ever doubt that we are supposed to be together."

After they made all the promises they could think of to secure their relationship, they just held each other. Finally, Alou kissed her and went home.

Chapter

28

Justice and Mark were both prepared for trial. The defendant was charged with aggravated assault and the state's offer was five years to serve. He had poured gasoline on his doctor and set him on fire. He claimed the doctor had given him a shot that contained poison during his last visit, and that his mother's death was caused by poison the doctor had given her. The man had waited patiently for his appointment with the doctor, and cooperated with the nurse who took his vital signs and information regarding his complaint. When the doctor walked into the room, he reached in his backpack, took out the jar of gasoline, threw it on the doctor, "flicked his bic", and set the doctor on fire. The doctor saved himself by rolling on the floor, but suffered first-degree burns.

Justice had filed a motion for a second psychiatric evaluation because she felt the evaluation made by the state's psychiatrist was incorrect. As the motion hearing began the defendant stood up and addressed the court.

"Your Honor, I think I'll take the five years to serve. I don't want to have to ever come back to court again. I have been here too many times already. Let's get it over ..."

Justice interrupted him. "Your Honor, I would like to have a few minutes to speak with my client."

"Very well," Judge Denver said. "Let's take a break, court will resume in thirty minutes."

Justice ushered the defendant to the witness room and just sat and stared at him. How *can the judge sentence this man to prison? He's obviously crazy, but then so is Mark and Judge Denver. And what about me, why am I here with these idiots?*

"Why are you doing this, Randy," Justice asked.

"Look, I appreciate all your help, but I'm not crazy. I knew exactly what I was doing. The doctor killed my mother. Now he has paid a small price, but he will pay in full one day. Oh, I won't do it, but someday someone will call his hand and he will pay for every evil trick he has preformed. But I have decided that prison is better than a mental institution. I decided to play crazy because I figured they would let me go. But I'm not going to spend the rest of my life in a crazy house." He folded his arms and stared at Justice. He knew that she would be forced to tell the judge if he told her that he planned to finish the doctor off. *Just take her out of the loop and my job will be easier.*

"Look, you obviously need some . . ."

"Are you saying I'm crazy? The psychiatrist said I was okay. I thought you were a lawyer, not a doctor. Let it go, Miss Fullilove. You did your job, and don't forget, it's my call."

Justice felt defeated. She wanted to go home and crawl into bed. She wanted to forget about defendants, judges, prosecutors, and courtrooms. *How did I ever get into this mess in the first place? Where am I making a difference? What's the point in all this? Aughhhh!*

"Okay," she said and sighed. "It *is* your call. Let's get on with it."

As they walked back into the courtroom, Justice could barely put one foot in front of the other. She was suddenly overcome with fatigue and frustration. Even the judge and Mark kept glancing at her. They had never seen her look so deflated. Frustration and disgust came through in every move. The defendant made it worse by patting her on the back and saying it was going to be okay. When they stood at the podium to enter the plea, Justice communicated by nodding or shaking her head. Even Judge Denver couldn't bring himself to demand that she speak up and checked to be sure that the court reporter was recording her responses.

"Is there anything else you would like the court to consider, Miss Fullilove," Judge Denver asked.

"Yes, your Honor," Justice tried to steady her voice and emotions. "I think five years is unreasonable. The defendant obviously ..." *Don't go there, you will only make things worse.*

"I'm asking the court to consider all the circumstances surrounding this case, and I recommend a sentence of one year."

"Taking into consideration both the recommendation by the prosecutor and the defense attorney, I sentence the defendant to three years in prison. You are remanded to the custody of the sheriff until you can be transported to the facility. This court is adjourned."

They stood while the judge left the courtroom. Then Justice slumped down in her chair. The defendant bent to hug her and told her that he was very pleased with her help and he was going to be okay. He waved to Justice as the deputy escorted him out of the courtroom.

Mark gathered up his belongings and turned to look at Justice. "Hey, are you okay?"

"Yes," she said as she stood and began placing her files in her briefcase. "I'm okay. Good night."

꒰

SHE WANTED TO call Alou, but told herself that she would not run to Alou every time something didn't go her way. She went to the mall instead. She sat on a bench and watched the crowd walk by and then went to have a salad in a small restaurant.

As she drove home, she was thinking about the case and wondering what she could have done differently when a car pulled in front of her and stopped abruptly. She slammed on the brakes and decided to back up and pull around it. When she looked in the rear view mirror, she saw a car pulling in behind her and then ram the rear end of her car. She tried to think. Her mind shut down. The car backed up and rammed her car from the side. She could see that he was trying to knock her off the road. She reached for the door handle but he rammed her car again and she unbuckled her seat belt and moved over to the passenger side. She lay down on the seat, put her hands over her face, and closed her eyes. There was no point in screaming, the sound of metal against metal was already deafening. She began to pray.

"Oh God, help me. Let your angels protect me. Oh, Jesus, oh God, oh God, oh God, in the name of Jesus." A thought came to her mind to put her seat belt back on. It was so strong it seemed like an audible voice, her voice. *Thank you, Holy Spirit.*

She could feel the car moving over the edge. She sat up and put the seat belt on just as the car started over the embankment. The car turned over several times as it rolled down the embankment. She heard the seat belt unbuckle and she felt herself moving through the air. She heard the explosion, saw the flames, and felt the heat. She screamed, and then watched her whole life flash before her. She closed her eyes and thought that death was not as bad as she had anticipated. Then blackness engulfed her.

Nito had called 911 when he saw what was taking place. The men had disappeared and her car was in the ditch and in flames when he arrived. But he thought that he had heard a scream coming from somewhere up on the other side of the ditch. He went to investigate. He could only hope. He was not looking forward to telling Snaggie what had happened. But she would have to tell Alou and not him. He did not envy her.

An ambulance, a fire truck, and a police car arrived at the scene. The car was completely engulfed in flames. The firemen raced down the hill and sprayed water on the car. They knew no one could have survived such flames. They all turned when they heard Nito yelling from the other side.

"Hey, someone help me, she's over here." The paramedics ran up the hill to help him. Justice was listless and covered with red Georgia mud. After they loaded her in the ambulance and headed for the hospital, Nito called Snaggie and gave her the report. He was sick to his stomach. He couldn't imagine what Snaggie felt, and he didn't even want to think about Alou.

Snaggie called Lela and Solomon, but went to tell Alou in person. When they arrived at the hospital, Justice was unconscious, but stable. She had a concussion and a few scrapes and bruises, but no broken bones. She regained consciousness around eleven o'clock that night. The doctor wanted to keep her in the hospital overnight for observation, but Justice signed herself out. She insisted that she would not feel safe in the hospital.

"We'll drive you home to get some clothes and you should spend the next few days with us," Lela said as they prepared to leave the hospital.

"Why don't you just stay at my place?" Alou asked.

"Because, I'm taking the rest of the week off, and she won't have to spend any time alone," Lela said. "Besides, Alou, why would you want to put Justice or yourself in that position? She's not in any frame of mind to make rational decisions at this time. And neither are you."

"And I suppose you are?" Alou asked. He didn't want to get into an argument with Lela, but she was taking a lot upon herself. "After all we are engaged."

"And she was my friend long before we knew you existed."

"Lela, Alou, please," Solomon said. Why don't you let Justice decide where she wants to go?" Justice just stood there looking confused with tears in her eyes.

"I'm sorry, Alou," Lela said. "I'm just so scared and worried about Justice."

"No, you're absolutely right," Alou said as he pulled Justice into his arms and kissed her on the forehead. "Have a good night's sleep and I'll come see you tomorrow. And we can go out for dinner, if you're up to it."

"Okay," she said and turned to Solomon.

"I'll talk with you tomorrow, kiddo," Solomon said and tussled her hair. He said good night to the group and headed for his car. Alou kissed Lela's hand, shook Ted's hand, kissed Justice on the mouth and went to his car. Ted sighed, took Lela and Justice by the hand and headed for his car. He was glad the confrontation was over. Now that he knew Justice was going to be okay, he just wanted to go home and watch a little TV. *Is that too much to ask?*

THE NEWS FLASH kept showing the burning car and said the car belonged to a local public defender. They did not give Justice's name immediately. But everyone who knew Justice knew it was her car. A car forced off the road and going up in flames was big news in Winston.

Ericka was mortified. "What if she's dead?" she said out loud. "And the last thing I did was try to destroy her relationship with Alou."

She walked to the mirror, looked at herself, and said. "Even if you were able to break up their relationship, Alou wouldn't want you. And Mrs. Hambrick would never accept you. She was only using you to keep Alou under her thumb. I pray to God that she's alive. And if she is, I am going to apologize to her and never get involved in anything like that again. That could have been my car rolling down that hill in flames."

Justice spent two days with Lela and Ted before returning home. "I can't live my life in fear," she said. "Besides, I trust God to protect me at home just as He did when my car went down that embankment. And you both know that none of us are leaving here until our time comes. And I still have a lot of work to do."

So, they allowed her to go home alone. What else could they do?

Nito knew that Justice was back home. He was concerned because it had been dark for more than 30 minutes and the lights were not on. He knocked on the door. Justice had been talking with Alou on the phone when it got dark and never bothered to turn on the lights.

"Hold on, Alou, someone's at the door."

"Are you expecting anyone?"

"No.'

"Don't open the door, Justice, find out who it is first."

"Okay, scary cat." She hurried to the door and looked through the peephole. She was surprised to see Nito and invited him in. Nito didn't want to come in, but she insisted. She wanted to know something about this man who followed her all the time. Justice returned to the phone.

"Alou, you will never guess who was at the door."

"Bat man and Robin."

"No, silly. It's Nito. I invited him in for a cup of tea. I'll talk with you tomorrow." They said their good-byes and ended their conversation. Nito told her about his life and she was so impressed with the way he turned his life around. As they sipped their tea, she told him a little about her life.

She told him about Lela's pregnancy and that she was going to become a godmother on December 20, 2007. Nito was always amused that women believed the doctor when he told them the exact date the baby would be born. Nito wondered whether she would baby sit sometimes and he would have to protect both of them. He shivered at the thought. He hoped Lela would have sense enough not to leave her baby with Justice. *It's much too dangerous!*

Nito finished his tea and went back to his station. They were both glad they had had an opportunity to get to know each other better.

"I am not going to allow that girl to take my son away from me," Auryola said. She picked up the phone and called her ex-husband.

"This is Tim Hambrick." He was leaning back in his swivel chair with his feet propped on his desk. He had had a very successful quarter and was feeling really pleased with himself.

"Tim, this is Auryola, I'm calling about Alou."

"What's wrong?" he asked as he sat upright and gripped the phone. He had not heard from Auryola in years, and his heart began to race. He just knew something was seriously wrong with Alou. *Oh, God, don't let him be dead.*

"He needs you, he's having some problems. I wish you would talk with him."

"What kind of problems, Auryola?" *Thank God he's alive. Perhaps I can still find a way to have some kind of relationship with him.*

"It's some woman. I swear she has hoodooed him Tim. He brought me some divorce papers a couple of months ago. He has signed these papers stating that he is divorcing me, and now he's engaged to that woman. And a few weeks ago he slapped me. Can you believe . . .?"

"What's wrong with the woman?" Tim relaxed. He knew the woman must be okay if Auryola didn't like her. And for Alou to *divorce* his mother, she must really be something. "What's her name, Auryola?"

"Justiana Jurisprudence Fullilove, nickname Justice. Can you image someone giving a baby such a name?"

"No, but then I can't imagine anyone naming a baby Auryola. That shows you how small my imagination is." Tim scribbled the name on an index card.

"Well, I don't know why I expected you to try and help your son; you haven't done anything to help him all these years. But he's in really big trouble now. If you let him down this time Tim, and allow him to marry that girl, well . . ." she hung up. She figured that would bring him to Winston and maybe the two of them together could talk some sense into Alou. She knew the accusation about not helping Alou was a punch below the belt. She always knew just how to get Tim's goat.

ALOU'S PLANE WAS landing in Detroit, where he hoped to find his dad, while his dad's plane was flying through the air headed for Atlanta, where he hoped to meet Justice. After the call from Auryola, Tim decided that he would not allow her to cheat Alou of a relationship this time as she had done with him. But first he had to know what the young lady was like. Because Auryola didn't like her, he figured she must be okay, but he had to be sure. His source in Georgia had referred him to Snaggie as the best private investigator in Georgia. As soon as his plane landed, he called her.

Snaggie placed her coffee on the desk and picked up the phone. "Jones & Associates, how may I help you?"

"Do I need an appointment to retain your services or can I just walk in?" Tim asked.

"You can just walk in; I'm free now if you want to come on in. Do you know where we are located?"

"Yes, I have the address and a GPS that should bring me there. My name is Tim and I'll see you in about 20 minutes."

"Okay." Snaggie went to the break room to make a fresh pot of coffee. *Private investigators drink too much coffee. And I head the list of over drinkers*

Snaggie was sitting at her desk blowing the steaming coffee when Tim walked in. She looked up and sloshed coffee on the desk, some spilled on her hand, then she knocked the mug over and coffee spilled on the desk and ran onto the floor. Tim moved forward to help.

"Are you alright?" he asked as he picked up the cup and pulled her away from the coffee running off the desk.

"Yes, I think so," Snaggie said. She stared at him as if she was seeing a ghost.

"Is something wrong?

"No," she stammered. "When you called . . . I didn't expect ...I thought you would be Asian or something. You didn't sound like a Native American."

"I'm not Native American, I'm African American," Tim said as he extended his hand. "I'm Tim Hambrick."

"I'm Snaggie Jones, pleased to meet you Mr. Hambrick." She shook his hand. "Have a seat, I'll get some paper towels and clean this coffee up. I'll be with you momentarily." Tim sat and watched her. He wondered why she was so nervous. Something about his presence seemed to shake her up. *Maybe it's the nature of her work.*

"Where are you from?" Snaggie asked. "I don't think I've heard that accent before." She knew exactly who he was. When he walked in the door she thought he was Alou. *Alou's father is here and Alou is in Detroit looking for him.*

"Detroit presently, I'm originally from Washington."

"Washington State, way out west?"

"Yes." Tim chuckled. "You say way out west like it's a foreign country."

"Might as well be, I've never met anyone from that far away before. People born in Winston tend to stay here, and people born other places don't tend to come here. Although we have had a few newcomers in recent years. I guess the world is getting smaller." She threw the paper towels in the trash and sat down.

"Sorry 'bout that, how can I help you, Mr. Hambrick?"

"I want you to *stage* a meeting for me with a young lady. In other words, I want to meet her on the sly."

"I take it you have a particular young lady in mind."

"Yes," Tim said and pulled the index card from his pocket. "It's Justiana Jurisprudence Fullilove, the nickname is Justice, and she works as a public defender here in Winston."

Okay, let me see if I understand what you want, you want someone to arrange for you to cross her path without her knowing that you were looking for her.

"Precisely, and my source says that you are the best private eye in the state of Georgia."

Snaggie kept her head down and continued to make notes. She was afraid to let Mr. Hambrick see her face. She had to pretend she didn't know Justice. Snaggie finally raised her head and look into Mr. Hambrick's eyes, she had her emotions under control and knew that he would not be able to detect a hint of familiarity with the target on her part.

"Actually, Mr. Hambrick, we refer all *staging* work to another source. They are experts in that area; we specialize in locating and surveillance. We learned a long time ago, that we serve our customers best when we stay within our specialty. I can call the other agency and see if they can see you today." He agreed and Snaggie made the call. Noah was in and said Mr. Hambrick could come right over.

They stood and Snaggie walked him to the door and told him that he would be very pleased with the services of Noah & The Eye. She wanted to call Alou and tell him that his father was in Winston. She wanted to tell the old man that Alou was in Detroit looking for him. But Alou had made it very clear that she was to do what he paid her to do and stay out of his personal business. *And I'm not about to get in his personal business when it involves Justice Fullilove. No way.*

⌒

ALOU DECIDED NOT to go to his father's office since he couldn't find him at home or reach him by phone. He knew that he looked a lot like his dad, and the people at his office would figure out that his son was looking for him. He didn't know if they knew he had a son. So he decided to give up and return to Winston. He slipped his contact information through the mail slot in his dad's door and headed to the airport to check in the rental car in and hop a plane back to Atlanta.

⌒

IT TOOK ALL of Noah's skills to develop a disguise for Mr. Hambrick. He looked so much like Alou that Noah had to use a wig, change the color of his skin, and add a beard. He was quite satisfied with the finished product and was sure that Justice would not recognize him as Alou's father. Then Noah arranged a scheme for him to meet justice. Mr. Hambrick was walking in front of the courthouse when Justice returned to the courthouse after lunch.

"Excuse me Miss, could you tell me where the Greyhound Bus is, my nephew dropped me off and said it was near the courthouse. I have walked around the courthouse three times and I can't seem to locate it."

"Oh my goodness, he dropped you off at the wrong courthouse," Justice said. "The bus station near the courthouse is in Atlanta. The bus station in Winston is way out on Memorial Drive." He sat his suitcase down and stumbled as he attempted to step up on the step next to her.

"Are you okay?" she asked.

"Yes, I guess I'm a little hungry. My nephew was in such a rush to drop me off so he could get to work, I didn't have a chance to eat breakfast before I left home. But I had a big supper last night. I'm on my way to Montgomery to spend the summer with my baby sister. Justice glanced at her watch. Noah was watching from across the street.

"Tell you what, why don't you wait for me and I'll give you a ride to the bus station. I pass right by it on my way home. I will probably be done in 30 to 45 minutes. What time does the bus leave?"

It's not by reservation, just whenever I get there. My nephew already purchased the ticket and a bus leaves for Montgomery every two hours."

"You can wait inside the courtroom or in the hallway if you don't like courtrooms. What did you say your name was?"

"Henderson, Thomas Henderson. I'll wait in the hallway," he said and followed her into the building. He gave Noah a slight nod and wave as they walked up the steps.

❧

JUSTICE WAS FINISHED and back in the hallway in 30 minutes. She came and found Tim nodding on the bench. She went over and touched him to wake him up.

"Okay, I'm done. I can take you to the bus stop. But first we are going to get you something to eat. It's a long drive to Montgomery."   She took him to Winston's Deli for lunch and Justice insisted that Tim eat a big lunch. Tim made sure she did most of the talking. He asked her lots of questions about Winston and her work. She loved talking about her cases. He was careful not to ask about her boyfriend. She eventually told him that Alou was out of town and that his mom did not like her.

"I would love to have a daughter-in-law like you," Tim said.

"Thank you, Mr. Henderson." *I sure hope Mr. Hambrick feels that way.*

❧

ALOU CALLED JUSTICE from the airport, "Hey precious, I'm giving up and heading back to the love of my life."

"Did you go to his office?" she asked.

"No, but I left my contact information at his house. Now the ball is in his court. I also addressed a letter to him at his office and marked it personal and confidential. I'm sure he will know I have been here. Whatever happens after that, I can live with."

"Alou, I'm sure your dad will call you when he gets the letter. When you get back to Winston, I'm cooking you a big meal and we're gonna watch a good movie, and I'm gonna kiss you until you're silly."

"That will take a lot of kisses," Alou said. "Are you prepared to stick with it until I'm silly?"

"Yes, I am," she said. "What's your flight number and time of arrival?"

"Flight 1403 arriving at 5:45 pm, but I'll take a cab. I want you to stay home and wait for me." Justice repeated the flight number and time as she wrote it on the napkin. Tim made a mental note of the information.

"Alou, it's not even dark at 5:45. I can pick you up."

"I will take a cab. End of discussion."

"Okay, but come straight to my place; don't run off with some other woman."

"If I'm tempted, I'll put up the strongest resistance and try to get to you before seven.

Justice said goodbye and clicked the cell phone off. "Sorry bout that."

"No problem. So, your boyfriend wrote his dad a letter," Tim asked. This was the first time he became aware that Alou was trying to reach him. *Go easy, don't ask too many questions; allow her to do the talking.*

"Well, it's supposed to be a secret, but I suppose that's for people who live in Winston." She looked around to be sure no one was in earshot. "He actually went to Detroit to look for his dad, but hasn't been able to catch up with him. He's coming home this afternoon. But he left a letter for him and a note in his mailbox. His dad will know he's trying to reach him, and I'm sure he will call Alou."

"I've seen that look before; I think you are in love with that young man."

"I am," Justice said and sighed.

"You don't seem to be happy about being in love with him?"

"I don't mind loving him; I just wish I didn't love him so much. His mom hates me and I have no idea why. She teamed up with his ex-girlfriend to try and break us up. Sometimes I feel like giving up, because I think she is going to win in the end. It seems that she has always won over Alou's will and desires in the past. But somehow he thinks that the two of us together can win this time. He has taken some pretty serious steps. If he finds his dad and he doesn't like me; I don't know what I'll do. In a way, I'm relieved that he didn't find his dad. But I hope he finds him eventually. I know that's selfish of me. But I just want us to be free from all this outside interference all the time. I guess you think I'm pretty awful, huh?"

"No, I think you are very precious and Alou is lucky to have someone like you. And he sounds like a fine young man also. I just know things are going to work out for you."

"Thank you. Well, we better get you to the bus stop. Your sister will be worried about you." He reached for his wallet, but Justice waved him off.

"You are in my town, and I'm paying. If I come to Montgomery this summer, you can pay."

⁓

AFTER JUSTICE DROPPED Tim off at the bus stop, she went to pick up a movie that she and Alou would watch. She was checking to see that everything was in place when the doorbell rang. She hurried to the door and wondered if by some mean Alou had arrived early.

"Hello," Ericka said when she opened the door. "Please listen to me Justice, I know you have no reason to believe me, but I came to apologize. I would like to come in, but if you don't want me to, I'll do it from right here."

"Okay," Justice said. "Go ahead." She folded her arms and stared at Ericka.

"I was wrong for allowing Mrs. Hambrick to get me involved in a scheme to try and break you and Alou up. It finally dawned on me that she didn't like me any more than she likes you, actually less. And Alou wouldn't want me even if we managed to break you two up. When I saw your car on fire, I was sick. I kept thinking that the last thing I had tried to do to you was awful, and if you died in that crash I would feel so bad about my actions. I was glad to hear that you were okay, and made up my mind that I would apologize to you if I ever got the chance. Well, I just wanted to let you know that I'm sorry for my part in that foolishness. Good night." Ericka turned and started to leave.

"Wait," Justice said. "Why don't you come in? I guess I'm just a little shocked."

Ericka walked into the living room and looked around. "Hey, this is a nice place you have here"

"Thank you," Justice said. "Have a seat. Would you like something to drink?

"No, I just wanted you to know how sorry I am about what happened. When I watched that video of you and Alou, I realized how much he loves you. Alou never pretended that he loved me. He wanted a piece of "poon tang", and I wanted to be on the arm of a handsome man, for him to spend money on me, and take me to The Club. We both got what we wanted, and that was it. He never looked at me the way he looks at you, and he never treated me the way he treats you . . .You know Justice, even though you were kind of silly for taking your clothes off the way you did that night. I kinda understand why you did it—I mean the reason why you were angry. No one wants their business about their sex live in the streets. That's private and personal. I was so angry when I say how Alou treated you. No one has ever treated me like that. But then Mrs. Hambrick pointed out, indirectly, that you were a lady, and I was not. She really helped to open my eyes that night, even though I know she was just being mean. I'm never going to sell myself cheap again, and I never want anything else to do with her. And I'm through talking."

"Thank you, Ericka. I don't know what to say."

"Well, will you accept my apology?"

"Yes, I accept your apology."

"Thank you, then I'll be on my way. Will you tell Alou that I'm sorry?"

"Yes, I will."

"Well, good night," Ericka said as she stood and moved toward the door. As Justice followed her to the door, she felt an urge to ask her about her eternal estate. She tried to ignore it, but it wouldn't leave. *Well, here goes.*

"Ericka, are you a Christian?"

Ericka turned and stared at Justice. "I went to church when I was a kid, and I haven't done anything really bad. Well, maybe sleeping around. But I've never done drugs or really hurt anyone. What I tried to do to you didn't work out, so I guess I am. . . But I haven't been to church in a long time. So, I guess not. But I do pray sometimes."

Justice felt such compassion for Ericka. She wondered how many people were walking around in limbo about their salvation. *We are doing a poor job of reaching lost, hurting, and confused people.*

She reached out and took both of Ericka's hands in hers. Ericka just stood there with her mouth open.

"You know Ericka, Christianity is not about going to church, or not sleeping around, or not doing drugs. It's about accepting a person, Jesus Christ. He's the one that has the power to change your life. Would you like a change in your life?"

"Yes," Ericka said without any hesitation.

"I can help you with that. Would you like to pray now and know for sure that you are a Christian?"

"Yes."

"Okay, bow your head and repeat after me. Dear Heavenly Father, I realize that I'm a sinner and I need a savior. I believe that you sent your Son to die for my sins. Lord Jesus, come into my heart and into my life. I receive you as my Lord and Savior. In Jesus' name I pray. Amen."

Ericka repeated the prayer after Justice as the tears streamed down her face. Justice embraced her and she cried and cried. Justice didn't know what to say. She had no idea why Ericka was crying. She just held her and patted her on the back until she was able to speak.

"I'm sorry for crying like that, but no one has ever shown any real concern for me before.

When I sat in Mrs. Hambrick's living room and realized that she didn't care one thing about me, I was so angry with all the people that have used me all my life. And none of them have ever cared about me. Alou was the only man who continued to speak to me after our affair was over. The others slept with me and called me all kind of sweet names, but looked the other way when they saw me later. I don't know how I allowed myself to be used by Mrs. Hambrick like that. And I don't know how you could be so kind to me after what I tried to do to you, Justice."

Justice placed her hand on Ericka's back as they walked to the door. "Remember when you said that my burning car could have been your car rolling down that embankment? Well, that could have been me looking for love and not finding it. Being a Christian is about loving everyone and forgiving people, even when they don't ask. That's because God always forgives us and never stops loving us, and He gives us the ability to do the same."

"How can I ever thank you?" Ericka asked.

"By always realizing that you are very special to God. And remembering that He loves you even when you mess up, and that He will always forgive you and give you another chance, if you ask."

"I will never forget that, and I will never forget this night. Good night Justice, I'll see you later."

"Good night, Ericka." Justice stood on the stairs until Ericka was in her car. They waved to each other and Ericka drove away. She could not stop the tears. *Why in the world am I crying!*

Chapter

30

Tim was waving a big sign with Alou's name on it near the baggage claim section. Alou saw him and stopped to stare. It was like looking at himself in a mirror. The range of emotions he felt surprised him. He felt anger, frustration, joy, confusion, and finally, relief. They both cried. Neither could think of anything to say. Alou had not checked his luggage, so he turned to his dad and said, let's go out front and get a cab."

"Okay," Tim said and silently walked along beside him. "It turns out that I arrived in Winston about the time you reached Detroit. I met Justice."

Alou stopped and stared at him. "You did what?"

"I met Justice, and I have only one thing to say about her."

"And what might that be?"

"If you don't marry her, I will."

"Did you tell her that?"

"No, she didn't even know who I was. I wore a disguise and told her my name was Thomas Henderson."

"Why would you lie to her?" Alou asked and frowned.

"I wanted to get to know what kind of person she was without her knowing what I was up to. Look, son, Auryola called and said that you were in trouble, that some girl had bewitched you, and all kind of crazy things. I came because I didn't want her to squeeze the young lady out of your life the way she did me. I wanted to do what I could to stop Auryola, but I had to know if she was right for you."

Alou was angry. "Since when did you become an expert on what's right for me? And how did you find Justice?"

"I hired a private investigator, and he staged a meeting with her in front of the courthouse. He made me a disguise and I wore a hat. I asked her for directions, pretended I was trying to find the bus station near the courthouse. She told me I was at the wrong courthouse, offered to take me to the bus stop and stopped to buy me lunch on the way. We were having lunch when you called and gave her your flight information. That was when I learned that you were looking for me."

"You owe Justice an apology. You had no right to deceive her like that."

"Okay," Tim said. "I hope she won't be angry with me. At least she knows I like her. Maybe that will earn me some brownie points."

They took a cab to Alou's house, dropped of his travel bags, hopped in his car, and headed for Justice's condo. They were both silent during most of the drive. Each was lost in his own thoughts. When Alou rang the doorbell, Justice opened the door and greeted him with a big smile.

"Welcome back . . ." She stopped, stared at Tim, then frowned. He had the face of Alou, fast forwarded a few years, but the clothes and body belonged to Mr. Henderson. For a moment she was confused. Then it hit her. *That's Alou's dad. Then why did he . . .*

She felt anger creeping up on her. "So, you never went to Detroit, you called me on your cell phone while your father led me around like an idiot. What is it with you Hambricks, what is it that make you people think you can treat me any old way? Why don't you two just leave."

Tim was mortified. He was so disappointed with himself. He had no idea he would create such confusion. He wanted to tell Justice that Alou didn't know he was in Winston, but he was unable to speak.

"Justice," Alou said. "I swear I didn't know . . ."

"Look Alou, it doesn't even matter any more. I am just so tired of all this confusion. So I would appreciate it if you just left me alone. She closed the door and left them standing there. *No point in slamming it, don't be angry, just forget him. Them.*

"I'm going to see Solomon," Alou said. "Maybe he can talk some sense into her. Why didn't you tell her what happened." He turned to look at his dad.

He simply shook his head. He tried to speak and couldn't. He look so dejected, Alou felt a ting of pity for him. *He meant well, but he sure didn't do well.*

⤙

SOLOMON STARED FROM Alou to his father. "This has to be you father, Alou. Now I know exactly how you will look a few years from now. It's like seeing into the future. Come in."

They walked in and Solomon motioned for them to sit on the couch. He sat across from them on the love seat.

"What's up?" Solomon asked.

"We had a big misunderstanding with Justice. Well, I went to Detroit to look for my dad, the same day he came to Winston to stage a meeting with Justice. He pretended he was looking for the Greyhound bus station, because he was on his way to Montgomery. She gave him a ride to the greyhound bus station. When he showed up at her door with me, she figured out he was my dad and thought we had planned the whole thing. I had no idea he was in Winston."

"And Justice couldn't tell that he was your father?"

"He had someone make him a disguise."

"Well, what did you expect her to think? You said you were going to Detroit, he said he was going to Montgomery. He obviously didn't go to Montgomery, is it so unreasonable for her to think you didn't go to Detroit either?" Solomon was just a bit ticked off with Alou and his dad.

"She should know I went to Detroit, she dropped me off at the airport."

"But she also dropped your dad off at the bus station, and he didn't go to Montgomery, in fact, he never intended to go. Being dropped off at the airport and going to another city is two different things." Solomon turned to Mr. Hambrick and his voice softened. The man looked like he was going to cry.

"So, what were you thinking, sir?" he asked gently.

"I guess I wasn't really thinking at all, at least, not too clearly. I was just trying to prevent Auryola from hurting Justice the way she hurt me, and depriving Alou again of someone who cared about him. There is no way I can tell you how many times I tried to see and talk with Alou. But she was so determined to keep me away from him. I'd come to the house or call or leave a note in the mailbox. She wouldn't allow him to answer the phone or door or pick up the mail. The few times he forgot and answered the door or phone, she would scream and yell until I couldn't stand it anymore. We went to court until I was out of money and fight. Many times she was sick, or in the hospital, or Alou was sick. She moved several times and it took weeks to locate her. So, I gave up . . . By the time Alou was old enough to make his own decision about who he wanted to live with, I figured I was just a stranger to him.

"So I came here fully prepared to spend all my time and resources to stop her from coming between Justice and Alou. But, I felt I had to know what kind of person Justice was before I embarked on that venture. Obviously, I went about it the wrong way. Now I have hurt Alou more than Auryola ever did. I have failed him twice; I don't know how I can live with myself."

"Hey, it's not as bad as it seems," Solomon said. "Justice is a reasonable young woman with a quick temper. She loves Alou and obviously took a liking to you. Believe me, she'll . . ."

The phone rang and Solomon stood and walked over to his desk. "Excuse me," he said as he checked caller ID. He grabbed the phone and sat on the desk.

"Hello, kiddo, what's up?" Solomon asked.

"I just shot my big mouth off at Alou and Mr. Henderson, and even though I acted better than I normally act, I know I somehow missed the Kingdom."

"Wait, back up, who is Mr. Henderson?" She explained what had happened and Solomon turned to look at Mr. Hambrick.

"I see. Well, you didn't get it exactly right, but you didn't get it all wrong either. So you are learning to press you way into the Kingdom, kiddo. In the Kingdom you should be *quick* to hear, *slow* to speak, and *slow* to wrath.' If you follow that order, you will very seldom get to wrath."

"I'm just so angry that they deceived me like that."

"Hold on, I'm going to put you on hold and get another phone." Solomon placed the phone on hold, held up a finger to let the Hambricks know he would be back in a minute, and went into the den to pick up the extension.

"Do you know for sure that Alou was in on it?" Solomon asked.

"Well, pretty sure, what other explanation could there be?"

"You should give him the opportunity to explain that. Remember, you should be quick to listen."

"Okay."

"Do you still love Alou?"

She sighed and frowned. "You know the answer to that Solomon; you don't just stop loving someone because they hurt you, even if you do hate them."

Solomon chuckled. "Then, don't you think you owe it to him to hear his explanation about what really happened, even if you do hate him?"

"Yes, I guess so. I guess I'll just call him and tell him I'm sorry for jumping to conclusions without hearing what he had to say."

"Good idea. You are pressing your way into the Kingdom, kiddo."

"Thanks Solomon, for listening to an idiot."

"You're welcome. It's not easy being young and in love is it, kiddo?"

"No," she said and giggled. "I'll make the call now, over and out."

☞

ALOU'S CELL PHONE rang as Solomon walked back into the living room. Solomon told him it was probably Justice and Alou looked at caller ID, flipped the phone open, and said, "Justice."

"Alou," she said, and they just held the phone. Alou stood and walked to the window and stood staring out. Solomon and Mr. Hambrick made small talk by whispering. They had no idea they were just holding the phone. Justice finally broke the silence.

"Can you two come back to my place?"

"Yes, and I really didn't know . . ."

"Alou, it really doesn't matter. You are here now, and that's all I care about."

"Okay, we will see you in a few minutes."

Tim looked at Alou as hope filled his heart. "This is wonderful. After I have a chance to apologize to her, I will keep my big mouth shut. I promise I won't say another word."

"Justice is not that kind of person, Dad. After she forgives you, it's all over. She doesn't hold grudges. She will insist that you talk. She's a wonderful person, you'll see. You will love her once you get to know her."

"Son, I know she's a wonderful person, and I already love her. You couldn't find a better woman to marry. I'll never understand Auryola. But I'm glad she called me. This is all going to work out in the end."

They said goodbye to Solomon and headed back to Justice's condo.

"Alou . . . can you ever find it in your heart to forgive me for not standing up to Auryola?" Tim asked as they walked down the steps.

"Yes, because I love you, and because I need Justice to forgive me for not standing up to her sooner. When Justice put mother in her place, it was the only thing that gave me the courage to stand up to her. I know Justice will forgive me and I forgive you."

Mr. Hambrick was apprehensive. He didn't know how Justice would react to him. When she opened the door she went straight to Mr. Hambrick, took both his hands in hers and looked into his eyes.

"The next time I meet an old man looking for the Greyhound bus station, I'm going to make him wash his face and pull on his hair and beard. No one will ever pull that one on me again. So, you see, I learned something from this; don't trust old men looking for the bus station. And now you know that your son is in love with a hot-tempered idiot."

"I don't know any such thing, but I know he has an idiot for a father. Now, will you forgive me for using such poor judgment?"

"Of course, I forgive you. Did you mean it when you said you would be happy to have a daughter-in-law like me?"

"I've never meant anything more. I told Alou, 'If you don't marry her, I will.' I think he believes you will automatically choose him over me. But I know I have as good a chance as he does, because young women like older men these days. They treat women better."

"Do I have to make up my mind now, or can I sleep on it?"

"I'll give you a few days."

Justice embraced Alou and he kissed her on the forehead. "Hey, did you miss me lady?"

"I did and I'm glad you're back. If you two are as hungry as I am, we should find a good restaurant and get something to eat. I know I said I would cook, but I had a visitor, which you will be happy to hear about, Alou. So you get a rain check on the homemade dinner."

Mr. Hambrick watched in silence as Justice and Alou tried to decide where to go for dinner. He was already enjoying his son and the lady he hoped would be his daughter-in-law.

⌒

SOLOMON WAS THINKING about Justice and Alou and the way trouble always seems to find them when his doorbell rang. He looked out the peephole and saw his Aunt Gracie.

"Hey," he said as he opened the door. "Should I beware of Romans, or should I say aunts, bearing gifts?" He took the salad from her hands and ushered her into his living room.

"I have pizza and tea in the car. Four of the women who were supposed to come to the bridge game tonight can't make it. Can you believe that? I go to all the trouble to make pizza for them and they tell me at the last minute that they can't come. And it's turkey pizza and quite delicious. Come along and get the pizza and tea, dear. Maybe you can share it with your friend, Justice. I have to get back before the other eight ladies arrive. I wanted to bring the pizza to you while it was still hot."

Solomon asked her about each member of the bridge club as he walked to the car with her to get the pizza and tea. He knew each one by name. He was always the fortunate recipient of the extra food; whenever one or more them did not show up for the game. He figured that remembering their names and a little about them was the least he could do for the delicious food he received when they didn't show. *Keep it up ladies. And enough for four, I'll take it over to Justice's. It will be my gift to Alou's father. I know they will love it. Besides, I certainly can't eat it all.*

⌒

SOLOMON RUSHED OVER to take the food to Justice's before they left to buy food. He knew his aunt's pizza would be better than anything they could get at a restaurant. The aroma was breath taking. They were delighted and insisted that Solomon stay and eat with them. Solomon didn't want to intrude, but was finally persuaded to stay. He was glad he did. The food was delicious and they had such a good time. Solomon hated to leave. Mr. Hambrick was humorous and reminded him a lot of his own father. He had forgotten how much he missed his father. He felt that he could discuss anything with Mr. Hambrick. He looked at Alou and thought, he has Justice and Mr. Hambrick, what do I have? He suddenly felt so lonely; he wanted to cry. He stood and shook hands with Alou and Mr. Hambrick, and gave Justice a hug.

"I better get home before I turn into a pumpkin. It was a pumpkin that the deserted person turned into wasn't it?"

They all laughed and Justice walked him to the door. Mr. Hambrick just sat there and smiled. He was so thankful Alou was willing to forgive him. He knew it would take some time for Alou to forgive him completely, but Justice had already forgiven him. *Well I guess I didn't do as much damage as I thought, and she will see to it that he forgives me. She's my kind of girl.*

When Alou and his dad got to his place, they talked well into the night. When they went to bed, neither was able to sleep. Alou tried to sort through his life and see how he could make some sense out of his current predicament. He was overjoyed with the fact that everything was okay with his dad and Justice. He wished he could forget his mother, but he could not. He thought of the fact that she had been such a good mother to him all those years. The only thing she had done wrong was deprive him of a relationship with his dad and try to break up his relationship with Justice. And now he would have the opportunity to develop a relationship with his dad, and she had been unsuccessful in her attempt to destroy his relationship with Justice. So why can't I have a relationship with my mother now, he wondered. But he knew the answer, he would have to give Justice up, and that he could not do. *Why is life so hard?*

31

Thursday, November 1, 2007, was Alou's 31st birthday. Justice made reservations at *The California*, a new restaurant in Atlanta. She was excited and kept calling Alou to ask him questions throughout the day on Wednesday.

When he arrived at her place, he didn't like her blouse. "Where did you get that blouse?"

"At Leslie's." Justice looked down at her new blouse.

"And they didn't have the kind you usually wear?"

"Yes, but I wanted to try something different."

"Why, what made you buy a blouse like that?"

Justice felt both anger and disappointment wash over her. The sales clerk had assured her that Alou would love the blouse. "Men like to see a little cleavage, but not too much," the clerk said. "And this would be perfect for celebrating his birthday."

"Alou, you are not my husband or my father, what make you think you can tell me how to dress?"

"Okay, I'm not your husband yet. So tell me, what am I to you? Do I have a right to just ask you a question about the blouse?"

Justice sighed, took Alou by the hand, and led him to the couch. He sat and turned to stare at her. He wanted to hear her explanation.

"I was excited about celebrating your birthday and going to a new restaurant in Atlanta. When I told the sales clerk why I needed a new blouse, she suggested this one. I guess

I just took her word for it because she was so old. She was at least 50 years old. And she said you would love it. I just wasn't thinking. I'll go change it." She started to get up, and Alou pulled her back down and put his arm around her.

"Justice, I'm not criticizing you, but you should never change you ideas and values to conform to someone else's. I love everything about you; just the way you are. Sure, I wanna see your cleavage. As a matter of fact, I wouldn't mind if you took the blouse and the bra off. I would like to see the whole thing. But that's not something I want every man in Atlanta to see." When he released her, she went to change the blouse.

She looked in the mirror as she tucked her blouse into her skirt. Her mind went to the conversation she and Lela had had with Lela's mom when they asked why they couldn't wear hot pants and a halter top to Lela's dad's company picnic. Miss Mary had been very descriptive in her objection.

"When you expose your breast and cleavage to men, you are letting them know that you want them to imagine or think about making love to you. Now there may come a time when you really feel that way about a man. But it should not be every man in DC, and it should never be when you are out in public. So those type clothing should be reserved for someone that you are in covenant with, and in a private setting. Exposing you body to men under any other circumstance is unbecoming and unladylike."

Both Justice and Lela had watched to see how men would react to women who wore low cut blouses and dresses at the picnic. Some men went to great lengths to avoid looking at the lady's bosom. They stared at their hands, their feet, and then they stared out across the park. They seemed so uncomfortable, Lela and Justice felt sorry for them. Others blatantly stared at the women's bosoms. Justice and Lela had agreed that they never wanted a man to stare at their bosom, or put forth so much effort to avoid looking. But that was eleven years ago. Justice wondered if the rules were the same. Today's men didn't seem to pay much attention to women with low cut blouses and dresses. She would have to talk with Miss Mary about that the next time she was in Tampa.

When she came back into the living room, Alou stood and smiled. "Now, that's my girl, and you are gorgeous, as always. Justice, you are perfect just the way you are. You don't need to change anything about you. And I ought to know; I'm an expert on how a female should look. Tell me you are not angry with me."

"I'm not. I have a mind of my own, I should have used it."

"Then you won't be angry if I insist on driving. I think you are too excited to make it all the way to Atlanta and back." He couldn't imagine why she was so excited about going to a restaurant in Atlanta. But pretty soon he was caught up in the excitement, and they sang, giggled, and told jokes all the way to Atlanta. When they arrived at the restaurant, Justice was blown away. The restaurant seemed to be setting in a desert. There were cactuses, palm trees, rocks, and beautiful tropical plants. They walked all the way around the building. Every few steps, Justice would stop and kiss Alou. He relaxed, smiled, shook his head, and enjoyed it. Once seated, Justice could not decide what she wanted to eat. After about 20 minutes, she decided on a chef's salad and red velvet cake. She wanted the cake served with the meal. The food was delicious, Justice talked non-stop, and Alou enjoyed every minute of it.

Both Alou and Justice had taken Friday off and planned to spend the day together. Alou wanted to take her back to Atlanta and show her all the streets named Peachtree. Then they would go to the Carter and MLK Centers. After a shopping spree at Hemp Hill Mall, they would have dinner at *The California* before returning to Winston. Justice was thrilled with the idea.

"How many streets can they have named Peachtree?" Justice asked.

"Well, there's Peachtree Chase, Peachtree Road, Peachtree Way, Peachtree Jump Up, Peachtree Jump Back Down . . . "

Justice began laughing and couldn't stop. She tried to tell Alou that she didn't believe him, but she couldn't stop laughing.

"Then there's Peachtree Holler, and the next street is Peachtree Be Quiet."

"You are making that up," Justice was finally able to manage. "There's no such street in Atlanta."

"No, I'm not. And there's also Peachtree Run, Peachtree Walk, and Peachtree Don't Walk . . ."

Justice placed her hand over Alou's mouth and they both laughed until they cried.

When she was able to talk, Justice reached over and took Alou's hand, leaned her head on his shoulder and giggled. "You know what I wish, Alou? I wish you didn't have to go home tonight. I wish you could spend the night with me and hold me in your arms all night."

"Stop it baby, don't do this to me."

"You don't have a baby, you're not even married."

"I would like to take care of both of those issues tonight. You really want me to stay; I'll sleep in the guest room."

"No, you can't stay. Nito would know you were there and he would think we were up there rolling in the hay. That would be a bad influence on him."

"What if I left, parked my car a few blocks away, and snuck back. He wouldn't have to know I was there."

"But he would see you when you came back to the door. Remember, he's watching the door."

"I don't pay those people to make me miserable. Why don't we go to my place and spend the night?"

"Then he would know I spent the night with you and would think we are at your place rolling in the hay."

Okay, Justice, let's just call Nito in and tell him that we are spending the night together but we are sleeping in separate rooms."

"Then he would be suspicious because we had to tell him. He wouldn't believe us and it would be a bad influence on him. Alou, we have to be careful how we impact the lives of young people—But we could tell him that I'm spending the night with Lela, and tell him to go home."

"But," Alou said. "He might wait for us to leave before he left and he would know if you didn't go to Lela's."

"It was a bad idea, Justice said. "Let's just forget it."

"No, I think it was a great idea. Let's find a way to do it."

"The answer is no, and this silly discussion is over. Period."

"Over and done." Alou wondered why they had spent so much time trying to figure out a way to spend the night together to sleep in separate rooms. And that had not been the original idea; she said she wanted him to hold her in his arms all night. *That would never work, what was I thinking?*

Chapter

32

When they got to Justice's place, they talked about moving the wedding date up. Justice wanted a June wedding. Alou tried to get her to move it up to the Thanksgiving weekend. She said that moving the date would not allow them enough time to make all the arrangements, and she also had a trial starting the Monday after Thanksgiving. They finally agreed on Valentine day of 2008 and Alou stood and walked toward the door.

He stopped and turned to Justice as she walked him to the door. "Why don't we take off our shoes, get into your bed, and I hold you in my arms for 15 minutes."

She giggled. "Okay, I guess that can't hurt anything."

Alou had meant it as a joke. But he was not about to turn it down. If she agreed to something like that, he would use the opportunity to teach her that that is not something she should ever agree to. They went into the bedroom and took off their shoes. Alou took off his jacket, picked Justice up and kissed her before he laid her on the bed. He could tell that she was a little flustered. He slipped into bed beside her and kissed her again.

"Alou, I don't think we need to be doing all this kissing."

"Okay," he said. "Just one more little kiss." When his lips touched hers, she moaned and Alou's mind went on vacation. He forgot all the promises he had made to her, to God, and to himself about waiting until after they were married. He held her gently and tightly and kept telling himself to let it go, but he couldn't. Instead of teaching her a lesson, he was leaning a lesson about the power of the flesh.

Justice slipped her arms around his neck and melted into his arms. She realized that she had no power to resist him. None whatsoever. Then she remembered her promise to Miss Mary and began to pray in her heart. *God, can you please help me. I need your help right now.*

The phone rang and they both ignored it. The ringing stopped and suddenly they heard Lela's voice. "Justice, what's wrong with you?"

They both sat up and turned toward the voice. They expected to see Lela standing by the bed. They breathed a sigh of relief when they realized it was the answering machine.

"You two were supposed to go to a restaurant called The California, and not head out west to the state of California. Did you get mixed up? It's after ten o'clock and you know I'm waiting up ..."

Justice picked up the phone. "Hello."

"Girl, are you in bed? Did you forget to call me or what?"

"Yes, I'm in bed . . ."

"I'm sorry sweetie; I should have known that you wouldn't sleep a wink the night before. Answer two questions for me, is The California as beautiful as it looks on the internet, and did you two have a good time?"

"Yes to both."

"Go back to sleep, we'll talk tomorrow. Bye."

Justice said bye and hung up. Alou had already slipped on his shoes and jacket. There were no words to describe the disgust he felt with himself. *She trusted me, and look what I almost did.*

Justice swung her legs over the side of the bed and looked up at Alou. He stood there with his hands in his pocket and stared at her. "Justice, what's the matter?" he asked as he took a step toward her. *He could see that she was shaking and he thought he saw fear in her eyes.*

"Nothing," she said and held up her hands to stop him. She wanted him to leave, but she didn't want to be rude. "Can we talk later? I just want to get to bed now."

"Look, I promise you, on my word of honor, I cross my heart and hope to die, this will never happen again until we're married. I don't know what happened, but I promise you, it's never going to happen again."

"It's okay," she said. *Now please go.*

"No, it's not okay, and I'm not leaving until you tell me what's wrong. What are you feeling, and why are you shaking?"

"Really, I'm okay. Please, Alou, can we talk later?"

"Okay," he said and sighed. "Call me when you get up tomorrow and let me know what time we are leaving for Atlanta." *How am I going to fix this?*

"Okay."

As soon as Alou left, Justice called his home number and left a message that she had changed her mind about going to Atlanta the next day, and that she would call him later that afternoon. *One can always take the coward's way out.*

The next morning, Justice waited until she was sure Ted had left for work before going to Lela's house.

"Hey," Lela said. "I was just about to . . . what's wrong; did you and Alou have a fight?"

"No. But I'm frustrated and scared."

"Of what?"

"Me . . . and what happened last night."

"What happened?" Lela's eyes narrowed as she stared at Justice.

"We got into bed together. He was just going to hold me in his arms for 15 minutes. He kept kissing me and I had no power to resist him. Absolutely none. Although nothing really bad happened, he had complete control over me. I never want to be in a situation like that again, and I will never allow anyone to have that kind of control over me again."

They moved to the kitchen table, Lela began to question Justice, and she told her everything that happened that evening. Lela was angry with Justice when she told her about the blouse and how she had said she wished Alou didn't have to go home, and then agreed to get into bed with him for 15 minutes. Lela wanted to punch Justice. *How did this girl get to be such an idiot?*

"What were you thinking?" Lela asked. "Were you trying to make the man seduce you? What happened to your brain Justice Fullilove?"

Justice closed her eyes and lowered her head. She wanted to cry. She was hoping Lela would understand and help her sort things out.

"You better not cry! You better not shed one tear! You instigated the whole thing. First, you exposed your breast to the man."

"I didn't, it was just a blouse, and it was not . . ."

"Then you suggested that he spend the night and hold you in his arms all night . . ."

"But I didn't really mean literally hold . . ."

"And what did you think a man would want from you if he held you in his arms all night? Alou is not a toy soldier, Justice; he's a flesh and blood man. And to take your clothes off and get into bed with . . ."

Justice stood up. "We didn't take our clothes off; we only took our shoes off." Justice felt like she had been slammed with a baseball bat. Lela had always made her feel better about her mistakes before. Justice knew she had to get away from Lela. She hurried through the living room and out the door. *I have turned Lela against me, now I don't have anyone to turn to.*

Lela just sat there. She saw the disappointment in Justice's eyes, but she was unable to speak or move. She and Justice had always tried to make each other feel better about their mistakes in the past. She wanted to call Justice back but her voice would not work. She was suddenly overcome with anger at Justice and her own guilt because she knew she was trying to make Justice live up to the promise they had made to her mother. She had to find a way to make Justice keep her promise, because she was unable to keep hers. And it's all so unfair to Justice. *But she has to keep her promise for both of us. I'll figure out a way to fix this later.*

Justice knew exactly why Lela was so upset with her, and she really couldn't blame her. She decided that she would find a way to help Lela get over her own guilt once she was able to work through her own issues with Alou. *Lela was right about what I did, but I didn't think of it that way at the time. What was I thinking? It was so unfair to Alou. But shouldn't he have known better too? I'm going to make an appointment with Solomon and learn how to live by Kingdom principles every day of my life.*

⌒

"Hey kiddo," Solomon said as he ushered Justice into his living room. "What's up?"

"I need to know how to press my way into the Kingdom and live my life by Kingdom principles every day."

"I like that determination. What brought you to that conclusion?"

She told him about her evening with Alou, her attempt to discuss it with Lela, and what Miss Mary said about a woman exposing her cleavage. "I know what I did was wrong, so, tell me how to recognize bad choices before hand. It's all clear in hindsight."

"Well, I can see you had some concerns about the blouse, but that was no big deal. It's just not who you are, and you recognize that now. For the most part, I agree with Miss Mary that most of the time, women expose their bodies because they want the attention of a man, or to feel sexy. But many of them do so because it's fashionable. Not all people who design clothing are Kingdom minded. But Alou told you he didn't like it, and you took it off. So that's history. I personally like a woman that can look sexy without exposing her body. I love looking at the female body, but I don't want my lady's body on display for every man in Winston.

"As to your telling him that you wish he didn't have to go home, that was just your way of saying that you were having a good time and didn't want it to end. You weren't saying let's sleep together. And I'm sure Alou understood that, and he probably felt the same way. So that's history.

"But his suggestion about getting into bed and his holding you in his arms for 15 minutes, I'm not sure what that was about. But I know it was not about trying to seduce you. Only Alou can tell you why he did that. But I think he may have been the one who was really surprised. Whatever his plan was, I think it backfired on him, and now you are hiding from him and he's disgusted with himself.

"There's nothing unusual about the way you felt. That's the power of carnality. We have very limited control over our flesh and what we feel, but we can always control our behavior and not get into those type situations. What you don't seem to recognize is that Alou didn't have any more control over you than you had over him. He couldn't resist you and you couldn't resist him. In the end you were afraid and he was disgusted. But it was for the same reason. So how do you gain the victory over that type of thing? Recognize the flesh for what it is and remember what the Bible teaches: Don't make room for the Devil.

"Now, let me give you some advice about Alou. He has probably been rolling in the hay since he was a teenager, but he gave it all up for you. I would say that's true love. Justice, don't end up married to some other man five or ten years from now and spend the rest of your life wishing you had married Alou. I can't tell you how many patients I see each year that are in that predicament. Life is never going to be perfect, but the kind of love you two have for each other usually comes around only once in a lifetime. Don't run away from that kind of love, you may never find it again. He has never been mean to you, he has never mistreated you, he has only loved you and tried to make you happy. What more do you want from him, or for yourself?"

"Thank you, Solomon. We will never need to have this conversation again."

BOTH ALOU AND Lela had been calling Justice all afternoon. Lela answered her phone on the first ring. "Girl, where have you ..."

"Lela, I'm a new person. Let's have lunch tomorrow and I'll tell you all about it."

"Okay," Lela said and got off the phone. She was too tired and frustrated to argue and she was relieved to know that Justice was okay.

Alou glanced at caller ID and picked up the phone. "Justice, where are you, what's wrong, Precious?"

"I'm an idiot."

Alou started to laugh and couldn't stop. "Is that all that's wrong?" he finally managed. But she was laughing also and couldn't answer. After about ten minutes they were able to talk.

"Hey, can I come over, I need to talk with you," Alou said.

"Yes, and I need to talk with you, too. Alou, I'm never gonna ... well, if I... Alou, would you do something for me?"

"Yes, what is it?"

"If I ever try to kick you to the curb again, don't let me."

"I won't, I promise." *That's what I'm talking about.*

33

The wrongful death trial for LaRita Willis began on November 26, 2007, in Watterson, Georgia, and Justice had been adamant that Nito was not to follow her to Watterson. She agreed that he would resume his duties when she returned to Winston.

"Look," she said. "Experience tells us that it's too soon for them to attack again, and they won't even know where I am. I want you to honor my request, Alou. Put it on hold until I get back to Winston." Against his better judgment, Alou had agreed. He was a little ticked off at Justice. She was much too stubborn. But what could he do?

Justice was lead counsel, and Lionel and Brad agreed to serve as co-counsel. Brad helped Justice with all the paperwork and requests for information from the defense attorneys. Lionel argued all the motions and objections in the Judges chambers. He was happy with the result. Justice was elated. The judge reminded her a little of Judge Denver. He was partial to the other side. She wondered if all judges were partial to men, or if it was just her. Solomon was on vacation from November 21 through December 4. He volunteered to stay with her and help her pick the jury. Justice was pleased with the jury of nine women and three men. She felt that she could handle the rest of the trial without Brad or Lionel.

It had been Solomon's idea that Justice wear the same dress every day. "Wear a navy blue or black dress and you can change the accessories each day, that way the jury will pay more attention to what you are wearing and how many attorneys are teaming up on poor little "ole" you and not pay any attention to the facts in the case." *Women are more concerned about clothes than anything else.*

"But I want them to hear the facts; we are right and they are wrong." Justice protested.

"But the judge has made it clear that he's on their side. He will keep as much of your evidence out as he can without being obvious. You are trying to fight fair with an unjust judge. Remember, they regard neither God nor man, or should I say woman."

She trusted Solomon and followed his advice. She bought a basic washable navy blue dress and changed the accessories everyday. When they entered the courtroom, Solomon sat on the front seat behind Justice and the Deputy came up to him and began to ask questions, the judge wanted to know who Solomon was. Solomon told him that he was a friend of Justice's and was there for support. Then he stood up and moved to the back of the courtroom. He sat and folded his arms. He wanted the jury to think that the deputy had asked him to move to the back. There were several paralegals sitting on the front seat behind the defense table. He could see the jurors frowning and whispering. He wanted the jury to focus on how the court was making a difference between the defense and the plaintiff because the judge did it in such a way that the jury couldn't pick it up. He and Justice had to fight fire with fire. The defense attorneys were not even concerned about Justice, because they knew she was a public defender with very little criminal experience and no civil experience. They were happy when Lionel did not show up the next day.

Although Justice, as plaintiff's attorney, had the right to give her opening statement first, the Defense attorneys requested permission from the court to go first. Solomon advised Justice to agree. The Defendant had four attorneys, and the lead attorney gave a long opening statement detailing the life of the defendant. He talked about how Mr. Hines, owner of the cement company, was born into a very poor family, and how he had worked and struggled to complete his education.

He detailed how he had embarked upon his entrepreneur endeavors on a shoestring budget and toiled diligently day and night to turn it into an enormous success. He explained how the Defendant had given back to the community by helping low-income families, and how he never forgot his struggles to escape the poverty of his childhood. He told the jury about how the defendant had assisted a young widow financially when she was involved in an accident after falling asleep at the wheel, because she had to leave home before day every morning in order to drive to her job in another town. She had two young children and no family to help her. He concluded by stating that the Defendant was always looking for an opportunity to help the less fortunate, because he had been born into that group himself, and it was his desire to lift as many from that predicament as possible.

When he finished, the judge told Justice that she could present her opening statement.

"Thank you, your Honor," she said as she moved to the podium and turned to face the jury.

"Good morning, ladies and gentlemen, my name is Justiana Fullilove, and I represent the Plaintiff in this case, Mrs. Josie Willis. I want to make it clear, that this is not a case about rags to riches. This is a case about a Breach of Duty and how that breach snuffed out the life of a six-year old girl. It was a clear day on September 7, a little over two years ago, when little LaRita was playing in the schoolyard. Suddenly, she heard the music and turned to see the flashing lights of the Jingles Ice Cream Truck. Automatically, she began to run across the street toward the truck. But, she never reached the other side of the street.

"Because a truck driven by the Defendant, Frank Jones, and owned by Hines Cement Company, crushed her into the pavement. That was the last time LaRita ran for ice cream. She died five days later in a hospital without regaining consciousness.

"Like most little children, LaRita had a passion for ice cream. When she saw the flashing lights and heard the ice cream music, everything else was over. For LaRita, the thrill of running to the truck with the flashing lights and ice cream music was second only to the joy of licking the ice cream as it ran down the side of the cone. So what happened that clear day in September when LaRita ran for ice cream?

"Ladies and Gentlemen, the evidence will show that the Defendant, Frank Jones, who was employed by Hines Cement Company, negligently drove his truck through an area where there were three obvious reasons to keep a proper look out for children.

"Number one: The area was clearly marked—school zone;

"Number two: The Defendant saw the Jingles Ice Cream Truck with the flashing Lights parked across the street from the school;

Number Three: It was the time of day when school dismissed and children would likely be crossing the street.

"Now I ask you, who had the 'last clear chance' to avoid the tragedy? Was it the little girl, who had her mind, attention, and thoughts focused on the ice cream truck? Or was it the Defendant who was required-- by law-- to keep a proper look out for children in a school zone and was warned and reminded to do so by the flashing school zone lights?

"I submit to you ladies and gentlemen, that it was the Defendant who had the 'last clear chance' and a duty to keep a proper look out to his right, and to his left, and to avoid the tragedy that occurred that day.

"So what are the issues for consideration in this case? Simply this:

- The Defendant had a duty to keep a proper look out for children in a school zone;
- The Defendant breached that duty;
- And it was that breach that took the life of six-year-old LaRita.

"We expect the defense to present evidence that the Defendant was only driving a few miles over the speed limit. But I submit to you that a driver of a motor vehicle has a duty, first of all, to drive within the speed limit, and secondly to watch out for children who may cross the street without first looking out for their own safety. After all, isn't that the whole purpose of the school zone signs, flashing lights, and decreased speed limit?

"I must admit that I was impressed with the details of the Defendant's education, how much he has accomplished in life, and how he has reached out to the less fortunate. But I want you to write in your notes what that has to do with the case before you today." She waited until they picked up their note pad and pencil. She moved along in front of them, looking each juror in the eye, then said, Nothing—absolutely nothing ... It's interesting how he encountered many obstacles and was able to overcome each one. I admire the fact that he never gave up hope, and his hard work was rewarded. He probably has more money than he or his children can ever spend. But I want you to write in your notes what that has to do with the case before you today. Nothing—absolutely nothing. Because how his life began and how hard he worked to succeed has nothing to do with how this little girl died? She died because of the negligence of the defendant. Let me conclude by listing once more the issues before you today.

- The Defendant had a duty to keep a proper look out for children in a school zone;
- The Defendant breached that duty;
- And it was that breach that snuffed out the life of that little girl.

"This case involves the Defendant, Frank Jones, and his employer, Hines Cement Company. Because the Defendant was driving the company truck and enroute to a job site when the tragedy occurred, he was acting within the scope of his employment.

"After you have heard all the evidence in this case, I will have another chance to talk with you. At that time I will ask you to return a verdict for my client, Mrs. Willis, the grandmother and LaRita, and against Mr. Jones and Hines Cement Company. Ladies and gentlemen, I thank you for your attention."

After opening statements, and a brief recess, the judge asked Justice to call her first witness. The plaintiff's two witnesses were Mrs. Willis and the psychologist for LaQuita, the twin sister of LaRita. Mrs. Willis testified about receiving the phone call from the hospital and how they waited by her bedside, but LaRita never regained consciousness, and the change in LaQuita's behavior after her sister's death. The psychologist testified about the effect the death of her sister has had on LaQuita and how the death of a twin is more traumatic on the surviving twin that on other siblings.

The defense called three experts who testified that children of such a young age readily adjust to death and usually suffer no real adverse affects in the future, and that the death of a twin is no more traumatic than that of any other sibling. The Defendants did not testify. Court was adjourned early on Thursday and the attorneys were instructed to be prepared to present their closing arguments Friday morning.

THE LAST THING on Justice's mind before she fell asleep was the ongoing trial. She agonized over how the judge seemed to favor the defense attorneys. "God can you help me with this," she mumbled just before she was overcome by sleep. During the night she dreamed that she had developed a strategy that would guarantee a verdict for her client. She crawled out of bed and scrawled the answer on a tablet on the dresser. When she picked up the tablet the next morning, she was disappointed because she had written, "Just cry".

She crossed out cry and wrote try. Then she threw the note in the trash and reviewed her prepared closing statement. She called Solomon she told him about her dream and what she had written.

"Just cry. That's interesting," Solomon said. "Jeremiah is the only weeping prophet I'm familiar with. In the end things turned out okay for him as a result of his weeping."

The defense attorney requested permission to do his closing arguments first, and again, Justice agreed. She felt the jury would see this as the other side taking advantage. The judge explained that the attorneys had agreed to change the order of presenting their closing arguments.

When the Defense attorney finished and returned to his seat, Justice moved to the podium. She adjusted the podium, shifted her papers, and just stood there for a few minutes. Then she went back to the Plaintiff's table and exchanged her blue pen for a black pen. She moved back to the podium, shifted her notes and then moved around in front of the podium. She looked at the jury and opened her mouth. No sound came out. She moved back behind the podium, tears were running down her face. She placed both palms over her face and quickly blotted the tears away. She turned and looked for Solomon at the back of the courtroom, where he usually sat each day. He was not there. The jury began to look for him as well. By this time tears were running freely down her face. She shifted through her papers and made a few notes. The court reporter pulled three tissues from her Kleenex box and moved over to hand them to Justice. She nodded her head to thank the lady. She blotted her face with the tissue, threw it in the trash, and moved back to the front of the podium. Tears kept running; a few jurors were dabbing at their eyes. She turned to look for Solomon again; he was not there. The jurors began watching for Solomon again. The judge sat there and waited patiently. Justice went back to the Plaintiff's table and exchanged the pens again. She moved back to the podium and the court reporter passed her three more tissues. She nodded to thank her, blotted her face, and turned to look for Solomon again. He was sitting there with a puzzled look on his face. Her shoulders slumped with relief. She picked up her notes and shifted them again. She thumbed through them and looked at the jury. She opened her mouth and tears rolled off her face and onto the front of her dress, but no sound came out. The court reporter passed her a hand full of tissue. She took the tissue and nodded thanks. The lead defense attorney cleared his throat.

"Is there a problem, Miss Fullilove?" the judge asked. Do you need a brief recess?"

She shook her head no, and held up one finger to indicate she only needed a minute, and she would proceed. She turned to look at Solomon again, and the jury looked at him.

Solomon moved up a few seats, and turned to look at the deputy. The jury looked at the deputy. The deputy went back to Solomon and told him that he could move up to the seat behind Justice if he desired. Solomon stood and told the deputy that he was okay, he preferred sitting in the back. As soon as the deputy walked away, Solomon moved back to the back seat again. The jury was furious. They thought the deputy had made Solomon move back to the back of the courtroom. That was just the effect Solomon had hoped for.

Tears continued to run down the front of Justice's dress. The court reporter continued to hand her a few tissues at a time. The defense attorneys, as well as the judge, wished she would give her the box and be done with it. Solomon was thrilled that she kept handing her a few at a time. He looked around, and even the spectators were dabbing at their eyes.

"Objection, your Honor," one of the defense attorneys said.

"To what?" the judge asked.

"She's crying in front of the jury."

"I'm not familiar with anything in the evidentiary objections that would prohibit her crying," the judge said.

The attorney sat down and folded his arms. The court reporter passed Justice another hand full of tissue. Justice blotted her face and went back to the Plaintiff's table and exchanged the pens again. She held up one finger to the judge to indicate that she only needed one more minute before proceeding. By this time all nine of the female jurors were dabbing at their eyes and the males were rubbing their noses. Solomon took note of the fact that, besides himself, the defense attorneys and the judge were the only people in the courtroom with dry eyes. He dropped his head and rubbed his nose. Justice dropped her pen, stooped down and picked it up. She stood and moved close to the jury box. She was determined to give her closing arguments. She opened her mouth, but no sound came out. She stood there with her arms hanging loosely at her sides and the tears ran freely down her face and onto the front of her dress. She wanted to remind the jury that what the Defendant had accomplished had nothing to do with why they were in court today, and that he had breached his duty to keep a proper look out for the child's safety.

The court reporter handed her more tissue, she blotted her face, looked at her watch, and realized that she had been crying for 15 minutes. She opened her mouth once more and no sound came out. By this time she was openly weeping. She nodded to the jury and returned to her seat. The court reporter hand her more tissue and the Plaintiff patted her on the back as she sat weeping at the table. The jury looked at Solomon, they wanted him to move up close and comfort Justice, but he just sat there with his head down and rubbed his nose.

"Are you done, Miss Fullilove?" the judge asked.

She nodded her head yes.

"Let the record show that Plaintiff's attorney indicated by a nod of her head that she was finished with closing arguments," the judge said.

According to the original agreement, the defense attorneys would have an opportunity to rebut Justice's closing argument. The judge turned to look at the defense table and the lead attorney stood.

"We don't have anything further, your Honor." He knew that anything he said would only serve to aggravate the jury.

"Very well," the judge said. "Do you have anything further, Miss Fullilove?"

Justice shook her head no, and the judge instructed the jury on the law that must be followed in the case. He passed the written instructions to the deputy along with the verdict forms to be given to the jury, and they were sent to the jury room to begin deliberations. The defense attorneys were frustrated, but felt uncomfortable and didn't know how to respond to a woman crying. They rushed from the courtroom. Solomon moved up to Justice's table as the jury was leaving the courtroom. They all stopped to look; they were relieved.

Justice was disappointed because she had not been able to give her closing argument. She felt that she had such a good closing, and all she did was cry. How pitiful. Lord, please touch the jury's heart, and have mercy on my client. Otherwise, all my time on this trial has been wasted, and justice will not be done.

Solomon reminded Justice of the "just cry" note she had written during the night, and told her that it was the hand of the Lord. What other explanation could there be?

The jury returned a verdict for the Plaintiff in the amount of six million dollars in a little less than three hours. Justice, Mrs. Willis, and Solomon were elated.

Lead counsel for the defense team stood and walked over to shake Justice's hand.

"Congratulations, I have never seen a more effective closing argument." He just stood there, held her hand, and stared at her. *How could this young, new, public defender, win over us. All she did was cry. What was the jury thinking? Other members of the defense team came over one by one and shook Justice's hand.* Although she was happy, the tears were still flowing. The judge granted a brief recess before post-trial wrap up. The defense team hurried from the courtroom.

34

Justice insisted that Solomon go home. He wanted to wait for her, but she said she would be finished with post-trial wrap up long before dark, and come straight home. Reluctantly, he agreed to go and headed home.

On the way home, Justice saw a lady with a baby, who appeared to be having car trouble. She stopped and asked if she needed a ride. The lady said she needed a ride to the gas station to purchase a can and get some gas.

"I'll give you a lift, get in," Justice said, as she unlocked the door. The lady moved over to the door on the passenger side and opened the door. As she started to get into the car she stumbled and fell. Justice jumped out of the car and ran around to help her.

"Are you okay?"

"Yes, I guess I lost my balance." Before the lady could get into the car a black SUV pulled up and a man jumped out and asked if he could be of any help.

"No, but thank you for stopping." Justice said. "She stumbled and fell, but I think she's okay now."

When Justice turned around to help the lady and baby into the passenger seat, the man moved up behind her and placed a handkerchief over her face. She tried to grab his hands, but lost consciousness and slid to the ground. He picked her up and took her to the SUV.

"Drive her car," he said to the lady with the baby. "Rob will pick your car up shortly. Go to Handy Mart, park near the grocery entrance, and leave the keys under the matt. Walk into the store and watch for Rob. When he leaves your car and takes hers, go out and get your car and go straight home. Don't call attention to yourself."

"Okay," she said. "Nothing's going to happen to her, right?"

"I told you, my boss just wants to talk with her." The lady got into Justice's car and drove away; she was already beginning to regret her decision to get involved in this. She had a sick feeling in the pit of her stomach.

Michael took Justice to Virgil's estate and laid her on the couch in the guesthouse. He thumbed through a magazine while he waited for her to come around. When she stirred, he threw the book on the table and walked over to her.

"Boss is waiting to see you, mam. You sure took your time about coming around . . . let's go."

"Where are we going?" she asked.

"I told you, the boss wants to see you."

"Who is he, and why does he want to see me."

"Now, you're just gonna have to ask him that. And he doesn't like to be kept waiting."

"What if I don't want to go?"

Michael smiled, folded his arms across his chest, and said, "We have ways of changing your *want to*." He opened the door and motioned to Justice. She walked out the door and looked around. *Nothing but woods as far as I can see. Where in the world am I?*

They crossed over to the main house, and Michael opened the door with a key and they proceeded to the office of Virgil Boatner.

"Well, well, well," Virgil said as he turned to stare at Justice. "So you are the little lady that has caused me so much heartache and sorry. I didn't expect you to be so pretty. It's a shame to have to get rid of someone so pretty. You probably could have made some man a nice little wife."

"But I don't know you, and I've never done anything to hurt anyone." Justice could feel fear creeping upon her. *God, please help me.*

"Thank you, Michael, I'll call you when I need you," Virgil said as he gestured with his hands for Justice to have a seat. She sat and stared at him.

"What did I ever do to you?"

"Well, let's not have any secrets between us . . . I got married almost a year ago. She was a beautiful woman. Everything I ever wanted in a woman. I gave up all the womanizing and fast living for her. Everything went well for a while. I hired a man to drive her around. I didn't want her to have to drive, just relax and enjoy the countryside and shop and do whatever she wanted. I hired a maid to clean and cook. But she insisted on cooking me a meal or two each week herself. Said that the way to a man's heart was through his stomach. And man could she ever cook."

Virgil's eyes glowed when he thought of the meals she prepared for him and how they dined by candlelight and then danced until midnight. He closed his eyes and folded his hands. He could see her pretty face and those big blue eyes as she smiled at him and told him how much she loved him and that he was a gift to her from God. He banged his fist on the table and Justice jumped and looked around for a way of escape.

"Don't make the same mistake she did, no one gets away from Virgil forever. One of these days, I'm going to find her. And him, and when I do, they will regret the day they were born . . . He was a young Black man, tall, handsome, and well spoken. He was so mannerable, always on time, and a good driver. Then, one day I came home and she wasn't here. I thought she was still out shopping. I waited and waited. Then something told me to go look in her closet. Her clothes were gone, not all of them, but enough that I missed them. She had spread the remaining clothes out to hide the fact that some were missing. But I didn't get it at first. Why would her clothes be gone, I asked myself. It took a while for my brain to process it." Virgil stood and walked over to the window. He stood there looking out, with his back to Justice. Tears ran down his face.

Suddenly, he turned to stare at Justice. "I realized that she was gone the same time I realized that he had not reported to take her to her piano lesson that Wednesday. He was due at two o'clock, and it was three before it all fell into place. But I didn't want to believe it. So, I called his cell phone number. His phone was not in service.

So I walked out to the guard shack, because I wanted to talk to the guard face to face. I asked him if Jonathan had taken Mrs. Boatner for her piano lessons. And he told me that she had gone early today, he picked her up around 9:30 that morning. That means they were planning it all the time, just waiting for me to leave. I left at 9:00; they gave me just enough time to get out of the drive way." Virgil gritted his teeth, closed his eyes, and balled his fist.

"I would dream that I had found them and tortured them for days. I would awaken feeling so good, only to find that it had all been a dream. I was tormented. Then I would have a nightmare and see his face mocking me. I gave him a job and he stole my wife. I had no peace. Then I decided to avenge myself by seeing that every young Black man is put where he belongs, in prison."

Virgil paced the floor as he clenched and unclenched his fist. His voice was full of rage. He almost forgot Justice was there. She was afraid to interrupt him, but she wanted to ask what this had to do with her. His remark about prison caused a sick feeling to form in the pit of her stomach. *So, I thought it was Mark, or Judge Denver, and at one time even Mrs. Hambrick. But it had to have been him, all this time, trying to kill me. And I was just doing my job.*

⁀

JUSTICE CLEARED HER throat; Virgil stopped and turned to look at her. "What would you say if I told you I wouldn't cause you any more problems?" she asked.

"I wouldn't believe you. Besides, you have already caused me too much grief. Everything was going my way until you came along. The attorneys had just about given up the idea of winning a trial in my courtroom. It's difficult to win a case if the judge is totally against you. At least that's the way it was before you butted your nose in. I even had one doctor who agreed go along with my plan. Man did he turn out to be a disappointment. He will have to figure out another way to pay off his student loans, and he will probably lose his license and end up in prison for perjury. Serves him right. But, you know, he refused to go along with us after that first case. Michael lied to him and told him that the guy had a long rap sheet. When he discovered that the guy had never been arrested before, he wanted out. I guess he never had the stomach for it, just needed quick money.

Virgil paced, stopped to stare at Justice, shook his head and paced some more. He told Justice how the police department was more than willing to help him any way they could, including the plot to set her up for arrest on drug charges the night she went to the Oaktree Downs to help Big Man. They agreed to stop any car with three or four young Black men and see what they could find. It was easy to find a reason to arrest at least one of them. One would have a ticket, or the driver would not have a driver's license or insurance on the car. If drugs were found in the car, bingo, they all went to jail.

"I would have been able to take over every courtroom in Winston sooner or later. Men will do *anything* for enough money, if you just give them time. Then I would have gone for the state, and then the nation. I wouldn't have stopped until I had every young Black male in the U.S. where he belongs, behind bars. It would be an insult to everything I stand for to have a young, Black, female, fresh out of law school, and a public defender on top of all that, hinder my progress. I am going to chop you into pieces too small for bait.

He turned to look at Justice. "You know, I've never made love to a Black woman, I hear you guys are tigers in bed. Is there any truth to that?"

Justice was so frightened she couldn't speak. She just sat and stared at the man.

She tried to remember what she had been taught in karate class. Her mind was blank. *God, can you please help me with this!*

"What's the matter, cat got your tongue?"

"No," she mumbled.

"No what, cat doesn't have your tongue or you guys are not tigers in bed."

"Both."

He laid is head back and laughed. "Well, I think I'll just find out for myself." He pressed a button and Michael appeared in the doorway.

"Take Miss Fullilove to the guesthouse, provide her with whatever she needs, she will be with us a few days. I'm gonna have myself some fun. Make up for all the misery she has caused me. Justice had no idea she could experience such fear. She was unable to move from the chair. The big man moved over, helped her to her feet, and led her from the room. She felt as if she was being led to the electric chair. She could barely breathe and felt that her heart would leap out of her chest.

"What are you going to do to me," she whimpered when they were in the hallway.

"Nothing," he said. "I'm just taking you to your room."

As if on cue, Virgil stuck his head out the door and said to the big guy, "Hey Michael, the report says she's a virgin. Take care of that for me before I get to her, I don't have the patience for virgins anymore. Justice thought she would die. Her throat felt as if it were closing. She wondered if those were death pangs. *God, you can't let this happen to me. You know I promised Miss Mary I would remain a virgin until I get married. Please don't let this happen.*

"Be my pleasure," Michael said and turned to look at Justice. He could see the tears welling up in her eyes.

"Look," he said. "I've been with virgins before. I'll make sure you enjoy it."

It was the first time in her life that Justice had wished someone would drop dead. If she had had a pistol, she would have shot him right on the spot. She had never been so afraid and angry. She wanted to kill both Michael and Virgil. *How could they be so cruel? There is no way I could survive being raped by two men in one day. I know I'm going to die. God help me.*

When they reached the guesthouse, Michael opened the

door and stepped back for Justice to enter. When she just stood there, he placed his hand on her back and gave her a little push. He motioned for her to sit on the couch. She sat and stared at him. He sat in a chair and smiled at her.

"Like I said, this doesn't have to be a bad experience. You hungry? Want something to eat first?"

"Yes," she said. "I 'm hungry." *He acts as if he's asking me to play a game of checkers. But this will give me time to think.*

Michael's cell phone rang. He listened, said a few words, and then hung up.

"That was Mr. Boatner; he had an emergency and has to leave. So we don't have to be in a hurry. You want hot food or a cold sandwich?"

"Are you going to cook?" she asked, hoping for more time. *This man is not in touch with reality. He is completely crazy. I'm supposed to be happy that we don't have to be in a hurry for him to rape me.*

"I'll make cold sandwiches, but hot food will have to be leftovers. But it's delicious. Mr. Boatner has a wonderful cook. So, you get to choose."

"Okay, I would like a sandwich with everything." She figured that would give her more time to plan her escape. She was surprised at how calm she sounded.

"Coming up," he said and left the guesthouse.

Justice raced over to the phone, picked it up, and listened for a dial tone. A male voice asked.

"May I help you?'

"Yes, I would like to make a phone call."

"What is your access code?"

"Access code?" she asked.

"Yes, you must have an access code to use this phone."

"Okay, I'll get it and try again." She replaced the receiver and sat back on the couch. She slipped down on her knees and began to pray.

"Please God, please help me. Oh God, please." She had a thought so strong it seemed like an audible voice. *Look in the closet.* She rushed over to a huge walk-in closet and began to search for something to use as a weapon. She didn't find anything. She stood there and wondered if she had misunderstood the thought. Just as she was about to step out of the closet, another thought came to her. *Lift the black plastic cover by the door.* She lifted the cover and there was a red phone attached to the wall. Her heart began to race. She lifted the receiver and placed it to her left ear, she reached to dial with her right hand, but there was no buttons for dialing. She was standing there in shock, her hope beginning to fade, when a male voice said, "Winston Journal."

She slapped her forehead and tried to remember the name of the reporter that had interviewed her about her fourth trial. "Hercules," she stammered. "I need to speak with Hercules Cole." *Thank you, Holy Spirit.*

"May I tell him who's calling?"

"Yes, it's Miss Fullilove." The next voice she heard was that of Hercules Cole.

"Miss Fullilove, to what do I . . ."

"Can I talk with you in the strictest of confidence, my life depends on it."

"Of course." He looked around quickly to see if anyone was within earshot. "What's happening, Miss Fullilove?"

"I've been kidnapped by a man name Virgil Boatner."

"Where are you now?" He wanted to ask all the crucial questions fast. He didn't want the line to go dead before he got the information he needed. "Are you okay?"

"Yes, so far." Then she began to cry and tell him all that had happened and what he said about his plans for her, and how he had left because of an emergency.

"And where is Michael now?"

"He went to make me a sandwich."

Hercules could feel his pulse racing and his blood boiling. He knew he had the makings of a story that would skyrocket his career at the Journal, but he had to help get her out of harms way and help keep her safe until Virgil was where he belonged. He knew that Virgil's son was undergoing surgery for appendicitis as they spoke.

"How did you get access to a phone?"

"I picked up the red phone in the closet; it doesn't have any buttons to dial, and connected me directly to the Winston Journal."

"Can I call someone for you?"

"Yes," Justice said and gave him Lela phone number. "And ask her to call Alou, he's my fiancé. Be sure they understand that they are not to call the police. Please give her all the details. I'll try to call again later, it seems like the charge is going out on this phone."

"Okay," Hercules said. "I think I know how I can help you, but I need your permission to quote you. I will try to run this article in the Saturday morning paper. Everyone in Winston will have access to it. That should stop the police from becoming involved in a phony rescue attempt. They wouldn't dare try that after the paper goes out, plus the corrupt ones will be trying to cover their butts. She gave him permission to quote her and he hung up and checked to be sure he could read his notes. He would call Lela in a minute; there was nothing she could do now anyway. He hurried to his computer and began transcribing his notes. He stopped, picked up the phone, and called Lela. He knew she must be worried; it was after ten o'clock.

"Hello," Lela answered on the first ring.

"This is Hercules Cole of the Winston Journal, and I have a message for you from Miss Fullilove. The first . . ."

"Where is she?   Is she okay?"   She was practically screaming

"She wanted me to be sure you understood that ..."

Then a male's voice came on the line. "This is Ted, where is Justice?"

"Who are you?" Hercules asked.

"I'm Lela's husband and she is in no condition to take down any information. So, tell me what's going on?"

"She has been kidnapped. She wanted me to be sure you understood that you are not to call the police, because the police are part of a scheme to kill her. The plot involves a setup in which the police accidentally kills her in a phony rescue attempt and the kidnapper will pretend that she came to his place on her own accord. Do you understand?"

"Yes. Look, hold on and let me connect you to her fiancé, Alou. He and Solomon are looking for her." Hercules tapped his hand on the table as he waited to be connected to Alou. When Alou came on the line, Hercules identified himself and got right to the point.

"Miss Fullilove has been kidnapped and wanted to be sure you understood that you are not to call the police. Apparently, the kidnaper has connections to some corrupt police officers in high places that he plans to use to kill Miss Fullilove and pretend it was an accident, and no one will ever know that he kidnapped her. He plans to say that she came to visit him regarding a contribution for her work at Oaktree Downs, and someone made a false report of kidnapping and in the process of trying to rescue her, the officers shot her by mistake. So you can see why it's important that we don't call the police."

"How did you get all this information?" Solomon asked. Alou had put his cell phone on speaker so that Solomon could hear.

"She called me. She had access to a phone that connects directly to the Journal. It doesn't have buttons to dial. She gave me Lela's number, and that's how I got connected to you. She also gave me permission to print this information in the paper and said she would try to call me back in a couple of hours. She is being held in the guesthouse. Mr. Boatner is currently at the hospital where his son had emergency surgery. Any message if she calls again?"

"Yes, tell her that I love her, and Solomon and I are coming to get her." Alou said.

"I'll tell her if she calls. And remember, those men are armed and dangerous, so you guys may want to wait until the paper hits the streets. She will be safer then."

"Thank you, sir. Can you try to put her through to us if she calls again," Solomon asked.

"Will do." Hercules hung up and rushed to finish the

story. He wanted to meet the Saturday morning deadline. After practically getting down on his knees and begging, he got permission from his boss to change the Saturday morning headline and print his story with no restrictions because the young lady's life was at stake.

~

JUSTICE LOOKED AT Michael and smiled when he entered the door with a sandwich and chips on a tray. She had the table set with two glasses of apple juice. "Aren't you going to eat?" she asked.

"Well, no, I hadn't thought about it, I'm not that hungry."

"I'm not very hungry myself. We can share this sandwich. It should be enough for both of us. I found some apple juice in the pantry."

Michael smiled. "So, you are going to be a good sport about this. Like I said, this doesn't have to be a bad experience, and I'll make sure you enjoy it." He set the tray on the table and moved over to the cabinet to get a plastic knife to cut the sandwich. Justice had already checked and knew that the only silverware in the kitchen was plastic. She was disappointed because she noticed that Michael did not have his cell phone. She left the wooden statue behind the paper towel holder, and watched Michael as he cut the sandwich in half. He opened the bag of chips and divided them between the two plates.

"Here you go," Michael said as he smiled at Justice and motioned toward the food. "We have plenty chips if you want more."

"Oh, that's plenty, I'm not very hungry. I'll get us a paper towel," she moved over to the counter and tore off two paper towels, folded them and picked up the statue with her right hand and moved back to the table. "This is my favorite potato chip she said. Only French fries can beat them out."

Michael looked down at the chips. "Actually I prefer French fries to chips . . ."

Justice raised the statue and crashed it into his head. Michael blinked once, staggered backwards, and then fell to the floor. She ran to him and felt his pulse. It was strong. She placed the statue on the table and stood there trembling and wondering how much time she had before Virgil came back. Whatever it took, she knew she had to stay alive and thwart Virgil's plan. She tried to break the window with the statute, but it was unbreakable.

She tore a sheet and tied Michael's hands and feet. Every time he appeared to be regaining consciousness, she tapped him again on the head and prayed that he didn't die.

She took his pistol, placed it on the table, and tried to figure out a way to get her purse from the trunk of her car in the guesthouse garage.

She fiddled with the combination lock on both doors. She used a pair of small scissors to try and pry the lock off the back door. The scissors finally broke but the lock would not bulge. She tried the red phone and was told that Hercules had just left. She didn't dare leave a message. As hope began to fade, she picked up the broken scissor blade and began trying to poke a hole in the back door around the lock. When she had chipped away for what seemed like hours, there was a crevice in the door so small that she wanted to give up. Her hand ached and she laid her head against the door as she stopped to rest. She froze when she heard a car pull into the driveway. She found the strength to grab the statue and scramble to the bathroom when she heard a knock on the door. She locked the bathroom door and listened to see if they would go away. She heard a crash and knew that the door had been kicked in. She slid to the floor and began to weep because she realized that she had forgotten to take Michael's pistol, and she was so tired of fighting men.

35

The paper hit the street at 1:00 a.m. Saturday. About the same time Alou and Solomon drove up to the gate of Virgil Boatner's estate. It had been Solomon's idea to rent a hearse and pretend they were picking up a body. Alou used his radar device to shut down the guard's phone. It would only last 30 minutes. They were pressed for time. They found the location by the tracking device Snaggie had placed in Justice's purse. Alou realized he needed to improve the tracking device. It brought them to the location, but it took much too long.

"May I help you?" the guard asked.

"We are here to pick up a body," Solomon said. He was careful not to use the word dead.

"You must be at the wrong place; there's no dead body here," the guard said.

Solomon picked up his clipboard and flipped a few pages. "Is this 120 Boatner Lane?"

"Yeah, but ..."

"We understand that the owner does not want the body here when he returns. And I know I don't need to remind you of the seriousness of refusing to allow the removal of a body. That's a serious crime." The guard had never encountered anything like this before, he didn't know if it were a crime or not. But it sounded logical to him, and he knew Mr. Boatner wouldn't want a dead body there when he returned. It has to be the girl. *Why would they kill her? It was Michael; I knew he spelled trouble.*

The guard tried to call the house, but his phone was dead. He tried his cell phone and it was dead also. He stepped out of the guard shack and looked toward the house. He was too far away for them to hear him. He scratched his head and moved back into the guard shack.

"Look, mister, this is not the only body we have to pick up. Are you going to let us in, or do we need to go back and report this to the state?" Solomon asked.

The guard opened the gate and turned to look at the house again. *Bloody Michael, I knew he was trouble.*

"Solomon drove straight to the guesthouse, which was not in the guard's view.

The guard tried his phones again. They did not work. He scratched his head again. He couldn't figure it out. *I'll certainly be glad when they leave.*

Alou didn't like the way Solomon was taking charge of everything. But he couldn't think of one thing to do on his own. He was almost listless. He felt as if he would stop breathing any minute. When he realized that they were probably within a few feet of Justice, he wanted to kick the door in, grab her, and run.

Solomon turned to look at him. "Hey, be cool. We are not the smartest two men in the world, but we have a common goal, to get Justice out safely. I'm going to lure the bodyguard to the vehicle, when he gets here, spray him with the pepper spray and we will both attack him at once. Don't allow him to get his hands on his weapon."

Alou simply nodded his head. He wondered what made Solomon think the man would walk out to the car without his weapon drawn. One can always hope. *God, give me the strength to do whatever is necessary to keep Justice safe.*

Solomon knew that the coroner's office usually picked up dead bodies, but he was willing to take a chance that these men had seen funeral processions and had no idea what happened before the body reached the funeral home. He knocked on the door and waited. No answer. They noticed the door had a combination lock.

"Justice," Alou said. "It's me and Solomon." There was no response.

"Let's kick it in," Solomon said. "We have to depend on the element of surprise. If the guy is here, he obviously didn't hear us knock and won't be expecting us, we can spray him before he draws his weapon." They both took a few steps back and rushed the door. When they kicked the door it flew off the hinges and they rushed in, looked around, found the bodyguard on the floor, out cold, his hands tied behind him, and his pistol lying on the table. They began searching for Justice.

They searched the house and quickly determined that she had to be in the bathroom. She picked up the statue and listened. *Lord, can you help me with this.*

Alou knocked lightly on the door and called to her. "Hey, Precious, it's me and Solomon."

Justice thought someone was playing a trick on her. *How could he have known Alou calls me Precious, and how does he know about Solomon? They couldn't possibly be here. How would they have found this place?*

"Hey, kiddo," Solomon said. "Open up, we have to get out of here fast." He looked at this watch and realized that the guard's phones would be working in five minutes. Justice opened the door when she heard Solomon's voice.

They helped Justice up. "Let's get outta here," Solomon said. "The guard's phones will be working in five minutes."

As they ran to the hearse and opened the door to get in, a car pulled right up behind them. All they could see were headlights.

"Freeze, one wrong move and you're dead men. Put your hands up ... We'll take the young lady, If either of you move, we'd love nothing better than to fill you with bullets."

One of the men moved up to them, grabbed Justice, and pulled her forward. She started to scream, he clamped his hand over her mouth, and she went limp. Alou and Solomon were in complete shock and couldn't move. They could see that the man was a uniformed policeman. Alou started to move toward him, and Solomon yelled at him.

"Stop!" That's exactly what they want you to do. Remember the warning!"

Alou stopped and stood with his fist clenched at his side. The second officer moved forward to cover the first one as he picked Justice up and hurried to the patrol car. Solomon stood there as his heart sank to his feet. *Me and my bright ideas. We have played right into their hands. How did the police find out she was here? What have I done?*

As the patrol car sped away, Solomon turned to Alou.

"Look, she's going to be okay, I have the big guy's pistol. Let's go catch them. We can't give up hope. I know she's going to be okay." He was trying to convince himself as well as Alou. *We did everything right; we didn't call the police. Who could have called them?*

The phone in the guesthouse began to ring. They knew it was the guard. They jumped into the hearse and headed toward the gate. Solomon was trying to think of something to tell the guard. He did not want a shoot out. He slowed and rolled the window down as they approached.

"Well, you were right; there was no dead body, so we'll be on our way. Good night, sir, we are sorry to have bothered you." Solomon saluted the guard and drove away. The guard had no idea what had just happened. He didn't realize the police had Justice. He had no idea where she was, and couldn't figure out why Michael wasn't answering his cell phone. One thing he knew for sure, he never wanted to see the girl, the two men or the policemen again. He was glad his phone was working. *Why doesn't Michael answer his bloody phone? Surely he didn't sleep through all this.*

☞

VIRGIL WAS LAYING on a cot in his eleven year old son's hospital room. He was unable to sleep. He checked on the boy and went outside to smoke a cigarette. He glanced at the newspaper as he passed the news rack. He stopped and stared at the Saturday Morning, December 1, 2007 headline.

There in bold letters were words that caused his heart to sink. LOCAL PUBLIC DEFENDER KIDNAPPED; A STORY OF CORRUPTION IN WINSTON. He took coins from his pocket, pushed them into the machine, and took a copy of the paper. He stood there and read the story of his plans, word for word, as he had told them to Justice.

Local businessman told his kidnap victim that he has the city in his back pocket. He bragged about how he is above the law in Winston. He tells of how he owns the judge and prosecutor in a certain Courtroom. And how they have agreed with him, for a fee, to send as many young Black males to prison as possible. All that didn't end up in prison on the first go round would go when they were unable to meet the conditions of probation. They were always given conditions that were impossible to fulfill. They would agree to anything just to get out on probation. They had no idea they were being set up for failure and would soon be in prison anyway.

He told a tale of wine, women, and fun for years. Then he fell in love and gave it all up for marriage, only to have his beloved wife run away with a young Black male. He describes his painstaking search for them for months before he came up with the idea of putting every young Black male where he felt they belonged, in prison.

He bragged about how he had even gotten others, outside the courtroom, involved in the escapade. He told of his plans to infiltrate every area of Winston with his plans. He said he was proud of the police department because there were so many willing to help him reach his goal, including persons in high places. They agreed to find an excuse to stop every car with three or four young Black males. They were sure to find a reason to arrest at least one of them.

It appears that everything had gone well until a certain young woman was assigned to *his* courtroom. She began to try and win cases in that courtroom and this inspired others to begin trying case again. The man told her that he had tried many times to get rid of her without bloodshed. But she would not go away. He tells of how he had someone write a letter to the Bar complaining about her conduct and expressing a fear for the safety of the judge in that courtroom. Seems the judge ran scared and squashed the inquiry. He had men attack her on three different occasions. Once her car went over an embankment and burned. On another occasion, her car was smashed and destroyed by a train. He complained that all he got for his money was the destruction of two cars and she spent one night in the hospital.

So, he had her kidnapped and brought to him. But before he did that, he reached an agreement with members of the police force that they would rush to his estate when they received the call that she had been kidnapped, and kill her accidentally in a phony rescue attempt.

In order to prevent any suspicion of wrongdoing on his part, he made notes of a make-believe discussion that they had regarding a contribution to help with her work at the local housing project.

He apologized to her, saying it was nothing personal. No one knows what will have happened to the young lady by the time you read this report. We can only hope she is still alive, and that the police have not yet staged the phony rescue attempt. The one thing that kept her alive long enough to give this interview is the fact that the man's son had to have emergency surgery. This is a son from his first marriage. Rumor has it that the first wife ran away with his cousin. Funny he didn't try to send every young white male to prison. Maybe there were just too many young white males.

In conclusion, let's do what we can to promote justice and get rid of corruption in our town. We are not haters, are we?

Virgil grabbed his cell phone and dialed Michael's number. No answer. Maybe he decided to spend the night with the girl. He dialed the guard shack. The guard answered and told him that a hearse arrived to pick up a dead body, and the police arrived shortly after the hearse. He said he had not been able to reach Michael on the phone, the hearse and police had left; and he had not seen the girl. Virgil was frustrated and angry.

"Did you see her with the police?"

"No, they just zipped out and I thought the hearse would bring the girl's body out, but they said there was no dead body."

"Why is Michael not answering his phone?"

"I don't know; I tried to call him when the hearse arrived, and he didn't answer.

Virgil was angry with the policemen. Why would they show up at his place before they were called? They were supposed to kill her during a rescue attempt. He wondered if all government workers were stupid sissies. He felt a little frustrated and angry when he realized that even with all his money, he could not always get what he wanted. Lately, he had gotten very little of what he wanted and someone was going to pay for his misery.

Virgil remembered the day he learned why the judge and prosecutor were running scared. Both had notified him within two weeks of each other that they wanted out. He was disgusted to find that a young, Black female, by the name of Justiana Jurisprudence Fullilove was the problem. He had called Michael in and explained the problem and his assignment.

"The two sissies in the courtroom are running scared. I have no gripe with Black women, just Black men. All I wanted was for her to go away. She would not. Every effort to get rid of her nicely and without bloodshed has failed. She has left me no choice. Pick her up and bring her to me."

"I'm on it, Mr. Boatner," Michael said and hurried from the room. Michael was a big tall guy. He came highly recommended, and this would be his opportunity to prove himself. He certainly had the size and strength to do the job.

As Virgil stood crushing the newspaper in his hands, he was almost overcome by anger, bitterness, and frustration.

He realized that the failure was in Michael. And wondered why he hadn't been able to see that size and strength were not enough for what he wanted. He recognized the fact that he had made a lot of bad decisions himself, but someone was going to pay for his misery, and pay dearly. His anger had shifted from Jonathan to Justice. He was going to crush that pretty face and destroy that shapely body. "Such a waste," he said out loud. "She should have gone away."

☞

SEVERAL PEOPLE IN Winston were unable to sleep and went to pick up the Saturday morning paper. Among them were Judge Denver and Mark LaNear. Judge Denver had been planning his retirement, on the bench, for months. He packed his bag and headed for the airport. He had no intention of ever returning to Winston.

Mark sat at his desk and began reviewing his actions for anything that could trip him up. He had taken all his money in cash. He had not deposited any of it in his bank account. Sharon had spent it all on foolishness. There was no evidence to connect him to Virgil's allegation. He had often suspected that Judge Denver was on the take, but always ruled it out. He determined he was not going down because of Justiana Fullilove. If his ability to earn a living diminished, he knew that Sharon would bail out. He had begun to think that maybe he had had enough of her anyway. She was not his worry now. If by some chance I survive this, he reasoned with himself, I am going to make some changes in my life. His heart broke when he thought of what would happen to his daughter. Sharon would use her to tear him into tiny pieces. *What was I thinking? How did I allow her to drive me to this?*

☞

Officers Clark and Davis pulled off the road and stopped. Officer Clark got out and went to the back seat to check on Justice. When he opened the door she screamed and scrambled to the other side of the seat.

"Hey, it's me, Officer Clark," he said as he slid into the back seat. "We saw the article in the paper about the kidnapping. Even though his name was not given, we knew exactly who it was."

Her eyes widen, and then she went limp and crawled into his arms. "Oh my God, oh my God," she said as the tears rolled down her face. Both officers told her that the article in the paper would cause any corrupt police officer to abandon any plan they had of harming her. Justice was angry with herself for crying, but she couldn't help but feel special. Alou and Solomon had risked their lives for her and now she realized that the two officers had done the same. Then it dawned on her, they had thought these were the corrupt officers when they snatched her.

"Hey, the two guys that you took me away from were Alou and Solomon."

"What were they doing in a hearse?" Officer Davis asked.

"I don't know, they never got a . . ." She grabbed Officer Clark's phone.

"I need to call Alou," she said as she flipped open the phone and dialed Alou's number.

"Hello," Solomon said. Alou was not able to drive or man the phone.

"Solomon, it's me, Justice."

"Justice, are you . . ."

Alou snatched the phone from Solomon. "Justice, are you okay, where are you, how did you get access to a phone?"

"I'm with Officer Clark and Officer Davis. They were the policemen that took me away from you guys. They thought you were the bad guys. Hold on, I'll let him tell you where we are."

When Officer Clark told Alou where they were, he realized that they were only five minutes away.

"We are headed your way, hold onto my girl."

"We'll do it, over and out."

Alou jumped out of the car before Solomon came to a complete stop. He ran toward the patrol car as Justice ran toward him. Solomon got out of the car and just stood there. The two officers walked over to him and they watched the two lovebirds. They were pouring their hearts out to each other. Justice told Alou about Virgil's plan to rape her and what he had said to Michael. Alou held her so tight; she thought he would crush her ribs. Solomon and the officers just stood and shook their head at how evil men can be.

"Thank you, Lord," Solomon said, and the two officers said, "Amen and amen".

The officers asked Solomon about the hearse, and he explained how he had come up with the idea, because he felt he could bluff his way in with it. He counted on the fact that the guard wouldn't know whether it was a crime to refuse to allow them to pick up a body or not.

"Man, was I sick when you guys took her away from us. I thought we had played right into their hands".

"So, what do we do now?" Officer Clark asked.

"We just need to take this hearse back and pick up Alou's car."

"I don't think anyone from the police department would dare touch her with that article in the paper, but she should probably spend the night with you or Alou," Officer Davis said."

"Better yet," Officer Clark said. "Why don't we take her to her Lela's house."

"I'm sure Alou will want to do that," Solomon said. "But maybe you guys can follow us to the mortuary; she may not want to ride in the hearse. And I hope it's a long time before I take another ride in one." They all laughed and headed for their vehicles.

JUSTICE CALLED LELA and told her she was okay and would come by and tell her everything later in the day. She told her she was spending the night with Solomon and two officers were patrolling the area. She hated lying to Lela, but she knew that was the only way to keep Lela from worrying and insisting that she come to her place.

Chapter

36

Justice insisted on spending the night at home alone. "If I don't spend the night at home, Alou, I will probably never be able to stay by myself again. I'll call you before I go to bed and first thing in the morning."

Neither Alou nor Solomon could get her to change her mind. The two officers promised to patrol the area. They did not like the idea of Justice staying alone. Alou dropped Solomon off first, and then drove Justice around to her unit. He wanted to stay a while, but she refused. Alou sat on her steps for a while, and then headed for his car. He was reassured when he saw the two officers drive slowly by her condo. Also, he had called Nito and he had taken up his post at Justice's condo. But he still didn't like it.

Justice flopped down on the couch and turned on the TV. There was nothing interesting on. She turned if off and began to pray.

"God, how did I get here? Why am I here? What did I ever do to deserve this? And what's going to happen to me now? She felt like crying but had no more tears. She went into her bathroom and turned the shower on. She had stripped down to her panties and bra when she heard the closet door open. She turned and Virgil was standing there with a sneer on his face. She screamed and he rushed over and slapped her.

"Shut up," he said as he pulled out his knife, grabbed her, and held it to her throat. Virgil pushed Justice forward and turned out the light. The automatic nightlight came on. Justice was in complete shock. She was unable to move. Her phone began to ring and he pressed the knife into her throat. She could fell blood seep out and run down into her bra. She closed her eyes and tried to die. He threw the knife on the nightstand and pull out a pistol.

"Look," he said as he pulled her to the window and pointed to Nito's car. He knew that Nito was not in the car, but figured she didn't. "This is a high-powered pistol with a silencer. If you say the wrong thing, I will shoot him dead. Do you understand?' She nodded and moved ovcr to the phone as he stood there pointing the pistol at Nito's car.

"Hello."

"Hey precious, it's me," Alou said. "Are you sure you don't want to go to Solomon's or Lela's?"

"I'm sure," she said. "I'm okay." But he could hear the fear in her voice.

"Okay then, I just wanted to check one more time before I turned in."

"Thanks, I'll call you later at your mom's house." Alou made a u-turn and called Nito. The words mom's house had confirmed his suspicion. He was glad he had given Nito his key to Justice's condo.

"Get into Justice's condo immediately. Walk softly, someone's in there."

"Okay," Nito said and felt for his pistol and pepper spray.

"You are not going to get away with this." Justice said. She knew Alou would call Nito. She had to get Virgil's attention back on her; she did not want Nito to get hurt. He could tell that she was filled with fear. He placed the pistol on the nightstand and moved toward her.

"Oh, but I will. You were a guest at my home when I left to go to the hospital. I will take care of you and get back to the hospital before anyone misses me. No one will ever know I was here. There is no evidence of a forced entry, and you won't get a chance to tell your reporter the plan this time. And no one will believe the story in the paper.

"How did you get in?"

"Let's not have secrets between us, my dear. One of my men followed you home from the courthouse one day and discovered that your next-door neighbor was a man he worked with at one time. The guy couldn't remember his name most of the time and always lost his keys and glasses. So he always left his patio door unlocked for the few times he came home. Getting from his apartment to yours was not that difficult. So, you see, everything is working in my favor. He grabbed her bra strap and snatched it off. He stood there with the strap in his hand as he gazed at her breast. Suddenly anger rose up in her so fierce she felt as if she was going to explode. She squatted, spun around, and kicked him on the left side of his head. He was startled; he just stood there with his mouth open as she kicked him on the right side of his neck. He stumbled and then lunged at her. She stepped aside and hit him in the face with the back of her fist. He grabbed her and threw her to the floor. He was on top of her when he felt a pistol barrel at the back of his head. He knew it was Nito. He squeezed his hands around her throat.

"Drop the pistol, or I'll strangle her!"

Justice tried to tell Nito to shoot, but she was only able to groan.

Nito took one look at Justice's face and stepped back.

"Drop it! Now!"

Nito dropped the pistol and Virgil released Justice and scrambled to get his pistol and knife. Nito tackled him and they sprawled on the floor, Virgil reached for Nito's pistol and Nito kicked it under the bed. Justice scrambled to her feet, grabbed Virgil's pistol and knife, opened the window, and threw them out. Virgil broke free of Nito, grabbed Justice, and held her in front of him and in a chokehold.

"Stay back or I'll break her neck!" He inched toward the window. He picked her up and held her up to the open window.

"No!" Nito yelled and rushed toward them. Virgil perched Justice on the ledge and sneered at Nito, who stopped in his tracks.

"One more step and over she goes. Now, get the pistol from under the bed and hand it to me. Nito moved back toward the bed, but kept his eye on Virgil and Justice. Justice felt something tug at her hand and tried to turn and look. She felt herself slipping over the windowsill. She screamed and closed her eyes. She wished she could have said good-bye to Alou, Ted, Lela, and Solomon. She wished she could have said thank you to Nito. She tried to block the look on Nito's face from her mind, and then she slipped into darkness.

Nito reached under the bed and picked up the pistol; Virgil rushed him and they struggled on the floor. Virgil wrestled the pistol away from Nito, pointed it at his chest and pulled the trigger. Nothing happened. Nito lay there frozen and stared. Virgil pulled the trigger again. Nothing happened. He tried to hit Nito in the head with the pistol. Nito blocked him; Virgil scrambled to his feet and ran toward the window. He could hear footsteps coming up the stairs. He jumped out of the window and grabbed the ledge below. He saw Officer Clark standing on the ledge holding Justice. He swung several times and dropped to the ground. He ran to get the pistol that Justice had thrown out the window.

"He jumped out of the window," Nito said as he struggled to his feet. Officer Davis ran to the window and spotted Virgil just as he picked up the pistol, pointed, and fired at Justice and Officer Clark. Officer Clark felt Justice jerk and he knew she had been hit. He turned and tried to shield her with his body as he saw Virgil aim the pistol again. He heard pistol fire above him and looked up. Officer Davis was standing in the window. He fired until Virgil dropped his pistol. Virgil staggered and fell to the ground, then turned to take one last look at Justice. *She won after all.*

"Can you pull her back in," Officer Clark asked.

"Yes." Officer Davis lifted Justice through the window as Nito ran over to help him. Officer Davis laid her on the bed and Nito lifted the bedspread and covered her body. There was a trail of blood from the window to the bed. Alou came through the door just as Nito covered her with the spread. He stopped in his tracks and stared at her. She looked so still and he could see the trail of blood. Alou tried to go to her, but his feet were stuck to the floor. He looked at Officer Davis and pleaded with his eyes for him to tell him that she was going to be okay.

"She fainted," Officer Clark said as Nito moved over to help him through the window. "He hit her in the leg, I'm sure she's going to be okay."

Alou moved over to the bed and sat beside her. He could hear the ambulance, fire truck and police vehicles outside. He felt for her pulse and was relieved that it was strong.

The emergency crew rushed through the door and began asking questions. They examined Justice, there were bruises on her neck and they couldn't tell how deep the wound was on the side of her throat. The bullet had hit her ankle. They wrapped it to stop the bleeding, placed her on the stretcher, and moved to the ambulance.

"I'll follow the ambulance," Alou said. "Would you guys pack some stuff and bring it to the hospital for her. I'm sure she doesn't want to come back here for a while."

"Sure, we're right behind you." Officer Davis said. When Alou left he turned to Officer Clark and said, "You pack the stuff, you know more about what she would want."

Officer Clark turned to Nito. "You 're in her age group, it might be best if you packed her stuff . . . did anyone call Lela?"

"No," Nito said. "Justice wouldn't want us to. Lela's pregnant and expected to go into labor any day. I'm sure someone will call her later today. That'll be time enough."

"What about Solomon?" Officer Davis asked.

"Since she's going to be okay, why don't we just let the man sleep, he'll find out all he needs to know later on today,"

Nito said. "I'll pack that stuff for you guys, then I, for one, am going home and go to bed. She's in the hand of the only people that can help her now, and I don't think even a corrupt policeman would tangle with Mr. Hambrick tonight.

The two officers took the bag that Nito packed to the hospital. When they arrived at the Emergency Room, Alou told them that Justice had been taken down for stitches in her throat and would have ankle surgery Monday morning, a second surgery the following Monday, and would probably be hospitalized for at least a week.

As the two officers were leaving the hospital, they saw Hercules Cole hurrying down the hall. "A reporter always gets his story," Officer Clark said.

"Yes, he does, and this one should keep the town talking for a long time. Have we ever had anything so crazy happen in Winston before?"

"Not on our watch. And I hope we never do again."

"Amen and amen."

37

When Solomon learned that Justice was in the hospital, he was angry that he had not been called sooner. When Alou got off the phone with Solomon, he was afraid to call Lela. He took the coward's way out, called Snaggie, and asked her to go and tell Lela and Ted what had happened to Justice.

Justice knew that Lela would be upset that no one had called her earlier, but she was happy that Nito had decided not to call Lela, and that she had insisted that Alou not call her when he reached the hospital.

When Lela arrived, saw the bandages on Justice's neck and ankle, and heard all the details of what had happened, she was angry with Alou, Justice, and Nito for not calling her sooner. Ted pulled up a chair and thumbed through a magazine. Justice tried to explain to Lela that she didn't want anyone to disturb her because pregnant women needed their rest, and she was getting the care she needed at the hospital.

Lela was angry. "And you would have been satisfied to lay in bed and sleep when someone had broken into my house, attempted to rape me, cut my throat, shot a hole through my foot, and threw me out of a window. You would have been content to lay your behind in bed and say I need my sleep?"

"No, I wouldn't have, I'm sorry Lela, I guess I wasn't thinking clearly."

"I would expect Justice to be a little crazy, but I didn't expect you and Nito to be crazy," she said to Alou. He just sat there, hung his head, and tried to look pitiful. Lela was sick at the thought of Justice's blood on her bedroom floor and the windowsill and ledge.

"Justice, I know you never want to go back to that place again. Why don't we have one of the men pick up your personal stuff and give your furniture to whoever can use it in Oaktree Downs? Since you will be having the first surgery tomorrow, why don't I plan a wedding ceremony for this Saturday, and you can go home with Alou from here. You guys should have gotten married months ago, and this wouldn't have happened."

"Lela, what makes you think we want to get married in a hospital?" Justice asked.

"Speak for yourself; I think it's a great idea," Alou said. "I'm grateful for friends who care about me and look out for my welfare. This is no time to be ungrateful, Justice."

"I *am* grateful," Justice said and turned to look at Lela.

"You sure have a funny way of showing it," Lela said as she folded her arms and stared at Justice. "Shall I proceed with the wedding plans or not? Look, Justice, I just want you to be safe and happy. I would be worried sick if you ever went back to that condo to live again. Girl, do you realized that you could have been killed? How could you even think about going back there? And remember, marriage is not about a big wedding, it's about coming into covenant with someone you love."

"No, I don't want to go back there." *But getting married in one week, and in a hospital. Anyway, all of this has to be a dream, so don't worry about it.*

Alou took Justice's hands in his. "I think it's an excellent idea. It would really solve all our problems. You will never regret it, I promise. We could go to Hawaii later on our honeymoon, or wherever you want to go. Whenever."

"Can I sleep on it?"

"Sure, I'll give you fifteen minutes, close your eyes."

By the time Lela left, she had convinced Justice that a hospital wedding was a good idea. She painted a picture of a small wedding so intimate and unique that Justice would be the envy of Winston. Justice agreed to the wedding to appease Lela, and going home with Alou sounded a whole lot better than going home alone. She knew she would never be able to sleep in her condo again. She had learned her lesson. Being headstrong had almost gotten her raped and killed. She decided it was time to listen.

"We'll keep it real small. It will be Solomon, Jan, Benny and Ted and me," Lela said.

"What about Nito, he saved my life so many times."

"Oh, I forgot about Nito. And what about the two policemen?"

"Oh, my goodness, it would be terrible to forget them. And the kids in Oaktree Downs, we can't leave them out. And Hercules, he started the chain that saved my life this time, and I'm sure he would want to take pictures."

When Hercules got the call, he rushed back to the hospital. He wanted all the details and asked if he could print the announcement in the paper.

"This is a hospital room, not a stadium," Lela said. "We don't want everyone in Winston to come."

"But I'll print it in such a way that only those people will come that hold Miss Fullilove in high esteem. Trust me."

Justice agreed to his request. She realized that she was grateful to so many people. It was the least she could do for Hercules. She felt a little sad when she realized that neither Alou's mother nor father would be there. She thought of her own parents and wanted to cry. But Lela's excitement lifted her spirit and the guest list grew to fifteen.

When Ericka saw the announcement in the paper, she called Justice and asked if she could come. Justice told her that she would be disappointed if she didn't come. Then Justice thought about Brad and Lionel. She realized that she could not invite Brad without inviting everyone in her office. It was a courtesy, she told Lela, she was sure they would not all come.

By Sunday afternoon, the guest list had grown to the point that they had to request permission to use the doctor's lounge, and Justice was wondering if the whole thing had been a bad idea.

"I'm worried Lela," Justice said. "Maybe we should just have the preacher and two witnesses. This is getting to be..."

"Look, silly, you only get married once. At least that's what we hope. So invite everyone you want to come. The hospital is being very gracious to you. So, rejoice at your good fortune."

☞

AURYOLA HELD THE paper and stared at the picture of Justice and Alou. She couldn't believe her son was getting married without inviting her to the wedding. She looked in her closet to see what she would wear if he called her. But she knew he wouldn't. She thought about his childhood and his adult life. Alou was all that any mother could hope for. She had thought she would spend the rest of her life laughing and talking with him. But he had thrown her over for Justiana. She faced the fact that she would never have a relationship with her son again unless she accepted Justice. *And is she really all that bad. But she did take my son away from me.*

For the first time in years, Auryola felt tears running down her face. She didn't even think she had the ability to cry. She looked at the phone and wished it would ring. But she knew it wouldn't. *I must be the most miserable person in Winston and I'm the only who can do something about it. But I can't. I just can't.*

☞

On the day of the wedding Justice insisted on seeing Alou. Lela tried to convince her that it was bad luck for her to see the groom before the ceremony, but she would not be dissuaded. Alou was there within 20 minutes of the call.

"Alou, I just want to know if you are going to be sad because your parents won't be here," Justice asked.

"My dad is already here. He snuck up on me about two hours ago. And no, I'm not sad that my mother won't be here. I'm not going to put up with anyone abusing either you or me anymore. She made her choice and we have to accept it. Look, precious, everyone who's supposed to be here will be here, I promise. And I want you to know that this is the happiest day of my life. My mother is satisfied with her choice, and I'm happy with mine because time will take care of all of this."

"Your dad is one sneaky old man."

"He didn't want us to be disappointed if he couldn't make it. Let's just be thankful for what we have. Don't you love me?"

"Yes, I do."

"Show me," he said and bent down for a kiss. She giggled and kissed him.

"Can I go and get dressed now?" She giggled and kissed him again. Alou saluted her and started to back out of the room. He stopped when he bumped into someone and turned to see a man and woman in dark suits. He could tell they were not hospital personnel.

"Can I help you," Alou asked as he blocked their entry into the room.

"We're with the FBI," the man said and they banished shiny badges.

Alou took a good look at each badge and then asked why they wanted to talk with Justice.

"Who are you?" the woman asked.

"I'm her husband," Alou said and looked at his watch. "At least I will be in about two hours and fifteen minutes."

"We're getting married today," Justice said. "What do you guys want to talk with me about?"

Alou moved out of their path and they moved over to the bed. "We wanted to ask you a few questions about Courtroom

D. But I'm sure it can wait," the woman said. "Why don't you give us a call at your earliest convenience."

They each handed Justice a business card and left. Alou came back to the bed and kissed her on the mouth. He saluted and backed out of the room without another word. Justice giggled and placed the cards on the nightstand. *I think Mark and Judge Denver are in trouble with the Feds.*

⌒

ALOU HAD HIRED professional decorators to decorate the doctor's lounge, under Lela's supervision. Lela had made a final check on Friday night and everything was perfect. Nito had designed a "rolling float" on which Justice could sit and it made her appear to be standing. She was not able to put any weight on her right foot.

The wedding began promptly at five o'clock. Justice had insisted that they start on time and Lela had threatened to kill anyone who was late. The room was packed and people were gathering in the hallway.

Justice entered from the side door with Solomon on one arm and Ted on the other. She sat on the rolling float created by Nito, which was operated by remote. The musician played soft music. Nito was grinning from ear to ear. He was proud of his invention. Lela, the matron of honor, and Benny, Alou's best man, also entered from the side door. When Lela saw all the people, she wanted to choke Hercules. She was afraid the fire department would make some of the guest leave. When Justice saw all the people in the hallway and standing along the walls of the room, she was moved to tears.

When Justice, Solomon, Ted, Lela, and Benny were all in place, the music changed and Alou entered from the back door. He took one look at Justice and stopped in his tracks. *She is the most beautiful bride that ever stood at an altar. And I'd give anything to be able to hold her in my arms all*

night tonight. How did we end up with a hospital wedding?
He had written a revised version of his favorite song by Ray
Charles. He substituted Justice for Georgia. *Ray Charles
loved Georgia and I love Justice.*

He began to sing as he walked down the isle:

Justice, Justice, the whole day through
Just one sweet kiss
Keeps Justice on my mind

Justice, my sweet Justice
No peace shall I find
Just one sweet kiss
Keep Justice on my mind

Other arms reach out to me
Other eyes smile tenderly
Still in peaceful dreams I see
That you are the only one for me

Justice, oh Justice, the whole day through
Just one sweet kiss
Keeps Justice on my mind

EVERYONE, EXCEPT BENNY, was surprised. They had no idea he
had such a beautiful voice.

Benny had listened to him rehearse it all week. Justice's
eyes were shiny with tears when she saw the crowd, now the
tears ran freely. When Alou reached the makeshift altar, Lela
lifted the veil, dabbed at Justice's eyes, and whispered, "Stop
crying, silly."

As Solomon and Ted passed her hands to Alou, Lela lifted
the veil to dab at her eyes again, and Alou bent to kiss her.

The preacher moved up to them and said. "Not yet, I'll
let you know when it's time to kiss the bride."

"Oops," Alou said, and everyone laughed.

"Dearly beloved," the preacher began. "We are gathered here today to . . ."

"Wait," Ericka said as she hurried down the isle. She wore a beautiful navy blue dress and was covered from her neck to her knees.

Everyone turned to stare at Ericka. She could feel daggers at her back. Officer Davis and Officer Clark recognized Ericka and started to move forward, Justice held up her hand, and they stopped.

"I don't have any objections to the wedding," Ericka said. "I just want to say something while everyone is here. We may never all get together like this again."

Most of the people began to whisper. They had never seen Ericka dressed that way before. Solomon chuckled. *Ericka looks like Justice and Lela.* The preacher turned to Justice and Alou. Justice mouthed, it's okay.

Ericka just stood there for a moment; she seemed a little embarrassed. Then she said, "Well, I would just like to say that I was a part of a scheme to try and come between Justice and Alou. And I know I have caused them a lot of pain. I was wrong, and I'm sorry for what I did. When I saw Justice's car rolling down that embankment on TV, I vowed that I would apologize to her if she survived. Well, she survived, I apologized, and my life was changed forever. In fifteen minutes, she forgave me, taught me how to become a Christian, and how to be a lady. Justice is the most gracious person I know, and the best Christian I know. And I'm through talking." Everyone laughed.

Justice held out her hand to Ericka, Ericka shook Justice's hand and went back to her seat. Lela lifted the veil, dabbed at Justice's eyes and said, "Stop crying, silly."

The preacher held out his hand as if conducting an altar call. "Is there anyone else? Anyone else who would like to have a word?"

Tammy came forward. "Yes, I would like to say a few words. I have worked in the public defender's office for seven years. At one time it was always Tammy, Tammy, Tammy, and then Justice came along and it changed to Justice, Justice, Justice. Well, I resented Justice, and Antonio and Vanessa thought she could do no wrong. When an office came available with a large window, I insisted that I was entitled to it because I had more seniority. I didn't care about the window; I just wanted to win over Justice. When she had an opportunity to put me down, she didn't. I tried to turn Shannon, another public defender, against Justice by suggesting that Antonio was allowing Justice to try all of her impossible cases, but that didn't work. So, I know how Ericka felt, because I felt the same way when I read about Justice being kidnapped. Then when I saw the announcement about the wedding, I had to admit that I have come to hold her in high esteem. So, Justice, I want to apologize to you and let you know that I moved back into my old office and we have moved your stuff into the office with the big window, and when you come back to work, we are going to throw a welcome back party for you."

Justice held out her hand to Tammy and she shook it and returned to her seat. Lela lifted the veil, dabbed at her eyes and said, "Stop crying silly."

"Is there anyone else?" the preacher asked.

Katrina and Leroy came forward. "We are speaking on behalf of My Brother's Keeper from Oaktree Downs," Katrina said. "We want Miss Justice to know that we think she is special and Mr. Alou is special. And they make the best couple in the whole wide world, and Oaktree Downs is a better place to live because of them."

"When Miss Justice first came to Oaktree Downs, I was fat and wouldn't take a bath," Leroy said. He held out his hand and looked down at his clothes, "And look at me now." Everyone laughed. "I started taking a bath everyday because Miss Justice danced with two or three of us each time she came, and I didn't want her to catch me stinking." Everyone laughed.

Leroy and Katrina motioned for My Brother's Keeper choir to come forward. "And now, we want to tell you how we feel about you Miss Justice and Mr. Alou," Katrina said and turned to the choir, and they pointed to Justice and Alou as they began to sing:

"You are somebody; you really are somebody.

You are somebody; you really are somebody.

You've been washed in His blood; you've been filled with His love.

And you're a child of the Most High King."

Each child went to shake hands with Justice and Alou. Justice could not stop the tears. Lela lifted the veil, dabbed at her eyes and said, "Stop crying, silly."

"Anyone else?" the preached asked. When no one came forward, he proceeded with the wedding ceremony. When he finished and told Alou that he could kiss the bride, Lela lifted the veil, and Alou bent and kissed Justice. Afterwards Lela dabbed at her eyes and said, "Stop crying, silly."

"Before I present the newlyweds to you, the doctor has an announcement to make," the preacher said.

The doctor came forward, stood in front of the couple, and smiled. "I have a surprise wedding gift for you from myself, Lela and Ted, and Solomon. Lela made the request and made all the arrangement for the needed services, I worked out the deal with the surgeon, and Ted and Solomon financed it. Alou . . . you may take your bride home with you for the weekend. But you must promise to have her back before six o'clock Monday morning." He turned and pointed to Lela. "She has taken care of all the details. Shane will provide food for each meal, you will be provided with a motorized wheelchair for Justice to get around, a nurse will visit on Sunday to dress her foot, you two will have no other guest at the house, and a limo is waiting out front to take the bride and groom home. Can you two follow those rules?"

"Yes, but I can't believe it," Justice said. "How could you have been so sneaky, Lela?" Alou was speechless. He turned to stare at Justice, swallowed, and nodded his head.

Solomon had been watching Lela for about 20 minutes. He suspected that she was in labor. When she whispered to

Ted and he turned pale, Solomon moved over to them and asked, "You need me to call Dr. Cosgrove?" Ted just stood and stared. Lela nodded yes.

"Now, ladies and gentlemen," the preacher said. "I present to you, Mr. and Mrs. Alou Hambrick."

All the kids from Oaktree Downs came forward and blew bubbles at Justice and Alou. Justice tossed the bouquet, Ericka caught it, and Alou picked Justice up and headed for the limo. Lela followed them and Ted walked beside her, held her hand, and looked like he was going to faint. Justice was too excited to notice.

Solomon informed Snaggie that Lela was in labor and told her to let Ted know that he would be waiting around the corner with a wheelchair. The crowd followed them out to the sidewalk and stood waving, cheering and blowing bubbles at Alou and Justice.

Snaggie hurried the bride and groom along, shooed the well wishers away from Justice and Alou, and whispered to Ted that Solomon was waiting with a wheelchair. When Alou placed Justice in the limo, Snaggie practically pushed him in the car behind her and closed the door. Lela knocked on the window. When the driver rolled it down, she leaned in and kissed both Justice and Alou. Then she dabbed at Justice's eyes one last time before they sped away, and said, "Stop crying, silly."